A TeamGlobus™ Adventure

THE ANCIENTS:
A GAME

Bernard J. Putz

The Ancients: A Game is a work of fiction. While many of the names, characters, organizations, places, and events are products of the author's imagination, some of them are based on history and are being used here in a fictitious manner. Any disparagements of people, places, or organizations are unintentional. This book is presented solely for educational and entertainment purposes.

The author and Amadeus Creative, LLC, have made every effort to ensure the accuracy and completeness of the information contained in this book. As the contents of this work are the product of the author's imagination and interpretation, any differences from actual facts are intended to enhance the educational or entertainment value of the work, and the author takes no responsibility for the interpretations of others even where that interpretation causes any loss, damage, or disruption.

The information is meant to supplement, not replace, proper lesson plans, curriculums, and education. We advise readers to take full responsibility to think critically about the topics presented herein.

Copyright © 2013 by Bernard J. Putz Ph.D.
All rights reserved.
ISBN: 1481132857
ISBN 13: 9781481132855
Library of Congress Control Number: 2012922848
CreateSpace Independent Publishing Platform
North Charleston, South Carolina

CONTENTS

ACKNOWLEDGMENTS

FIRST, I WANT TO THANK MY WIFE, DAGMAR DOLATSCHKO.
She immediately believed in my vision of adventure stories for students six years ago when we first talked about my idea at dinner on a beach in Greece. With the day-to-day demands of life, it has taken some time to complete this first book. She has kept the faith since the first day and has provided amazing support in so many ways.

My son, Adrian Putz, is also wonderful. A middle schooler when this book was written, he was my first and continuous sounding board and critic. Sometimes wise beyond his age, his questions and comments helped me better understand my audience and better shape the story. He reminded me over and over how youth can get excited and engaged, how with their youthful energy they dare to explore, dare to question—something we adults must never forget.

Both my parents, Frederica and Artur Putz, who instilled in me a love of learning, a desire to question and look beyond the obvious, and a philosophy that achieving worthwhile goals takes a lot of hard work, should not go unnoticed.

The curriculum of Professor Ross Dunn, project director at World History for Us All helped me make sense of all the history content swirling around in my head. For years as a consultant, I have focused on the patterns that drive behavior, trying to understand how a holistic system functions, and then intervening at critical junctures to help drive change. The curriculum he and his colleagues developed at San

Diego State University resonated with my vision that students need to understand the big patterns. His approval to allow me to tie my story to the curriculum was very helpful.

Thank you to Mr. Ninaltowski and Mr. Nazar at Tierra Linda who took the time out of their busy schedules to share their insights after reading my draft. Also, thank you to the middle school, high school, and college student readers, specifically Gavrielle Lent, who read a final draft of the novel and provided honest and very insightful feedback. The unvarnished truth they provided helped make this book so much better.

The authors listed in the appendix were an important part in the creation of this novel. Without them writing and publishing their books, I would have never been able to come up the learning curve about history, the Internet, and science so quickly.

Finally, thank you to the folks at CreateSpace for their support, good work, and for providing me a platform to bring my story and ideas to market.

PREFACE

THE ANCIENTS: A GAME IS PRIMARILY A WORK OF FICTION. The main characters and the adventure story come from my imagination. However, as the characters embark on their quest and venture through world history from 10,000 BCE to around 600 CE, I have tried to accurately describe and include historical facts, people, and events. Drawing on many published sources and the vastness of the Internet, I have included this historical information as described by these nonfiction sources. Like any science fiction writer, I took liberty with the technology aspects of this story and extrapolated many of the specifics. However, many of the technology and science concepts I used are based on advanced research that is currently happening in labs around the world, such as the research on nanobots in medicine that can work at the level of atoms and molecules.

History is a dynamic field with new evidence, new theories, and new interpretations emerging all the time. We can understand history at the granular level of one person and one event, or at a big-picture level, such as humans and their relationship with the environment. Every author makes important decisions about what to include and what to leave out that ultimately affect his or her story. In this story, I have tried to weave together specific names, dates, and events as well as convey major historical themes and patterns.

The primary focus of the TeamGlobus™ series is to help young adults see how major patterns that shaped the past can affect the future, and to better understand different cultures. The goal is to help them develop creative, critical, and historical thinking skills. With the massive amounts of information available in the twenty-first century, we need to help people, especially students, not only see and understand the facts, but also look beyond them to see and understand the underlying patterns that affect the world. Only in this way can they see the connections, understand the relationships between the parts, and make informed decisions.

This is not a tome on world history. The intent is to engage students in a fast-paced, exciting adventure story that fits into the modern world, an adventure that both entertains and educates, and most importantly a story that motivates students to explore further, on their own.

If, after reading this book, a single young adult is motivated to look up one additional item that caught his or her attention, ask one additional question, or follow up on one reference, then I feel I have succeeded. If one teacher uses this story and finds the associated Curriculum Enhancer effective in enhancing his or her lesson plans, and if one parent uses the associated Conversation Starter to have a meaningful discussion with his or her child, then I believe I have made a worthwhile contribution.

The ultimate goal of these stories and associated tools is to engage readers to think critically, creatively, and historically, to ask the tough questions that will shape the future for all of us.

Bernard J. Putz, PhD
Amadeus Creative, LLC
www.amadeuscreative.com
www.dare2question.com
www.dare2explore.com
San Carlos, California
July 2013

BERNARD J. PUTZ

For more about the power of story in 21st century learning and education
see: www.AmadeusCreative.com

For more about the adventures of TeamGlobus™ see:

www.Team-Globus.com

PROLOGUE

WE ARE NEARING THE MIDDLE OF THE TWENTY-FIRST century. The Internet has become an essential part of life.

Humans use the Net for everything—to communicate, to socialize, to play, to pay for goods and services, and to find whatever information they need. People are no longer tied to their computers to access the Internet; small, portable devices, handheld or even wearable, have become the standard communication tool. People live in a world where everyone is connected to everything, everywhere. Cars talk to each other. Devices in the home talk to each other. Machines talk to each other. More and more information is exclusively digital, with hard-copy books, articles, and paper becoming rare.

Three laws govern the spread of technology:

- Moore's Law: The processing power of a microchip doubles every eighteen months.
- Gilder's Law: The total bandwidth of communication systems triples every twelve months.
- Metcalfe's Law: The value of a network is proportional to the square of the number of nodes.

Those three laws continue forward unabated, now driven by nano-technology, biochips, and quantum computers that have taken the place of silicon.

Technological development continues to accelerate, and human society chases it to keep up. This is the world of seventeen-year-old Jared,

Megan, and friends. Unknown to them, this world finds itself at war, and they are dragged into a battle that has been raging for years.

CHAPTER 1

"SHOOT! ARJUN, AIM LOWER AND SHOOT ALREADY," YELLS Jared into his microphone. "Watch out. Here he comes." Jared chooses a crossbow with exploding bolts. It takes a little extra time to reload, but it has one of the highest damage ratings of all the available weapons.

"I'm trying, but I can't get this stupid thing to work," shouts Arjun as he struggles with the glove controller to draw the string of his oversized bow. Arjun, with a strong upper body from surfing in the Pacific, finally gets the arrow centered just as the two-headed werewolf-like beast leaps off the eight-hundred-foot cliff, spreads its wings, and dives toward him.

Jared looks up as Arjun's arrow sails over the werewolf's head. He quickly cranks the handles that pull back the cable on his crossbow and aims his laser sight at the animal's belly. He tracks the beast as it dives toward Arjun. The belly is the biggest target and where his exploding bolt will do the most damage. He slowly moves his fingers to the trigger, constantly keeping the diving werewolf in his crosshairs. He aims and then pulls the trigger just as he sees a flash out of the corner of his eye.

Megan, riding on top of a silver, almost-transparent dragon, whooshes by and with one slice of her huge, six-foot sword decapitates the werewolf in midair.

Where did she come from? wonders Jared, as his bolt slams into the rump of the dragon instead of the werewolf, explodes, and obliterates the animal. Megan tumbles out of the air and lands next to Arjun with a thump, dead.

"You idiot!" she yells into her microphone as she re-spawns. She rips the virtual reality helmet from her head and throws it to the floor. "It took me almost twenty hours to get enough points for that dragon. And you obliterate it with the only weapon that can kill it. I'm outta here."

Jared stands alone in his bedroom. He mumbles into the microphone, "Hey. I didn't see you coming. Sorry. You could've warned me." Thank goodness, he and Megan are friends. You do not want to mess with Megan when she's angry. For a second, Jared thinks about the co-ed soccer game last weekend. Megan totally flipped out after she was fouled, and the referee gave the red card to her instead of to the person who committed the foul. She grabbed the card out of the ref's hand and tore it in half.

"Megan…Megan," calls Jared into the microphone. "You there? You're still picking me up tomorrow, right?"

There is only silence. Megan does not answer. She has already signed out, and her character and online name disappear from the screen.

"I'm sorry," Arjun says softly into his own microphone. "I didn't think it would be this difficult."

"That's what happens when you spend so much time out at the ocean instead of playing online games," replies Jared jokingly. "These new glove controllers require a lot of practice, and these weapons aren't the easiest to learn."

"No kidding. I did pray to Varuna, the Indian god of the sky and ocean, for help, but it looks like he's better at sending me a good wave than at helping me with a video game."

Jared chuckles. "I understand. I've got a ways to go myself. You should see Ethan, though. He's a master."

"Where is Ethan, anyway? Wasn't he going to join us?" asks Arjun.

Jared begins to unbuckle his gloves. "Knowing Ethan, he's probably been here for hours and is at least five or six levels ahead of us. He even got sponsored to play a different game last year."

"He must play a lot," replies Arjun. "My mom and dad are really strict about how much screen time I'm allowed. I'm not supposed to be online this late." Arjun pauses. "Uh-oh! My grandparents are coming from Chennai, India, tomorrow. I almost forgot. I better sign out."

Jared tosses the gloves into the recliner in the corner of his room. He lifts his visor and unbuckles his helmet. "Later. See you in class tomorrow." Jared gently places his helmet on his desk when he hears a knock on his door.

"Jared, it's almost midnight. I hope you're not still playing," calls his mother. "Tomorrow's a school day."

"I'm not, Mom." Jared smiles to himself. Technically, he is not playing anymore. "I'm going to bed right now."

"All right, good night. I've still got some work, so I'll be up a little longer if you need anything." Jared's mom returns to the dining room table, shaking her head. She wishes Jared would spend less time playing games, but his grades are good and the counselors suggested it might be a good way for him to cope with the incident.

"'Night, Mom." Jared pulls the covers over his chest and stares up at the ceiling. His thoughts drift between how angry Megan will be in the morning, given that he obliterated her dragon, and how he really does not want to go to school. Classes are so boring. Soon he is fast asleep and deep in the world of dreams.

>> >> >>

"Here we go," says his dad as he pushes the ignition button. "We haven't gotten a tardy slip yet, so let's not start now."

"Good morning, Master George," says the car in a British accent as they settle into their seats and fasten their seat belts. "And you too, Master Jared."

"Good morning, Jeeves," replies Jared. He loves this new voice-activated technology. His dad let him name the car and download various voices from the Internet. The car has all the newest technologies: windshield-integrated digital display, always-on Internet connection, voice-activated controls, and an automatic drive-itself feature. Jared's uncle, Alberto, owns the same model except he has the two-door Cabriolet. Jared touches the large display screen to warm up the Corinthian leather seats. They can be set to warm, cool, or six different massage settings. His father puts the transmission in automatic mode, since the car has both an automatic and a manual setting. They drive away sounding like a moped.

"Dad, can you change the engine sound?" asks Jared. He knows that if he arrives at school in a car sounding like a moped, his friends will give him a hard time. He can hear the jokes now: "moped boy!" or "lawnmower man!"

He adds, "Uncle Alberto usually makes his car sound like a Ferrari."

Normally, the hydrogen hybrid car runs silently, but the automotive engineers built in a dial-a-sound feature that allows the driver to simulate the sound of any vehicle manufactured in the last fifty years.

To be different from his brother, Alberto, his dad chooses a Porsche sound instead. A few yards from the first streetlight, he pulls out a device that looks like an old credit card and places it on the dashboard. "I've got to give a lecture about the history of technology at the university this morning so we need to make up some time. Don't tell anyone what you're about to see. It's still in development. One of Alberto's newest inventions. Watch! We're guaranteed to never be late again."

His dad breaks out into a big grin and taps the device. A deep-red glow illuminates the sides of the card. They come up to an intersection, and the red stoplight automatically turns green. At the next intersection, the same thing happens. At every intersection, as soon as they get close, the card turns from red to green and the stoplight turns from red to green. At first, Jared thinks it is a coincidence, but by the fourth light, he catches on. All the way down the street, as they get within ten yards of an intersection, every red light turns green, even when there are cars ahead of them.

"Dad, this is awesome. How does it work?"

George glances briefly at Jared. "Years back when traffic was going to overwhelm cities, the traffic authorities decided to connect all the traffic lights within a metropolitan area into a huge, wireless network. A central traffic-command center monitors the traffic flow and adjusts the traffic pattern. This device interrupts those wireless signals, only for a split second, and sends its own signal to turn the light green."

"Neat. Can it be detected?" asks Jared.

"Not really. The computer algorithm that controls the traffic sees the pattern change, for a brief second, but the people at the traffic-control center can't tell what's causing it."

They settle back into their seats and drive toward school, confident they will not be late. Jared thinks about the good times with his Uncle Alberto. He loves to spend time in his uncle's lab whenever he gets a chance, tinkering with all the cool devices and computers. His uncle is a computer genius. On a few occasions, his uncle has shown him products in development, and he has let him observe some of the scientists. Jared had to swear to keep anything he saw secret. Lately though, his uncle has not had much time. His dad says it is because he has been working on a very important project.

Suddenly, Jared is ripped from his thoughts as his dad shifts the car into manual mode, downshifts, and steps hard onto the accelerator. The car lunges forward, making the high-pitched whining sound that is distinctively Porsche, and speeds down the street.

Jared braces himself against the dashboard with his arms. "Dad, what the…? We're not that late."

Looking into his rearview mirror, his dad's face grows intense. "I know. We're being followed, and I don't like it. Jared, if anything happens to me…" At that moment, a large black Mercedes SUV with tinted windows rams the back of the car.

With an expression of both fear and confusion, Jared looks at his dad. "What are you talking about? Why should anything happen?" He has never seen his father this way before. Jared senses his father's fear and is truly frightened.

"I'm afraid it might be about my research. I came across some important information."

"What information?" asks Jared as the SUV hits them again with tremendous force, sending the car skidding onto the sidewalk. His father does everything he can to keep control. He spins the wheel, pressing Jared into the door as the car skids onto a side street. He passes slower cars and weaves between parked cars and oncoming traffic.

Jared wonders where his father learned to drive like this. He closes his eyes for a few seconds just as a head-on collision is imminent. He opens them again as soon as he feels his father swerve back into his own lane. The big SUV, still behind them, clips a few mirrors and scrapes a few cars as it barrels down the road.

As they enter the next intersection, another SUV comes at them from the right and slams into Jared's door with tremendous impact. The side post crumples inward, almost knocking Jared unconscious, and instantly the side airbag deploys. The car spins diagonally across the street over the sidewalk and onto the wet grass of a deserted park, slamming into a large sequoia tree. The front of the car crumples, as it is designed to do, to protect the passengers. The remaining airbags deploy.

Jared feels nauseous as he climbs out of the car and falls to his knees. He throws up next to the rear wheel, and then moves forward to get away from the smell. He cowers behind the car, shaking and shivering. He is motionless, paralyzed by fear.

His father is trying to unbuckle the seat belt when two big hands reach in through the airbags, click the button on the buckle, and pull him out by the lapels of his blazer. A bodyguard as big as a football linebacker and dressed in a black suit and sunglasses drags him out onto the grass. "Get up," he growls. "You've got a meeting." Two other men climb out of the SUVs to aid their comrade. They slap his father around.

Jared hides behind the car. He cannot bear to look at his father being roughed up. He wonders if he should try to help or stay hidden. Those guys are huge, even bigger than his father is, and they look like professionals. He cannot decide.

Then a fourth man, wearing an elegant designer suit, steps out of the second SUV and calmly walks toward the scene. "That's enough!" he says. "You haven't been cooperating, George! Now, you won't have a choice."

His father looks up with puffy, bruised eyes and mumbles through his swollen lips, "Victor, since when do you do your own dirty work?"

"You're going to be our special guest. Too bad you're going to miss your meeting at the university. I hope they continue your funding," Victor says sarcastically, then breaks out laughing.

Jared can just barely hear what they are saying. His father is in serious trouble. He continues to watch, crouched motionless behind the car. The big black SUVs look almost like those used by the Secret Service, but that cannot be. What would the Secret Service want with his father?

All of a sudden, his father runs. He is maybe three yards away when Jared sees one of the men casually pull out a gun and aim it at his father. A second later, he hears a "pop," and his father falls to the ground.

"No!" screams Jared. He begins to shake and tears come to his eyes. His palms are sweaty, and he feels a numb emptiness in the pit of his stomach. His muscles seem frozen. He cannot run to his father or run away. He is paralyzed by indecision.

Jared forces himself to focus through the tears. He sees the two men walk over to the crumpled body; one pulls two electrodes from his father's chest and retracts two wires. Jared breathes a huge sigh of relief. The gun was a Taser, a nonlethal electroshock weapon often used by police to subdue a fleeing person.

"Take him, and make sure he doesn't wake up for a while," commands the man named Victor.

The two men grab the limp body of Jared's father like a sack of potatoes and dump him into the back seat of one of the SUVs.

"No! No! Leave him alone!" screams Jared as he bolts upright in his bed. It is three a.m. His bed and pajamas are soaked in sweat. His hair is matted to his head, and his eyes are wide open. He is trembling.

His mom rushes in, sits on his bed, and takes him in her arms. "That dream again?"

Jared wipes his nose and nods.

"I'm so sorry, dear. The counselors thought that six months after the incident the dreams would start going away."

Jared shrugs. "They are becoming less frequent. The one about my interrogation by all those government agents has almost disappeared."

"This one will go away, too," his mom says in a soothing voice, holding him tightly. "The FBI promised to let me know if they get a lead in the case."

Jared sighs heavily. "Yeah, but it's been six months and nothing. Do they even have an idea where he might be?"

"Not yet," replies his mother, stroking his hair. The kidnapping has been tough on Mom as well—the constant interrogations, the disruption to their normal routines, the surveillance. She massages Jared's back. "Try to get some more sleep."

"Will you stay here?" asks Jared, a bit embarrassed. Normally, seventeen-year-olds do not ask their moms to wait until they fall asleep.

"Of course! I'll be right here."

CHAPTER 2

"MEGAN'S HERE," HIS MOM YELLS TOWARD THE BEDROOM. Jared walks out of his room, pulling his long, dark brown hair into a ponytail and securing it with a hair tie. "You don't have to yell, Mom, I'm right here." He is wearing black jeans, a black T-shirt with the word "anarchy" on the front, and fluorescent-green Nikes that have seen better days.

His mother looks at him with a concerned look. "Anymore dreams?"

"After the one, nope, slept like a baby."

She smiles. "That's good." She looks at his clothes. "You're not wearing that T-shirt to school, are you?"

"Yeah. Why not?" He passes the kitchen table and grabs a granola bar.

She shakes her head. After these last six months, she has no energy to argue about what he wears to school, or the length of his hair. He has let it grow ever since his father was taken. When she asks him about it, all he says is that he now looks like his uncle Alberto, and if he can do it, so can Jared.

"Aren't you going to eat?" she asks.

He waves the bar in her direction as he walks toward the door. "I am eating."

"Don't forget to ask your teacher about the term paper. What was it called? Cultural mindedness? Or was it historical thinking?"

Jared opens the door and sees Megan out front in her red, classic Triumph Spitfire with the top down. He turns back to face his mother.

11

"I got it, Mom. Cultural mindedness is Megan's topic. Bye." He slams the front door and bounds down the steps.

Jared's mom fills her coffee cup and leans against the counter. Most days he seems like any normal teenager, but there are other days when the fact that his father is missing takes a toll. He has suffered after the interrogations especially, when agents suggested that his father might be part of an enormous conspiracy. On those days, Jared buried himself in his video games. He and his father were very close, and Jared is sure his father is not mixed up with anything illegal.

"Hi, Megan!" Jared waves from the bottom of the front steps, carefully gauging whether she's still angry about her dragon.

Megan smiles and waves back, her deep green eyes glistening in the morning sunlight. She then gathers her red dreadlocks with both hands and centers them on her back. "Let's go. I know you couldn't live with it if we were late to school," she jokes.

"Ha, ha. Funny. I might not like school, but I like keeping my perfect record," replies Jared as he squeezes his six-foot frame into the sports car. His head barely fits under the top of the windshield and the aftermarket roll bar. "Hey, sorry about your dragon."

"No big deal. It's only a game. Luckily, I had saved an earlier version. I only need a couple of minutes to get him back." Megan pulls away from the curb. "You seemed a bit distracted yesterday. What's up?"

"My mom. She's worried about me playing video games. She says ever since the incident with my dad, I play more, and it's going to affect my schoolwork."

"It doesn't look like it has. You're still doing well."

"Yeah. I only play when I think about my dad. It helps me take my mind off him and wondering what's going on. Why would anyone kidnap a history and communications professor?"

"That's kind of odd. What does your mom think?"

"She doesn't say much. She's buried herself in her own work." Jared does not want to talk about it any longer. He looks at the sports car and changes subjects. "I can't believe they still let you drive this old piece of junk."

"What?" replies Megan, as she accelerates, making the four-cylinder engine whine. She weaves between several emission-free hybrids like a slalom skier. "This is a classic, introduced at the London Auto Show in 1962. My dad bought it at an auction in Europe."

"Exactly. That's really old. It's an old piece of junk," replies Jared with a big smile. He knows how to push Megan's buttons.

"Piece of junk, huh? Watch this." She floors the accelerator, and Jared is pushed back into his seat. He understands why she needs the roll bar. Megan, who can barely fit in the car herself, given her height, looks like a WWI fighter pilot, but instead of a scarf wafting into the sky, it is her dark-red dreadlocks. She pilots the Spitfire car not like its namesake, the British Spitfire single-seat fighter aircraft, but rather like a modern-day jet fighter. The speedometer quickly climbs to seventy miles per hour. With a top speed of only ninety-five miles per hour, it doesn't seem like a fast car. However, when flying down a two-lane road inches from the ground in an open-top convertible, seventy miles per hour is fast. Old oak trees and dry bushes race by. Jared can easily touch the bushes if he extends his arm outside of the car.

As she nears the left turn onto the school's long, private driveway, Megan takes her foot off the accelerator and barely touches the brakes. She turns the wheel left, and the car, with its low center of gravity, begins to spin. She keeps holding the steering wheel, gently taps the brakes, and the car spins 360 degrees twice. She then turns the steering wheel to the right and, in perfect control, straightens out the car and continues up the drive.

"Woo-hoo! I've been practicing that maneuver," she yells excitedly.

Jared says nothing. He knows Megan can drive better than most adults can. A few months after she received her driver's license, her father enrolled her in a twelve-week professional driving course. He probably hoped that it would teach her to drive more conservatively. Unfortunately, it backfired. Megan drives like a Formula 1 racer. It is never boring.

The school driveway, a narrow, two-lane, paved road, winds through dry grasslands and under old oak trees, Douglas firs, and redwoods. The road then opens up into a large, gravel parking lot with a drop-off zone and parking for teachers, parents, and students. Megan passes a few historic buildings and pulls into the student parking lot in front of a beautifully restored mansion from the early 1900s. The school sits on one hundred acres of land straddling the North American and Pacific tectonic plates in Northern California. The campus consists of two separate schools about a quarter-mile apart. There is a middle school and a high school. Globus Academy for the Gifted (GAG) was started in the early twenty-first century by a wealthy individual who figured there was a different way to prepare students for the future. Students love to joke about the acronym, "GAG."

GAG is a large, private school with close to eight hundred students at the California campus, but it has more students if you count the satellite campuses around the world. High school students have access to teachers from around the world through technology and a virtual network infrastructure that is the envy of many high-tech companies. In some of Jared's classes, there might be eighteen students, with a few attending from different parts of the world via tele-presence. Their images are projected on a screen, and it is as if they are in the classroom. GAG prides itself on being an early adopter of some of the newest educational technologies on the market.

Megan slowly lets the car roll to a stop, and after a gigantic grin, pretends to speak into a microphone. "Flight ninety of Megan Air has now safely landed without incident at GAG International Airport. You may now unbuckle your seat belt, and please take care when removing items from the overhead bins, since objects may have shifted."

"Yeah, my granola bar shifted all right," jokes Jared. "You're crazy, you know."

"Maybe, but we're safe and on time—the hallmark of any good airline," Megan quips. She steps on the driver's seat, grabs the roll bar, and launches herself over the side of the Triumph without opening the door. She snatches her backpack from behind her seat and jogs toward her first class. "See ya!"

"Yeah, later." Jared extracts himself from the seat and slowly wanders into math class, entering the room seconds after the bell rings.

"Welcome, Mr. Reyes. So glad you could join us," says the teacher as he hands Jared his latest exam. Another 90 percent. Jared glances at the result and crumples the paper into his backpack. He makes no effort to put it into a folder or to fold it neatly. He drops his pack next to his chair, hooks his feet under the front legs, and tilts backwards. School is totally boring. He hides his smartphone under the lip of the desk, since students are not allowed to use smartphones in the classroom. He scans several text messages.

Jared sees a message from Arjun, teasing him and reminding him to make sure he stays awake in world history today. Jared reflects on how he liked history last year, especially when his dad translated all the details into big historical questions and major themes. His dad used to say, "Think of looking at world history with the magical lens of a camera. Turn the focus ring one way and see a broad, panoramic landscape— the large-scale patterns that have shaped human existence on earth for millennia. Turn the focus ring the other way, and you have a macro lens with which you can see the minute details of an individual life. The power rests in your ability to adjust your focus and ask the critical questions." But now history has become a chore and a bunch of disconnected facts. Even Megan says that she does not understand the point of learning all this ancient history, a bunch of stories and facts about dead people.

Whenever his dad spoke about history, he would always finish with, "And always remember, history is a powerful force, for as George Orwell wrote in the novel *1984*, 'He who controls the past, controls the future; and he who controls the present, controls the past.'"

CHAPTER 3

JARED, MEGAN, AND ARJUN ENTER SIXTH-PERIOD WORLD history. They sense something is different. There is a nervous excitement throughout the class, and it is not because the weekend is only fifty minutes away. The bell rings, and all fifteen students settle into chairs at various tables. Jared, as usual, takes his seat in the back.

Ms. Castro, his teacher, moves toward the front. "Good afternoon. Today, I want to welcome Dr. Jones. Many of you already know him from your other classes. He is Globus Academy's newly hired vice principal for technology, and he is going to talk to you today about a wonderful opportunity."

Jared sighs and rocks back and forth on his chair.

The vice principal boots up the three large, flat-screen monitors in the front of the room. He smiles at the class and then begins. "Thank you, Ms. Castro. As you know, our school prides itself on being on the leading edge of technology in education. And in that regard, we do have an amazing opportunity. Our school was chosen, as one of ten schools around the world, to participate in a new, highly innovative educational program."

Jared rolls his eyes as he thinks about how a new, innovative program is launched almost every month—Internet-based this or tablet-based that—and they all stink. Megan sees his face and smiles across the room.

Jared tunes out as Dr. Jones drones on. Then, his ear catches the word "dragon."

Dr. Jones asks again, "How many of you play 'Dragon Scrolls' or other massive multiplayer online role-playing games?"

Jared's attention is piqued. Why is he talking about online games? He, along with the other fourteen students in class, raises his hand.

Dr. Jones sees he has caught everyone's attention. "Now imagine a game where, while you're playing, you're learning all the world history you need for this class."

"Totally cool! What can we win?" calls out Ethan, only glancing at Dr. Jones through his disheveled brown hair. Heads turn toward him, and he shrinks back down in his chair making sure to avoid making eye contact with anyone. Everyone knows that Ethan would be excited. Ethan loves action role-playing games. He is a total gamer and techie. He often looks like he stays awake most of the night playing his games.

If only Jared's mom could see how much time Ethan spends online, she'd cut him some slack. However, this game does sound interesting.

"What's it called?" asks another student.

"*The Ancients*," replies Dr. Jones.

With a look of disappointment, the twins Damian and Ivy reply almost in unison, "That doesn't sound as exciting as Dragon Scrolls."

Jared looks at the twins. Although they are fraternal twins, they look almost identical with gray eyes and shoulder-length blond hair. Moreover, they definitely think the same, often answering each other's questions before the question is even asked. It is as if they think in unison, always on the same wavelength—except for when Ivy plays up her role as the older sister and tries to boss around her ten-minute-younger brother. That is funny. Damian gets so frustrated.

"Oh, believe me!" replies Dr. Jones. "This will be exciting. You have never seen a game like this before."

"What's the plot?" interrupts Ethan. "What do we need to do?"

"Think of it as a quest. Someone hid a set of clues in world history from 10,000 BCE to around 600 CE that lead to an artifact in the real world. You need to find these clues, fight a variety of enemies, compete against other players, and then find this artifact."

A slight groan ripples through the students. Many students have played educational quest games before. Most of the time is spent answering questions, and they are not a lot of fun. Damian captures the feeling of the entire class. "Dr. Jones, this doesn't really sound like an action game. It actually sounds kind of, ah... boring."

"Trust me. This will not be boring. Let me explain." Dr. Jones taps on his handheld pad, and several slides appear on the screens. "It's a network game. It resides on the Internet. Scientists have created an amazing game based on a second World Wide Web, a virtual Web, a simulated Web that is identical to the one that everyone sees. It grows and changes just like the real Web. Every time a Web site is created, updated, or deleted, the same happens in the virtual Web, instantaneously. Except for one big difference: it is fully interactive—a complete, immersive, simulated reality indistinguishable from true reality. In this game, you actually enter the Web. You interact with each other, the content, and anything that is on a particular Web site."

Lien, another student, raises her perfectly manicured hand and asks, "How is that possible? There are probably over a billion Web sites, and the Web is constantly growing."

Dr. Jones chuckles, then replies, "You're right. You'll be playing in a subset of the Web—specifically, on history sites. That's why we're here in your world history class. We figure there are several million sites with historical content. I don't want to get too technical, but this game taps into very powerful computers, known as servers, and into the largest networks and data centers around the world."

Arjun, worried about those glove controllers, asks, "Do we use virtual helmets and glove controllers?"

"Not in this game. It's totally immersive. You're the controller," replies the vice principal.

"I remember in one of those old science-fiction movies, or was it a television series, they had something called a holodeck, which was a virtual reality room. Is it like that?" asks Damian.

"That's a good guess," replies Dr. Jones. "However, this is not a room or a holodeck. This is new, revolutionary technology. Let's say you go to a site on the Roman Senate; instead of watching or reading the content, you will be in the Senate chambers interacting with the senators. Totally interactive, completely immersive, simulated environments based on real history, or at least what historians and archaeologists know about history. There are characters on the site with whom you interact; some are other students who are playing the game, and others are characters controlled by the computers. Imagine talking with a Roman citizen during the rise of Christianity. He wants to believe in the new god but can't quite let go of his belief in the old Roman gods. You'll learn concepts like historical empathy, just by interacting with the characters."

"Sounds pretty educational to me," Damian calls out skeptically. "And boring," he whispers under his breath. Several students smile.

"Sounds like a lot of other games," adds Ivy, before Dr. Jones can reply. "I choose a character that I want to be, outfit her, and play."

"Not quite," answers Dr. Jones. "There are no avatars, no surrogates, nothing besides you. You are the one in the game. Let me explain. A team of neuroscientists, computer engineers, and psychologists worked on this for a very long time. It consists of a three-part system."

Although he knows he is not allowed to use his smartphone in class, Jared secretly texts Megan anyway. "This sounds OK. Beats using our textbooks."

Dr. Jones walks over to the table and removes a cloth cover, revealing a beautifully packaged box. The box is matte black with a gold, embossed network that looks like a huge spider web with millions of nodes. "The Ancients: 10,000 BCE–600 CE" is stenciled in gold. He touches the side of the box, and the spider web transforms itself into a hologram, projecting gold rays and nodes in a two- to three-foot radius above the box. He opens the box.

"First is this wrist bracelet. It is similar to any metal bracelet that a man or woman might have worn during almost any era in history."

Except in the Stone Age, thinks Jared, when the bracelet might have been made out of ivory instead.

"It looks quite normal, like any bronze-and-iron wristband," continues Dr. Jones. "Except it isn't. The bracelet is a high-powered transmitter and receiver. This will ensure that you have a wireless connection to the virtual Web as long as you're near a high-speed Wi-Fi network, like your home network.

"Second, we have these contact lenses. The lenses project high-resolution images directly onto the retina of your eyes—in this case, search results. The text and the images will be somewhat transparent so that you can still see what is happening around you.

"And third is what makes it all happen: full-immersion, virtual reality that encompasses all of your senses. You will feel as though you are there. Your body will think you are in the game. These are biological nanoelectricalmechanical systems—bioNEMS, for short. They are tiny circuits or nanobots that send signals to a receiver and receive signals from a transmitter. Thousands of these little bots will position themselves in close proximity to interneuron connections from all your senses. When activated, they replace the real signals that your brain would receive from your senses with signals from the virtual environment—from the Web site you are visiting. You will think you are there. If you run in the virtual environment, your muscles will get tired, and you will be out of breath, yet you haven't really moved. However, your brain thinks you have, and is signaling and receiving information that your muscles are running and your lungs are breathing harder. If you get hit, you will feel pain."

Lien straightens her designer top, twirls her long, black hair, and scrunches her almond-brown eyes. She raises her hand again and, before Dr. Jones calls on her, says, "Sounds intriguing. And I'm looking forward to exploring the places my Chinese ancestors may have lived. But I have one question. In normal video games, if a character gets killed, it can respawn or come back to life in some way. In this game, can a player get killed?"

Silence engulfs the class. Jared looks at Lien and smiles. That's exactly what he wanted to ask. He's amazed at how she always asks such critical questions in such a nice, non-threatening way.

Dr. Jones clears his throat and pauses for a moment. "Let me explain. The computer-generated characters can die. However, real-life players that enter the game with the nanobots can only get hurt. The developers built in safeguards against a player dying. I doubt any parent would let a son or daughter play a game without such safeguards." He smiles and then continues, "However, to make it lifelike, the players can experience real injuries and pain. The nanobots interpret the signals from the Web site and make them happen inside of the body." He quickly adds, "So, that's why this game is strictly voluntary, and your parents must sign a release form before you can begin."

No one says a word as the students process what Dr. Jones just said. Finally, Ethan raises his hand and shouts, "That's so cool. Finally, a game with some real consequences." He leans back in his chair and rubs his chin. "That's pretty intense." A few seconds later, he adds, "I like it. There's no other game out there like this."

Other students hesitatingly nod in agreement.

Lien, skeptical about how this will all work, asks, "While we're in the game, what actually happens to our real bodies?"

"Your body will be as if you are asleep," answers Dr. Jones. "So you need to make sure that when you engage the nanobots, you're some place safe and private. It will be like falling asleep instantly. You should be in your home, bedroom, on a couch or chair. Someplace where you would normally sleep or rest."

"You mean like this class," whispers Damian. Several students around him laugh. Ms. Castro, who is standing just off to the side, frowns at him. Damian avoids her eye contact, rolls his eyes, and whispers to his table-mate, "Oops."

Dr. Jones senses the concern in the classroom and continues. "The company that developed this game is offering thirty thousand dollars in scholarship money to every member of the team that locates the clues and finds the artifact first, and one hundred thousand dollars to the winning school. Plus, I've spoken to Ms. Castro and the principal, and everyone who participates will automatically have his or her grade raised by a letter grade or receive extra credit."

Megan secretly texts Jared, "This is getting better all the time."

Jared replies, "Cool game. But nanobots sitting at my synapses in my brain? I don't think so." Jared is torn. He is excited about the potential of the game but hates the idea of thousands of tiny nanobots in his body. It does not feel right. What happens if something goes wrong—they send the wrong signal or fry his brain? He shivers.

Megan types back, "I'm sure they tested it."

"Yeah, but something seems odd," Jared texts back.

"Excuse me, Mr. Reyes," says Ms. Castro, catching Jared off guard. "Is there something you'd like to share with the class?"

Jared knows he is not supposed to text in class, and he hates being singled out. He likes cool games as much as anyone does, but he has many questions about this one. He wants to ask them, but most of his classmates think his questions are stupid. They don't take him seriously.

"Actually, there is," Jared replies quietly. He turns toward Dr. Jones. "I have a couple of questions. You mentioned nanobots. Who controls these nanobots?"

Dr. Jones replies, "No one controls them. All they do is receive the signals as if you were actually in the virtual environment. That's what provides the full-immersion experience."

"OK, I guess," replies Jared. He is not quite satisfied with the answer but decides to go on anyway. "You also mentioned the 'winning team' several times. Does this mean we'll be competing against someone?"

"Yes," replies Dr. Jones. "You can work individually or with some of your classmates. But you will be competing against the others who aren't on your team. And remember, there are ten other schools all looking for the same clues."

"OK," replies Jared, looking back down at his desk.

Qadim raises his hand and asks, "Are there any other risks?"

"Not really," replies Dr. Jones. "There could be some minor glitches like in any other game, but nothing you won't be able to figure out once you get into it."

Jared secretly whispers across the aisle to Arjun, who is sitting at the next table with his head turned to the front of the classroom. "I don't trust this. Probably good to be careful."

Arjun whispers back without turning his head. "If we have to learn history, it might as well be this way. I read about a similar type of technology in a science magazine a few weeks ago."

"I don't know," replies Jared. He looks down at his phone and sees another text from Megan.

"Others don't seem worried," she wrote. "Ethan asked me if I want to work with him."

"Good for him," replies Jared, typing while looking up to make sure Ms. Castro does not catch him using his phone again. "You could do worse. He knows games, and technology."

Megan looks up and glares at Jared across the room. She was hoping that telling him about Ethan might motivate him to join her. Jared smiles back.

"OK," says Dr. Jones. "If there are no more questions, I'll turn it back over to Ms. Castro. Please read the detailed instructions for the game, and then make sure your parents sign the disclaimer and release form online. All they need to do is respond to the e-mail, and then you can participate. Oh, and don't forget, the deadline is Monday morning. We've been told that a lot of students want to participate, so if you're late there's a chance you can't join. OK?"

The class claps with enthusiasm as Ms. Castro returns to the front of the room. "Thank you, Dr. Jones. This sounds like a good opportunity for our school and this class."

Jared detects uncertainty in her voice. It sounds like she is not fully convinced about the game. Maybe she has questions, too. A few minutes later, she dismisses class for the weekend. Jared is tempted to walk up to her desk and ask, but figures that might not be the best idea right now. As the students stream out of the classroom, teams begin to form immediately. Damian and Ivy grab a few of their friends and head down the hall. Ethan walks over toward Megan. Everyone talks excitedly about the new game, *The Ancients*. They all seem to have forgotten the risks involved.

Jared is one of the last to leave the classroom, followed by Lien.

She catches up to him in the hallway, which is filling with students from all classrooms. "Those were good questions. I have the same concerns."

"Thanks. It's probably nothing, and the game sounds cool. It's just the thought of the nanobots."

"Something to think about over the weekend, I guess," replies Lien. "Take care." She walks off, leaving Jared in the hall. He stops at his locker and then heads off campus. He cuts across the open field and emerges a few miles from his suburban neighborhood of single- and two-story homes. He is walking along the side of the street when he feels his smartphone vibrate. He picks it up, pushes the text-to-speech button, and listens to Megan's text message.

"You sure you don't want to join me? It would be great to have you on my team."

He pushes the talk button to respond, "I don't know. Let me think about it." He hits the send button as a four-door convertible comes to a screeching halt next to him.

"You scared of a little competition?" shouts Ivy, leaning out over the edge.

"You're probably afraid of being known as a loser after we smoke you in this game," continues Damian.

"Oh, I'm sorry. You're already a loser," adds Ivy, bursting out laughing at her own wittiness.

Jared ignores them, continues to walk, and then abruptly turns and sprints toward the car with a scowl on his face. "Careful what you wish for. I'm not afraid of two clones like you."

Damian smokes the tires and quickly peels away from the curb. "The game is on. Don't come crying to us when we win," he yells.

Jared throws his plastic water bottle after the car. He continues down the street and asks himself, Am I scared? He then remembers a quote from Mark Twain that his dad would recite: "Courage is resistance to fear, mastery of fear—not absence of fear."

A while later, he walks up his driveway with a smile. At least it's the weekend, and there could be worse things than learning world history while playing a game. He will have to give it some thought.

CHAPTER 4

MEGAN CONVINCES HER FATHER, WHO IS TRAVELING WITH her mother in the Middle East, to go online and electronically sign the release form. To her surprise, a special courier delivers her personalized virtual Web kit first thing Saturday morning. Only a few miles from Jared's house, she's tempted to let him know what she is about to do. She then decides against it, settles on the couch, and tears open the outer shipping package. She carefully removes the shrink-wrap from the matte-black box and lifts open the cover. Inside, cradled in the same deep green that she saw in the classroom version, are the three items: the bronze-and-iron bracelet, contact lenses, and a pill. On the inside of the cover, in the middle of a gold, network diagram, is a button that says, "Push here first."

She pushes the button, and the network image transforms itself into a screen. A voice begins to describe how to use the different components of the kit, and how to start. After listening to the instructions, Megan figures, why wait until Monday? It looks like everything is ready; she can take it for a test drive and get proficient before the others do. She slips on the bracelet and carefully places the soft contact lenses on her corneas. She picks up the pill and turns it around in her fingers for a moment, staring at its color. Feeling a bit strange, she hesitates.

Then she hears her father's voice in her head. They'd often spoken about the risks associated with his diplomatic missions. "Sometimes you have to be a risk taker, but it should always be a calculated risk," he would remind her. Then she thinks about all the clichés he uses: "When swinging from one tree to the next, you have to let go of the first rope to grab the second. You have to leave sight of the shore if you want to discover new horizons. Nothing ventured, nothing gained."

She grabs a nearby glass of water and with one gulp swallows the nanobots. She makes herself comfortable on the large couch, spreading her feet and tucking a pillow under her head. A few minutes go by, and nothing. She takes a couple of deep breaths. For a second she thinks about what Jared said about all those nanobots streaming through her body, but then she thinks of what Yuri Gagarin, the first human to travel into outer space, must have felt as he strapped himself into the rocket for the first time. She waits, and nothing happens. Five minutes go by, ten, fifteen minutes; still nothing happens. Then she remembers the video. She touches the "home" image on her bracelet and says, "Go home." Instantly her breathing changes and she looks as though she is fast asleep.

For Megan, however, it is anything but sleep. She is standing on a transparent platform in the middle of what looks like deep space. But it is not any space she knows. All around her are millions of soft, pale-gold strands connected with millions of spheres. The strands and nodes that are closer are bigger and more pronounced; those farther away get smaller and smaller. Some nodes are connected to many strands, more than she can count. Even below her, the nodes and strands seem to extend into infinity. New nodes and strands are constantly being added; others disappear. As she looks around, she feels as if she's standing inside an enormous, dynamic spider web radiating three-dimensionally in every direction. For a second she thinks about a large spider coming to get her food but dismisses the thought as soon as she realizes it is only her fear. She is standing in the middle of an enormous network—the Net—the World Wide Web.

Megan slowly twirls around. This is amazing, she thinks. What a home page! It's like standing in the middle of the universe, and all the stars and planets are connected by tiny strands of shimmering silk. She touches the question-mark image and says, "Dinosaurs." In less than a quarter of a second, over sixty-five million search results are located. Several of the top search results project on her contact lenses. There is so much information; she needs to scroll through the sites quickly to find one that interests her. She experiments with moving her eyes up and down and from left to right, but nothing happens. She tries all sorts of options. She holds the question-mark image and moves her eyes: nothing. In her excitement to get going, she did not read about how to navigate search results. After several minutes of trying with no results, her patience runs out. She is ready to deactivate. In her frustration, she angrily says, "Scroll down." To her disbelief, the screen scrolls down. This must be one of the advanced features. She whispers, "Scroll right," and the screen moves to the right. She says several other commands in an even softer tone, "Zoom in, zoom out, open, go, more detail," and they all work. She is amazed. What an awesome device. She continues to experiment with the feature and then tries a barely audible whisper, only moving her throat muscles, "Scroll down." The screen scrolls down. After a few minutes of scanning the different dinosaur sites, she finds one that looks interesting. She touches the thunderbolt image on the bracelet and names the Web site. Then she says, "Go."

A few minutes pass and nothing happens. She waits longer and still nothing. Finally, she tries it again in a low whisper. Again, she waits. Then in the blink of an eye, she finds herself running through waist-high grass on a rolling meadow. The sun beats down on the savannah. Large, birdlike animals lazily circle high in the clear, blue sky. She passes a Paleolithic pit house ringed with mammoth bones, half covered in hides;

the other half has blown off. In the distance, a forest climbs up gentle hills. Megan slows down and turns around just as a band of prehistoric hunters scream and yell as they sprint out of the forest toward her. She looks down at her clothes and sees that she is dressed in a similar fashion and that she can understand what they are screaming. They are yelling, "Run. Hide. Faster. Go." Dr. Jones was right, she thinks. Not only does the computer automatically translate the language of the place and its people at the time, but it probably translates her words as well. In addition, the technology makes the player look like he or she belongs in that time. Advanced stuff.

Three Tyrannosaurus rexes, two adults and a baby, come through the trees fifty yards behind the hunters. The two adults are enormous, weighing close to ten tons and standing over twenty-three feet tall. One young hunter makes a deadly mistake. Instead of running as fast as he can and hiding, he decides to stop. He plants his feet and throws a spear at one of the huge beasts. The spear bounces off the tough hide as if hitting a coat of armor. The T. rex lunges forward and with one swoop grabs the screaming hunter in its powerful jaws. A sickening crunch silences the screaming. The big dinosaur breaks the hunter's back and proceeds to eat him while continuing to run after the others. The T. rex is still hungry and charges after his next victim.

Megan tries hard to remember how to avoid a Tyrannosaurus. She knows that dinosaurs most likely evolved from animals in the ocean and that they then ruled the earth for one hundred million years or so. They were omnivores and existed everywhere. Dinosaurs were the most successful of the early land animals and roamed all over the world. Then, some kind of mass extinction event occurred sixty-five million years ago. Some say a massive meteor smashed into the Earth, and the environment changed. She remembers there were several different theories and ideas of why the dinosaurs became extinct. Within a few hundred thousand years, they were all gone. She does not have time to look that up right now. She is aware that this information is not helping her much in trying to escape the beasts. She tries to think of something else. She remembers seeing an old Hollywood film a few years back. In it, the main characters avoided detection because a Tyrannosaurus supposedly had poor eyesight. She stops, does not move, hoping the big beast will not see her. She stands as still as a statue.

Across the way, another hunter sees what she is doing and yells at her to keep moving. She answers that if she stands completely still the T. rex should not see her. The hunter yells back that she is crazy. They can see and smell quite well. He then waves his hand in dismissal and adds that if the T. rex eats her, maybe he will have a chance to escape. Maybe Hollywood had it wrong, she thinks.

Megan, now unsure, gets ready to run as well when she realizes what a dunce she's been. She can just hit the home symbol on her bracelet and be out of here. She touches the home image and nothing happens. In the excitement, she completely forgot about the time delay mentioned in the introduction video. They called it a little glitch in the software. But it's a glitch that could be quite dangerous.

She realizes it is time to run. She sprints forward and, in her rush, does not see the jagged rocks sticking up under the grass. She trips and rams one of the sharp edges into her right shin. She clenches her teeth and swallows a scream as she lands on her stomach. Blood begins to trickle from the cut. These nanobots sure make it real. She lies flat on the ground, covers her shin with her palm, and covers herself with grass. She feels the tremors in the ground as the two heavy animals run past her. Farther away, she can still hear the hunters screaming as the dinosaurs pursue them. She lifts her head from under the grass and sees the second T. rex pursuing a hunter who is sprinting toward a few lone trees. Thinking it's safe, she is about to get up when she feels a puff of warm air on the back of her neck. She slowly turns around and almost gags at the stupendously bad breath. She does not breathe and stares straight into the face of the young T. rex. She can't believe she forgot about the baby. He has located her under the grass. All she can hope is that he has already eaten and is not very hungry. He nuzzles closer. Megan pretends to play dead and closes her eyes. The T. rex does not leave.

She lies motionless for what seems like an eternity. Several minutes go by. Finally, she opens her eyes expecting to see gaping jaws. Instead, she sees a golden web. She is no longer in the meadow; rather, she is back on the platform. She never thought she would be so grateful to find herself in the middle of a spider web. She exhales with a big sigh, and then whispers, "Deactivate." Seconds later, she wakes up on her couch at home.

She looks down at the sharp pain in her shin and sees the blood continuing to trickle down her leg. She heads to the bathroom to get a Band-Aid and looks at herself—her disheveled hair and sweat-covered body—in the mirror. Her clothes are not torn. That makes sense; the nanobots cannot leave her body so they could not have torn the clothes in the real world. She smirks. These nanobots take their jobs seriously, maybe too seriously. What an awesome game! She has to tell Jared. He will learn to love it. She hopes.

CHAPTER 5

IT'S MONDAY MORNING, AND JARED IS STILL THINKING about whether he is going to play *The Ancients* game. He talked with his mom about it, and all she said was that she would support his decision, whatever it is. That does not exactly make it any easier. He wishes he could discuss this with his dad.

He is rummaging through his locker when Lien and Arjun interrupt his thoughts. "Hey there."

"Hey," replies Jared, turning around. He looks directly at Lien and thinks, She always looks so cool and fashionable.

"Have you decided whom you're going to work with in the game, or are you going solo?" asks Lien.

"Not really," replies Jared. "I don't know if I'm going to play."

"What? With your mind for history?" says Arjun.

Jared shrugs and gives him an I-don't-know look.

"Teams are already forming," continues Arjun. "Several formed over the weekend. Everyone's so excited."

Lien looks into Jared's eyes and hesitates. "I'd, ah … I mean, if you do decide to play, I'd like to be on your team." She is not sure why she likes Jared, but there's something about him.

"Me, too," adds Arjun.

"Let me think about it," replies Jared, not wanting to disappoint them, as he stuffs his backpack into his locker. He closes the door and turns around just as Megan limps up.

"Jared, you signed up yet? This morning is the deadline."

He grabs his books. "Not yet. What happened to you?"

"Nothing." Megan then lowers her voice so only the four of them can hear. "You know, it's not that bad."

"What's not so bad?" asks Jared.

"The nanobots, the Web, the game. All of it."

"What do you mean?" asks Arjun.

"Well…" Megan hesitates for a moment, looks around, and then leans toward the lockers. "I tried it this weekend."

"You what?" says Jared with a look of concern. "What are you talking about?" He knows Megan can be impetuous, but this is a bit much.

"Cool!" blurts out Arjun thinking about the amazing science behind this new game technology. Several students in the hallway look toward him.

"Shhh. Not everyone needs to know," replies Megan.

"Are you nuts? You entered the virtual Web alone?" asks Jared.

Lien looks at Megan, half admiring her boldness and half jealous that Megan went into the Web first.

Megan shrugs. "Yup, and it's awesome." She taps her chest with the palm of her hand several times. "These little nanobots sure make it realistic. You've never experienced anything like it. They're deactivated right now, of course."

"Of course," replies Jared sarcastically. "Is that where your limp comes from? What about the risks?"

"Don't start that again. What about the first astronaut, the first person to explore Antarctica, the test fighter pilot, do you think they—"

"I get it," replies Jared. "Adventurers take risks. Still!"

"Seriously. It wasn't bad once you get used to the quirks. It's so cool. Best game I've ever played. I mean, I almost became a T. rex snack. But other than that, no big deal. There's this time delay when you touch the home button on the bracelet. It took a while before I got off the Web site. I got a little banged up, but nothing a Band-Aid couldn't take care of."

"A *what* snack?" asks Arjun.

"T. rex. I went to a dinosaur Web site and hung out with a bunch of Paleolithic hunters. A few got eaten, but I escaped," replies Megan, as if running from a T. rex is a routine daily activity.

"Wait a minute. Slow down. Hunters? Dinosaurs? How can that be?" asks Lien.

"Like I said, I was running and two—"

"How can there be hunters?" interrupts Jared, understanding what Lien is thinking. "Dinosaurs died out sixty-five million years ago, and the first ancestors of humans didn't show up until millions of years later, more like two million years ago. They never lived during the same period of history. What site were you on?"

"I can't remember," replies Megan, stepping back and thinking for a moment. "You're right, dinosaurs and humans never met each other. See, that's why you need to join my team. You know more about history than anyone I know."

"That's strange," replies Jared.

Megan continues, "I didn't have time to think about dinosaurs and humans never meeting. I was too focused on running!"

As if looking through her, Jared stares off down the hall, thinking. He then focuses on her again. "It does make sense. If they're instantly copying the real Web, we'll have to look at the information and the sources very carefully. Information on these Web sites is a modern perception of history—what we know about the past, today. Hopefully, the information is based on solid evidence. But we also know that there are many bogus sites. I mean, anyone can publish anything. That particular Web site doesn't sound historically accurate. Maybe it was just an entertainment site. Did you use the contact lenses?"

"Yeah," replies Megan, "to initially find the site. Why?"

"That's another thing we're going to have to watch for. The search engine uses an algorithm to find sites; what it delivers first may not be the best site."

"That's correct," chimes in Arjun.

Megan touches Jared's arm and looks him in the eye. "Did I just hear you say, '*We're* going to have to watch for'?"

Jared takes a deep breath. "I don't like it, but I'll like it even less if you go alone."

"I won't be alone. Ethan's already agreed to be on my team. If you have such doubts, maybe you shouldn't go. But I'd love to have you on my team." She smiles and gently punches him in the shoulder. "C'mon. You'll love it."

"I guess," he replies. "Someone has to keep an eye on you." A look of disappointment flashes across Lien's face.

Jared sees her look and quickly adds, "I was going to work with Lien and Arjun. They should join our team, too, then."

In that moment, Lien is reminded about one of the things she likes about Jared. One rarely gets to see it through his carefully cultivated "I don't care about much" image. Besides being smart, he is more perceptive and sensitive than most other guys.

"Sure, if they want to," replies Megan. "This will be good. I'll let Ethan know."

"Cool," replies Jared. "I need to text my mom to make sure she registers me this morning. I'd hate to be late and then not be able to help you." He breaks out into a big smile.

"Funny. I thought I was helping you," replies Megan. "I'll see you in class."

The rest of the school day is uneventful except that everyone is talking about the new history game. Ethan is a bit disappointed. He had hoped to work only with Megan, but he figures it's better to be on her team with others than not to work with her at all. He can't wait to get to sixth period and start playing.

In sixth period history, to the disappointment of all fifteen students, instead of talking about the game, Ms. Castro begins class with a review from the week before. She quickly taps on her tablet, and several slides emerge on the monitors at the front of the room. She looks around.

"Much of human history happened in secret, since without written records there are only archeological artifacts. Here are some slides with information you'll want to know for your quiz this week." She reviews the slides.

Paleolithic (Old Stone Age) ~ 2.6M–10,000 BCE

- Two million years
- 200,000 years ago Homo sapiens, ancestors of modern humans appeared
- "Extensification" - human nomads spreading across Earth's land-masses and adapting"
- Sedentary hunter/gatherers
- Had language, exchanged ideas, learned collectively

Neolithic (New Stone Age)/Agricultural Revolution ~10,000 BCE–6,000 BCE

- Several stages, lasted thousands of years
- Major transition from hunter/gatherer to agriculture and settlement
- "Intensification" - humans settled and thrived in one place, numbers of humans and population density increased
- Cultivated plants and domesticated animals
- Stayed in one place longer. Shift in thinking—saw land as their own; if others entered, they were seen as intruders

Jared secretly takes out his smartphone and sends a text to Megan. "This is killing me. Everyone knows this stuff."

Megan smiles as she scans Jared's text. It is so great to have him on her team.

"Mr. Reyes!"

Startled, Jared looks up. Ms. Castro is looking directly at him. "Is there something you'd like to add?"

"Not really. I was just thinking how some say the Neolithic Revolution made things better; others say it made things worse."

Several students give him a confused look, not understanding how the agricultural revolution could have made things worse. It led to the domestication of animals and food, higher productivity, and the building of towns and cities. He looks around the class and can see several kids thinking, What a stupid comment.

"You're correct in looking at both sides of the argument," replies Ms. Castro. "Would you like to explain?" She has known all along that Jared is much brighter than he likes to let on.

"Not really," Jared replies as he quickly puts away his phone.

Ms. Castro looks around the class. "Actually, it's a very important question. I won't go into it now, but for Friday's discussion, be prepared to discuss how the Neolithic Revolution changed nutrition, health, and social relations. And did early humans make a critical decision way back then that put us on a different trajectory?"

Several students glare at Jared. If he had only kept his mouth shut, they would not have received extra work. Ms. Castro continues with the next slide.

<u>Major Patterns That Created Change around 4000–1000 BCE</u>
- Growth of civilizations
  - » Complex societies came into existence around 4000 BCE–1000 BCE.
  - » Classical civilizations in India, China, Mesoamerica, and the Mediterranean arose around 1000 BCE–600 CE.
- Development of agricultural societies
  - » Approximate dates for domestication.
    ~10,000 or 9000 BCE, Fertile Crescent in Mesopotamia
    ~8000 BCE, Yellow River in China
    ~6000 BCE, Indus Valley in Southeast Asia and around the Nile River
    ~4500 BCE, Americas
- Pastoral nomads migrated from the steppes of Central Asia.

Ethan raises his hand. "Ms. Castro, I thought this world history class would now focus on playing the game. Not all this other material."

"You will get plenty of time to play, Ethan. But you will not be searching for clues during class time. The game is in addition to classroom work. Class time will continue to be for discussions, debate, group work, presentations, and some individual activities, but not for disappearing into an online world."

A collective groan comes from the class, and several students slump their shoulders; they had so hoped they could just play. Ms. Castro then continues by explaining that part of connecting the past, the present, and the future in world history is not only knowing key events and dates, but also recognizing broad areas of change, or themes. Jared listens halfheartedly.

He and his dad often had long discussions tracing themes from the earliest of times all the way into the future, or taking themes from today and tracing them back in time. His dad used to call it "history in reverse." The most interesting to Jared was how power has been used and abused throughout history. He thinks about those discussions, which often took place while they were biking. They used to go together at least every other weekend. He misses his dad. He snaps his pencil as he remembers the day they took him. He wonders if he should have done more, not just hide behind the car.

Halfway through the period, Ms. Castro introduces a video titled *The World's First Temple. Changing Our View of Civilization*. It is a video about Göbekli Tepe in Southeastern Turkey, one of the greatest archaeological finds of all time. Jared perks up. He is surprised that he has never heard about this before. None of his textbooks ever mentioned it. The video explains that the complex was built around 12,000 years ago—7,000 years earlier than Stonehenge and 6,500 years before the pyramids at Giza. Archaeologists still debate its meaning, since this dig site is challenging how they think about the rise of civilizations. It used to be that historians thought agriculture led to cities, and then later to other things like art, writing, and religion.

The commentator says it was first believed that the rise of civilization was due to environmental changes that allowed people to cultivate plants and herd animals. This new research proposes that the Neolithic Revolution occurred across a huge area over thousands of years and that Göbekli was the beginning of a new pattern, in which the human sense of the sacred and love of a good spectacle may have given rise to civilization. Maybe worship led to civilization. Only Jared and a few other students, Lien included, grasp the significance of the archeological find. Fascinating, he thinks, and makes a mental note to research more about Göbekli.

Ms. Castro turns off the video and walks back to the front of the classroom. "That was it on historical themes and patterns. Your homework assignment for Thursday will be to analyze the video and identify several other key themes that span the major eras of world history." Some of the students sigh loudly enough for others to hear.

The class is about to break out in laughter when Ms. Castro abruptly says, "OK, let's change subjects and spend the remaining few class minutes talking about *The Ancients* game." Instantly, all students pay attention and focus on her. Damian looks over, and as soon as Jared makes eye contact, he runs his index finger across the front of his throat. Jared ignores him and looks straight ahead.

"Before we begin, remember that search engines rank material based on what they think is relevant," says Ms. Castro. "It may not be what you want, so don't just go to the first thing you see. Second, I suggest that you always check the sources, reliability, or credibility of the site. Understand the source of the information."

At the back of the room, Jared gazes out of the window. He talked with Megan about this when she came back from the dinosaur site. Any time you research anything, you need to check the sources.

Ms. Castro continues, "Dr. Jones said you start the game by looking for clues in one of earth's earliest settlements during the Neolithic Revolution."

Kazuo interrupts, "Did he give any more details?" He pulls out his own smartphone, unfolds the screen, and types several key words. "I get close to forty-one million search results. It will take several lifetimes to look through all that information."

"Didn't Dr. Jones say the game is limited to sites with history content?" adds Alexa. "With that I get thirty-five million hits. We'll never find anything."

"If you would let me finish," says Ms. Castro, taking back control of her class. "I received word from Dr. Jones. He says you'll need to start with one of Earth's earliest settlements. There is also a riddle; the solution probably helps to narrow down your search. It says: *I represent the challenge with archaeology and ancient history. Hanging on the wall, I am one of several things. Will anyone ever know?*'"

"That's it?" asks Damian. "What kind of riddle is that?"

"Unfortunately, that's all I've been given," replies Ms. Castro. "I suggest you make your best educated guess and begin. Use the research techniques we learned earlier in the year, and I'm sure you'll be fine."

With only a couple of minutes left in class, Ms. Castro asks how many students have received confirmation that they are signed up for the game. All hands except Jared's go up. His mother hasn't responded to the text he sent her earlier in the day. The bell rings, signaling the end of the period. "Remember, next week is spring break. That might be a good time for you to start. Some of you might even finish. Class dismissed."

The students all rush to leave except for Jared, Megan, Lien, Arjun, and Ethan. They huddle and look at Arjun's tablet computer.

"What happens when you search for early settlements or towns?" asks Lien.

"I already did and found this table right here," says Arjun, scrolling down the page.

Examples of Early Towns with Approximate Dates
~9000 BCE: Jericho, West Bank, Palestinian Territories
~6500 BCE: Çatalhöyük, modern Turkey
~4000 BCE: Hamoukar, modern Syria
~2600–2500 BCE: Harappa and Mohenjo Daro, Indus Valley
~Various dates—Many more in Mesopotamia

"Maybe we should split up and start with the first two," suggests Megan. "Jared and I can go to Çatalhöyük and the rest of you go to Jericho."

Ethan is about to protest but decides to hold off. It was Megan's suggestion, and he doesn't want to challenge her in front of the others. He'll have to figure out another way to show her that he is a better partner than Jared. He looks over at Lien, thinking that she might be a good ally in helping him spend more time with Megan. He knows that she would rather go with Jared. Lien, however, quickly masks her disappointment and looks away.

Arjun shrugs and replies, "Works for me. When do we start?"

"How about tonight around eight? We can play for a couple of hours and get a head start on everyone," replies Megan.

Jared lowers his eyes. "Maybe. I don't know if that'll work for me."

"Are you still worried about the nanobots?" teases Megan.

"A little," replies Jared, "but I don't know if I'm registered yet."

Ethan sees an opportunity. "If you can't make it tonight, you can always join us later. I can go to Çatalhöyük with Megan."

"Sounds like a plan," replies Megan as she stands to leave the group. "Why don't we wait until around dinner and see what happens? I'll check in with everyone." They all agree and leave campus.

Later that afternoon, Jared looks at the box that arrived by special courier and opens the confirmation e-mail where his mom gave approval for him to play the game. He scrolls down and sees pages and pages of disclaimer text written in a legalese he cannot understand. He looks at the pill full of nanobots in his fingers, and then carefully places it on his desk. He thinks back to when Lien asked about dying and the game. Dr. Jones's response was a bit odd. Just for the heck of it, he asks his Web browser to search the legal text for words such as "death," "deceased," "expiration," "demise," and several other terms that could be synonyms for dying. After a few minutes, he leans back in his chair and runs his hands through his hair. He knew it! Buried deep in the disclaimer, where 99 percent of users would never look, are words that barely sound like English. It says that although safeguards were put in place to guard against any player dying, there are still bugs in the system. Therefore, the developer assumes no responsibility for what happens in the game, or as a result of the game.

His gut is right. Something is off. Yet, at the same time, he cannot imagine that the game would let anyone die. It would be a disaster and a public relations nightmare for the developer. He picks up the pill, looks at it for another few seconds, and then pops it into his mouth and washes it down with a glass of water. He wonders if he should say anything to the others about what he just read. His first day in the game should be interesting.

$$\gg \gg \gg$$

At a secret computer lab somewhere in North America, a technician sends an encrypted message. *"All players from Globus Academy are now active. All schools are ready to go. Tracking feature is regrettably still in development and offline."*

CHAPTER 6

LATER THAT EVENING, MEGAN AND JARED COORDINATE
with Lien, Ethan, and Arjun and enter the game. Within seconds, Jared
and Megan are transported to a promising Web site about Çatalhöyük,
Turkey, and stand behind a clump of trees looking at a dirt road that leads
to the settlement. Megan confidently steps out from the trees and blends
in behind a group of people walking on the road.

Jared says quietly, "Megan, get back here! What's the plan? People
will see you."

"They're not going to recognize us in this crowd. The game ensures
that we're dressed like the locals and can speak the language. Just mingle."

"Yeah, like your red dreadlocks and white skin don't stand out."

"Think of me as a visitor passing through."

Megan pushes the question mark icon on her bracelet and searches
her contact lenses for any information on the ancient Neolithic settlement. She turns to Jared. "Çatalhöyük is one of the largest concentra-
tions of humans on the planet, and right now we're in 6200 BCE. The
town probably has close to ten thousand inhabitants."

"How do you know that?" asks Jared.

"I just looked it up. Let me show you how these lenses work. If
I had these things in class, I could have aced every test without ever
having to study."

"True, but if they'd caught you cheating, you would have been kicked
out."

"I was only kidding," replies Megan. "Don't take everything so seriously."

They continue to walk toward two large mounds ahead; one rises about sixty feet above the plain. Off in the distance, they can see a marsh formed by the Çarşamba River. The town rises from these two mounds of alluvial clay. One mound is close to thirty-two acres in size. They notice that farmers are carrying their loads. There are no wagons or draft animals. The wheel has not been invented. Farmers tend their crops on a vast, fertile expanse known as the Konya Plain. Irrigation ditches crisscross the fields as hundreds of people work with a variety of stone, bone, and obsidian tools. They also seem to be weeding to get rid of non-food-producing plants.

Far off in the distance, huge plumes of dark smoke waft into the sky. Megan wanders over to one of the farmers and asks what is happening in the distance. He tells her that it looks like a field is no longer producing so they are burning trees to create a new area to plant. As he hears the farmer's answer, Jared thinks about the Amazon rainforest and how even in the modern world, some farmers still use slash-and-burn agriculture—8,500 years later.

They keep walking. As they near Çatalhöyük, they see that it is a major trading center filled with artisans making pottery, baskets, woolen cloth, beads, leather, and wood products. They see copper, lead, silver, and gold. The buildings are clustered together in a honeycomb fashion; the rooftops are the streets. People enter the one-story domestic buildings through holes in the roof. Some have windows up high.

"This place reminds me of the Pueblo structures in the Southwestern United States," says Megan.

"Yeah. There are similarities," replies Jared. "Those came much later, though." He remembers that Indians had lived in the Southwest for thousands of years, but they didn't start building pueblos until around 750 CE.

They continue to walk across the rooftops.

"This community is so alive and active," comments Megan, "and look at all the vivid murals painted on the walls and all the clay and stone figurines."

Occasionally they peer down into rooms. In some, the walls are covered in cream-colored plaster with paintings; in others, the walls are decorated with reliefs, and benches line the perimeters. As they move about the town, they pass a building that looks like any other from the outside. But inside it looks like a shrine. Unaware of the eyes that follow them, they come upon an artisan who shapes arrowheads out of black obsidian.

"We're looking for a shrine," says Megan.

The craftsman eyes them warily, and then chuckles. He says, "There are many shrines. Shrines are everywhere. Which one do you want?"

Jared had been thinking about the riddle all afternoon before entering the game. He brings up the same site he found earlier that describes Çatalhöyük, a mother goddess, and a wall painting. He finds a picture of the modern-day excavation and dig site and quickly scans it.

"What is with your companion? Is he all right?" asks the craftsman. "He stares off into nowhere."

Megan looks at Jared and gives him a slight nudge. Jared focuses back on the craftsman. "We're looking for the shrine with the mother goddess and the painting on the wall."

"We are visitors and were told it's a place we can leave an offering," adds Megan.

The craftsman thinks for a moment and points to a building several rooftops away. Megan thanks him, and they walk in that direction, passing several rooftop openings.

Once they are out of earshot of the craftsman, Jared says, "That's not where we need to go. I did a search, and we need to head this way." He points off to the left. "I figured out the riddle right before we got here."

"How? What was it?"

"Remember, it said, 'I represent the challenge with archaeology and ancient history. Hanging on the wall, I am one of several things. Will anyone ever know?' One of the biggest challenges with ancient history is that there is often little evidence, so people have many different hypotheses or theories."

"How do you know all this?" asks Megan.

"What do you expect? My dad is a history professor. We talked a lot. In ancient settlements, usually only a few things hung on the walls: bull skulls, reliefs, wall paintings. Most were pretty clear, but there was one wall painting in Çatalhöyük. I looked it up. Some think it's the earliest landscape painting ever known; others think it's a map. Some think it's a painting of a leopard skin, and others think it's just a geometric design. That fits with the riddle—'I am one of several things' and 'Will anyone ever know?'—because unless more evidence is uncovered, we won't ever know."

Megan looks at him and shakes her head. "Sometimes you really scare me. Your brain works in some weird ways."

"Hey, it's worth a shot." He scrambles up a ladder and across several rooftops, heading west, with Megan close behind. The craftsman watches where they go. On their way across the rooftops, Jared holds his nose and points out the garbage in the spaces between the buildings and courtyards.

"Unique garbage disposal system," replies Megan.

As they reach the location, Jared suggests, "Maybe one of us should stay outside and keep watch."

"For what?" replies Megan. "We need both of us looking. These places aren't large; it should only take a few minutes."

First Megan and then Jared climb down the wooden ladder into a room approximately fifteen by fifteen feet. The colorful, highly decorated walls astound them both. There are paintings depicting hunters, farmers, and animals. Reliefs in plaster and animal skulls protrude from the walls. Alcoves, most containing single female figurines and some male figurines, dot the walls. Plant-fiber mats cover the floor. They search the room. Nothing. After several more minutes of searching, Jared climbs up the ladder while Megan continues to look. He looks back down into the hole. "Megan, are you coming?"

"I'll be right there."

Jared shakes his head, wondering why they did not find anything. He brings up the online map of the modern-day dig site of Çatalhöyük and tries to locate where he is standing. It is hard to compare the dig site with the old settlement. "Damn," he says to himself as he walks over to the hole in the roof. He yells down, "Megan, I was off. We should be two buildings over."

"Now you tell me," replies Megan as she scrambles out of the building. "Did you know they buried their dead right in the floor of their houses, and then continued living in the place?"

"Yeah. I saw that. Different time, different values," replies Jared as he heads to the next building. Neither one notices the men who have gathered around the craftsman. Jared climbs down the ladder, facing forward. Rays of sun filter in through the opening, illuminating a spot on the wall. "Hey, I think this is it." He stands next to a nine-foot-long wall painting. It seems to depict the settlement at Çatalhöyük itself, with graded terraces, rectangular buildings, and the twin cones of a volcano.

Megan joins him. "That explains all the obsidian," says Megan, looking at the drawing. "It comes from the volcano. What are we supposed to look for?"

"I don't know," replies Jared. "Something that stands out or is different. A clue."

They both stare at the painting for several more minutes until Megan finally says, "I don't see anything." She steps away from the painting and stumbles over a bowl, spilling sand across the floor.

That's odd, thinks Jared. Why would anyone have a bowl of sand in a shrine? A bowl of water, as a possible offering, makes sense. But sand? He picks up the empty bowl. The outside is highly decorated with blue, green, purple, brown, yellow, and red pigments.

"I think it tells a story," he says, marveling at the intricate drawings. "I don't understand it."

"Let me take a look," says Megan, reaching for the bowl. She looks at the drawings and then peers into the inside. On the bottom, written in white, are a few sentences. "That's odd. I didn't know they wrote on the inside of pottery." She holds the inside of the bowl toward the sunlight coming in through the opening.

"They didn't," interrupts Jared. "We're in around 6200 BCE. Writing didn't come along for another three thousand years, and then in Mesopotamia. We're in Turkey."

"Maybe this is the first clue," Megan replies with excitement in her voice.

They hear voices from above.

"Quick, we need to get out of here," Jared says as he begins to climb up the ladder. "Bring the bowl."

Megan cradles the bowl in her shirt and follows Jared up the ladder. As they emerge into the sunlight, two burly men grab Jared. He struggles to get free, but the men are strong and pull his arms behind his back. The craftsman, standing in front of Megan, points an obsidian spear at her stomach. "These are the two." Looking directly at the bowl in Megan's hands, he asks, "What do you have there? Robbing our shrine?"

Without answering, Megan takes off. She runs over the rooftops as fast as she can while carrying the bowl. She figures that since Jared's wearing the bracelet, he can take care of himself. Looking backward one last time, she rounds the corner of a building and runs directly into a group of farmers returning from the fields. With the craftsman yelling that the two visitors desecrated a shrine, the farmers drop their tools and grab hold of her arms and legs. Like a wild cat, she kicks with her feet and punches at anything within striking distance. Her left hand protects the bowl in her shirt. One of the farmers, growing tired of this crazy female, grabs the wooden handle of a stone hoe and swings it at her arm. Megan instinctively twists her body so that the handle misses her arm, but it strikes the bowl in her shirt dead center. It shatters into several pieces.

The craftsman, not much taller than Megan, walks over to her and, with his face inches away, says with deep contempt, "You will pay for what you've done. Take them away and lock them up. We will decide what to do with them later."

The farmers and the two burly men drag Megan and Jared across several rooftops to another hole. They order Megan and Jared down the ladder. Megan refuses, and two of the farmers grab her and hold her upside down over the entry hole. Shards of pottery spill from her shirt. They then throw her into the hole. Megan grabs onto the ladder, twists around, and tumbles downward, feet first. Jared is thrown into the hole as well. He grabs onto the ladder with both hands and, luckily, stops his fall. The room has no doors and no windows, only the hole in the roof. As Jared continues to climb down, the broken pieces of the bowl rain down around him as the farmers kick the shards after them. The men remove the ladder and roll several large tree trunks over the opening. They are trapped.

"Nice going," Jared says sarcastically. A few rays of sunlight filter through the cracks.

"Hey. That wasn't only my fault. You could at least ask how I'm doing."

They sigh, sit down, and lean against the wall and look around. The room is packed with artifacts: female statues of stone and clay, human skulls lying beneath ox heads, bags of obsidian spear tips, shells, copper and lead beads, flint, obsidian mirrors, wool textiles, wooden cups, and stone axes.

"Looks like a storeroom," says Jared. "Things they traded."

"Yeah. A lot of good that's going to do us now," replies Megan.

"We still have most of the pieces. Maybe we can puzzle it together," Jared says.

"I hate jigsaw puzzles," replies Megan. "Always take too long."

They collect the pieces of pottery and sit on the reed mat covering the lime plaster floor. They begin to reassemble the bowl. After a few minutes, they have most of it put together.

"This looks to be a riddle," says Jared as he tries to decipher the phrases. He reads aloud: *"Complex societies grow. Water flows, trade flourishes. Seek the portal opposite the wonders of the ancient world.'"*

"I have no idea how this ties together," says Megan, shaking her head. "I assume the phrase 'wonders of the ancient world' refers to the seven wonders."

"I think so. It's easy if you remember your ancient history," says Jared.

"I actually slept through that part, remember?" jokes Megan.

"Oh yeah, I remember you were snoring so softly. Everyone else knew, but Ms. Castro never caught on."

"Funny. What's the phrase mean?"

"Water flows, probably refers to rivers. Many early civilizations were located in river valleys: Mesopotamia, between the Tigris and Euphrates; Egypt, on the Nile; Indus Valley, on the Indus River; and the Shang Chinese on the Hwang He or Yellow River. This fertile land was great for agriculture and helped create these urban societies. Soon they ran out of materials such as wood, metal, rock, and precious stone. They needed to trade."

"I am going to stop asking how you know all this," says Megan.

"This is cool. With these lenses, I can look things up immediately." He reflects for a moment, and then says out of the blue, "The Americas were different."

"Excuse me?"

"Sorry. I just remembered that societies in the Americas didn't grow along large river valleys," replies Jared.

"What do you think 'portal' means?"

"I don't know. I think you're right. It has something to do with the Seven Wonders of the Ancient World. Those were remarkable feats of art and architecture, but as soon as the list was created, people started to debate what should be included."

"It says seek the portal *opposite*," replies Megan.

Jared shrugs. "That part I don't understand."

They hear the men return on the rooftop above and figure it's time to leave. They both touch the home button, but nothing happens. The men argue about what to do with the prisoners. The back and forth continues for several minutes before the craftsman and several local men finally remove the tree trunks. Megan and Jared squeeze themselves against the wall behind sacks of shells so they can't be seen.

"This is the delay I was telling you about," whispers Megan. "Touching the home button doesn't mean you go immediately."

"I see how this can become quite exciting," replies Jared.

The craftsman yells for them to come out, but there is no answer. Finally, he climbs down the ladder into the room, spear in hand, to pull them out by force, or dead, if necessary. The room is eerily silent. He looks around and finds nothing. He jabs his spear into various sacks hoping to hear a grunt or see blood. Nothing. Except for the supplies, the room is empty. The broken shards of pottery lie scattered across the ground. The prisoners are gone.

Several minutes later, the bowl reforms, refills with sand, and returns to the room with the wall painting. The Web site has refreshed itself.

CHAPTER 7

ETHAN STANDS HALF A MILE FROM THE OLD SETTLEMENT at Jericho (Tel-el-Sultan), one of earth's oldest town sites and the lowest in elevation. It is somewhere between 10,000 and 6500 BCE, but dates that old are very subjective. It's hard to know the exact year. He stares at the twelve-foot-high and six-foot-wide town wall and its massive, round tower. This was the first place in history where stone walls were built on a large scale to protect a settlement and its newly accumulated wealth.

Where are Lien and Arjun? he wonders. They all agreed to this site and touched the thunderbolt activating the nanobots within a few seconds of each other. Before coming to Jericho, he remembers looking at a Web site that described how the Ice Age ended with what archaeologists call the end of the Paleolithic era—the Old Stone Age. Ice melted, seawaters rose, and three distinct landmasses emerged: Afroeurasia, Americas, and Australia/Papua New Guinea. Forests and meadowlands appeared. Huge areas of water separated people who had settled in these different lands earlier. Communities and settlements existed throughout the world, and the global population started increasing.

Ethan watches as a lone farmer leaves his field and walks to the Ain es-Sultan, Elisha's Spring, which supplies water to Jericho and the surrounding fields. The farmer walks up a wide path that winds between several large boulders. Just as he disappears behind the first boulder, Arjun appears on the same path a few feet ahead of the farmer. Before the man emerges, Ethan leaps forward and tackles Arjun. They tumble through bushes, down an embankment, and come to a rolling stop.

"Ouch. What the…?" complains Arjun, brushing off his clothes and looking at the minor scrapes on his hands and arms. "You're a big guy."

"There's someone coming up the path. I don't think we want to be seen."

They slowly get up. Hiding behind the bushes, they watch as the farmer walks toward the spring. The sun is beating down on the Jordan Valley, easily pushing the temperature above 110 degrees. Upon reaching the water's edge, the farmer strips down and wades in. He holds his breath and dunks underwater. He knows he should be working in the fields and not cooling off in the spring, but it's so hot and the water feels refreshing.

The farmer begins to climb out of the water when his eye catches a bright glimmer. He looks over and sees a black-and-white object lying in the mud. Intrigued, he carefully climbs along the edge of the spring until he reaches it. It looks like a piece of obsidian or flint. Most of it must still be buried in the mud. He tries to pull it free, but the suction of the wet clay holds it tight. He tries one more time, summoning all his strength as he pulls. Suddenly, the suction releases, and the man falls backwards into the spring. In his hand rests an obsidian scythe about a foot in length. His eyes grow wide as he looks at the scythe's handle. It's been shaped from a human thighbone. He wades to shore and then nervously wraps the scythe in his clothes. He tightens his grip and heads toward town.

The farmer is lost in thought and unaware that besides Arjun and Ethan, two pairs of eyes have watched him since he first found the object. He rounds a corner and sees the city walls off in the distance. He breathes more easily knowing that he is only a short distance from home. His older brother will surely know what to do. When he walks between two large boulders, a young man steps in front of him. Ethan and Arjun can only see the back of the other man.

"What do you have there?" the man asks.

"Nothing," replies the farmer, trembling.

"I saw you pick up something in the water. Give it to me," he says. Without warning, he hits the farmer in the stomach and punches him in the jaw.

The farmer falls to his knees and drops the scythe.

"Now that's better," says the assailant, picking up the old tool. He takes a step back, moving out of the way, as a flint-capped spear, normally reserved for hunting animals, flies through the air and hits the farmer in the stomach. The tip and part of the spear come out the farmer's back. He screams in pain and falls backward, propped up by the wooden shaft. Another person, his face covered in cloth and a bow and arrow slung around his shoulders, comes near. Without saying a word, he grabs the scythe from his partner and slits the farmer's throat.

As life slowly drains out of the farmer, Ethan and Arjun pull back. They can't believe what they are seeing.

Then, one of the assailants wipes the blood from the blade on the farmer's clothes, and Arjun gets a glimpse of his face. "He looks like a teenager," he whispers to Ethan.

The assailant looks at the handle of the scythe. "This probably came to Jericho through trade. This better get us some points."

"Maybe it's a clue," responds the other.

Ethan and Arjun look at each other. "Did you hear that?" whispers Ethan. "These guys are players. Maybe we should introduce ourselves." He leans forward to stand up.

Arjun pulls him back to the ground. "I don't think I want to mess with them," he says. "Not after what they just did to the farmer."

"It's a game character. Who cares?" counters Ethan.

"You didn't read the disclaimer for this game, did you?" asks Arjun.

Ethan shrugs and shakes his head. "Who reads that stuff? I just clicked on 'accept.'"

"Exactly. In small print, it warned that if you get injured too many times, they can yank your privilege to play."

"You mean you can get kicked out of the game? How lame is that?"

"That's what it says," repeats Arjun.

"That sucks. If you want to get rid of someone, all you have to do is injure him several times and he's gone?"

"I don't know. I'm just telling you what I read."

"That's interesting," says Ethan absentmindedly as he thinks about how he might take advantage of that information. "We'd better get out of here." He reaches for the home button.

"Wait!" says Arjun as he grabs Ethan's arm. He points toward the two assailants. There, several feet in front of them, stands Lien.

Surprised, the two assailants make their way toward her. The first has his spear ready. The second places an arrow in his bow. "Who do we have here?" asks the taller one as he stands several yards from Lien. "Looks like another player. And a pretty one, too. Looking for the clue? You're a little too late!"

At that moment, Arjun jumps up from behind the boulders, yelling to distract the assailants. Ethan rises also, only much more slowly. With one fluid motion, the second assailant turns and fires an arrow. It grazes the rock in front of Ethan and bounces off to the side, missing him by less than an inch. Arjun and Ethan both drop back to the ground behind the boulder.

Lien takes the cue and immediately launches herself at the attackers. With a well-timed kick, she knocks the spear out of the first one's hand

and then punches the side of his head, knocking him unconscious. The second assailant is not so easy. He throws his bow and arrow to the side as they both move around in a circle, trying to anticipate each other's next move. When the assailant has his back to one of the boulders, Arjun launches himself from above. He lands on top of the assailant, and they tumble a few feet. As Arjun gets up, the young man disappears.

"A player," says Lien, lifting her long, black hair to cool her neck. "He was wearing a wristband."

"Yeah, I saw it."

"Nice move," she says.

Arjun brushes the dust off his clothes and bows. "At your service, milady." He says with a fake British accent, then smiles. "Where did you learn to fight like that? Looks like you know martial arts."

"Uh-huh, the basics," replies Lien, not wanting to reveal too much. Her parents always told her to downplay her fighting skills. "You seem to be pretty good yourself."

Arjun only nods.

Finally, Ethan appears, slowly making his way down from behind the rocks. His brown hair is drenched in sweat. "You know, most of my other games aren't this way. I fight and stuff, but I don't…um, never mind."

Arjun and Lien break out laughing. "We understand," says Lien. "You don't physically fight."

They look down at the other player, still unconscious. "What are we going to do with him?" asks Ethan as he nudges the fallen boy with his foot.

"Leave him here. He'll wake up soon enough," replies Lien.

"For fun we could take his wristband. That'll freak him out," adds Ethan as he bends down and grabs the other player's wrist.

"Ethan, get serious. We can't do that," says Lien. "Without the wrist-band he won't be able to deactivate the nanobots. He'll be in, like, a coma wherever he is, with no way to get back." She can't believe Ethan would even suggest such a thing.

"Hey, it's a game. No rule says we can't."

Arjun and Lien both frown. "There are moral and ethical rules," replies Arjun.

"If you guys don't want to, fine!" says Ethan with a disappointed look. "But don't come to me when this guy turns up somewhere else in the game and attacks us."

"His partner will probably come back to help him," comments Arjun.

"What about the scythe? It could be a clue," says Ethan.

"I don't think so," replies Arjun. "You can't take physical items back into the real world. I doubt it's a clue unless something is written on it."

They examine the scythe closely and find no writing. They decide to go home. Several minutes apart, they land back on the home page. Each player says, "Disengage." The nanobots go dormant until the next time they want to enter the game. Lien sits upright on her bed, Arjun rises from the family room couch, and Ethan gets up from the beanbag in his bedroom.

Arjun tries to contact Jared, but there is no answer. He's got to tell him about what happened. This game is more dangerous than they thought.

CHAPTER 8

IT'S TUESDAY AFTER SCHOOL. NEAR THE CAMPUS POOL, Damian and his friends are watching a video on a smartphone. When his twin sister walks over, all eyes stop watching the video and look up. She is coming from girls' swim practice, and her shoulder-length blond hair is still wet. She wears a frumpy, dark blue sweat suit similar to her brother's, with GAG stenciled across the front. Whereas the suit makes her brother look like any other athlete, it makes Ivy look very cute. All the guys, except Damian, turn toward her. After all, it's only his sister. Ivy is quite popular, even though everyone knows she can be ruthlessly competitive. If she gets a chance, she'll readily break a rule to win. "Hi, Ivy," say the boys.

"Hey." She takes Damian's elbow and pulls him away from the group so she can't be overheard. "I know it's only two days until spring break, but we need to start playing *The Ancients* game tonight. At lunch I overhead Arjun and Ethan talking. They've already checked out two places in the ancient world."

"What did you learn?" replies Damian, moving closer. He's no less competitive than his sister is.

"I know they found the first clue, but I didn't understand the second part. I think they noticed that I was trying to listen." Ivy pulls her brother farther from the group.

"So what did they say?" asks Damian.

"They said something about civilizations and rivers."

"That's it!" Damian thinks for a moment. "Actually, that makes sense," he says with excitement. "I think I know where we can start. Mesopotamia."

"Why there?" asks Ivy. Her brother is smart, but she's not sure she believes his quick answer.

"It's considered the cradle of civilization in the West; it's the land between the Tigris and Euphrates Rivers, where the Sumerians built many cities. Sumer, Babylon, Assyria. Civilizations and rivers." He gently knocks her head with his knuckles. "Anything in there?" he jokes.

"OK, I get it, I get it. It could be what Ethan and Arjun meant. We'll go there tonight."

"Sounds good," replies Damian, heading back to his friends. He turns around one more time. "Ivy, don't tell any of the others yet. Let's do this one on our own first. See what the game is like."

Ivy frowns, preferring to have her friends along, but she understands her brother's reluctance. She goes to look for her friends, Alexa and Maria.

Later that afternoon, Ivy comes home and finds her brother researching by using a hologram projection of ancient Mesopotamia and all of the city-states.

"Find anything?" she asks.

"Listen to this," replies Damian. He begins to read aloud. "'The growth of these city-states; the intent to control the rivers, transportation, water, and irrigation; and the desire for wealth and luxury goods led to continued conflict. These constant wars, for almost two thousand years, reinforced the rapid development of military technology and techniques during the Bronze Age.'"

"As a military buff, that's right up your alley," replies Ivy. "You love this stuff. But there's a lot here." She looks over his shoulder. "Where do we even start? Without knowing the clue, we could search forever."

"One of the first empire-builders was Sargon the Great of Akkad. He and his sons conquered the city-states throughout Mesopotamia. We should probably start there."

"Sounds as good a place as any. Any place is better than sitting here. Let's go," replies Ivy.

They look at several Web sites and agree they don't seem right. After searching for another fifteen minutes, they locate one that looks promising. Ivy goes to her bedroom, settles on her couch, and touches the thunderbolt image on her bracelet. A few seconds later, sitting in the adjoining bedroom, Damian does the same thing. Within seconds they are in the game.

"Whoa. Whoa. Slow down," yells Damian. He bends down and grabs the sickle sword at the same time that he grabs the reins from the driver, who is slumped over. He tries to settle the out-of-control donkey-like animals known as onagers. Damian and Ivy stand on the back of a four-wheeled wooden chariot as they race headlong into an advancing army. This particular chariot is not an offensive weapon, but in battle, soldiers used whatever they could. Ivy realizes that being whisked into a simulated environment has its risks.

"Nice," she says sarcastically. "Right into the middle of a Sumerian battle. I should have known."

"Hey, I didn't plan it this way!"

"Well, don't slow down. Turn over there. We need to get out of here!" yells Ivy as loud as she can. The noise of swords and shields clashing against each other is almost unbearable. Ivy looks at the driver. To see if he is still alive, she touches him, and he mumbles something about the color blue. She cannot understand the rest and quickly dismisses it.

"We need less weight," yells Damian. "Get rid of him."

"He's still alive," says Ivy.

"So? Dump him over the side!" shouts Damian. "Or take the reins!"

Ivy takes the reins. Damian grabs the driver by his armored cloak, breaking the arrow in his chest as he pushes him over the side. "We need to move, and fast. Stop and we're dead."

"That's what I said. Look, I've never driven one of these before. There's no accelerator or brake," shouts Ivy. "The last thing I need is a backseat driver."

Not listening, Damian points and yells, "Maneuver over there, to the edge of the battle field. Maybe we can disappear among those trees."

The noise of crunching wood, screams, arrows, and spears whizzing by is louder than Damian imagined. There are hundreds of soldiers everywhere—infantry, a few chariots, archers, and spearmen. It is total chaos. Even during the heat of battle, Damian notices that some of the enemy bowmen are using simple bows and firing them from ranges of fifty to one hundred yards. At that distance, the arrows are not penetrating the leather armor of the enemy. On the other side, the Sumerian/Akkadian army is using a composite bow. Composite bows are a significant military innovation. Damian knows that for the next 1,500 years, this bow was a primary tool of war. Sargon and his grandson's continuous wars of suppression and conquest spurred constant military innovation. The Sumerian bowmen are firing half as many arrows and from twice the distance, yet they easily penetrate the leather armor of the enemy. Damian has played enough of these battlefield video games to know that the side with the superior technology usually wins. He realizes that they are on the wrong side. He hopes that one of those archers doesn't target him or Ivy.

Ivy looks out for attackers, spotting three warriors out of the corner of her eye as they make their way toward the chariot.

"Damian, watch out!" she yells.

Damian takes two spears and, in rapid succession, hurls them at the soldiers. His aim is almost perfect, and two soldiers crumple to the ground. The third soldier jumps up on the back of the chariot just as Damian tries to reach for the last spear. Ivy lets go of the reins. She grabs a sickle sword, twists around, and thrusts it into the soldier's neck above his chest plate. "Take that," she yells. She severs the carotid artery, and blood splatters everywhere, covering her chest and face. "Ooh," she screams as she watches him fall backward off the chariot. Damian grabs the reins as she leans over the edge of the chariot and throws up. She and Damian have played a lot of fighting games, but none this realistic. She's never actually felt the warm blood of an enemy.

Damian is steering the chariot away from the battle when a bronze socket axe with a narrow blade coming to a point flies toward him. At the last moment, he twists out of the way, and the axe only leaves a cut on his forearm. It flies by and embeds itself in the wood of the chariot. He drives the onagers toward the side of the field as fast as he can. They need to get as far away from the main battle as possible, but the animals are exhausted and frightened.

"This is way cooler than any video game I've ever played," yells Damian as he whips the onagers to keep them running.

"It's realistic all right—maybe a bit too realistic," replies Ivy, wiping the blood from her face.

As they near a fork in the road, they agree to jump out while the chariot is still moving. Damian snaps the whip several more times to motivate the onagers to keep running.

"Letting go of the reins now!" yells Damian. "Jump!" They both leap, rolling and tumbling toward cover in the high grass. Luckily, no one sees them, and they escape with only minor scrapes and bruises. The chariot keeps bouncing down the road for another two hundred yards before the onagers realize there are no more riders and slow down. Moving deeper into the grass, Damian and Ivy hide, making sure that no one can detect them.

They wait a few minutes to catch their breath and then make their way through the hilly grasslands, avoiding the marshes and swamp, and head north. At an irrigation canal, they wash their hands and faces. Ivy tries to wash the blood off her shirt. They continue and soon reach another road that leads away from the battle. Strangely, only a few miles from the battle this road is almost empty except for a fast-moving cart bearing two men who are fleeing the carnage. Several yards ahead, the cart comes to an abrupt stop. As they catch up, they notice the older man is well dressed, and the other looks like a messenger.

Figuring Damian and Ivy must be of a high social class, given their clothes, the older man asks, "Can we be of assistance?"

Recognizing the man as a wealthy merchant, Ivy answers, "Yes." Remembering the site they looked at earlier, she quickly adds, "We are heading to the city of Kish."

Damian looks at her as if to ask, How can you be so dumb as to tell this man where we want to go?

"Ah. We are headed there as well," replies the older merchant. "These constant battles are so annoying. They always disrupt my trade. Join me."

Ivy and Damian climb onto the cart and sit in the back. Ivy looks at the messenger. He has many items; some are wrapped, and others look like letters with royal clay seals.

The merchant notices Ivy's eyes and says, "Yes, even the royal postal service requires my help today."

As they travel along, the merchant is captivated by Ivy. He can't keep his eyes off her. Her blond hair, pale skin, and gray eyes intrigue him. He completely ignores Damian, addressing his conversation only to her. "The Tigris and Euphrates Rivers have caused us much trouble this year, flooding so unpredictably and so often. The farmers spend half their time fixing canals and irrigation ditches. We all suffer every time the farmers lose a crop. These heartless gods."

Ivy nods. She remembers reading how the Sumerians saw their gods as powerful and merciless since they lived between two rivers, the Tigris and Euphrates, which flooded unpredictably, creating harsh conditions for the people. They honored and respected the Sumerian gods, but looked at things pessimistically. It was quite different in Egypt. The Nile flooded predictably and provided a fertile basin every year. Egyptians often depicted their gods as animals, suggesting a close relationship between nature and the gods. The Egyptians felt they must keep the gods happy to ensure order and stability in the universe. Because of this predictability, the Egyptian gods were seen as more merciful.

At one point, the merchant stops talking. Ivy whispers into Damian's ear, "What year are we in, anyway?"

"I'm not positive, but I think we're somewhere around 2200 BCE," replies Damian.

The merchant, quite talkative, continues, saying how thankful he is that King Sargon has unified the land and that the cities are growing. This has helped his trade business flourish. However, peace never lasts for long. There are always those who resist unification, he says. It's so disruptive—unless, of course, you are trading arms; then it can be quite lucrative.

They travel for a little while longer and then reach the city of Kish. They stop near the red ziggurat, a pyramid-like monument to local religions. The merchant looks directly at Ivy. "There is going to be a huge feast tonight at the palace. I need to meet with friends and partners, but you are graciously invited to join my party."

Assuming that's where they should probably go to learn more, Ivy responds, "Wonderful. Thank you. We'll be there."

The merchant nods with a slight frown. He had hoped that Ivy would come alone and leave her companion elsewhere, but that is not to be. He shrugs.

Ivy and Damian look around. They don't have much time before the feast, and they should check out Kish to see if they can find a clue or anything that will tell them what to do next. They walk the city with little success and then decide to rest a bit before joining the feast.

The celebration begins with music, exotic food, and dancing. Domestic slaves, often prisoners, orphans, and debtors, cater to the guests' every need. In this ancient society, one was either free or a slave. Aside from farmers, slaves did much of the work. This allowed some Sumerians to pursue other activities, such as pottery, artistry, religion, and crafts. It is easy to identify the wealthier Sumerians at the festival. They wear colorful clothing with gold and silver bracelets and earrings, and necklaces of bright, precious stones.

Three women dance a temple rite to worship the goddess Inanna, the queen of the heavens. As the festivities continue, several men withdraw and sit by themselves in private. One of the traders, noticing Damian's fine clothing, asks if he would like to join them, saying that the woman should go to the other women. Ivy is about to protest, but then catches herself. She understands that this is a very different time and culture. The role of women is very different. She heads toward the other women.

At first, the men discuss business and the trading of gold, silver, lapis, bronze, stone, clay, and ivory. The conversation changes to stories of adventure and intrigue. Most of the stories focus on the exploits and heroism of individual merchants fending off pirates, rescuing women, and making great trade deals. One of the traders rambles on about how, over the years, the Sumerians and Akkadians have conquered many cities and people. By adopting customs and tools, things are always changing. This change can be highly profitable. He continues talking, even though the others are no longer listening. Half the men have left to find entertainment elsewhere. The others are asleep. Undeterred, he rambles on, boasting about his business skills. Tired and frustrated by the long-winded story, Damian stretches out, leans against a large stone, and closes his eyes, pretending to be asleep. Maybe the trader will get the hint and shut up. Instead, a few seconds later he feels cold metal against his throat. Damian's eyes snap open. Swaying above him, barely standing, the trader laughs.

"Ha-ha-ha! You're awake. This is the future, young man." The trader pulls the iron sword away from Damian's throat and starts to wave it back and forth. "This metal is the future. Most still use the older bronze, but once they see the strength of this metal, more and more will use this new material. The trade in this metal will make me rich."

Damian realizes the man is talking about the transition from the Bronze Age to the Iron Age. As the sword sweeps by his face, Damian grabs the merchant's wrist and pulls him to the ground. "You're drunk. Stop waving that in my face, or I'll show you how I can use it."

The merchant lands on his back, laughing. "I tell you, friend. This is the future." He pats the sword. "This has already helped me to great riches." He then sits up and leans close to Damian's face. Damian can smell the wine on his breath.

"Shh. Don't tell anyone," he whispers. "Just yesterday, it helped me steal a tablet with strange symbols from the time of Gilgamesh and the city of Uruk. It must be quite valuable. I'm sure I can get several sacks of obsidian for it, or wine, or maybe even silver and gold."

Damian wonders if this is the clue. Flattering the merchant to get more information, he says, "That must have been a very daring attempt. Weren't you worried about getting caught?"

The man leans close, as if telling Damian a highly guarded secret. "I overpowered a guard at the palace, and…" The merchant begins to sway back and forth and is ready to pass out. Damian needs to learn more. He gently slaps him several times to ensure he doesn't fall asleep. The merchant burps and continues, "I hid it in my tent. It's safe." Then his eyes roll to the back of his head, and he passes out. Damian heads to the dance in search of Ivy.

As he rounds a brick column, the merchant with whom they traveled steps forward. "Leaving so soon, my friend? I have a business proposition for you."

Damian tries to avoid him and keeps walking. The merchant grabs his arm. "Wait."

"Yes?" replies Damian.

"I've been watching that woman of yours. If you are tiring of her or can no longer provide for her, I would give you much gold. All you have to say is, 'You are no longer my wife,' and you are divorced. A secret trade, maybe?"

Damian doesn't tell him that she is actually his sister. He politely declines and moves on. The merchant follows and doubles the offer. Damian declines again. The merchant does not want to give up easily. In a much more frustrated and animated voice, he makes his last and final offer.

Ivy, who meanwhile had come up behind the merchant, catches Damian's eye and winks. She jumps at Damian and, to his surprise, slaps him hard across the cheek. "You have no right to divorce me or sell me. I am an individual, and you will treat me as such."

Damian is about to hit back when he remembers her wink. He intuitively understands that she must have a plan. He just stands there, hunching his shoulders.

The merchant sees Ivy's behavior and immediately backs away. He crashes into a pile of neatly stacked pottery. Only a woman of royalty or one with a very powerful husband would act as an individual outside of her family. He cannot believe she slapped her husband. He does not want to deal with this type of woman. The merchant turns quickly and hurries away without saying another word.

Damian rubs his cheek and looks at Ivy. "Nicely played, I guess."

"Thank you. I thought it might work. Women's rights were very different and depended on social class."

"I know. Let's go," says Damian, moving back into the shadows. "I learned we need to steal a royal tablet."

"A what?"

"A royal tablet," says Damian, matter-of-factly.

Ivy uses her lenses to quickly search for ancient Sumerian laws and the penalty for robbery. She finds a reference to the Code of Ur-Nammu, the oldest-known tablet containing a law code that survives today. "You realize it says here that if a man commits a robbery, he will be killed."

"Then we better not get caught," answers Damian, moving toward a group of tents. They locate the tent and sneak up to the front. Inside they see a guard fast asleep with the tablet lying next to him. Ivy quickly lifts the tent flap, scrambles inside, and quietly pulls out the tablet while Damian keeps an eye on the guard. He then joins her on the side of the tent and looks at the tablet. Recognizing the wedge-shaped writing as cuneiform, he shrugs, indicating that he can't understand any of it. All he knows is that writing was a powerful invention. It fostered trade and commerce, helped people to communicate, and unified parts of the empire through providing a means by which to pass along history and ensure laws were understood. It helped King Sargon control his vast lands.

With gestures, Damian silently indicates that he has an idea. He uses his contact lenses and an online program to translate the basics of the message.

"This doesn't make sense," he finally whispers to Ivy.

"What's up?"

"This quotes Hammurabi's Code. It's the first known set of laws to govern everyday life in Babylon and the basis of modern-day legal codes. But it was written four hundred years later—around 1780 BCE. We're around 2200 to 2050 BCE. This shouldn't exist yet."

"Maybe it's the clue," suggests Ivy. "Or a glitch in the game."

"I don't think it's the clue. It's nothing but a bunch of laws. I think it's a dead end, or maybe even a false clue. Let's go home."

"Are you sure?" asks Ivy, not quite willing to give up.

"Yeah, I'm pretty sure," Damian replies without hesitation.

"No. Are you really sure?" Ivy presses, not quite trusting her brother's reply. He tends to jump to conclusions quickly.

"Yes. Dead end." Damian touches the home button on his wristband and a few seconds later disappears. The tablet falls to the ground.

Ivy picks up the tablet to push it back under the tent and pushes her wristband, too, when a loud voice startles her. "You should know the law. If anyone steals the property of a temple or of the court, he shall be put to death, and also the one who receives the stolen thing from him shall be put to death."

Ivy turns around slowly and faces a heavily armed soldier as the guard inside stirs awake. This is not good, she thinks. The nanobots better kick in soon and get her out of here, but nothing happens. Why would her brother disappear within a few seconds, yet she seems stuck here for what feels like an eternity? She also wonders why a soldier would quote one of Hammurabi's Laws? Or did he quote from the Code of Ur-Nammu? Ivy is confused. She is sure one legal code built on the other, but right now that doesn't really matter. The soldier begins to move toward her, and she realizes that she has no other choice. Without any warning or hesitation, Ivy swings the tablet with lightning speed, hitting him squarely on the side of the head. His bronze helmet tumbles to the ground, and he falls backward. Seconds later, to Ivy's amazement, he respawns and stands up again. She's trapped. Then, before the soldiers can take action, the nanobots finally engage, and she disappears.

CHAPTER 9

JARED, STILL UNABLE TO CONVINCE HIS MOM TO LET HIM take the car to school, rides his bike home and up the driveway. It is a bit embarrassing to ride his bike home at seventeen, especially when other kids have cars; but he figures it keeps him in good shape, and he just ignores what the others say. He hops off his mountain bike and places his hand on the glass panel next to the garage door. The door rolls open. He's surprised to see his mom's car.

"Hey, Mom!" he yells as he enters the house.

"Shh!" His mom places her finger on her lips. She hits the mute button on the phone and turns to Jared. "Hi, I'm on a conference call."

"What are you doing home so early?" asks Jared as he heads into the kitchen.

"A couple of my meetings were canceled, so I decided to work from home the rest of the day."

"OK," answers Jared, grabbing an apple from the counter. He heads toward his room.

"By the way, Uncle Alberto called and left a voicemail saying he needed to see you at the lab right away," Mom calls after him.

"Now? Do you think it's something about Dad?" asks Jared hopefully. Jared knows that his uncle started his own investigation into the kidnapping of his father.

"I don't know. All his message said was that it's critical you come now."

"Can I take the car?" asks Jared with a pleading look in his eyes. When his mom doesn't answer, he adds, "It's several miles, and I still have a ton of homework tonight."

Reluctantly his mother agrees. "Be careful, and don't drive too fast. You're not Megan."

Jared gives her a quizzical look, wondering how his mother knows about Megan's driving habits. "Thanks. Hopefully, I'll be back in a couple of hours." He jumps into the car, placing his iPod on the seat next to him. It automatically syncs to the car's onboard computer and starts to play his favorite songs. He speaks the lab's address into the onboard GPS and lets the car figure out the best route. As he backs out of the driveway, he relishes the freedom the car provides. If only he could talk his mom into letting him drive it more often—or even better, convince her to let him get his own car. But he knows things are financially tight. Without his father, his mom can barely make ends meet. Luckily, Uncle Alberto is helping them out. As he drives down the street, heading out of the residential area, he thinks about his uncle, the crazy genius scientist.

His uncle looks as if he belongs on the beaches of South Florida rather than in a California computer lab. His closely cut and precisely manicured beard frames an elegantly chiseled face, and he pulls his long, gray hair back in a ponytail. He always wears the same lab coat, covered with multicolored squares, circles, and triangles, letting it hang open in the front to reveal a pastel-yellow linen suit. His handcrafted Italian leather loafers make almost no sound. His light olive–colored face, similar to Jared's, is accented by intelligent, deep brown eyes and always carries a smile.

His uncle is cool and well off. He runs one of the most successful contract research-and-development computer labs in the country. He often does work for the government. His lab deals with nanotechnology, virtual reality, technological singularity, network infrastructure, min-iaturization, and quantum-level computing. When his uncle talks, Jared doesn't understand half the words, but it sure sounds interesting. His uncle always says that today, people live in an always-on, always-connected society. Humanity is moving toward a world where everyone is connected to everyone and everything is connected to everything, everywhere. This new world is full of new opportunities and full of new dangers.

As he continues to drive, Jared has no idea about the software that has been secretly downloaded into his mom's car. It's tracking where he drives and sending this information to an unknown monitoring station every two minutes. If he places a call over the car's phone system, the software will record the call, filter the information, and send that to the monitoring station as well.

He drives to the industrial section of town, which consists of several blocks of one- and two-story offices and warehouses. This area contains a variety of businesses, including plumbers, contractors, metal shops, cabinetmakers, architects, biotech labs, and engineering firms. Some of the buildings have "for lease" signs out front, and others look aban-doned. Jared passes an old, decrepit cement factory and a ceramics store, and then he makes a sharp left through the open gate of a high, barbed wire–topped chain-link fence. The lot, between two warehouses, spans the entire block, all the way to the next street. Jared drives for a few yards on a large, concrete pad full of cracks and overrun by weeds. He parks in front of a World War II Quonset hut, a building made of lightweight, cor-rugated, galvanized steel that has not been touched since the end of the war in 1945. A rusted sign on the front says R3 Technologies.

He enters through the door into a windowless lobby. He hasn't been here in a while. The room looks as if it hasn't been updated since the early

1980s. A sitting area, consisting of an old, beat-up couch and two mismatched chairs, stands off to the right. In front, next to a steel entry door, is a chipped and dusty reception counter with a dark glass top.

Jared walks up to the counter, and a female hologram appears out of nowhere, almost startling him.

"Hello. Welcome to R3 Technologies, Mr. Jared Reyes. Dr. Reyes is expecting you," says the hologram.

"Hello," replies Jared, not quite sure how to act in front of a hologram.

"To check in, please place both hands on the glass counter and look at the picture you see," continues the hologram. "You will feel a scratch on your palm."

Jared does as he is told. A computer reads his palm prints and takes a sample of the genetic material from the skin cells of his palm, and a laser scans his retina as he looks at the picture.

"Your identity has been confirmed. You have clearance to enter," says the hologram.

Jared hears the click of the metal door and walks toward it. The door lifts up and slides open with a deep swoosh, revealing a huge space, forty by one hundred feet, filled with worktables and strange-looking computers.

Jared looks up as Uncle Alberto, wearing his trademark lab coat, bounds down the stairs. "*¡Hola!* How's my favorite nephew?"

"I'm your only nephew," says Jared with a smile. "I'm good."

His uncle gives him a big hug. "I'm sorry about the urgency."

"No problem," replies Jared. "You know I always love coming here. It's been a while."

"Yes, it has. Your hair is starting to look like mine. I like it," says Alberto, tugging on Jared's ponytail.

"Is that hologram new? I can't remember seeing it last time," Jared says.

"It is new, but she's a prototype. We're already on version 2.0."

"How did it know I was Jared?"

"Simple," replies Alberto. "When you entered, it took a picture of you and then compared key features to all known pictures of you on the Internet. It then looked for pictures associated with your name. After comparing the data with other data, and once the probability reaches 99.99 percent that the person in the lobby is truly associated with that name, the hologram says the greeting out loud."

"Wow!" Jared shakes his head. "That's amazing and a little scary."

"The wonders of technology. Come. We need to talk." Alberto smiles, takes Jared by the arm, and walks farther into the lab. He leads the way to a large space behind several machines. It is a sitting area similar to what one finds in any company break room: plastic chairs, tables, a sink, a coffee machine, and two vending machines with a variety of foods and drinks. Alberto walks to one of vending machines and punches in the code for a granola bar. There is a short hum and whir as the robotic arm reaches up for the bar, but instead of depositing the bar in the tray, the two vending machines swing open, revealing a huge double door. He places his hand on the palm-scanner and looks into the retinal scan. The doors open. Jared peers into a large, industrial-size elevator.

As they enter the elevator, Alberto asks, "Did you leave your bike in the lobby?"

"No," replies Jared. "I convinced Mom to let me take the car."

"Damn!" says Alberto as he taps the descend button. He begins to frown, and runs his hand through his ponytail. "I thought for sure with your mom at work, you'd take your bike, so I didn't say anything. We could have a problem."

"What's wrong?" asks Jared, looking at his uncle with concern. His uncle looks visibly nervous.

"It's probably nothing. Don't worry about it. It's just some people have been looking for an excuse to shut us down. I hope this doesn't give them a reason to proceed."

The elevator doors close, and they head down into the basement. Jared feels a slight suction as if he's being vacuumed. The doors slide open, and he stares into another room almost as large as the Quonset hut above, but nothing like it. This room is ultramodern and boasts the newest technologies. It is filled with person-sized computers, desks with flat-screen monitors, lab tables, huge microscopes, and state-of-the-art machining tools. He shivers. It is at least fifteen degrees colder than upstairs. There is no sound except for the slight whirring of the computers and negative air fans that ensure that the space is dust-free.

"Gia, my assistant, is in the computer clean room in the back. Other than her, we're the only ones here," says Alberto, motioning for Jared to sit on one of the desk chairs. "I needed to talk to you about this new game at school in private."

"How did you know about that?" Jared asks with a look of surprise.

"It's a long story," answers Alberto. "It goes all the way back to—" He's interrupted by Gia's voice over the intercom.

"Alberto, we've got a problem. My computers tell me several agencies are mobilizing and will be here in less than ten minutes. Recommend we go to security shutdown, priority one."

Alberto jumps from his stool, quickly moves to a keyboard, and types in a few key strokes. "I knew it! I'm sorry, Jared, this is going to have to wait." In a clear, commanding voice, Alberto calls out, "Initiate security shutdown, priority one, voice authorization Alberto. Gia, clear out the clean room and exit."

"Initiating shutdown procedure, moving all files to secure location, purging all records," replies a computer voice that emanates from all around the room.

Alberto jogs around the room to grab a few remaining file folders.

"What's happening?" Jared asks with a bit of fear in his voice.

"Come with me. I'll tell you along the way," says Alberto, walking quickly to the back of the basement room. Jared follows. Alberto pulls an old computer book from a large metal-and-glass bookcase and then places his left hand on the metal side. The large bookcase swings to the side, revealing a brightly lit tunnel roughly three feet wide and six feet tall. "The government thinks that your father and I are involved in a conspiracy. They've had your mother and me, and to some extent, you, under surveillance since your father was kidnapped. They've been going through all my business records trying to find any excuse to shut us down. Looks like they might have found something."

"Why?" asks Jared as he follows his uncle down the long tunnel and through several steel doors.

Alberto stops and turns. "In 370 BCE, Plato wrote, 'Things are not always what they seem; the first appearance deceives many; the intelligence of a few perceives what has been carefully hidden.' And so it is again today, almost 2,400 years later."

"I don't think I understand."

"It's about the game. It's much more than just a game."

Alarm bells start wailing. Back in the lab, they can hear the computer voice indicating that the security procedure is complete and several cars are en route, estimated arrival time five minutes.

"Come, we need to hurry," says Alberto. He begins to jog down the tunnel. The steel doors slam shut behind them. "For now, just keep playing like nothing is happening. We need to meet again, in a different and more secure location. Memorize this address, and meet me there the night after next. Make sure you're not followed."

"OK. But how do I make sure I'm not followed?" asks Jared nervously.

"You'll figure it out. Remember what your dad taught you. Now listen, this tunnel empties into another warehouse several blocks away. But your mom's car is still back at the lab. You're going to have to go back. They know you or your mom came here tonight. So they're going to question you no matter what. Better now."

Jared doesn't like where this conversation is going. He remembers when he was interrogated right after his father was kidnapped. He was just getting over those dreams. "What am I going to say?"

"Tell them you got a call from me, came down, but the place was locked and you were just checking around back. Keep it simple, and don't change your story."

"I don't know if I can do this. What if I slip up?" Jared runs his hand through his ponytail just like his uncle. This is getting much more intense than he ever thought possible.

"You won't. You don't know much. Plus, I have full confidence in you," replies Alberto, putting his hands on Jared's shoulders. They exit into an abandoned warehouse a couple of blocks away. "Believe me, you can do this. Keep reminding yourself that this is the only way you can help your father and me. We need you, Jared. Until the day after next."

Jared stands there looking after his uncle as he disappears into the shadows of the old building. He wonders what this is all about. It did seem a bit odd how quickly the game was introduced at school, but he did not give that much thought. And now this. He quickly exits the warehouse and jogs back to his uncle's building. He hopes Gia got out safely. He passes the back door and turns the corner toward the front as six unmarked cars screech into the driveway. Several men dressed in black suits run toward him. For a second, he's transported back to when men jumped out of black SUVs and grabbed his father. He stops in his tracks and raises his arms. Two men grab him and lead him to one of the unmarked cars.

"Jared Reyes! FBI! We got a few questions for you down at the office," says one of the men in business suits.

Great, Jared thinks. More interrogations. He summons his courage and asks bluntly, "Can I see some ID, please?"

The man pulls out a badge bearing the words Federal Bureau of Investigation.

Jared looks at it closely and politely says, "Hmm. FBI. Can you tell my mom where I'm going to be? She might worry if I don't get home."

"She's waiting for you at our offices," replies the agent.

A few hours later, Jared is exhausted after questions from the FBI, the National Security Agency (NSA), the Defense Intelligence Agency (DIA), the Central Intelligence Agency (CIA), and the Computer Crime and Intellectual Property Section (CCIPS). He's surprised at how much attention he's getting. This must be serious. He only had one question for them: Have they made any progress in finding his father? Unfortunately, the answer was no. Finally, after realizing that Jared and his mother know very little they release them both on the condition that they remain available for more questions, if necessary.

They drive home together in silence.

CHAPTER 10

SOMEWHERE IN ASIA, AN IMPORTANT MEETING TAKES place; the location is as anonymous as the attendees are. The ultramodern skyscraper has an eightieth floor, but the elevator doesn't stop there unless one enters a special code. Few even know that the floor exists, and none of the attendees knows the floor number. This is one of the cartel's seven secret meeting places around the world. Stepping off the elevator, one feels transported into an ancient Chinese temple. The ceiling is laced with intricately carved and upwardly curved wooden beams to ward off evil spirits. Plush, hand-knotted Oriental carpets cover the dark, wood floor, dampening all sound.

All one can hear is the slight murmur of hushed voices as two dozen powerful executives mingle and talk. In an age of disappearing privacy, these are some of the most private people in the world. Everything they do stays anonymous and remains untraceable. They have come together from all parts of the world. A few look out the windows at one of Asia's busiest harbors. The windows, camouflaged to look like part of the building facade, are bullet- and rocket-proof. One can never be too careful. With remote-controlled drones (unmanned aerial vehicles) and satellite weapons, an attack is not out of the question. The decor consists of a mixture of Western and Eastern artifacts.

Outside on the roof, men secure the helipad to receive an incoming helicopter. Inside, a gong sounds, inviting the attendees to enter the boardroom. The room looks like it could belong to any multinational conglomerate, except for one visible exception. There are no windows. For protection, the room is in the center of the building.

The walls are covered by dark panels from which hang authentic paintings by Picasso, Rembrandt, Shen Zhou, and Qian Xuan. Sculptures from India, Africa, and the Americas stand on illuminated pedestals around the room. This collection of antiquities would be the envy of the finest museums in the world. In the center of the room, a conference table of solid African-blackwood dominates the space. An inlay of a world map made from the rarest trees in the world, most of which no longer exist, underscores the cartel's focus on global domination.

The twenty-four men and women of the cartel take their assigned seats around the enormous table. Everyone knows exactly where to sit, although there are no names listed or mentioned anywhere. Throughout the proceeding, only first names are used, and these are usually pseudonyms. No last names are known or used, ever. One of these men is known only as Victor.

Finally, the chairperson arrives and takes her seat at the head of the table. With a forceful, steady voice, she calls the meeting to order. "Ladies and gentlemen, let us begin. I hope you all took extra precautions when you traveled here today. More and more governments are improving their cyber capabilities. They have been scanning vast amounts of information for years. But now there is a new threat. Several governments are working on developing algorithms that can search millions of videos and find specific events or specific objects from the images online. A few weeks ago, a government agency located one of our operatives as he tried to get away from a rally in Europe consisting of several thousand protesters. By looking at videos from street cameras, drones flying overhead, satellites, and videos posted online by everyday users, they are now able to spot specific people, events, or objects.

"We're also seeing more and more computer viruses that are essentially reconnaissance tools. They grab images from computer screens, monitor key strokes, record e-mail and instant messages, monitor network traffic, and turn on microphones and cameras remotely. They can also erase your entire hard drive in less than a second. These viruses can also spread to other devices—even if the computer is not connected to the Internet. In the coming weeks, we will send you a security bulletin and software updates that will boost your security levels and protect you against this spying.

"And now to the business at hand. Victor, can you give us an update on your latest efforts?"

"Thank you, Madam Chairperson. We launched our latest educational game, *The Ancients*, in ten schools earlier this week. It is our newest attempt to try to locate the clues and the hidden artifact. As many of you know, several years ago we learned about the existence of a unique artifact. All we know is that it is critical to our overall plan to dominate the Internet and the World Wide Web. Our largest competitors have already been searching for years, but no one has had any success. Then, last year we learned that a professor in California, a Professor George Reyes, was also searching and had made more progress than any of our teams had. We suspected that Professor Reyes's research was being funded by some other entity, but we don't know for sure. So, six months ago, we decided to kidnap him before he could present any findings. We thought that we might be able to convince him to work for us."

"And how has that worked out?" asks one of the other senior members who routinely competes with Victor for political power among the executives. The member is not sure he trusts Victor and tries to mask his skepticism with a weak smile. Victor notices the false smile and makes a mental note to keep an eye on that particular board member.

"Professor Reyes is a very stubborn man and was quite uncooperative. Finally, after much convincing, he told us that clues to the location of the artifact were hidden on world history Web sites, starting with Earth's first settlements."

A newer member of the group asks, "World history Web sites? That's odd. Why?"

Victor chuckles. "It's actually a brilliant idea. Most people don't see the relevance of history. Many students today find it boring, and not relevant to their day-to-day lives. They say, 'Who cares about the ancient Greeks or Chinese?' They only see isolated events and facts. Many adults often feel the same way. Since people are so focused on living in the present and the future, the past would be a good place to hide the clues. Most people would never go looking."

"Do we know who hid these clues?" asks the oldest member.

"We don't," replies Victor. "After much more persuasion, the professor finally revealed his latest findings and where he thought the first clue might be. He also confirmed that we were on the right track with the development efforts we started six months ago. We tasked our top technical-development team to work with our creative folks to develop a new approach, a way we could involve more people in the search without them ever knowing what we are doing. They came up with a brilliant idea: a massively multiplayer online role-playing game, or MMORPG. The idea was to involve students to help us locate the clues. So, we created The Ancients: A Game. Following Professor Reyes's confession, we went 'live' with the game a couple of days ago. There are only a few minor bugs in the software."

"So you're going to leave finding this highly valuable artifact up to a bunch of teenagers?" another senior member asks loudly, leaning forward in his chair. "That's crazy."

"And in a game located out on the Internet, in the cloud. No game console necessary? No controls?" asks another.

Victor nods. Not letting himself be intimidated, he takes a sip of water and then turns to the senior member. "In the game, computers instantly mirror all the Web sites that have history content. And teenagers tend to be the best at playing quest-type games. We are recruiting more schools to compete for the prize. They don't know the importance of what they are looking for. They just want to win. Who knows, some students might actually be willing to work for us, unknowingly, of course. Or we may even put our own players into the game, if necessary. We're hiring several former mercenaries who are also avid gamers. If there's a clue out there, they'll find it. We have several strategies in mind to make sure we end up with the artifact no matter who finds it. Plus, the Internet only looks free, but it is full of controls. We'll be able to monitor what happens." He then raises his voice just a little to show his conviction. "Believe me, this will work!"

"With soldiers in the game, what are we going to do if anyone does die? We have safeguards, but our engineers say there are bugs in the code," says another senior member. "I read your presentation. It could be a public-relations nightmare. Even with signed release forms."

The head of public relations replies, "Now that the game is on the Internet, we've eliminated all traces of the developers or the publisher. No one can tie it back to us. Our plan is that if a death does occur, which is unlikely, we keep it a secret for as long as possible, use a disinformation campaign to obscure the facts, and pay off anyone who has an issue. Most people are so overwhelmed with information, they don't pay attention for very long. Then, once we have the artifact, it doesn't matter."

"If the game is on the Internet, or, as you say, in the cloud, what about security, and hackers?" asks another.

Victor pauses, then slightly lowers his voice again. He doesn't want this to become a debate about the game. All he wants to do is inform the other executives. "We are aware of all the issues, the risks, and are addressing them. Of course, if any of you has a better idea, one that will bring us more success than what we've tried in the past, I'm willing to listen."

The other senior member sinks back into his seat. "Point taken. Please proceed."

The meeting is interrupted by a knock on the door. "Enter," calls the chairwoman. Victor's executive assistant quietly enters the room with her eyes cast toward the floor. She doesn't want to look at any of the members of the executive committee. She hands Victor a piece of paper and quickly exits the room.

Victor skims the note and feeds it into the shredder. "It looks like the government has finally moved on R3 Technologies. It looks like Alberto Reyes's lab has been shut down."

"Isn't he the brother of George Reyes, the professor we grabbed?" asks a junior member.

"Yes. The government is becoming much more aggressive. We will need to watch our steps as well and make sure our contingency plans are in place," says the chairwoman.

Victor nods and continues with the meeting, not mentioning that one of the players is the professor's own son. The executive members of the cartel do not need to know everything. He concludes his presentation, saying, "There is not much else to say, except that the game begins."

CHAPTER 11

AFTER SCHOOL, MEGAN, JARED, LIEN, ARJUN, AND ETHAN huddle off-campus at a picnic table in a nearby park.

"Did you notice how exhausted Damian and Ivy looked in class today?" starts Lien.

"Yeah," replies Arjun. "Almost like they stayed up most of the night."

Jared turns to Ethan and Arjun. "I noticed Ivy was hanging around you guys yesterday."

"Did you talk about the game during school?" asks Megan.

"I don't think so," replies Ethan.

"Actually, at lunch we did talk a little," adds Arjun.

Ethan shifts uncomfortably on the bench. "It was nothing."

"Do you think she heard you?" asks Megan, with frustration in her voice. She knows it's not beyond Ivy to spy on another team.

"She didn't hear anything," Ethan says abruptly. He hates to be interrogated, even if Megan is only asking a few basic questions.

"Looks like we have to be extra vigilant," says Jared. "Let's make sure we don't talk about the game at school. We only have a few more days until spring break. Let's not let anyone else know how far we've gotten."

"Jared, c'mon. We know that. Don't treat us like idiots," replies Ethan, now feeling insulted.

"Ethan, it's just a reminder…to all of us," snaps Jared.

Ethan shakes his head and looks away. He hates it when Jared acts as if he's in charge, especially in front of Megan.

They all agree to watch out. Lien then pulls out her smartphone, unfolds the screen, and they review several sites based on Megan and Jared's finding in Çatalhöyük—"Complex societies grow. Water flows, trade flourishes. Seek the portal opposite the wonders of the ancient world." They agree to meet on a promising-looking portal site later that afternoon.

At five p.m., Jared, Megan, Lien, Arjun, and Ethan independently activate their nanobots. They arrive at a train station in a relatively modern city within a few minutes of each other. "Those nanobots always take their time whenever we touch the thunderbolt," says Jared.

"Adds a little excitement," replies Megan as she looks around. "A modern train station, huh? They didn't have any train stations in ancient times."

The five teenagers stand in the middle of an island platform with seven train tracks radiating in different directions. The entire station is covered with a massive steel-and-glass canopy that lets light in and keeps the weather out. Passengers hurry about, not giving the students a second glance. Stores, kiosks, and restaurants line the perimeter of the platform.

"Can this be right?" questions Ethan.

Jared looks around. "I think so. Look." He points to a large arrival-and-departure sign hanging at the end of the platform. In digital letters it lists the Great Pyramid of Egypt, the Hanging Gardens of Babylon, the Statue of Zeus at Olympia, the Temple of Artemis at Ephesus, the Mausoleum of Halicarnassus, the Colossus of Rhodes, and the Lighthouse of Alexandria.

"Those are the Seven Wonders of the Ancient World," says Lien, repeating part of the clue.

"And a train station with trains going to different sites could be a portal," adds Arjun. "But didn't the clue say something about the portal *opposite?*"

"Yeah," replies Megan. "Let me go ask." She walks toward a crescent-shaped booth with a large, green "i" stenciled on the side near the main lobby of the train station.

"Where are you going?" asks Jared.

"I noticed an information booth. I'm going to see if they can help."

Ethan, Jared, Arjun, and Lien trot after her. Megan reaches the information booth and sees a green button with the same green "i" as on the booth's wall. She pushes it. A few seconds later, an animated holographic figure materializes from behind the half-round counter. Jared steps back in surprise. The hologram receptionist looks to be a similar technology to what he saw in his uncle's lab. He doesn't say anything.

Megan whispers, "She looks like a charming old grandmother." Her hair is pinned in a bun, and glasses rest halfway down her nose. Jared can't decide if the hologram looks like a grandmother or a reference librarian he once knew in middle school.

"May I help you?" asks the hologram.

"Yes," says Jared, moving in front of Megan. "What is this place?"

"It is a train station, young man," answers the figure.

Megan is about to make a wisecrack when the figure continues, "It is a special train station. It is the departure station for the Seven Wonders of the Ancient World Tour. Pick any track and enjoy the amazing wonders of the ancient world."

"I've never heard of these," says Ethan from the back of the group. "Except for the pyramid in Egypt."

"Young man, they are all very old. All except the Great Pyramid are gone, destroyed in earthquakes, wars, and other human mayhem."

"What about Stonehenge?" asks Megan.

"And the Great Wall in China? Why isn't that on the tour?" asks Lien.

The hologram looks at Lien. "Excellent question, my dear. This list of seven wonders was compiled over time by ancient Greek writers." She pauses, as if thinking about how to say something diplomatically. "So they highlighted their own culture. They did not know about those other places back then."

The hologram freezes.

"The riddle mentioned the portal opposite," whispers Megan.

Then the grandmotherly hologram comes back to life. "Here, why don't you take a ticket and enjoy the rides?"

Arjun takes Ethan aside and says quietly, "I think something just happened." Both Ethan and Arjun are into computer technology and understand how games work. Ethan is more of a techie and a gamer; Arjun is a techie and more into science and math.

"It's like someone just inserted some additional code into the hologram's program," replies Ethan.

"Yeah. It was like an automatic update, and then the hologram rebooted."

"This game is on the Internet, right?" asks Ethan. "Could someone have altered the computer code of the game as we play?"

"I don't see why not," answers Arjun. "A simple update. Programmers can change the code engine that makes the game run at any time."

Several feet away, Jared continues to talk with the hologram. "No, thank you. We're really not interested."

"They are actually wonderful places. You'll have the time of your life. The Hanging Gardens are beautiful this time of year," replies the hologram more forcefully.

"Thank you, no," Jared replies, turning toward Megan, who is standing a few feet from the counter.

"You must go!" insists the figure. "You will love the Hanging Gardens. I will even make you a special offer."

Jared turns to the hologram and more forcefully says, "I'm sorry, but we're really not interested." The five students begin to walk away.

Not giving up, the hologram begins to talk like a salesperson rather than a helpful provider of information. "Wait. It will provide you with what you are looking for."

Startled, Jared walks back to the booth. "What did you say?"

The woman hologram has a big grin on her face and replies, "It will provide you with what you are looking for." Then she repeats, "I promise, it will provide you with what you are looking for."

Jared turns to Megan and whispers, "Weird. This thing is trying really hard to influence us to go to the Hanging Gardens."

"Maybe we should go," replies Megan. "It could lead us to the next clue."

"I don't know," replies Jared. "The clue in Çatalhöyük said to seek the portal opposite."

"Hold on, guys," says Lien. She senses the hologram is watching very closely and then reacting. She thinks for a moment and then turns toward the hologram. "Thank you for your very kind suggestion. That sounds very interesting, but before we go there, I have a question. I was told there's a portal opposite this one. Maybe one with tours about the complex societies in the ancient world. We might want to do that first. Where would I find that?"

"Oh! You want the other tour," replies the hologram, now using a helpful voice again. "You are currently in the south terminal. That tour departs from the north terminal. Take the escalator down to the next level, and walk down the long tunnel linking the two terminals. Take the escalator back up. You will arrive at your destination in approximately five minutes. You can then pick up your free tickets at a counter just like this one."

"Thank you very much," replies Lien bowing slightly. "You have been most helpful."

"You are welcome, young lady. Have a nice day," answers the hologram.

They turn to walk away. Jared gives Lien a thumbs-up and walks toward her. "You do realize you just bowed to a hologram, right?"

Lien nods.

"Still amazing how you got it to give you the answer. How did you know that?" he asks in an inquisitive tone.

"She is primarily programmed to be helpful. And I know that these programs can also assess human behavior online. They factor that into their algorithms. So, I figured that if I was really friendly and changed the topic, her programming would allow her no other choice but to tell us."

"Brilliant," replies Jared. He is walking away from the information kiosk when he feels a slight pat on his back. He wheels back around toward the information booth, but the hologram is gone.

As they walk toward the escalator, he thinks about the pat on the back. Finally, he asks Lien, "Did you just pat me on the back?"

"No. Why would I do that?"

"I don't know. It felt like someone patted me on the back."

"Not me. Where did you feel it?"

"Right under my left shoulder."

Ethan walks up behind him and takes a closer look. "Look at that. There is something here," says Ethan. He uses his fingernail to peel a translucent disk a half-inch in diameter off Jared's shirt and sticks it onto one of the stone columns.

"What was that?" asks Jared.

"A tracking cookie," says Ethan. "This Web site probably planted it on you to see where you're headed next. Or maybe they want to send you a few ads about their next great tours." He chuckles. "It's all about ads these days."

"Is that possible? We're in a simulated world."

"It's been happening in the real computer world for decades, so I guess it can happen in a simulated world, too," adds Arjun.

"Or someone is trying to track our moves," adds Lien. "We need to stay alert."

Megan, already on the escalator, motions for them to hurry up. Jared, Lien, Arjun, and Ethan jog toward her and down the moving steps.

CHAPTER 12

THEY RIDE UP THE NORTH TERMINAL ESCALATOR AND emerge in a great hall covered by a glass-and-steel canopy similar to the one over the south terminal. Around the central platform, seven train tracks radiate outward, just like those accessible from the south terminal. In front of the five teenagers hangs another digital departure monitor spanning the width of the platform.

Arjun heads to a strange mechanical sculpture in the middle of the platform. Inlaid in the granite floor are two intersecting circles. They touch at two points, like a Venn diagram. The left circle spins to the left, and the right circle spins to the right.

"What are these things?" asks Megan, coming up behind him.

"This is so cool," replies Arjun. "One is a positive feedback loop, and the other is a negative feedback loop. The right circle shows how better farming led to population growth, which led to more agriculture, which then led to more population growth again. It keeps repeating. A positive feedback loop. The left circle also connects agriculture to population growth, but it spins toward the left. More population led to problems with the environment, which led to conflict, more disease, and food shortages. That in turn led to more innovation to control the environment, which then led to more agriculture and more population. A negative feedback loop."

"I get it. Yeah, and…?" asks Megan.

"It shows how societies are getting more complex and how sometimes there are unintended consequences," replies Arjun.

Ethan, who is standing with Jared and Lien, points to the monitor and asks, "Did you see the video that just played?"

"I wasn't paying attention," replies Jared.

"Look up there," says Ethan, pointing to the right of the departure board with his index finger. Ethan, Lien, and Jared look at the enormous video screen. "Watch. Here it comes again."

First, text scrolls across the screen, "25 percent off—Smartphone Encyclopedia." Then a video starts to play, depicting a young girl sitting at home and struggling with her homework. She asks her mother and father, "Do you know the elements of complex societies?" Mom and Dad both shrug and say, "No." The girl looks very disappointed. She reaches for her smartphone, activates the encyclopedia app, and speaks into the device. "Do you know the elements of complex societies?"

A few seconds later, the device answers while projecting 3D images from the phone. "*Hi, Emily, good to see you again. I can help. Several different elements characterize complex societies. For example, they can include the existence of cities, central governments and law codes, writing and record keeping, highly organized religions, specialized jobs, social classes, and complex technologies. There are other examples as well. Here are other sources you can check.*"

The video ends with the girl replying, "Thanks. You're a lifesaver—or at least a homework saver. I'll check them out."

"Interesting," comments Lien as she walks to the nearby information counter.

The others scan the rest of the departure monitor. On the left-hand side, next to advertisements for moon and undersea vacations, is a listing of train tracks and their destinations.

- Track 1: Sumer in the Tigris and Euphrates Valley
- Track 2: Egypt in the Nile Valley and Africa
- Track 3: Harappa in the Indus Valley
- Track 4: Shang Dynasty in China
- Track 5: Olmec in Mesoamerica
- Track 6: Chavín in South America
- Track 7: Minoan Crete in the Mediterranean

A few minutes later, Megan and Arjun come back to the group. "We really are in the right place," she says proudly.

"Yes. We know," replies Lien walking up behind them, having picked up five tickets.

Megan gives her a puzzled look.

Jared points up to the large video monitor.

Megan watches part of the ad and nods. "Now what?"

"My guess is we have to get on one of these trains," suggests Jared.

"Sounds good," adds Arjun. "But which one? There are seven tracks and only five of us."

"We have no choice. We have to split up or it will take forever," adds Megan.

"I'd like to go to the Shang Dynasty," says Lien. "I've always wanted to learn more about my ancestors and explore ancient China."

"Me too!" Arjun says excitedly. "I mean, learn about my ancestors and explore ancient India and Harappan culture." He remembers reading that Harappa reached its peak around 2600 to 1900 BCE. It was an incredible place. The architectural planning was so advanced that they used a standard-sized brick; towns had sewage canals and houses had bathrooms. The sludge was reused on the fields as fertilizer. They used a binary decimal system. Then, around 1900 BCE, the cities were abandoned, and historians still don't know why. Some say there were climate changes that caused century-long droughts. Others say that nomadic tribes, the Aryans, arrived from the north and destroyed the ancient cities.

"Sounds OK with me," replies Megan. "If no one else wants it, I'll go to Egypt."

"I'll go to the Minoans," says Jared.

They all look at Ethan, who seems to be in a trance, staring off across the train station.

"Hey, Ethan!" yells Jared. Ethan doesn't respond. "Ethan!"

Megan grabs his shoulders and shakes him. "Earth to Ethan, are you there?"

"Oh, sorry. I was checking out something on the lenses and didn't hear you."

They all look at each other, not sure they believe him.

"No, really," Ethan says. "I just got a text message. It looks like we reached another level in the game. Our lenses have been upgraded to communication devices. We can send each other text messages."

With disbelief Megan asks, "What, with our eyes? Sure."

"Actually, yes. Look, I'll show you." Ethan chuckles at his own humor. He then gives a quick lesson on the new feature. "The only tricky part is we need to remember each others' screen names. Otherwise, I don't know where the message will go."

"Ethan, you missed choosing a track, so you get to go to either Sumer or the Americas," Lien says.

Ethan looks at the ground. "I suppose … If I don't really have a choice, I'll go to the Americas."

Jared notices Ethan's lack of enthusiasm. "Hey, Ethan, would you rather go to Minoan Crete?" he asks, realizing that the team will be more successful in finding a clue if everyone is excited to play.

Ethan looks up. "Yeah. The Palace of Knossos, the maze, the Greek legend of the Minotaur. Much better."

"I'll switch, if you want," replies Jared. "I'll go to the Americas, starting with the Chavín, and you can go play with a Minotaur."

"Cool. Thanks," says Ethan, now in a much better mood.

"This looks like a big portal with a lot of links," Arjun says. "There could be hundreds or thousands of Web sites linked to any one of those trains. To be safe, let's meet on the home page in three hours. OK?"

"That's around nine p.m., right?" asks Lien.

Megan nods.

"How am I supposed to keep track of time? I'm not wearing a watch," continues Lien.

"You can check in the contact lenses," replies Arjun. "Hit the question mark and ask what time it is on the home page. Good?"

Jared and Megan look at Lien and Ethan. They all nod.

"What should we be looking for, anyway?" asks Ethan, turning to Megan and Jared. "You guys found the first clue. Any suggestions?"

"Anything that looks out of place or looks too modern for the time period," replies Jared.

Megan throws a glance toward Track 2 and sees the Egypt and Africa train slowly pulling out of the station. "Whoa, got to go. See ya back on the home page." She grabs a ticket out of Lien's hand and sprints after the train, reaching it just before the platform comes to an end. She jumps, grabs the handle of the last car, and pulls herself aboard. She turns and waves. Jared looks after her until the train is out of sight.

He then turns and takes a ticket from Lien as she heads to Track 4 for the Shang Dynasty. Arjun heads to Track 3 for Harappa. Ethan, on his way to Track 7 for the Minoans, is sidetracked by another advertisement. Jared slowly walks to Track 6, heading to the Chavín in the

Andes Mountains. As he walks, he throws one last glance at Lien as she boards her train. She looks at him and waves. He waves back. As he gets to know Lien, he thinks she's actually pretty neat. He's happy she's on his team. Grabbing the handle, Jared steps onto the train. A few minutes later, the large, magnetic levitation train pulls out of the station, headed to the highlands of ancient Peru.

Jared has settled into a seat when he notices a tiny icon blinking in the lower left-hand corner of his contact lenses. That's the new message feature. He focuses his eye on it for several seconds, and the icon changes color. He whispers, "Open," and two additional menu items pop up. One says, "Compose," and the other says, "Read." He focuses his eye on the "Read" button, and it expands into a short text message. Thinking it might be Megan, he's surprised when it says, "Good luck in the Andes—Lien."

CHAPTER 13

MEGAN RECLINES COMFORTABLY IN A FIRST-CLASS SEAT
after leaving the coach section of the train. She hears the announcement
over the speaker system. "Last five stops coming up." She is wondering
what the stops will be when she notices a travel brochure in the seat
pocket in front of her and pulls it out. The title on the cover page says,
"Adventures in Ancient Egypt & Africa." Below it is a full-color map of
the African continent. At the bottom, in big print, it says, "Come visit
five exciting Web sites filled with adventure." She turns to the first page
and reads the headline: "Tour 1: Ride the Rapids from Upper to Lower
Egypt."

Inadvertently, she touches the headline, and the page transforms
itself. This is interactive digital paper. She's read about this technology,
but she's never seen it. A voice narrates, accompanied by images:

- "Go rafting on the Nile, the longest river in the world and one of
  the most predictable in ancient times.
- "See how Egypt, the longest-lasting civilization in the ancient
  world, thrived for close to three thousand years.
- "Meet King Menes (also known as Narmer) who first unified
  Egypt around 3100 BCE.
- "Witness the inundation (Akhet), when the Nile floods, deposit-
  ing rich, fertile silt on the riverbanks.
- "Understand how a predictable river and sun led Egypt to become
  an organized society with a strong central government.

- "Have lunch with a pharaoh. Learn how, as the head of civil admin-istration, the supreme warlord, and the chief priest, the male or female pharaoh's main job was to keep order."

She turns to the next page and touches the headline, "Tour 2: Bungee Jump and Watch the Rise and Fall of Dynasties."

The narrator begins again, accompanied by other images.

- "Travel through Egypt's thirty dynasties—rulers belonging to the same family.
- "Help build a pyramid during the Old Kingdom (2700–2200 BCE), the age of pyramids. Bury a pharaoh who was like a god on earth.
- "Explore a tomb during the Middle Kingdom (2100–1800 BCE) when pharaohs were no longer buried in pyramids but rather in hidden tombs. In this Golden Age, trade, arts, and literature flourished.
- "Fight with the Egyptian army during the time of the New Kingdom (1500 BCE–1000 BCE) as Egypt expanded her borders, becoming a world power. Visit the Valley of the Kings, the next burial ground of the pharaohs.
- "Enjoy lunch with Egyptian and Nubian women, and discuss their relatively high status and how they enjoyed more rights than women in other major civilizations of the ancient world."

Megan reads a sidebar article that describes how Egypt's emphasis on massive building projects and its desire for luxuries drove an increase in trade and commerce. She turns the page and touches the headline, "Tour 3: Pan for Gold in the Great Kingdoms South of Egypt—Nubia/Kush and Aksum."

The narrator begins again.

- "Witness how the Nubians founded the Kingdom of Kush and became very wealthy, while Egypt was fragmenting around 1000 to 600 BCE.
- "Fight alongside the Nubian king as he conquers Egypt and becomes Egypt's pharaoh.
- "Visit the first capital, Napata, and then the new capital, founded farther south in Meroë after the Assyrians defeated the Kushites.
- "Create iron tools in one of the iron-smelting centers of the ancient world, or work with merchants trading in Africa, Arabia, and Egypt.
- "Spend an afternoon with the Kandakes, powerful Nubian women (warriors, queens) who ruled Nubia for hundreds of years until the first century.
- "Experience the decline of the rich Kushite culture and the rise of the Kingdom of Aksum, located to the southeast on the Red Sea.
- "See when the Aksumites adopted Christianity in the fourth century and how this changed the culture of the entire region."

Megan turns to the last page, which contains descriptions of the two remaining tours. She touches the headline, "Tour 4: Fly over Africa South of the Sahara in a Jet Helicopter" and listens to the narrator.

- "Fly over kingdoms and cities of sub-Saharan Africa, like Djenné-Djenno.
- "Attend a performance that explains why African history outside Egypt is often forgotten.
- "Learn how these societies had strong oral traditions. Oral histories were not considered legitimate historical evidence until well into the twentieth century.
- "Witness one of the largest migrations in human history—the millennia-long Bantu migration."

Finally, she touches "Tour 5: Attend a Play, *Who Wrote Africa's History?*"

- "Watch a riveting play depicting how much of African history was written by nineteenth-century Europeans, often based on biases, stereotypes, and a view that Africa was 'uncivilized.' Witness the consequences.

- "Learn about the achievements of the other great kingdoms of Africa that existed during the first millennium, such as Ghana, Mali, Songhai, Kanem-Bornu, Nubia, Kush, and Aksum."

Megan pauses and rereads the title of the fifth tour. She stares out the window into nothingness, thinking that she has never given much thought to the question of who wrote Africa's history. She realizes that not only is this question important for history, it's also important for anything she reads. Understanding an author's background, assumptions, and the context is key for critical thinking. She places the brochure back into the seat pocket in front of her and rests her head on the seat back. An announcement over the loudspeaker interrupts her thoughts. "Next five stops: Upper and Lower Egypt, Rise and Fall of Dynasties, Kush/Nubia, Sub-Saharan Africa, and *Who Wrote Africa's History.*"

After riding on the train for close to fifteen minutes, Megan realizes that she has no idea where to get off. Egyptian history is so long and has so many aspects; where does she even begin to look for a clue? Should she go to Nubia and Kush or sub-Saharan Africa? There are too many places. Normally very decisive, in this case, Megan cannot decide. She relaxes a bit as she gets the feeling that she should stay seated. But for what? she wonders. After the fifth stop, the train tilts forward and begins to travel down a steep grade. After several minutes of silence, the loudspeaker finally crackles, "Last stop: the Afterlife." The train stops, its doors open, and the interior lights go off.

Megan steps onto the platform, and the train dissolves into nothingness behind her. No turning back now, she thinks. She stands on the stone platform and looks around. Torches provide the only light. Off in the distance, she sees a faint neon sign that reads "Afterlife Tour." No one ever mentioned an afterlife tour. It seems to be the only exit. She walks through the exit and emerges in a big room with tables, chairs, and sinks. For a minute, she wonders if she's back in Globus Academy's chemistry lab. Two people sit on bar stools at each of the counter-height tables. Posters depicting the afterlife are pinned to the wall. Megan's eyes travel over illustrations of Ba, Ka, Akh, and the ancient Egyptian soul; the temple complexes at Karnak and Luxor; the different types of burial structures, from a pile of rocks to elaborate pyramids; the Valley of the Kings; and a step-by-step diagram of the mummification process. Megan recalls that the afterlife played a critical role in ancient Egyptian society. An older woman stands at the front of the room. She is wearing a long, white, cotton gown; a gold-plated vest; and a beautiful gold-and-gemstone necklace, earrings, and matching bracelet. Megan assumes that she must be a high priestess. Based on their clothing, she figures the others standing off to the side must be priests, craftsmen or artists, and workers.

"Welcome. Please join us. We are just about to begin," says the priestess, turning to Megan.

Megan grabs a stool at the last table in the back, near the door. The woman begins to speak. "Welcome to the afterlife in Egypt. Humans' relationship with a higher force, a god or gods, and the afterlife has always been linked to the environment. In ancient times, people could not explain what happened in the environment, so they said it must be the gods, since the gods controlled the natural world. They developed elaborate stories and myths to provide explanations.

"You've all heard about mummies, I'm sure," says the priestess. "In Egypt they are essential to ensure a safe passage to the afterlife. A little side note: Did you know that although Egyptian mummies are the most well-known, early South Americans were embalming their dead even before the Egyptians? The Incas were still involved in preserving their dead many years later. There are also accidental mummies all over the world in European bogs, in Greenland with its subzero weather and dehydrating winds, and in the brutal dryness of China's Taklamakan Desert."

Megan looks around the room at the different people. All are dressed in the best-quality finely decorated, and almost see-through linen. They also wear jewelry, make up and wigs. Megan realizes they must be upper class or wealthy Egyptians with a different sense of modesty. It makes sense, she thinks. Only the wealthy could afford mummification. They sit very quietly, watching the priestess. This certainly is different from her chemistry lab, where no one can ever sit still. She remembers that much knowledge about Egyptian clothing comes from studying hieroglyphs. Did they really dress this way, or were the hieroglyphs exaggerated and the actual clothing much simpler? She looks down at her own dress, and then quickly looks back to the front of the room with some embarrassment. She is wearing a similar, almost-transparent linen dress like the other women. She quickly grabs the shawl from the back of her stool and covers herself.

The priestess continues, "Ancient Egyptians value an orderly life with little change and where everything can be controlled. They also value an orderly death where everything is properly organized. Death is basically a step toward a better life in the next world. The body inherits the life force, Ka, at birth and continues to live as long as the body receives sustenance, such as food and drink. Upon death, the Ka leaves the body but requires a separate existence. The Ba is another force. Some say it's a little like the soul. It is the nonphysical aspects that make up personality, and it is unique to each individual. It stays attached to the body."

Megan raises her hand and asks, "Seems there's a lot of preoccupation with death and the afterlife. Why is that?"

"Yes. After death, the Egyptians aspired to life in a perfect existence in an ideal Egypt, full of happiness and peace. They provided for this afterlife based on their earthly means." The priestess continues, "But that's not the only reason we should care. It's because the idea of an 'immortal soul' predates the founding of today's major religions. The Greek historian Herodotus says that the Egyptians were the first to teach us the notion that the soul is separable from the body. A spiritual life beyond the physical."

As she listens, Megan feels her eyes losing focus. She's also getting a little light-headed. What is happening to her? She slips off the stool and stumbles to the water fountain in the back of the room. Before she reaches it, she passes out and crumples to the floor. A few minutes later, she awakens, sitting on the floor in the back of the room. Staring at her skin, she notices how dry and flaky it has become. She would do anything for moisturizing cream. The room feels very dry. She raises her head to look around and stifles a scream. She's in a mummification room, but it's nothing like she's read.

Now, instead of two people sitting at each table, two bodies in varying degrees of mummification lie on each table. At a few tables, priests are removing vital organs and the brain. Intestines, liver, lungs, and stomach are placed in special jars and stored. In other mummies, the organs are wrapped and put back into the body. Instead of being dried by natron, a preservative used in embalming, several bodies dry under high-intensity heat lamps to speed up a drying process that normally takes forty to fifty days. Others are being wrapped in linen.

Megan, never squeamish at the sight of blood, looks around horrified. She's read about mummies, but it's different being next to one as it is prepared. One of the priests sees Megan's look of horror and walks over to her. "Don't worry," he says. "Only a few more minutes. Your turn will be next on the table over there."

Megan, still a bit light-headed from the smells of embalming fluids, stands and wobbles to the door. Her head is pounding. A priest grabs her left arm. "You can't leave. We haven't started with you yet." Megan, summoning all her strength, hits the priest's forearm with her fist as hard as she can. "Yes, I can!" she mumbles as he releases her. "I'm not dead," she adds and stumbles through the door.

Outside the room, she stands in a narrow, dimly lit tunnel. The air, although musty, smells better than it did in the mummification room. Her head clears quickly. Behind the door, she can hear the priest summoning others. To her right the tunnel heads uphill. To her left it slopes downhill and disappears into the darkness. If she is inside a pyramid, this might be a maze built to confuse any intruders. Unfortunately, she hasn't gotten a hint of where a clue might be. She decides to head downhill, and she stumbles along, barely noticing the images on the walls. The only thing she's sure about is that she is entering a tomb. One hieroglyph catches her eye, and she stops. Not noticing the slight indentation in the ground, she takes a step back to get a better perspective. The floor gives way, and she begins to fall down a hole the size of a sewer cover. Reflexively she extends her arms to her sides and locks her elbows. Her locked arms crash to the floor with a thud as she stops her fall. She can't see the bottom of the deep, dark pit. Her hips and legs dangle beneath the floor in midair for a few seconds before her arm muscles begin to twitch. She closes her eyes and visualizes her muscles getting stronger. She brings up her legs and braces them against the side of the hole. Pushing against her back, she slowly inches her way up and out. Once out of the hole, she roles over on her back and stares up at the tunnel ceiling, catching her breath. She will never make fun of those reflex and visualization exercises in PE ever again.

She gets to her knees, looks around the tunnel, and thinks. The developers of this site must believe that Egyptian tombs were often booby-trapped. Another trap could be anywhere. She wonders if that's even historically correct. She reminds herself that although this game might have Hollywood elements, the traps are real.

She gets up, brushes the dust off her pants, and takes a few steps. Out of the corner of her eye, she notices the shimmer of a flame bouncing off something in the middle of the passageway. She stops and tentatively extends her arm into the dim light. The shimmer is gone. She continues forward slowly, gently, carefully swinging her right hand in front of her as if she is feeling for spider webs. Then she feels it as it cuts into her palm ever so slightly. Several thin, razor-sharp wires, made to look like strands of a spider web, stretch across the passageway at neck level. She ducks and scoots underneath. Another trap, she thinks.

She passes two unlit side tunnels that head off into the darkness. The decorations become more and more ornate. Megan recognizes that this must be the tomb of a noble person, maybe even a king or queen. Hearing footsteps, she quickly backtracks and ducks into the shadows of one of the unlit tunnels as two men walk by.

She recognizes them as craftsmen, ending their work for the day. As they walk by, they discuss how to remove some of the precious metals, oils, and spices before the body arrives and how they can take even more before the tomb is sealed. Megan listens intently. She can't believe she's run into genuine tomb robbers, but it was plausible that workers robbed the tombs, since it would have been much easier to steal from the tomb while it was under construction than after it was sealed.

She's about to move on when she hears more voices. She shrinks back. Two priests from the mummification room walk by. She overhears one of the priests talking about a "letter to the dead" asking for help from the deceased. A relative, still living, has asked a scribe to write a request on the inside of a bowl. The living individual wants the dead person to intervene in the afterlife, maybe at the court of the underworld. Megan realizes how much more there is to know about the Egyptians and their dead.

Soon, the priests pass, and she can continue with her search. The workers and the priests have left several torches burning, and she continues to head downhill when she hears a loud thump in the distance behind her. She fears that the workers have just closed the entrance. Now she has no choice but to keep going. After walking for a few minutes, she arrives in a large burial chamber. Megan realizes that she's reached the inner chamber. Although still under construction, it is already being filled with the deceased's earthly possessions. Half the room is dark, and a soft glow from the torches illuminates the other half, which is filled with gold, jewelry, pottery, spices, and linen and other fabrics. In the corner of the pit, she sees an open sarcophagus.

She kneels on the stone floor and leans over the sarcophagus to look inside when a voice from behind startles her. "Whom do we have here? Someone who wants to join the dead?"

Megan loses her balance and falls into the sarcophagus, landing face first on a newly finished mummy. She screams, but the mummy's bandages stifle the sound. She lies on top of the mummy, thinking this is definitely not her day, when the bottom of the sarcophagus crumbles away.

She and the mummy both fall through the floor into a great hall below, the Hall of Two Truths.

Luckily, the mummy cushions her fall. When she lifts her head, she recognizes the gods Anubis, Osiris, Thoth, and Ammit, the Devourer of the Dead, from her textbook. In front of her is the scale of justice in Duat, the Egyptian underworld. On one side of the scale is a heart, containing the deeds of a lifetime. On the other side is the feather of truth. The deceased starts to recite the Negative Confession. In this uncommon case, the heart is heavy with falsehoods told by the deceased. Thoth, one of the more important Egyptian gods, records the results. Ammit, who is part lion and part hippopotamus, with a crocodile-like head, looks at the scale and then snatches the heart and devours it in a single bite, dooming the soul to eternal death.

Megan flattens herself against the stone wall. This person surely did not enter the perfect afterlife. How does she get out of here? she wonders. Looking around, she sees the outline of a door hidden in the stone wall only a few feet away. She crawls toward it slowly, keeping an eye on Anubis and Osiris. Reaching the stone door, she is gently pushing it open when Anubis looks directly at her. She freezes and makes eye contact. He looks away and ignores her, realizing that she is not yet dead. She quickly crawls through into another tunnel and pushes the door shut. It only leads in one direction, upward. She runs up the passageway as fast as her sore body will allow. She has little strength left but wants to get above ground as soon as possible. Up ahead she sees daylight. As she nears the entrance, she turns around to look down toward the great hall one more time and collides with an Egyptian soldier who is heading her way. They tumble to the ground. As she gets up and starts to walk away, the soldier calls out, "Megan. Is that really you?"

Megan stops, turns around, and looks more closely at the Egyptian. "Sizwe. No way!" She can't believe it's her classmate from Globus Academy.

"It is you!" replies Sizwe with a broad smile.

"How in the world did you get here?" asks Megan. "I didn't even recognize you in all that Egyptian gear."

"It's a long story," he replies, getting up and wiping some of the sweat and dust from his curly black hair and off his dark skin. "I started the game in Djenné-Djenno, one of the earliest settlements in sub-Saharan Africa. Then I went to the Nubian Kushite Kingdom, and then followed the trail here."

Megan wonders how Sizwe got to this site so quickly. Are there equivalent clues hidden on multiple Web sites? Or was he only a few steps behind her team the whole time? "Where's the rest of your team?" she asks.

"I decided to work alone. You guys were gone, and I certainly didn't want to join the crazy twins."

"It's good to see you. Did you find a clue?" asks Megan.

"Nothing. You?"

"Not here," replies Megan. "Why don't you come back with me? Join our team."

"You sure that will be OK with the others?" asks Sizwe.

Megan pauses. "Actually, I should ask them first, but it'll be OK. If you want to join us."

"Yeah, maybe I will," replies Sizwe. "I wouldn't mind some company."

"Excellent," replies Megan.

They touch their wristbands. Within minutes of each other, they both land on the home page.

CHAPTER 14

WHILE MEGAN IS EXPLORING EGYPT, JARED HEADS TO
South America. The train car is empty, and Jared chooses a seat near the
back, kicks off his shoes, and puts his feet up on the seat opposite. Settling
into the comfortable cushion, he thinks about how little he knows about
ancient cultures in the Americas. Humans reached the Americas through
many migrations from Asia starting around 35,000 BCE, and the people
there were virtually isolated for fifteen thousand years. He remembers
that there were many different cultures and tribes in North and South
America, but the two most prominent ancient civilizations were the
Chavín, a pre-Inca culture, and the Olmec, a pre-Maya, pre-Aztec culture.

Jared touches the question mark button on his bracelet and whispers,
"Olmec." In his contact lenses, a series of Web sites pops open. Most of
the sites direct him to the tropical, swampy lowlands of south-central
Mexico, bordering the Gulf of Mexico. He learns that the Olmec had
polytheistic beliefs, hieroglyphic-like writing, the concept of zero, a calendar, and maybe even an early form of compass. He notices the absence
of any reference to metal tools or the wheel. There are also some discussions about the possibility of bloodletting and human sacrifice.

He continues to scan a few additional sites that raise some questions.
Some sources compare the environment in Mesoamerica, with its well-
watered soil and the transportation network of the Coatzacoalcos River
basin, to the Nile, Indus River, Yellow River, and Mesopotamia. Large
river systems often contributed to population increases and fostered

119

societies with different social classes. Others argue that the Olmec did have streams and small rivers, but just like the Chavín, no major river system acted as a generator for agriculture or transportation, or as the hub of culture. Therefore, the civilizations in the Americas are different from the ones in Eurasia in that they didn't develop along one large, singular, river system.

Jared reflects for a moment and looks out the window of the train. His dad once told him that to understand history, one can never stop questioning, analyzing, and interpreting. History is constantly evolving, based on historians' changing perspectives and the new evidence they uncover, even to this day.

He focuses on the Web sites again and reads how most of the Olmec lived in villages and how the three largest ceremonial and civic centers were part of an extensive trading network of city-states. He watches a short video that describes huge, thirty-ton, carved stone heads that rise over ten feet tall. They were made of basalt from the Tuxtla Mountains far to the north. The only stone heads he remembers are those on Easter Island. He wonders if there was any contact between the Polynesians and the Olmec.

The doors to the next train car open, and the conductor walks in, interrupting Jared's thoughts. The conductor yells, "Chavín de Huántar, arrival in five minutes," as if the car is entirely full of passengers.

"Excuse me," says Jared softly, quickly removing his feet from the seat opposite. "What is Chavín de Huántar?"

The conductor looks through the doors to the last cars and sees that there are no other passengers. He takes the seat opposite Jared and loosens his tie. "Let me tell you. It's a site north of present-day Lima, Peru, at the headwater of the Marañón River. A great mystery. One of the oldest archaeological sites in South America. A culture that vanished before written sources appeared. Archaeologists think that it was probably occupied around 3000 BCE."

"What year will it be when we arrive?" asks Jared.

"Around 600 BCE," answers the conductor. "Archaeologists think it was a large ceremonial and religious center where the local people believed that a group of elites had a divine connection. It was not a city, not a military complex, but rather a gathering place. A temple complex— the center of the Chavín culture. Located in the middle of an important connection between sea, mountains, and jungle, it had the opportunity to control several trade routes where merchants sold pottery, stone resources, wool, metals, dried fish, and textiles."

The conductor rises and starts to walk down the aisle. He then turns and looks back over his shoulder. "Before I forget, you must take the tour of the temple; it's a remarkable example of architecture and sculpture. Maybe you'll see the Lanzón. Beware the shamans, though; they are very powerful. Many believe these priests can become jaguars and interact with the divine."

The directness of the conductor's comment surprises Jared. He wonders why a conductor would tell him where to go. Was he simply a friendly conductor pointing out the tourist attractions, or is this possibly part of a clue? Before Jared can ask him another question, the conductor walks through the doorway into the next passenger car. A shrill horn signals the train's arrival in Chavín de Huántar. As the train doors open, Jared steps onto the platform and looks around. He feels a bit disoriented and dizzy. He looks up and stenciled on the wall are the words "Elevation: 3,180 meters." That's more than ten thousand feet above sea level. No wonder he's dizzy.

He exits the door and finds himself in a sunken circular plaza. This must be one of those strange Web page links, he thinks. You're in one place one minute, and then you step through a door and find yourself in another place the next. The surrounding walls are lined with granite. An eight-foot granite obelisk stands in the center of the plaza and points to the sky. On it are carved reliefs depicting jaguars and people. Several stone staircases lead up to three temples. Jared looks up in awe. Beyond the buildings, mountain peaks shrouded by the gathering clouds surround the circular plaza. He's already so high, and the mountains go even higher. A shepherd herds llamas, some with packs, to a shelter. He realizes that he is in the main plaza of Chavín de Huántar, the religious center and capital of the Chavín people.

As he peers around the plaza, storm clouds envelop the mountain peaks, and the light drizzle turns into a pounding rain. He is looking around for cover from the downpour when he hears a voice. "This way, quickly!" someone yells.

Jared turns to see a young man motioning for him to come. "This is our only chance to get into the temple."

Jared's instincts tell him to go. He follows the young man up the staircase and into an atrium made of black limestone and white granite. The young man reaches around the corner and then wraps himself in a richly adorned cloak made from llama wool. He uses the cloak to obscure his face. He hands Jared a similar cloak and tells him to do the same. They then join a group of worshipers who are ready to enter the temple.

"Why our only chance?" whispers Jared.

"The temple only houses priests, and only the elite are allowed to visit. Our social class does not belong. I had a friend steal—or I should say, borrow—these cloaks. With them, it looks like we belong. It may be the only time we can see the temple from the inside."

Jared realizes that when he came through the link to this particular Web site, he was put into a lower social class. For an instant, he wonders why he was put in a lower social class. He remembers from the departure monitor that elements of civilizations include organized religions and social classes. Social hierarchies were very rigid in the ancient world.

"Why are you taking me?" asks Jared.

"I have been provided to you as your guide. My name is Chimalli."

Jared wonders about Chimalli's choice of words. A hushed silence falls over the worshipers, and they begin to move forward. Jaguars, eagles, and feline figures, as well as tenon heads depicting the transformation of human to feline forms, decorate the temple walls. Up ahead, a few pilgrims gather between the two priests. Outside, the rain begins to fall. As Jared and the young man walk with the worshipers, the priests enter a narrow passageway formed by stacked boulders supporting a roof made of limestone or granite. The passage is about six feet tall and so narrow that individuals have to walk in a single file. They turn right, then left, and then make another right, passing chambers filled with religious artifacts. The only light comes from the flickering torches held by the priests and the pilgrims. The worshipers at the end of the line have smaller torches and less light. This is just fine with Jared. The less light, the better. Jared, disoriented, would not know how to get out of this subterranean maze if his life depended on it. He wonders how deep they've gone. Jared notices several smaller shafts in the tunnel network. They walk farther and farther, and then they finally enter a dimly lit subterranean gallery. At the center of a confining space stands a fifteen-foot-tall obelisk carved from white granite. Its base is embedded in the dirt floor, and its top pierces the ceiling. It's the Lanzón. Jared recognizes the image carved on it, a mix between a human and a feline with claws and fangs curved sideways in a smile. Her hair and eyebrows consist of writhing snakes.

He looks at his guide and absentmindedly says, "Her hair looks like Medusa from Greek mythology."

"Who are the Greeks?" asks the young man.

"Never mind," replies Jared, realizing that an ancient Chavín would know nothing about the Greeks. He then takes a closer look at the obelisk.

"Beware, the priests will get angry," warns Chimalli.

"Look," says Jared, pointing to the base of the Lanzón. "There is something written on the back. I need to get behind that obelisk, but with the other pilgrims in the chamber, I can't make it." Jared looks around, picks up a small rock and throws it into one of the other tunnels. It makes a long, echoing sound as it bounces against the walls. The worshipers all look in the direction of the noise and then follow the two priests who go investigate. No one wants to remain in the chamber alone. This gives Jared the few seconds he needs to scramble behind the obelisk. He is safe from view. Written near the bottom of the white granite obelisk is a short phrase. It looks as if the writer lay on the ground and wrote the message with a burned piece of wood just a few inches off the floor, possibly to ensure it would not be detected.

Jared realizes that he'll have to crouch on his hands and knees, even if it will expose his legs, in order to read the message. It might be the next clue. He looks around the corner of the obelisk to see if the priests are still occupied and drops to his knees.

Jared is trying to decipher the riddle when he hears a priest yell, "You! Stop! No one is allowed near the supreme god!" A young priest pushes his way through the pilgrims and heads straight for Jared.

Jared quickly tries to rub out the phrase. His hand now covered in black soot, he scrambles to his feet and begins to run down one of the tunnels.

The priest sees Jared's black hand and yells, "Catch him! He has defiled the Smiling God."

One of the male pilgrims who had obtained permission to enter the temple sees that Jared is about to escape and tackles him around the ankles. Jared falls to the floor, landing hard. The breath is knocked from his chest. He twists, turns, and tries to escape, but the man's grip is too tight. They tumble down the narrow tunnel, banging knees and elbows against the hard stone, when all of a sudden, the man's head transforms into the head of a jaguar.

Then, coming out of nowhere, Chimalli launches himself at the pilgrim and furiously kicks the half man, half animal in the head. The beast releases its grip, and Jared scrambles to his feet. He runs, stumbling, down the tunnel.

"Left," yells Chimalli, passing Jared. "Up the staircase."

It takes a few seconds before the other priests and pilgrims realize what is happening. They chase after Jared, who hobbles after the young man as fast as his bruised legs will allow. They head up a series of steps, around several corners, and emerge in the rain-drenched plaza. Jared is unable to remove the cumbersome cloak he is wearing, and he struggles to get across the plaza. The young man grabs Jared under one of his arms and helps him along. The downpour has become torrential, and they are soaked by the time they reach another staircase. The young man helps Jared, who is out of breath and a bit dizzy due to the altitude, up the stairs. They enter another temple and get out of the rain.

"I don't think they saw us. During the rainy season, the water never stops," says Chimalli.

A deafening roar emanates from deep inside the temple. Jared slowly walks toward the sound, down a long passageway. He turns the corner. Not looking where he steps, Jared almost twists his ankle in a hole in the floor. He notices that the floor is dotted with these square holes. They are stone-lined vents that channel the roaring sound. Down below, he can see water rushing by.

"The roar of the jaguar," yells Chimalli, trying to be heard above the sound. "Keep going."

"Great. Another jaguar," replies Jared.

They hear the priests nearby, and the young man runs ahead. "Come, the priests must not catch you."

Jared tries to keep up with Chimalli as he disappears around a corner. Jared, distracted and still slightly dizzy, doesn't anticipate having to make another sharp turn. His bruised muscles cramp up, and as he rounds the corner, he loses his balance and falls straight into a large canal. The water is icy cold and snaps him out of his dizziness. He is swept along by the rushing current. He kicks furiously, trying to keep his head above water. He tries to wriggle out of the cloak, with little success. The water flows through an open, subterranean canal leading into an enclosed stone drain. The volume of water is so great that Jared has no chance of keeping his head above the surface. He takes a big breath, spins around so that his feet go first, submerges, and lets the torrent take him into the pitch-black underground canal.

Jared can feel the stone walls all around him when he stretches out his arms. Luckily, they are smooth. He hopes that the tunnel doesn't narrow, or he'll end up like a cork stuck in a bottle. His lungs begin to burn, and it seems as if he's been underwater for an eternity. He slowly drifts in and out of consciousness as he thinks, What a way to die—600 BCE, high in the Andes, and in a game, no less.

He forces himself to focus; he's not going to give up that easily. He kicks his feet to move more quickly when he notices the flow of water slowing. A hand reaches into the water, grabs him by the collar of his cloak, and with one forceful motion, using the energy of the remaining current, yanks him out onto the stone walkway. Jared gags, spitting up water, and gasps for air. There, looking down on him and slapping his face, is Chimalli.

"Are you alive? Are you all right?"

Jared nods slowly.

"We don't have time," says the young man. "They will soon know where you are. We must go."

Chimalli grabs Jared around the chest and pulls him to his feet. They stagger along the underground walkway toward the surface, where the rain has turned into a light drizzle. The black-and-white portal, made of intricately decorated white limestone columns surrounding a wall of black granite, stands off to the side. They continue up a set of stairs to the roof of the old temple, four stories above the ground.

"Why have we come back here?" asks Jared, standing at the edge of a large air duct that leads down into the basement of the temple.

"They will not suspect us doubling back. You must continue your journey," says Chimalli.

Jared, drained of energy and barely able to stand, takes deep breaths. He replies weakly, "Thank you. Who are you?"

"I am Chimalli. I have been programmed to shield you."

Jared tries to make sense of what the young man said. He figures his mind isn't quite working at this altitude. Did Chimalli say he was programmed? As Jared ponders the question, three stone axes slam into Chimalli's back. He grabs Jared, and together they fall down the large air duct. About halfway down, Chimalli lets go of Jared and pushes him away. Jared lands on a narrow stone outcropping. He watches as Chimalli falls and, a few feet from the ground, transforms himself into an eagle and soars out of the air duct.

Jared can't believe what he is seeing. He hears voices from above and presses himself against the wall of the duct, hoping the priests won't see him. As he looks up, an eagle swoops down, and he hears as the priests yell and scatter across the rooftop. He sees spears flying into the air.

Jared lies with his back against the cold stone and presses the home button. He wonders if Chavín de Huántar truly looked like this or if this is a slightly-fictional computerized reconstruction of history. While he waits, he searches his contact lenses and finds out that some archaeologists believe that the Chavín culture used the San Pedro cactus as a hallucinogenic drug for religious purposes. Some say it was a way to reinforce the perception that priests had supernatural power. He reflects on how that would explain the human transformations or shape-shifting he saw in the temple and with Chimalli. But he didn't eat or drink anything, and especially not a San Pedro cactus.

CHAPTER 15

IT IS A FEW MINUTES AFTER NINE P.M., AND LIEN, ETHAN, and Arjun wait in one of the dozen sitting areas of the home page. They talk and stare off into the millions of golden strands and colorful nodes—the gigantic web that makes up *The Ancients* game. Every time a new light emerges, it signifies a new site that has been created; every time a light goes out it means a site has shut down.

"Where are those two?" asks Ethan, becoming a bit irritated that Jared and Megan are both missing at the same time.

"No idea," replies Arjun. "How'd you do? Find anything?" he says to no one in particular.

Lien shakes her head. "Nope. There wasn't really a clue. But I did come across something interesting. Slaves. Some argue that a slave society was critical to the success of the Shang economy."

"What's the big deal?" replies Ethan. "Lots of agricultural societies used slaves."

"True," answers Lien. "But in this case, the slaves were owned by the state; in the other parts of the world, the slaves were mostly privately owned."

"That *is* different," Arjun says. "Anything else?"

"No, not really. I found oracle bones with an ancient script carved in tortoise shells that I thought might be promising. And then I saw enormous royal tombs, but nothing that looked like a clue." She turns to Ethan. "What about you, Ethan?"

"Not much, either. I almost got lost in the maze of the Minotaur. Besides learning that the Minoans were an amazing society with impressive architecture, great art, and strong women's rights, nothing turned up."

"You didn't get attacked by the Minotaur?" jokes Jared as he steps out from behind a large recliner.

"Very funny," replies Ethan. "What took you so long, anyway?"

"I got attacked by a half man, half jaguar; almost drowned; and then fell down a four-story air duct," says Jared.

"Sure. And you survived," replies Ethan with a trace of skepticism in his voice. At least Megan isn't around to hear Jared's outlandish story, he thinks.

"A few cuts and bruises," replies Jared, rubbing the back of his neck where the jaguar's claws left deep scratches in his skin.

Lien walks over and gently runs her fingers over the wounds. "Does it hurt?"

"A little," replies Jared. He's about to continue when he sees Sizwe walking toward the group. "Hey, Sizwe. What a surprise!"

"Hey, guys," replies Sizwe. "Not as big a surprise as Megan finding me in ancient Egypt."

They all look at him except for Ethan, who looks at the floor. "What do you mean? That's a heck of a coincidence. Who are you working with?"

"I'm working alone. I went through ancient Africa, Kush, and then Egypt, and wham, outside of a temple in the Valley of the Kings, Megan knocks me over. By the way, where is she?"

"Don't know," replies Ethan. "She's almost a half hour late."

"Did you find anything?" asks Arjun, figuring it can't hurt to ask Sizwe while he's here.

"Nothing," replies Sizwe honestly. He hesitates for a moment. "When we left the Egypt site, she said she didn't find anything either. She should be here any minute." He pauses again. Standing, he starts to fidget with his hands.

Jared can tell that Sizwe is nervous. "What's up?" he asks.

"I hoped Megan would be here. She said she wanted to ask you guys first." He pauses again.

"Ask what? Out with it, already," says Ethan in an unfriendly tone.

Sizwe clears his throat. "She asked if I wanted to join you guys," he says with a crooked smile.

There is a moment of silence. Arjun, who has worked on several class projects with Sizwe, finally replies. "OK with me."

Lien shrugs her shoulders. "Sure."

Jared and Ethan say nothing. The silence is creating an uncomfortable tension when Megan walks up. "Hey, guys. Sorry I'm late. Sometimes these nanobots really take their time. Almost had to fight off more Egyptians." She turns. "Ah, I see Sizwe got here. Good."

"Can we talk?" asks Ethan, rising from his chair. Ethan puts his hand on Megan's back and tries to move her out of earshot of the others. Megan spins free. No one, not even her teammates, pushes her to go anywhere, even if it is only a gentle nudge. Jared gets up and joins them.

Ethan furrows his brow and tries to assert himself. "You can't just invite anyone to join us without talking with us first. It's not just your team." Anger and jealousy mix in his voice. He talked to Megan about working together before anyone else did. Then Jared and the others joined, and now this. He can't believe Megan would invite another guy to the team, especially Sizwe. He's one of the most popular students around.

"Don't lecture me," she says loudly enough for the others to hear. "I told Sizwe I needed to talk to my team first. End of story."

Ethan knows he's on the verge of angering Megan. He sighs heavily and quietly says, "OK."

"Timing was a bit bad, since he arrived before you did," adds Jared. "I'm OK with him on the team. We just need to realize that as the team gets bigger, it's going to get more complicated and harder to work with a bunch of people. We have to be clear about who leads."

"Fine," replies Megan. "And I know that," she adds as she angrily turns to walk back to the others. How dare they give her a hard time?

"Wait!" says Ethan. He signals for Megan and Jared to walk farther away from the others. "I didn't want to say anything, but at school I did notice Sizwe talking to the twins right after the game started. They seemed real chummy."

"Are you suggesting that Sizwe is really working with them?" asks Megan in disbelief.

"Sizwe is on the swim team with Damian," replies Ethan with a shrug. "I mean, they are already teammates. And all of a sudden he shows up. All by himself."

"That's right," adds Jared. "But I can't see Sizwe being a spy. That's not like him. Yet at the same time, we do have to be careful."

"I'm not sure, guys. Sizwe wouldn't do that," adds Megan.

"I don't know either," says Ethan making sure to not smirk as he looks past Jared at Sizwe. "I'm just telling you what I saw."

Jared leans in. "OK. Maybe we hold off and say we need to talk to Arjun and Lien about this first. We'll let him know."

Megan frowns but nods in agreement. Ethan nods as well. They walk back to the others.

"I'm sorry if I caused any problems," says Sizwe.

Megan throws herself into one of the recliners and stabs at the massage button. "I almost get mummified, and then this."

"Sizwe, the timing was off, and we were a bit surprised," says Jared. He then looks at Arjun and Lien. "We need to talk about this as an entire team. Since moving forward, we need to agree on how to deal with stuff like this ahead of time. So, let's hold off on you joining our team until we've had a chance to talk about it. We'll let you know. I'm sorry."

A look of disappointment crosses Sizwe's face as he looks from Jared to Megan to the others.

"Like I said, I'm OK with him joining," says Arjun.

"Me, too," adds Lien.

"Nothing against you, Sizwe," says Ethan quickly. "We just need to agree on some team ground rules first. After all, you never know when someone else might want to join."

"I think I understand," replies Sizwe as he begins to walk away from the group.

Jared gets up and walks with him to another sitting area on the home page. "Hey, just some weird group stuff. We'll get it figured out."

"Whatever," replies Sizwe as he grabs a chair and sits down. A few minutes later he disappears from the home page.

Jared stands and looks out into the golden web, past where Sizwe was sitting. He then heads back to the group.

"What was that all about?" asks Arjun. "Sizwe looked pretty bummed."

Turning to Ethan, Megan says with an edge to her voice, "Tell them!"

Ethan casually describes what he saw early in the week. Lien and Arjun look at each other in surprise. Neither one of them believes that Sizwe would actually be a spy. But who knows? Especially if he was seen talking with the twins right after the start of the game.

"Let's worry about this later and focus back on the game," suggests Megan, hoping to avoid a long discussion about Sizwe. "In Egypt I was an upper-class Egyptian woman that almost got mummified, but I didn't find anything."

"Hmm," says Jared. "In Chavín de Huántar I was in a lower class. Why were you put into the upper class?"

Megan shrugs. "No idea."

Ethan looks out at the web, deep in thought. He looks back at the group with a smile. "This is so cool. I bet the programmers developed a social class randomizer."

"A what?" asks Lien.

"A social class randomizer," replies Ethan. "A bit of code that randomly determines the social class you end up in when you go to a site."

"That could get…ahh…interesting," adds Jared. "Nobility one day, slave the next."

Lien looks at Ethan. "If this is true, it will certainly make the game more exciting."

"OK. A new twist. But it looks like we turned up a big zero," says Arjun. "I didn't find anything among the Harappans, either. But if you ever get a chance, you need to check out the cities of Mohenjo Daro and Harappa. Some of the stuff they built was really cool."

"I wouldn't say we got a complete zero," replies Jared. "Looks like the Chavín had a clue after all."

Megan sits up in her chair, now paying full attention. "Why didn't you say something earlier?"

"What! Knowing about a social class randomizer is important." He grins at Megan.

Ethan, not sure whether Jared is being sarcastic or truly appreciates his insight, kicks himself. He was originally supposed to go to the Americas until he switched with Jared. If he had found the clue, maybe then Megan would notice him more.

Jared continues, "Sure, with all that was happening. Anyway, on the back of the Chavín Lanzón it said, '*Seek a vanished civilization at Empire Plaza.*'"

"That sounds like a clue to me," Megan says without even the slightest trace of her earlier anger. She can never be angry at Jared for long. "It's late and I'm exhausted. Let's talk about this tomorrow," she says, rising from her recliner.

"I agree; we should call it quits," says Jared, getting up. "It's only a couple more days until spring break. We'll have more time then."

"We can talk about this at lunch," suggests Ethan.

"We agreed to not talk about the game at school," replies Arjun.

"Too many spies," adds Lien, chuckling.

"How about we meet after school tomorrow and decide what to do next?" suggests Arjun.

"I can't make it tomorrow. I've got an appointment that will take most of the afternoon and evening," replies Jared. "But you guys can continue. You don't need me."

"Actually, we kind of do. You found the next clue," says Lien. "We can wait and meet after school on Friday. I mean, we're going to have all of spring break."

"I suppose," Ethan says reluctantly. "See you at school." He deactivates the nanobots and disappears from the home page.

Megan and Arjun do the same.

Lien watches Jared, noticing that he hasn't deactivated his nanobots. He's reclining on the couch, staring out at the millions of nodes. Finally, she says, "Aren't you heading back?"

Jared replies, "Soon."

"Do you mind if I join you?" asks Lien, quickly adding, "Just for a bit."

"Sure," replies Jared. "But I might not be the best company."

"No worries," replies Lien.

To Jared's surprise, she gets up, sits next to him on the couch, and snuggles close. Jared is about to say something, but then stops himself. It's actually nice having her next to him.

Lien looks at him as he smiles and stares off into the distance. She'd give anything to know what he's thinking. Lien notices how the web looks like a colorful, starry sky where all the sites are connected with golden strands. They don't notice the first few students, but soon the home page is swarming with them, even though it's late. Lien and Jared scoot apart as they watch different groups of teenagers, all wearing the bronze-and-iron wristbands of the game. Some show up for just a few seconds and then disappear again; others linger a little longer; some even meet in the various sitting areas.

"What's happening?" asks Jared.

"I suspect these are students from other schools," answers Lien. "Let me find out." She walks to several groups. Every time she approaches, the talking stops, and the students look at her suspiciously. She smiles and asks where they're from. She then walks around and asks various individuals the same question. When she returns, Jared seems to be dozing; his eyes are closed.

She gently nudges him. "Jared, wake up. Are you asleep?"

He opens his eyes. "No. Just resting."

Lien sits on his armrest, looks down at him, and whispers, "Yup. They're all students from other schools on the same quest. Some of the schools are in different countries and time zones, so for them this is afternoon or morning."

"They all spoke English?" asks Jared.

Lien thinks for a moment. "Actually, yes. But their English was too perfect. Maybe the game was instantly translating what they were saying.

"I wouldn't be surprised. This is a lot of people," Jared observes. "Dr. Jones said ten schools were involved."

"Exactly," replies Lien. "Looks like more than that to me."

"The more students who search, the better for them," Jared says, "and the worse for us."

"What do you mean the better for them?" asks Lien, looking at him suspiciously.

"Nothing. The more students, the more competition."

Lien doesn't probe any further even though she suspects something else is going on. "I'm tired, and I still have to finish a paper for tomorrow." She leans over and gives him a peck on the cheek. "Good night."

Jared, surprised, stammers, "Good night." He had no idea that Lien liked him. For a few seconds, he thinks about how he feels about Lien.

Then he deactivates the nanobots and emerges from the Web back in his room, where he started earlier that day. He's exhausted. He brushes his teeth, puts on his pajamas, and climbs under the covers, ready to fall fast asleep. But his mind won't stop racing. Something is bugging him. He grabs his smartphone from the nightstand and checks his e-mail and text messages. There is only one text message. His mom sent it at seven p.m., saying she's still at work and won't be home until after midnight. There's cold turkey in the refrigerator for dinner.

He thinks about the riddle, wrestling with it in his mind. He's about to doze off when he remembers what was bugging him. He dictates a short text message. "Besides the clue '*Seek a vanished civilization at Empire Plaza*,' there was something else. I'll tell you later." He touches the send button and curls up under his covers. Now he can sleep.

CHAPTER 16

THROUGHOUT THE MORNING, JARED GOES BACK AND forth, debating whether he should ask Megan to accompany him to the address his uncle gave him. Megan probably wouldn't be followed, and he can get there unseen. Overall, she has a good heart, and besides his family, he trusts her more than he trusts anyone else.

During lunch, he sees her at one of the picnic benches with a few of her friends, laughing while looking at a smartphone. He casually walks up to the group. "Hi, Megan, can I talk to you for a minute?"

Megan turns. "Sure." She hands the smartphone back to one of her friends and gets up. Jared and Megan walk across the lawn to an area where they can speak in private.

"I need to ask you a favor," says Jared.

"Yeah, what is it?"

"Can you take me to Sausalito this afternoon?"

"That's a bit of a drive. Can't you borrow your mom's car instead?"

Jared moves closer and turns away from the other students on the grass. "I met with my uncle yesterday. You've got to promise to keep this to yourself. OK?"

"Believe me, I can keep a secret," replies Megan quietly. She takes Jared's arm and walks farther from the other students.

Jared swallows. "Well … it turns out the game is much more than just a game. Something else is going on, and I need to visit him today." Jared glances over his shoulders and lowers his voice even further. "Two nights ago, the government came to my uncle's lab and then interrogated my mom and me for almost two hours. This is the second time I've been interrogated by federal agents."

Megan steps back. With some excitement in her voice, she asks, "You're kidding. What did they want to know?"

"About my dad and uncle. They asked about a bunch of computer and technology stuff—cyber crime and computer viruses."

"Wow. That sounds intense. Did they ask about the game?" asks Megan.

"No. Interestingly, they didn't. But they must know. I'd like you to come with me."

Megan, always up for an adventure, replies, "This is turning into a regular mystery. I don't have anything planned. So yeah, I'll drive you."

"Cool. I don't know what we're getting ourselves into, but thanks." Jared turns and gives Megan a quick hug.

From behind the other students, Ethan watches as Megan and Jared talk on the grass. His blood pressure increases, and he kicks a rock across the walkway as he sees Jared hug Megan. I'm not giving up on her that easily, he thinks to himself.

Later that afternoon, Megan picks up Jared. They drive for almost an hour, crossing the fog-enshrouded Golden Gate Bridge as the sun begins to set. Mount Tamalpais and the city of San Francisco are barely visible. They take the second exit, and Jared directs Megan to the side streets. After a while, Megan notices that they keep traveling in one direction and then going back in the opposite direction.

Finally, she asks, "Jared, what the heck are we doing? We seem to be going in circles. Do you know where this place is?"

"Yeah. We're doubling back to make sure we're not being followed," he replies casually, as if every teenager knows how to throw off a tailing car.

"What!" says Megan. "Where did you learn that?"

"My dad taught me the technique after I finished reading a spy novel a few years ago."

Megan wonders why a professor of history and communication technology would know how to lose a tail, but decides not to ask.

They reach a community of houseboats nestled against the shore, and park in a dingy parking lot. Walking toward the main pier, Megan comments, "I've never been here. All these unique homes. Different sizes and styles."

"Yeah. Neat place to live," replies Jared, while looking at a directory of the houseboats. He wrinkles his nose as he smells a hint of garlic. Unexpectedly, an old homeless man wearing a tattered old coat and a wool seaman's cap steps out from behind the directory. Jared, startled, takes a step back.

"Don't like garlic, eh?" jokes the old man.

"Excuse me?" says Jared, trying to ignore him. "Are you talking to me?"

"Who else?" replies the man. "Do you see anyone else here? Do you think I ask myself questions? I might be down on my luck, but I'm not crazy."

Jared keeps his eyes focused on the directory and doesn't say a word. Megan comes up to his side. The old man dips his hat in greeting.

"Good evening, young lady. Looking for someone? Maybe I can help. You know, things are not always what they seem; the first appearance deceives many."

Jared, surprised by the comment, looks at the old man. Did he hear what he thought he heard? That was the same phrase his uncle had used. After carefully looking over the teenagers and checking them out, the homeless man says, "What you seek is on the last pier, the last row of homes, the last houseboat on the right, in the deeper water of the bay." The old man then bends down, grabs two empty aluminum cans, and throws them into his shopping cart. As he ambles away, he whispers into his overcoat, "Doctor, your visitors are on their way. Two of them."

Jared reaches the houseboat and looks down into the water as he crosses a gangplank to the front door. He notices that the boat's hull isn't anything like its neighbors'. It looks much more like that of a ship, but not a normal ship. A few inches above the waterline, he can see surface-piercing hydrofoils. The structure above water looks like any modern, square-shaped houseboat, but he senses that something is different about that, too. Before he can knock, the door swings open. An elegant woman, probably in her mid-sixties, dressed in a flowing, earth-tone caftan embroidered with gold, stands in the doorway. Her raven-black hair, pulled away from her face and secured with leather strings, flows down her back in a singular column. Her deep, black, obsidian-like eyes, not quite the shape of almonds, glance around behind Jared. She welcomes Megan and Jared inside, and then quickly closes the door, locks the latch, and touches several buttons to engage the security system.

She smiles, bows slightly, and places both palms together below her face. "Welcome to my home, Jared. I am Gia. I've been expecting you." Megan feels the affection in the greeting and recognizes its cultural significance. Having traveled to so many countries when her father was more active in the diplomatic corps, she knows that the gesture means "I respect the divinity within you that is also within me." *Namaste* is gesture that comes from Sanskrit, and is well recognized in Eastern religions.

Jared returns the gesture. "A pleasure to meet you. I've only heard your name. This is my friend, Megan. My uncle said I needed to come here tonight."

"Yes." Gia repeats the greeting gesture with Megan. "We must talk. I see you met my guard."

Jared looks at her with surprise, then chuckles. "Ah, yes. I didn't have a clue. Very good disguise."

Gia smiles. "Things are not always what they seem. Please come in." She leads them to the great room overlooking the water. The front of the boat consists of floor-to-ceiling windows facing both the mountain and the water. Jared notices that the windows are at an angle and curve inward like those on high-speed yachts. The interior décor, with its warrior-like simplicity, reminds him of a yurt from the steppes of Asia. Woven carpets cover an old wood floor. Ancient weapons and artifacts hang on the walls. The only modern elements are digital displays so well integrated into the walls that they are barely noticeable.

Jared has a strange feeling. The place is warm and inviting, old and new, almost as if the future and the past are embracing each other like the Taoist yin and yang. He wants to relax and be comfortable, yet there is also a coolness, a warrior-like hardness that keeps him on edge. The sunken floor is littered with large, overstuffed pillows, and there, reclining on one of them, is his uncle.

"Your uncle Alberto and I have been close friends for many, many years," Gia says as she leads them down a few steps.

Alberto gets up and gives Jared a big hug. "I'm so glad you're here. And we checked; you weren't followed." He then turns his attention to Megan. "Señorita!"

Megan stretches out her arm for a handshake, but Alberto takes her hand and gently brings it toward his lips. She initially resists. Then she remembers traveling with her father to Spain, where the traditional greeting is still used by some gentlemen. She also senses Alberto's respect and warmth. He places his lips to within a millimeter of the back of her hand. She blushes.

"Who is this charming lady?" he asks, looking at Jared.

Jared has never seen Megan actually blush, nor has he heard the word "charming" associated with her. He is about to reply when he is interrupted.

"I'm Megan, Jared's friend." She gives Alberto a big smile, showing her beautiful white teeth, and then curtsies. "And you must be Dr. Alberto Reyes."

Jared can't quite believe his eyes. Megan is a different person. He's never seen her so sweet and charming. Even her voice is different. "Forgive my uncle," Jared chimes in. "He clings to some old historical practices."

"Jared," says his uncle, "this is the way a gentleman greets a lady."

"Yes, Uncle. Maybe in the royal courts of seventeenth- and eighteenth-century Spain, but not so much today."

"I suppose I could send her a text message instead," he replies, laughing, as he grabs Jared's shoulder.

Megan looks at Jared, and her facial expression tells him, "It's OK. It's sweet."

Jared acknowledges her look, reflecting for a moment. He'd never considered her a romantic. Maybe some of her father's diplomatic training rubbed off on her.

Alberto steps back and looks directly at Megan. In a serious tone, he asks, "I assume that if Jared brought you here tonight, he trusts you completely, and you him?"

Megan's brain moves in slow motion. Wow! This conversation just got very serious, very quickly. She's never dealt with that question before. She's never given it much thought. But if she thinks about the past couple of years, and listens to her intuition, she knows. "As the daughter of a diplomat, I know a little about the importance of strong relationships. And, yes. I trust him." She makes eye contact with Jared. "Completely!"

"Good, because what you are going to learn tonight will affect your life from now on," continues Alberto.

Jared gives him a questioning look. "Is it related to the lab? What happened?"

"Federal agents shut us down," answers Alberto. "They froze my bank accounts and now have issued a capture order. They think I'm involved in some large conspiracy with your father."

"That's ridiculous. What would Dad be into, besides teaching and research?" asks Jared. He can't believe what he's hearing. Six months ago, someone kidnapped his father, and now someone has shut down his uncle's business. What's going on? He sighs and looks at Megan, who wears the same perplexed look.

"There's more to your father than you might think," says Alberto.

"Let me try to explain," Gia interjects in a quiet voice. "Come with me. There are powerful forces that want to destroy your father, your uncle, and the freedom we all currently enjoy. We need to stop them. We will stop them."

She descends a staircase to the lower level of the boat. They emerge into a large, windowless room with a highly polished wood floor. Dehumidifiers hum quietly in the background. The lighting is soft and inviting. Jared stares around the room in awe. The entire back wall consists of an array of huge touch-screen monitors curved in a large semicircle. Each displays a different image. Jared walks toward the wall and notices that by standing in one particular location he can see all of the monitors at once. He turns around and sees bookshelves and a desk strewn with papers against one wall. But it's the other side of the room that grabs his attention. The wall spans the length of the houseboat. It is matte black and completely empty. It looks like one of those old-fashioned chalkboards he once saw in a magazine from the 1960s. He walks up to it, and a voice says, "Good day, Jared."

Startled, he replies, "Hello."

A computer instantly scans his facial features and uses his voiceprint to confirm his identity. After verifying his identity and permissions, the computer says, "Jared, you have the necessary permissions to view the last search conducted." The computer then projects several holographic maps. They float about a foot from the wall.

One of the maps shows ancient Mesopotamia. Jared reaches toward it and notices that he can move it up, down, or sideways, and increase or decrease its size with the movement of his hands. He brings up one holographic map after another, zooms in, zooms back out, and then swipes it to the side. The maps can be looked at in several dimensions, even 3D.

Jared turns to Gia and Alberto. "This is incredible. Who built this system?"

"Your uncle," replies Gia. "When looking at a lot of information, it helps to see it in its entirety, not just one screen at a time. This way, you can begin to see connections and patterns. A few years ago, scientists started thinking about the future of life in a digital world. Research money became available to study how society will change in a world where everyone is connected to everyone, and everything is connected to everything, everywhere, all the time."

Jared looks at his uncle. "You have been saying that for years."

His uncle nods.

"Yes," adds Gia. "Our lab received millions to study how life will change as everything moves online. Several other labs around the world received funding, too."

Megan points back to the holograph. "What are these six maps? I recognize the first one, but the others? Is that a time line up on top?"

"Yes. These are maps of the world over a period of eight hundred million years. Notice how the landmasses move and change through the ages, six hundred million years ago, two hundred million years ago, all the way to today," replies Gia.

"I never knew the Earth changed so much," Megan says.

Jared looks up at the time line floating out from the wall near the ceiling. At the front of the room, where the staircase comes down, is the label "Universe Comes into Existence, Thirteen Billion Years Ago." Under the title, there is a note that lists different theories about the beginning: Big Bang, God, and Creation Myths. To the right are many feet of blank space and then another label, "Sun and Earth Form, 4.5 Billion Years Ago." Finally, all the way to the right, after several more feet of blank space, squeezed into the last few inches of the time line, is a third note: "Humans First Appear."

Pointing toward the time line, Jared asks, "What does that mean?"

Gia walks over to him. "It shows the different views of how the universe and the Earth came into being. Some say it was a Big Bang, others say God created it, and some other cultures have creation myths that describe the beginning. For example, the Iroquois Indians believed that the world was created on the back of a giant sea turtle."

"A sea turtle?" asks Megan. "Neat."

"Yes," replies Gia. "The time line depicts how long the Earth has been in existence compared to how long humans have been on the planet.

Even though it seems like a long time, all of human history is only a fraction of geologic time, and ancient history is a fraction of human history."

Gia walks to the end of the time line. "See these last few inches over here?" She makes a few hand gestures under the label "Humans First Appear," and another time line, nested under the first, appears. She moves it into the center of the wall. It extends from left to right for almost twenty feet.

Jared notices that it forms a cascade. At the top is the time line; different labels float below. One says, "Agricultural/Neolithic Revolution," then "Rise of Civilizations" with a list of several societies. He looks at "Babylonia." Below that, it says "Hammurabi." He touches the floating word "Hammurabi," and it floats upward. Beneath it, a series of images emerge and float in front of him: Hammurabi's Code, several videos, pictures, letters in cuneiform script, translations. He quickly scans Hammurabi's Code of Laws and then swishes across the images with his hand. They all float back up and nest under the name Hammurabi, king and chief priest of Babylon, 1792 to 1750 BCE.

Gia continues, "This fully interactive, nested time line is another of your uncle's inventions. With history, it's critical to think broadly—what happened across the world and across big spans of time—yet also to be able to drill down into the details, to a specific event or person. To look at historical records and understand the context in which they were created. To understand and interpret different types of evidence. Much of ancient history was described through the lens of individual observers, with their own cultural perspectives and biases. So it's good to look at multiple viewpoints, different angles, to see connections and relationships."

"I understand," replies Jared. "My dad used to tell me that it's important to try to look at more than one viewpoint, ask questions, and analyze assumptions. Then develop an answer based on solid evidence."

"Good advice," adds Gia. "That's historical thinking."

Jared looks around the room and back at the maps. He turns to Gia. "This is cool technology, but why did my uncle want me to come here?" Before Gia can speak, Jared answers his own question. "My dad worked here, didn't he?"

"Yes. This was his private office."

"But wait, I thought he worked at the university," Jared says.

"He did," replies Gia. "But he came here whenever he needed total privacy where no one could trace what he was doing. Here, he could work securely offline and online. Use secure computers to access information, use primary and secondary sources from libraries around the world."

"Why all the secrecy?" asks Jared as he plops himself into one of the chairs. Megan grabs a stool nearby.

Gia continues, "About a year ago, your father received a message from a very old, very wealthy man. He originally made his money with technology, but he'd had an interest in art all his life. His family had one of the largest private antique collections in the world. He tracked down your father. He said that he owned artifacts going back centuries and a few items even going back millennia. The collection was absolutely amazing.

"It contained texts from the ancient great libraries. The Great Library in Alexandria in Egypt from the third century BCE. Palm-leaf manuscripts from Takṣaśilā, Nālandā, and Vikramśīla, ancient Indian centers of higher education on the Indian subcontinent. Archived texts from Ebla in Syria, over five thousand years old. Others from the Library of Ashurbanipal in Iraq and the Academy of Gundishapur in Iran. Greek and Roman works. Even works from the Imperial Libraries of China going back to the Qin Dynasty. There were Mayan codices written in hieroglyphs on bark cloth. Everything was catalogued, digitized, and available remotely.

"He knew your father was a well-respected historian with high morals and ethics, so he gave your father full access to the entire collection. He could access everything from here. Alberto invented this technology to make it easier for him to search."

"I know my dad was well known in his field, but why all this and why here?" asks Jared, waving his arm around the room.

Gia sits on the armrest next to Jared. "The old man uncovered a prophecy about an artifact or device that could change the world as we know it. If it were to fall into the wrong hands, it could destroy human civilization. Your father has a reputation for uncompromising integrity, so the collector felt that your father would do the right thing. It took almost a week to download the digital versions of the old man's collection to our computers. Then, several days after we finished, and before your father had a chance to talk with him again, the old man disappeared under mysterious circumstances. Some evidence points to his being killed."

"Your father spent every free moment going through the materials, looking for clues about the artifact," continues Alberto. "A week before he was kidnapped, he told me he made a major breakthrough, but he wasn't specific."

"We looked everywhere but couldn't locate a thing. A few days ago, I found this under his desk." Gia hands Jared a plain piece of paper with his initials on top.

"Those are Egyptian hieroglyphs," comments Megan as she looks over at Jared.

Jared recognizes his father's handwriting. Years earlier, while Jared was doing an Egyptian unit in middle school, his father had taught him a secret code using hieroglyphs. They would use it around the house to stump his mom. His dad would write a few symbols and post them on the refrigerator, and when Jared came home from school, he would decipher the message and find the prize.

His father told him that for hundreds of years, Egyptian hieroglyphs were like a secret code. Then, in 1800, the Rosetta Stone was found, which included hieroglyphs, Coptic text, and Greek text. It took another twenty years to decipher and unlock over a thousand years of ancient Egyptian history. However, as with much history, even this is surrounded by controversy and debate. Another academic suggests that a Muslim scholar may have translated the hieroglyphs much earlier.

Gia continues, "I went to see Alberto in the lab to let him know what I found. We were sure everything was secure, but we saw what happened a few days ago."

Jared begins to translate. Although he hasn't used the code in years, it takes him only a few minutes to translate the few glyphs. It says to look at book seven of *Natural History* finished by the Roman scholar Pliny the Elder around 77 BCE. It's one of the largest single works to survive from the Roman Empire. His father owned a translated reproduction. Jared looks around the room. On the sidewall, in one of the large bookshelves, he sees the thirty-seven-volume set. In volume seven, halfway through the pages, he finds a piece of paper lightly glued into the spine. He carefully pries it out of the book. In his father's handwriting, the note says:

Prophecy
New Lords of the Clouds seek to dominate our world.
Choice disappears; freedom and independence are at risk.
Have the courage to use your own mind—sapere aude.

Follow clues hidden in the web of humanity's history.
Find this powerful artifact, before it falls into the wrong hands.

Megan, looking over his shoulder at the note, asks, "What does 'sapere aude' mean?"

"It means 'dare to be wise' or 'dare to know,'" answers Jared, looking to Gia for confirmation. But she is not paying attention. She is listening to something else. For the first time, Jared notices that she is wearing a skin-colored earpiece. He does not have a chance to read the rest of the note.

"I can't believe it. If it's not one, then it's the other," she yells to no one in particular. Gone is the quiet, humble woman. As if commanding an army into the field of battle, she barks orders. "We need to get out of here now. We only have a few minutes. Engage camouflage sequence one." She grabs a smartphone from the desk and hands it to Jared. "This is a secure satellite smartphone if you ever need to get a hold of us. Don't lose it," she says, seeing Jared's questioning look. He stuffs the phone and the note from his dad into his pockets as he follows her up the staircase. Megan and Alberto are right behind him.

Over a speaker in the main salon, Jared can hear a voice. "Two attack drones on the way. They passed under the Golden Gate Bridge a second ago. Suggest you leave ship immediately."

"Attack drones?" shouts Jared. "I thought those were only used overseas."

Alberto, a few steps behind Megan, replies, "Awhile back it started with drones used in foreign wars. Then the US government gave various agencies permission to fly drones over domestic airspace for surveillance. That soon led to weaponized drones, even at home, and not long after that private corporations and individuals started to buy them. Drones are now everywhere. They are used for almost anything you can think of: surveillance, surveying, aerial videos and pictures, even package delivery. It's a global phenomenon. They have become so commonplace that most people don't even think about it anymore. They are a very seductive technology—imagine donning a set of goggles, and the next thing you know, you are flying. It's a technology that gives us amazing powers."

"Sounds like technology racing far ahead of our ability to manage it," replies Jared.

"Yes, to some extent," replies Alberto. "There are always multiple sides to technological development."

Gia, Jared, Megan, and Alberto exit the houseboat and sprint down the gangplank and onto the pier.

"Get our own drones into the air to counter the attack," says Gia into her hidden microphone.

Jared glances at his uncle, who shrugs.

"OK. If it's too late, jam their signal!" says Gia. "The fog is coming in fast, and it will hopefully give us cover."

They continue to run as fast as they can toward shore as they hear the drones approach. Instead of firing missiles, the two drones slam into an abandoned houseboat moored in the bay. The explosion shoots a ball of fire into the night sky and sends water and debris everywhere. Windows in houseboats and multimillion-dollar homes on the shore are knocked out. Gia and Jared are thrown off the dock. Gia falls into the water, and Jared tumbles headfirst into an inflatable dinghy. Alberto and Megan land on the pier.

Soaking wet but not missing a beat, Gia climbs up the dock ladder and grabs Jared, whose head is pounding from the blast. They both head toward the shoreline. They walk past frightened residents and take cover behind a row of trees.

"What kind of drones where those?" asks Jared.

"Kamikaze drones, remote-controlled missiles no larger than toy helicopters. Probably sent by someone trying to slow us down," replies Gia quietly. "Your presence here was hopefully just a coincidence." She then turns her head and speaks into her microphone. "That was too close. Start posting online that two old gas tanks on that abandoned boat exploded. And make ready to depart."

Jared looks out toward the houseboat and cannot recognize it anymore. It has been transformed into a derelict boat and is slowly pulling out of its berth. He reaches into his back pocket and pulls out the note from his dad, now a bit wet and smudged from the water in the dinghy. He reads the rest quickly.

Dear Jared,

I'm sorry to drag you into this, but if you're reading this, your uncle and I desperately need your help. Forces are aligning against us. We need to find this artifact before anyone else does. Gia and Alberto can help you from afar. I hope that you have some others you trust to help. We need to win this game, this battle, this war. The fate of humanity depends on it.

Love, Dad

Jared is lost in thought. What kind of artifact is this? What battle? Win this game? Does he mean *The Ancients* game?

Gia touches his arm to go. "You never know what's on those abandoned boats," she says loudly, then adds quietly, "We'd better get out of here."

Jared, a bit shaken, walks beside Gia. Even Megan, who's normally not afraid of anything, looks alarmed. Twice in less than eight months, Jared has been part of a serious attack.

Jared looks around himself, his confidence shaken. This cannot really be happening. What is his father involved in? he wonders. Gia wraps an arm around his waist and smiles up at him. He can feel her strength as she strides forward with the courage of an experienced warrior. Slowly, his confidence returns.

Jared and Megan say little on the way home. Megan stops in front of his house and lets the car idle. "A simple trip to Sausalito, huh?"

"Yeah, interesting evening," replies Jared as he gets out of the car.

Megan turns to him and smiles. "You and me, we're going to win this thing and figure out what happened to your dad."

Jared returns the smile. "Thanks! Sounds like a plan." He slams the door, and Megan drives off. She sure is confident, he thinks as he walks up the driveway. He wishes he had a little more confidence himself.

That night it takes Jared a couple of hours to fall asleep. He tosses and turns violently throughout the night. The next morning all he can remember is that Megan was in his dream. Strange, he thinks; he's never dreamed about Megan before.

CHAPTER 17

FOR MOST OF LUNCH, ARJUN AND ETHAN HANG OUT together, trying hard to avoid talking about the game, knowing that others might try to listen. As they sit at one of the tables, Sizwe walks by.

"Hey, Sizwe!" says Arjun, trying to start a conversation. Sizwe moves away and does not even acknowledge Arjun's presence.

"Did you see that?" asks Damian, nodding toward the grassy area visible from the hallway.

"See what?" replies Ivy. She hates it when her brother asks such vague questions, assuming that she can read his mind.

"Arjun is over there with Ethan, and Sizwe just walked by totally ignoring Arjun."

"Yeah, so?"

"Arjun and Sizwe sometimes hang out together. Why would Sizwe not even acknowledge him?"

"Good point," replies Ivy. "Let's see if I can get Maria or Alexa to find out what's going on. Alexa kind of likes Ethan."

"OK. There's still twenty minutes for lunch. I'm going home to pick up my eavesdropper. The one I built in science. We could use it in class and see if they say anything."

World history, the last class before spring break, is total chaos. Ms. Castro realizes there is very little that will occur today. The students are all much too wound up and ready for a break. She asks several questions about the game. Every reply is vague. She's surprised by how competitive the class has gotten. Near the end of the period, she breaks the class into groups and gives them a short exercise about primary and secondary sources.

Megan, Jared, Arjun, Lien, and Ethan work together at one table. Damian and Ivy, with several of their friends, congregate in one of the front corners. Damian sits with his back against the wall to make sure he can keep his notebook pointed toward the other groups. The pen-shaped microphone of the eavesdropper is hidden inside it, set to record.

After the group exercise, the period ends uneventfully, and everyone streams out of the classroom. Spring break is here. Students hurry to their lockers, grab backpacks and books, and head off campus.

As the hallways empty, Ivy meets Damian at his locker. "You were right. Something was up. Sizwe wanted to join Megan and Jared's team last night, but they didn't let him."

"Wow. Why not?" asks Damian.

"I'm not sure. Alexa couldn't get Ethan to tell her." Ivy looks over her shoulder to make sure no one else is around. "Did you pick up anything on your microphone?"

"I didn't listen to it yet. Luckily, that last exercise was only ten minutes."

"Go through it now," says Ivy. "It might be important."

"Here? Now?" asks Damian. "Someone might see us."

"I'll shield you. Pretend like you're listening to your iPod in your locker."

Arjun, after spending some time with Ms. Castro after class, rounds the corner and sees Ivy next to Damian at his locker. Something is odd about the way she is standing there. It's as if they're trying to hide something.

He purposely walks up right behind them. "Hey, guys. What's up?" he asks.

Ivy twirls around and glares at him. "What do you want?" she asks.

"Nothing. Just passing by. On my way to my locker." He points down the hallway.

"Oh, OK," replies Ivy, backing up against the open locker.

Damian looks over his shoulder. "See ya, Arjun," he says, trying to sound like nothing is going on.

Arjun keeps walking. After a few feet, he turns. "Have a good spring break," he says. From that angle, Arjun can look directly into the locker, where he sees Damian holding the oversized pen-like device. He immediately recognizes what it is, since he was in the same science class when Damian built it. All of the students thought it was the coolest science project ever. Arjun quickens his step. He needs to stop off at the local electronics store before he meets up with the rest of the team.

"You, too," replies Damian, turning back toward his locker.

Damian slams his locker door and walks to his car with Ivy. He likes to call it his car, but it technically also belongs to his sister. They have to share. "So, they're meeting off campus in the park at around four p.m.," says Damian, throwing his backpack into the backseat.

"You need to be there with this listening thing. What's the range?" asks Ivy.

"Three to four hundred feet," replies Damian. "That should let me hide where I can't be seen."

"Good. Can you take me to Alexa's house and then drop my stuff off at home?"

"Yes, ma'am," replies Damian. "I will gladly be your humble servant and chauffeur."

As he drives off, Ivy punches him on the arm. "You can always let me have the car instead."

At four that afternoon, Jared, Megan, Lien, and Ethan are making themselves comfortable at a picnic table in the park when Arjun comes running up. "Wait! Don't start yet."

He pulls out a rectangular device with a speaker, turns the dial, and places it on the picnic table. "OK. Now we can begin."

"What's this?" asks Megan.

"It's an audio white-noise generator. I just bought it."

"A what?" asks Jared.

Arjun repeats, "An audio—"

"No. What's it used for?" asks Megan.

"It provides an audio-masking sound so that no one can listen to our conversations with, like, microphones or surveillance equipment," replies Arjun.

"Why do we need that?" asks Ethan.

Arjun goes on to explain how he saw Ivy and Damian at the lockers after school with the microphone Damian built as a science experiment. He was going to let everyone know that maybe they should meet somewhere else, but he didn't have time. Plus, Damian's device would even work if they were indoors.

"I can't believe they would stoop this low," says Lien.

"I can," Jared counters. "To some, this game is very important."

They all look at him for a moment.

Off among the trees, Damian fiddles with his dials. For some reason, he can't hear anything but scrambled white noise. After trying for several minutes, he finally rips the earphones from his head and walks back to his car. Something isn't working.

Back at the table, Megan says, "OK. Now that we can't be heard, where are we? Any thoughts on the clue?"

"The clue said, '*Seek a vanished civilization at Empire Plaza.*' So I started searching for ancient vanished civilizations," says Jared. "Looks like there were a bunch. Some sources say ten, others twelve, all the way up to forty."

"You mean like Minoan or Mycenaean?" asks Arjun.

"Yeah, exactly. But I came across a lot more. Like the Anasazi in the Americas and the Khmer in Asia. It would take us forever to go through all of them."

Lien pulls out her tablet. "After I got your text message, I started to search, too. But I looked at it differently. I searched for ancient empires first." She brings up a comparison table on her screen. "There's a lot of debate about definitions, and the dates are approximations, since it all happened so long ago. These were called empires because they had a single government and a class of elites of a particular origin, like the Han Chinese or the Persians or the Romans, who ruled over people with diverse languages, ethnicities, and religions."

Megan, Ethan, and Jared stand up and gather around Lien and Arjun. They look at an online table. In the first column are names like Achaemenid, Assyrian, Greek, Gupta, Han, Hittite, Kush, Kushan, Mayan, Mauryan, Parthian, Roman, Qin, Xiongnu, and several more. The time period is in the second column, the geographical area of the empire in the third column, and key facts in the fourth.

"Wow, I never knew so many ancient empires came and went," says Ethan.

"Look at this," says Arjun. "I didn't know that the Assyrians and Babylonians often used propaganda about the ruthlessness of their battles to instill fear in people, thereby maintaining obedience."

"Or that they used mass deportations as a method of control and punishment," adds Ethan, reading over Arjun's shoulder.

"Yeah, no kidding," replies Lien. "And this table keeps going and going." Lien scrolls and scrolls until she finally reaches the bottom of the Web page. At the bottom are two speaker icons. One is labeled "why empires rise," and the other is labeled "why empires fall."

Before she can continue, Ethan reaches over her shoulder and touches the first icon. A voice begins to speak. "Many factors contributed to the rise of ancient empires. One was new technologies that allowed rulers to extend their systems of central command farther and farther from the capital. A second was—"

Megan touches the stop button on the recording. "This goes on for another forty-five minutes. I don't want to listen to this right now. We need to find out where to go."

"I agree," says Lien. "Around 100 CE, Afroeurasia looked like a continuous chain of states with several large empires. But that's still too many. So, I changed my search to focus on 'Empire Plaza' instead, since the clue said 'at Empire Plaza.' Look what I found." She taps the screen and brings up a new Web site. "It's a portal site. I can't tell who owns the site, but it looks reputable. Contributors include universities, schools, and philanthropic organizations around the world."

"Nice work, Lien," says Megan. "This definitely is the best we've found so far."

"And it ties to the earlier clue," adds Arjun.

"Can we all meet there tonight?" asks Jared.

"It's Friday night," replies Ethan. "I don't know if I can make it. It's our family dinner night."

"Well, whoever can make it, show up at this Empire Plaza site at seven p.m.," says Jared.

They all agree and head home.

CHAPTER 18

LATER THAT EVENING, JARED, MEGAN, LIEN, AND ARJUN activate the nanobots. Within a few seconds, they are standing in the middle of an enormous plaza at the edge of a large, lagoon-like pool. In the middle of the crystal-clear water, a fifty-foot round sundial with blocks of blue glass, each containing a number, rises out of the water like a tiny island. Next to it, seemingly floating in the water, stands a multi-story, cubist building consisting entirely of dark glass. Pairs of transparent glass tubes radiate at forty-five degree angles from the top of the cube to each of five high-rise towers.

"This is amazing," says Arjun, first looking at the lagoon, and then tilting his head back to stare up at the five steel-and-glass high-rises surrounding it. "I can barely see the tops. It looks like they're touching the clouds." High in the air, a network of long bridges and walkways connects the five towers to each other.

Looking between the skyscrapers, past several smaller buildings, off in the distance across an even larger expanse of water than the lagoon, they see two additional high-rises. "What are all these towers?" asks Arjun.

"I have no idea," replies Lien, as she looks around the plaza. In front of each tower, a huge fountain feeds into the lagoon. The shade from palm trees and the sound of splashing water provide relief from the bright sunlight and oppressive heat. Some people are sitting next to the fountains, some are cooling their feet in the lagoon, and others mill about the buildings.

Megan looks around. "Who are all these people?"

"Probably just computer-generated visitors," answers Jared.

"Them, too?" asks Megan, pointing to several groups of teenagers trying to get into the various buildings and towers.

"They're students—all part of the game. I recognize some of them from the home page," replies Lien.

"How did they get here so fast?" asks Arjun, scanning the crowd. "No one could have found the clue we found so quickly."

"Have any of you said anything to anyone since this afternoon?" asks Megan.

They all shake their heads.

"Look over there, behind that large fountain," says Lien, indicating the direction with her head.

"I don't believe it," says Jared as he looks directly at Damian. Damian returns Jared's look with an arrogant smirk. "How did Ivy and Damian and the others get here?" He turns back to his team.

"There may be alternate pathways," says Arjun.

"I'll be right back," says Jared. "I need to check something back home." Without waiting for an answer, he touches the home button on his bracelet. Several seconds later he is standing in one of the sitting areas of the home page. No one is there. He deactivates his nanobots. Back in his bedroom, he searches for the phone that Gia gave him, and he gives her a quick call.

"Jared, good that you called," says Gia. "You are calling me on the phone I gave you?"

"Yes. What's going on?" asks Jared.

"I think your moves in the game are being tracked. And someone is monitoring your communications outside."

"What? Why?" asks Jared.

"I suspect it's because you were ahead. But first, tell me exactly what's going on," says Gia.

Jared explains the search to date and tells her that when they showed up where they thought the next clue should be, there was a crowd of students. They are not ahead anymore. Someone has leveled the playing field. Everyone is scrambling to get into the buildings.

Gia senses Jared's disappointment. "I understand your frustration. Let me try to explain how this might have happened. I suspect that everyone is watching everyone else. To combat terrorism, and for security purposes governments often track communications—millions of e-mails, phone calls, and text messages—to ensure that nothing illegal is occurring. Some countries even censor all Internet communication. Years ago, the United States government declared the Internet an 'operational domain of war.' That meant that to ensure the security of strategic networks, the United States would mount a more robust defense and would threaten retaliation against any cyber attacks. At the time, many of the attacks on US cyber networks came from other nations, but threats from transnational groups are on the rise as well. So the government has gone on the offensive to locate these transnational groups."

"Great. After the government interrogated me about Dad, they probably put me under electronic surveillance. They've been watching me the whole time."

"Maybe. They didn't have any reason to suspect you initially, but now I'm afraid it's probably different."

"What's all this tracking about? It seems to be happening everywhere," Jared says.

"Security, power, control," replies Gia. "Governments seek information about organizations or people that can affect security levels or in some cases the government's power—terrorist organizations, freedom fighters, other nations, and so on. And even security surveillance can become too much, to the point where people feel like 'Big Brother' is watching everything they say and do."

"What's going to happen to our privacy?" asks Jared.

"I don't know," Gia says. "There's a real trade-off between privacy and security. Some people don't seem to worry about it too much. Then, of course, there are the commercial enterprises. They want data about you so they can sell your information to others and also make targeted advertisements. You'll be more likely to buy if an ad is targeted specifically to you."

Jared sighs over the phone.

"Then there's control," adds Gia. "Control over information. Those who can control what people see or can influence how people behave have more power than those who can't. In the ancient world, scribes were powerful because they knew how to read and write, and priests were powerful because of their ability to communicate with the gods. Today, the power lies in the information that organizations can get people to consume."

"Wow. I kind of knew about some of this, but I didn't give it much thought."

"Most people don't," replies Gia. "Remember the concept of 'balance of power.' Think about what happens to society, to individuals, or to the world when one entity or a handful of entities becomes too powerful."

Suddenly, Jared jumps up. "Uh-oh. I'm such an idiot. I sent a text telling my team where we needed to go. That may have been tracked."

"I hate to say it, but that was probably it," replies Gia. "Someone probably tracked your message and shared it with the others—increasing the level of competition and making sure you don't get too far ahead."

"I should have known," Jared says, letting his head fall into his hands.

"Don't beat yourself up," says Gia in an understanding tone. "We all tend to forget that almost nothing is private anymore."

"Thanks. I guess it's better that this happened now and not right before finding the artifact."

"Exactly," replies Gia. "Tell your team they need to be extra careful. Jared, I've got to run. Call me any time you need help."

"Thanks. Oh, Gia. Wait. Can you find out if there has been any progress with the FBI investigation into my father's kidnapping?"

"Let me see what I can do," she replies.

Jared turns off the phone and returns to the others, who are still waiting at the Empire Plaza. Ethan was able to get out of the dinner with his family after all, and he stands casually next to Arjun.

"Hey," Jared says, walking up to the team. "I'm really sorry. I totally screwed up. We were doing so well. I figured for sure that we were ahead, and now everyone's here."

"What happened? Did your message get hacked or something?" says Ethan half-jokingly.

"Actually, yes. How did you know?" asks Jared, giving him a questioning look.

Ethan glares back. "I was only joking, but every idiot knows that texting isn't secure. You should be smart enough to know that." He then leans over and jabs Jared in the arm with his index finger. "Hackers can get into anything," he continues, with a sense of admiration in his voice. "Everything's tracked these days. You screwed up."

Jared pushes Ethan's arm away. "Look, I said I was sorry. I'm also the one who found the last clue. Give me a break."

Ethan's face gets red. "I was the one—"

"Cool it, guys!" interrupts Arjun. "It could have happened to any of us."

Lien leans over and gives Jared a hug. "No worries. We'll outrun them again."

Megan squeezes his shoulder reassuringly. They all ignore Ethan.

"But your text said that there was something else besides the clue," says Arjun.

"Yes! You're right! With everything else going on, I had completely forgotten," replies Jared, his confidence returning. "The Lanzón had one more piece of information."

"Well, that's nice. At least that's something," Ethan says. "What was it?"

Jared hesitates. He's not sure what to make of Ethan's behavior. Then he replies, "It was a set of letters and numbers: 'T3:F30:R10.'"

"What does that mean?" asks Lien.

"I don't know," replies Jared.

"Whatever it means, we need to make sure no one else finds out," says Megan.

"Or can follow us," adds Arjun.

"Exactly," replies Megan.

They walk toward one of the larger water fountains, where their voices will be drowned out by the falling water. They discuss what the letters and numbers could possibly mean. After considering several hypotheses, they decide to walk around the plaza. Maybe something there will give them an idea of what to do next.

CHAPTER 19

MAKING THEIR WAY THROUGH THRONGS OF STUDENTS, all five walk toward the edge of the plaza and stare out over the enormous expanse of water.

Megan is mesmerized by the small waves. "This looks and feels like the ocean."

In front of them, one hundred steep, wide granite steps descend down to a stone pier. A bridge, under construction, leaves the pier and extends out into the water.

Arjun points to one of the high-rises off in the distance. "I bet this bridge will go to that tower over there."

Jared thinks of the steep steps of the ancient Mayan pyramids in Mexico and Central America as he looks down.

"Could be," replies Megan. Then her eye is drawn to a large granite block as big as a midsize car, at the bottom of the steps. "I'll be right back." Before anyone can say a word, she leaps off the edge and jogs down the steps. Lien follows her.

Jared calls after them, "We'll stay right here and keep a look out." He sits down and watches Megan and Lien. He's never seen anyone move down and then up such steep steps so quickly and with such agility. Within a few minutes, the girls are back, and only slightly out of breath.

"It is one of the entries to this plaza," says Megan. "This plaza is the top of a huge pyramid. The granite block below marks the entrance. There are probably other blocks on the other sides. There are four-foot-high letters and numbers carved into the granite. On top of the block, it says 'Empire Plaza—Afroeurasia Complex and Towers.'"

"Below that it says '~2000 BCE–600 CE'—dates," adds Lien.

"We need to check out this complex and the five towers," says Megan.

"Wait!" says Jared, pointing toward the glass cube in the lagoon. "I think we should check out that building first."

"Why?" asks Ethan, trying to support Megan. "The towers sound like a good idea."

"We'll probably have to go there, too," replies Jared. "But notice how this cube seems to be in the center of everything, especially with the glass tubes coming out of the top. I want to see what that is first."

"Yeah," says Megan, "makes sense to me." Ethan looks away. He hates it when Megan takes Jared's side.

"Plus, look," says Arjun, pointing to the other buildings. "All the doors must be locked." All across the plaza, students are trying to get into the buildings. Some get frustrated and begin to kick the doors, hoping they will open. One group even takes a metal bench and throws it at a door, hoping it will shatter the glass and provide a way in. Instead, the bench bounces harmlessly off the glass without even leaving a scratch.

The five teenagers walk across the plaza toward the edge of the lagoon closest to the glass cube. "Now what?" asks Ethan. "There's no way to get across. The cube is surrounded by water. This lagoon looks way too deep. Even if we did get over there, what would we do?"

Jared, only half listening, stares at the wall of glass across the water. He looks away and then looks at the wall again. "Guys, there's something there. It's hard to see because the glass reflects the towers, but I think I see a set of doors."

Lien follows his gaze and squints her eyes. She turns around, looks at the tower behind her, and then turns back. "Yeah, I think you're right.

There are doors—barely visible from here. It looks like there's some kind of stone material on the sides. At first I thought it was a reflection from the tower behind us, but it's not."

"Good. What are we waiting for? I say we swim for it," says Megan, as she dives off the edge into the lagoon—only to land on her stomach in a foot of water. "Ouch!" she yells. "What's going on?"

The others can't keep from laughing.

Arjun kneels over the edge, puts his hand in, and then lowers his head to look underwater. "This is crazy. The entire floor of the lagoon seems to be glass. It makes it look a lot deeper than it really is."

Megan quickly gets up. "We better get going. As soon as the others find out, I think we're going to have company."

They all jump into the lagoon and run across the water as quickly as possible. Three-quarters of the way across, Arjun, who is bringing up the rear of the group, strays a bit to the side. He takes one more step and instantly finds himself under water. His surfer instincts take over. He looks around and quickly kicks his way back to the surface. He sees Lien and Jared turning back toward him. "Keep going! Hurry!" he yells. "I'll catch up with you!" He begins to swim with powerful strokes. It doesn't take him long to catch up with the others. As he stands up next to them, he catches his breath. "It looks like we were on some kind of underwater glass walkway. It started retracting." He looks down and notices that they are standing on one small portion of the walkway that hasn't fully retracted yet. "We better hurry. I don't know how long we'll be able to stand here."

"That's not the only reason," replies Megan, pointing back to the edge of the lagoon. Several other students have noticed how Megan, Jared and the others ran across the water, and they are quickly beginning to follow.

The walkway, however, has already retracted most of the way, and when they enter the water, there's nothing to walk on. They are forced to swim.

Ethan first tries to peer through the tall, nearly black, glass entry doors with little success; then he tries to push them open. "These doors won't budge. Probably locked. Looks like we're done."

"I don't think so," replies Megan, "but we better figure it out fast. We only have a few minutes."

Jared, Megan, and the others are still the only group at the glass cube, but other teams are quickly approaching. To the right of the doors is a large gold plaque bearing the phrase "Afroeurasia Complex Lobby." Jared stares at the intricate carvings on the stone pillars next to the entrance.

Lien joins him. "This is what I saw. What do you suppose these are?"

Jared looks more closely. "I think they're alphabets of ancient languages that have gone extinct."

"Look at this one," says Lien, pointing to a set of symbols at waist height. "It looks like ancient Sumerian cuneiforms."

"Interesting," says Jared. "I wonder if it's old Akkadian. Sargon the Great built one of the first world empires in Afroeurasia, and we're at the Afroeurasia Complex." Jared imagines what that empire must have been like, and absentmindedly traces the cutouts of the cuneiform symbols with his finger. As he finishes the last one and lifts his finger, one of the stone blocks slides backwards, revealing a screen with scrolling text and an old black phone.

"Excellent!" says Megan, pulling her teammates together. She looks back over her shoulder at the lagoon. "C'mon. Hurry up."

"No way! What's the text say?" asks Ethan.

Jared reads the message silently. "Great, another riddle," he says after he finishes. "It says, '*Neither good nor bad nor neutral, it opened the door to great empires.*'"

"Hmmm," says Arjun. "Look at the phone. The dial has holes in it with numbers and letters. That's pretty old technology."

They all stare at the twentieth-century device, and then Jared suddenly says, "Dude. You're awesome!"

"Thanks, why?" replies Arjun.

"'Technology,' that's the answer." Jared quickly scans his lenses and says, "Yes. New technology allowed rulers to build empires. It helped them extend their systems of central command farther from the capital. Horse riding—a technology—changed the communication of orders, news, how the military was used. Roads and canals—both technologies—helped grow empires.

"And listen to this!" He begins to read aloud. "'Technology is neither good nor bad, nor is it neutral. Think about it. A spear can be good when it helps you find food to survive, or it can be bad when it helps someone kill for no reason, but it can't be neutral since it will certainly have some type of impact. It all depends. The context and application of the technology determine the results.'"

"But it also depends on your perspective. One person might see something as good; another might see it as bad," adds Lien.

"Now I understand," mumbles Megan, turning to Jared. "Is that what worried you about the nanobots?"

"I didn't think about it quite like that, but in a way, I guess so," replies Jared. "There are definitely two sides."

"OK. Now what?" asks Ethan.

Lien lifts the phone receiver and dials the numbers corresponding to the letters that spell "technology." Nothing happens. She puts the receiver back on the cradle, and a few seconds later, the phone rings. She picks it up quickly.

"Yes? Hello?" she says.

"May I help you?" says a voice on the other end.

Thinking quickly, Lien replies, "Can you open the doors...please?"

There is a click as the connection is severed. She puts the phone back on the cradle, and the stone block slides back into place. Seconds later, they hear a clunk as the magnetic locks that hold the door closed disengage.

"Quick, let's go," says Megan.

The five teenagers rush through the door just as the first swimmer reaches the platform. Unfortunately, several others see them open the door, and they begin to shout loudly that someone's figured out how to get into the buildings. More than a dozen swimmers in the water kick and grab at each other, each now trying to get ahead of the other. In the plaza, a mad rush occurs as those students who didn't jump into the lagoon now realize their mistake and sprint to the water, trampling those who can't keep up and knocking others out of the way. It only takes a few seconds for Lien, Ethan, Megan, Arjun, and Jared to get through the doors. Then the doors shut automatically, and the magnetic locks reengage. They can hear and see other students pounding on the glass outside.

Ivy, Damian, Alexa, Kazuo, and the others on their team do not rush headlong into the fray. They sit back and watch everyone else.

"Did you get it?" Damian asks Kazuo, who has been hiding high in a nearby palm tree and staring intently at the glass cube.

"I got some of it, but not when they huddled together. They blocked my view."

"At least you got something. We'll wait awhile and then create a diversion. Maybe we can get this crowd to check out one of the other towers, and while they all rush over there, we'll check out the cube and follow Megan and Jared."

Jared, Megan, Lien, Arjun, and Ethan walk across the lobby on a highly polished, white-marble floor. Each of the four walls is a floor-to-ceiling, one-way solar window fifteen stories tall. They produce electricity and no one can see in, but looking out is astonishing. The square roof is made of the same solar glass. The floor reflects the sky and the sunlight shining in through the windows. Passing clouds are reflected on the highly polished floor, making the students feel as if they are walking on clouds. The center of the atrium is dominated by an enormous waterfall that rises twelve stories and cascades into a large, deep pool of water. A model of the towers sits to the side of the waterfall.

"This is the main lobby to the Afroeurasia Towers," says Jared. He and Megan walk over to take a closer look. The plaza, lagoon, and Afroeurasia Complex and Towers all sit on top of an enormous pyramid emerging from a large body of water. The five towers include an Africa Tower, a Europe Tower, a Middle East Tower, an Indus Tower, and a China Tower. The two high-rises off in the distance, across the water, are labeled as the Americas Complex and Tower and the Oceania Complex and Tower. They see that the angular glass tubes emanating from the roof of the cube are pairs of glass elevator shafts that go to each of the towers. The elevators emerge from the tubes and then ascend up the outside of the towers. Bridges and walkways several hundred yards up in the air connect the towers to each other.

"Why do you think those two towers are so far away?" asks Megan.

"My guess is because Oceania and the Americas were more isolated," answers Arjun, who has quietly come up behind Jared and Megan. "After the first humans arrived on those continents, they had little contact with the outside world."

"True," says Jared. "But there is some evidence—genetic data—suggesting that there may have been a wave of migration from India to Australia."

"Really? Wow! I didn't know that," replies Arjun, thinking about his Indian ancestors.

Jared runs his hand across the model. "History is dynamic. It continues to evolve as scientists use modern techniques to uncover more and more evidence." He stares absentmindedly at one of the towers. "That's what my dad used to say." He sniffles and smiles.

Megan gently touches his arm in support. She knows how much he misses his dad.

As they look around the lobby, Lien and Ethan notice several large directory plaques mounted side by side next to the elevator bank. They are rectangular and made of solid bronze. As Ethan walks closer, he sees that they are blank except for the title engraved at the top. The first plaque is labeled "Tower One–Africa," the second plaque, "Tower Two–Europe," and the third plaque, "Tower Three–Middle East." As Ethan gets within a few feet of the three plaques, they sense his presence, and the bronze metal transforms itself into a liquid.

"Check this out," yells Ethan. "You guys have to get over here and see this."

The bronze liquid floats in front of the wall and begins to transform itself again. The metal takes the shape of words that begin to scroll upward and then disappear back into the wall. New words come out of the wall at the bottom of the plaques and scroll toward the top. The words are Sumerian, Minoan, Egyptian, Kush/Nubian, Phoenician, Persian, Macedonian, Hittite, Lydian, Hebrew, Greek, Carthaginian, and Roman. The names keep coming in random order.

Lien stares at the names and realizes that Empire Plaza includes civilizations not only from classical antiquity but also other ancient civilizations like the Sumerians, the Minoans, and the Egyptians.

"This is crazy," says Ethan excitedly. "These must be the major civilizations in Towers One, Two, and Three. I wonder why there isn't anything about Towers Four or Five."

"Maybe it's because no one is standing in front of them," Megan offers as she walks over to the Indus Tower plaque.

As she comes within a few feet of it, the bronze transforms itself, and the words Aryan, Mauryan, and Gupta emerge in large letters and hover in the air a few inches from the wall. Lien walks a few feet to Megan's right, and the Tower Five—China plaque forms the words Shang, Zhou, Qin, and Han.

Megan walks back to the model.

"Jared, look at this," says Arjun. "I think this Web site recognizes that someone is here. The model now includes a listing of all the civilizations. This wasn't here before."

Jared joins him.

"Can a Web site recognize who is visiting it and dynamically change its content based on who you are?" asks Megan.

"Probably," replies Ethan. "If there's some way to recognize you. Maybe through tracking cookies, an IP address, or a log-in name. Or maybe by your online habits or search behavior. It may even recognize your image. I'm sure there are other ways, too. You can learn a lot about people based on what they do online."

"Hmmm. Going to be hard to stay anonymous," Megan comments as she looks at the Americas Complex and Tower. "Look, this only lists the Maya. What about the Aztecs and the Inca?"

"My guess is that they don't exist yet. Remember how you saw the numbers 2000 BCE to 600 CE? I guess this plaza only covers the ancient and the classical civilizations or empires until around 600 CE. The Aztecs and the Inca came later," replies Jared.

"Makes sense," Lien says. "That's probably why the Americas Complex and Tower doesn't include the Chavín, Moche, Olmecs, or all the tribes in North and South America. The Americas didn't have any large empires at that time. From what I read, some don't actually consider the Mayan civilization an empire since there wasn't a single Mayan political center. Similar to the Greeks, the Mayan people shared a common cultural background but encompassed many different groups. And the third building complex only says 'Oceania.' Although that area was populated, there weren't any empires in the Pacific until much later."

They walk to the elevators and notice that each floor in the towers is associated with a time period. For example, the twentieth floor in the Africa Tower is associated with 1200 BCE, and the top floor is associated with around 600 CE.

"My guess is that this is a portal site. It's made to look like a modern high-rise complex," says Arjun. "And it has links to all the ancient empires and civilizations."

Megan points out the window. "If this is a portal, then we can probably go from floor to floor. And to different towers or regions on those walkways and bridges."

"True." Jared walks back to the large model of the complex and stares at the various buildings. "Remember those numbers and letters that I mentioned earlier, T3:F30:R10? I had no idea what they meant, but now that I look at this model, I think they refer to a location."

"You mean like Tower Three, Floor Thirty, Room Ten?" asks Lien.

"Exactly—the Middle East Tower," wonders Jared aloud. "How did you know?"

"I'd like to say great minds think alike and all that," replies Lien. "But if you look real closely at the model, you'll see something similar written in it."

"My guess is that's where we should start," says Jared, walking toward the elevators.

"Agreed," replies Megan, following right on his heels.

They all take the elevator leading from the glass cube-like building to the Middle East Tower and step out into the thirtieth-floor lobby. They could be in any of the world's most elegant hotels. As they walk down the hallway, the deep, plush carpet silences their footsteps. There are no signs on the doors, just numbers, like a hotel. They walk past rooms one, two, three, and so on. When they reach room ten, Jared grabs the door handle. "You ready?"

"Always," replies Megan.

He turns the handle, and the door swings open. All five walk into a dimly-lit stone alley. Behind them, the door automatically closes, latches, and disappears.

CHAPTER 20

JARED LOOKS BACK AT THE WALL WHERE THE DOOR USED to be. "Guess we're not going back that way."

They make their way down the alley. The sun's oppressive heat beats down as the five wander the streets and alleys of an ancient seaport on the eastern shore of the Mediterranean. Within minutes, they are soaked in sweat.

Finally, Megan sits on a low stone wall under the shade of a palm tree and kicks off her sandals. "It's too hot. Why the Phoenicians, anyway? Were they an empire?" The others sprawl out next to her.

"I think they were a trading empire," replies Lien.

"Let me look it up," replies Jared.

He quickly accesses the Web on his contact lenses and scans information about the Phoenicians, citing key points to the others. "It says here that most of what we know about the Phoenicians comes from Greek and Roman authors who didn't like them very much. For centuries, the Greeks, Romans, and Phoenicians battled each other for political and commercial control of the Mediterranean."

"So the authors were a little biased; what else is new?" says Arjun.

"From what I remember, they were excellent navigators and seafarers. Weren't they a major naval and trading power in the Mediterranean region around 1200 to 800 BCE?" asks Lien.

"Yes," replies Jared. "They built a huge network, exchanging goods and ideas over vast distances."

Before Jared can continue, Lien jumps in, "These networks of economic exchange really developed during this era. Almost sounds like the basis for the world economy today."

"I suppose," Jared answers. "But the Phoenicians were a bunch of independent city-states that would fight each other one day and then cooperate and collaborate in leagues or alliances the next. They expanded westward, establishing city-states and colonies, and developed a huge maritime network trading wood, slaves, glass, and dye. This made them rich. They disseminated Egyptian, Mesopotamian, and Greek culture, and they adopted practices from throughout the Middle East. They had good natural harbors and large cedar forests. The cedars of Lebanon were heavily harvested, since the Egyptians and Mesopotamians didn't have much wood. This allowed them to build seagoing ships, a navy, and sell the timber across the Middle East."

Megan leans back and closes her eyes as Jared continues to talk.

"Here's a question for you all. Besides trade, what one other major item can be attributed to the Phoenicians?" asks Jared.

"I'm not sure I care," replies Ethan in a tired voice. "It's too hot."

"I know this one," says Arjun. "They invented glass and navigated by the stars."

"True," replies Jared, "but that's not what I was thinking about."

"The Phoenician alphabet," guesses Lien. "Didn't it become the most widely used writing system and the basis of modern-day alphabets?"

"Yup," replies Jared. "It was easy to learn, and it broke down social class divisions. Before, writing had been an instrument of power because the elite could control access to information, but now anyone could learn to read and write."

"Pretty big change," says Megan. Her eyes are closed, and she is only partially listening to the conversation. "Kind of like the Internet. That gave people access to all sorts of information, too."

Ethan looks toward the ocean and occasionally steals a glance at Megan as she tries to make herself comfortable on the stone wall.

Arjun, Lien, and Jared all search on their lenses and talk about how the Phoenicians were very secretive and private. They discuss the Phoenicians' democracy, their lack of a standing army, and their island trading posts.

Megan is about to drift off when the wind changes and a slight breeze comes up from the waterfront. "Ooh. What is that awful smell?" she asks.

"No idea," replies Ethan. "It's hideous."

Holding her nose, she sits up. "I'm going down to the harbor to check it out, and find out where we are."

"I'll go with you," replies Ethan.

"We'll be right there," says Jared, "as soon as we finish reading about the achievements of the Phoenicians. It might give us an idea of where to look."

"Later," says Megan as she and Ethan walk down the alley. They round the corner and emerge onto a stone pier that provides a full view of the harbor entrance. Megan points to three ships leaving under full sail and with rowers pulling on the oars. One ship with an off-white, rectangular sail lies low in the water—it's a seagoing cargo ship. Two Phoenician triremes follow on either side of it. Not all the rowers have their oars in the water so as not to overtake the heavily laden merchant vessel.

"I wonder where they're headed?" asks Megan.

Ethan shrugs.

She walks up to a bearded merchant who is pushing his cart along the pier. He looks at her cautiously. "Where are those ships headed?" she asks.

He shrugs his shoulders and nudges her with the cart, indicating that she should get out of the way.

She approaches several more people. No one has any idea.

"Leave it. Who cares?" says Ethan. "Jared mentioned how secretive the Phoenicians are. We'll never get information from these folks. Let's go figure out what smells."

Megan sighs and agrees. They turn and walk down the pier to investigate the origin of the hideous stench when they pass an old fisherman sitting on a wooden bench, mending his nets.

As they walk by, he says in a low voice, "They're headed to Carthage, Tyre's colony in northern Africa."

Megan turns. "I'm sorry. What did you just say?"

The old man gets up and folds his net. "Carthage. They're headed to Carthage." He then opens the door to his stone house and steps over the threshold. He turns back, quickly glances up and down the pier, and says in the same low voice, "What you seek is on board the cargo ship." He then slams the door before Megan or Ethan can react. Megan jumps to the door and tries to open it, but it's locked. She knocks and knocks, but there is no response.

She looks toward the ships; they're almost out of sight. Megan, filled with frustration, hurls a rock into the water. "How are we going to get on board now?"

Ethan begins to search his lenses, thinking that maybe there is a site describing Tyre. A few minutes later, he smiles. "I think I've got it. There's an image here showing three Phoenician ships leaving the seaport of Tyre for Carthage about 550 BCE."

"That must be it," replies Megan with excitement. "Is there a link?"

"Yup." Ethan cites the link.

"Let's go," says Megan impatiently. "I'll text Jared."

"We don't have time. We need to get on those ships. Text him later," says Ethan, partly because he wants to spend some time with Megan without everyone else around.

Megan decides to wait and send Jared a text from the ship. She then touches her wristband.

Jared, Lien, and Arjun take a different alley toward the harbor and end up much farther south. They are walking along the quay when Lien sees a series of large vats up ahead.

"Ooh! That's where that terrible smell is coming from," she says, pinching her nose and pointing. "It's disgusting."

As they get closer, Jared peers over the edge and sees thousands of decomposing snails. "This is one of the most luxurious products of the ancient world," he says. "This violet-purple dye made from the Murex snail was one of the most sought-after items, and the Phoenicians grew rich trading it. Some say that the Minoans might have actually been the ones who figured out how to extract this dye."

"I don't care," replies Arjun. "It smells disgusting."

As they continue to walk, the smell decreases, and they finally come upon a cauldron of mostly-purple liquid. Jared stops and looks around to make sure no one sees him. "This is such a cool color." He quickly pulls off his white outer tunic and drops it into the cauldron of dye.

"Jared, what are you doing?" asks Lien with an appalled look on her face.

"What does it look like? Do you want to dye anything?" replies Jared with a big smile.

Lien, who is draped from head to foot in the ordinary clothes of a Phoenician woman, replies with some embarrassment, "I can't take this robe off."

"Oh yeah, sorry. I forgot," Jared replies with a coy smile. Lien finds his little smile cute. Jared turns to Arjun. "What about you?"

"I'm good," replies Arjun. "You realize this dye is one of the most expensive and luxurious items of this time. I don't want to know what the penalty is for stealing it"

"I'm not stealing anything. I'm only testing it," replies Jared as he takes a long pole and fishes his now deep-purple tunic out of the cauldron. He places it on a flat stone and rolls the pole across it to squeeze excess water out of the fabric.

"Doesn't smell too bad," he says, running his nose along the cotton.

Several men come running up the pier. "Hey, you!" one of them shouts. "You're not allowed to use that dye!"

"No time to argue now. Let's go," says Jared as he grabs the tunic and sprints away from the men. Lien and Arjun follow closely behind as he weaves up and down the streets of Tyre. Soon they're out of range of the men, and Jared stops to catch his breath.

"Was that necessary?" asks Lien.

"Probably not," replies Jared. "I couldn't resist. This is just such an awesome color. I wanted to see how I look in a robe like this." He slips on the almost-dry tunic and feels a slight tingling sensation course through his body. "That's odd," he says.

"What?" asks Arjun.

"I don't know. I felt, like, a small shock go through my body." He looks down at his tunic. "I feel kind of strange."

Arjun and Lien laugh.

"You're wearing imperial colors now," says Lien. "Only the very rich could afford this."

"We'll call you 'Your Highness' from now on," adds Arjun. "That'll make you feel better."

Instead of reacting to their teasing, Jared replies in all seriousness, "No. It's not that. Something is different. I feel different. I can't explain it."

Arjun and Lien continue to chuckle as they walk.

"Probably static electricity from the fabric, Your Highness," says Arjun.

They are slowly making their way back to their arrival point when they get pinged by a text message with a link from Megan.

"Looks like it's time to go," Arjun says to Lien. "We'll see how Jared's new purple tunic does now."

Jared rolls his eyes. "I heard that. Not funny." He looks down at his tunic. Strange, he thinks, the purple seems to be getting more intense in the sunlight. He follows Arjun and Lien's lead and touches his wristband.

CHAPTER 21

A FEW MINUTES AFTER ACTIVATING THEIR WRISTBANDS, Megan and Ethan stand deep in the hold of an enormous Phoenician cargo ship filled with pottery vessels, wine, salt, dried fish, boxes of precious metal, jewelry, and even some glass. The storage area is almost one hundred feet long and twenty-five feet wide. But with all the goods they barely have room to stand.

"Great. Now we're stowaways," says Ethan as he ducks away from the opening to the cargo hold to ensure that they are not seen.

"C'mon. We need to explore the ship," Megan says. "The old man said that what we seek is here. I'm going up on deck to look around." She starts to climb out of the hold, taking care not to be spotted.

"There aren't a lot of places to hide. We may want to wait here until nightfall," whispers Ethan.

Megan continues to climb up the ladder. "We don't have time to wait until nightfall."

Ethan turns away from the ladder. "OK. I'll look around down here. I can always help, if you need me."

Megan nods and disappears onto the deck. She sees that the ship is under full sail—its one large sail is deployed—and making good westerly progress. Off to her left she can see the distant shoreline. A few hundred feet behind the vessel are the two large Phoenician trireme warships. As she continues to climb around the ship, she wonders why they are sailing so close to the shoreline and under the protection of two naval vessels. This ship must contain some valuable cargo. The sky becomes a deep orange as the sun begins to set on the horizon. The wind blows through her hair; a fine salt spray stings her face. She can't believe that this is Web-based simulation.

Ethan, meanwhile, makes himself comfortable sitting against a burlap sack in the back of the hold where no one can see him. He scrolls through more information on Carthage, located in modern-day Tunisia, on his contact lenses. He reads that Carthage was a Phoenician settlement founded around 800 BCE by Queen Elishat (Dido to the Romans and Elissa to the Greeks) from Tyre. She was clever, determined, powerful, and beautiful. Through trade, she built what was possibly the richest city in the ancient world. Some called it a Carthaginian hegemony.

Ethan continues to read that something rarely remembered about Carthage are the achievements of the Carthaginian engineers. They were the first to build apartments up to six stories high. They were also the first to have tubs, sinks, showers, and a whole system for water and sewage. These engineers helped Hannibal, one of Carthage's—and the ancient world's—greatest generals, fight against the Romans in the Punic Wars around 200 BCE. They helped him get across the Rhone River and over the Alps with his war elephants. The Carthaginians also had one of the most powerful navies. One of the things that helped Rome win the Punic Wars was that Romans reverse engineered a Carthaginian ship and then built a secret weapon, the corvus. It was a movable bridge that could be dropped onto the deck of an enemy ship, making a skirmish more like a land battle. After each Punic war, the victorious Romans made the Carthaginians pay a huge indemnity and tribute.

Ethan continues to scan the text while he climbs around the ship's hold looking for anything that might be a clue. Megan is still not back. He's about to climb toward the opening when he spots a piece of wood sticking out of a simple-looking linen bag. He wonders why the Phoenicians would put wood into a linen bag, unless they were trying to hide something. Often the best way to hide a special object is to make it look plain and hide it among ordinary things. He opens the bag and peers inside. It contains a wooden box bearing the image of three ships, similar to what he saw online, and what looks to be a royal seal. Not waiting for Megan, Ethan breaks open the lock to reveal a beautifully adorned scroll. He unfurls it and recognizes that it describes trade routes from the Great Royal Road, the Silk Road, and many other routes throughout the Mediterranean region, the Middle East, and Asia. The scroll also includes wind patterns and tide tables. He realizes that he has found a highly confidential and extremely valuable document. No wonder the triremes are protecting this vessel. If this scroll were to fall into the wrong hands, it could be quite detrimental. He quickly rolls up the scroll and puts it back into the box. Just as he's about to close it he notices a phrase written on the underside of the lid in white chalk. He takes a closer look and tries to figure out what it says.

Meanwhile, on deck, Megan is trying to hide behind a large coil of rope. Staying hidden on the deck of a Phoenician cargo ship is no easy feat. Not finding anything of importance, she turns to head back to the hold when she is grabbed from behind. Her arms are bent backward so hard, they feel ready to snap. She lets out a loud scream.

Belowdecks, Ethan drops the scroll.

"Look what we have here," growls a large, muscular sailor, his biceps rippling as he holds her tight. "How did you get on board?"

Megan struggles to get free, but the sailor's grip is too strong. She tries to kick backward. He anticipates her move, steps out of the way, and tightens his grip. Megan relaxes for a moment, thinking about her next move. She can't reach her bracelet.

The sailor yells, "Captain! Look what I've found. A pretty stowaway. She's a bit of a wildcat." He then turns to whisper in her ear, "Worst decision you ever made. You'll fetch a good price—maybe even the best price—at the slave auction in Carthage."

Ethan hears the commotion on deck, climbs up the ladder, and pops his head out of the hold. He sees Megan in the grip of the sailor. He slumps back into the hold. This is not good, he thinks. What should he do? If only she would…

He climbs back up just in time to see the sailor punch her in the stomach. She groans. He sends her a quick text message by quietly speaking: "If you can see my text, nod. Pretend to be royalty. See attached link." He hits the send button and watches, but Megan does not react. What happened? The message was sent, but Megan is still not reacting. He wonders where it went. He repeats the text and tries again. Instantly, a look of recognition crosses Megan's face, and a few seconds later, she nods.

As soon as the captain climbs down the steps from the oar deck, Megan begins to yell at the sailor as she struggles against his grip. "Unhand me, you animal. I am of noble birth. You will be the one sold into slavery if I have something to say." She continues to rant and rave, pretending to be a noblewoman. As she yells, she mentions the names of prominent nobles from Tyre and Carthage that she sees in Ethan's message.

The captain, now less sure of himself, moves toward her carefully. Is she a stowaway? A spy? Or truly a noblewoman, who was put on board to test his allegiance? She knows much more than a normal stowaway would know.

Megan keeps twisting to get free of the sailor's grip and ranting about the injustice of her capture. "Upon my arrival, I will inform Queen Elishat of how I've been mistreated on this vessel."

At that point, the captain's face changes. He steps closer and, without saying a word, slaps Megan hard across the face. "No stowaways on my ship." He then gently pats her on the head. "This voyage has just become so much more profitable. We don't have any slaves we can trade, but now we have you." He gently runs a dirty finger across her cheek and strokes her dreadlocks. "You, my dear, will be in high demand."

Megan kicks out, trying to hit him between the legs.

The captain jumps to the side and laughs as he walks away. "Fiery, too. That will surely get us a bonus. I do pity the man who has to tame her." The rest of the crewmen laugh at the captain's comment. "Tie her up and take her below," he yells. "And no one touch her. We don't want her harmed before the auction."

Ethan realizes Megan's mistake. She must have forgotten that they are in a Web site describing the trade in 550 BCE. Queen Elishat has been dead for close to 250 years. The captain knew Megan was lying when she mentioned the queen's name. Ready to duck back down, he feels a slight tug on his leg. This cannot be good. Ethan glances over his shoulder and sees a sailor who must have been sleeping in the hold. The man is looking up at him.

Ethan knows he has to act quickly, but what should he do? He kicks backward, luckily striking the sailor squarely in the forehead. When the man tumbles backward into the hold, Ethan grabs a clay pot and scrambles up the ladder to the deck. He runs toward Megan and her captor, and throws the clay pot at the sailor's head. The sailor raises his arms to defend himself, releasing Megan, who rewards him with a kick to the groin. She runs toward the stern of the ship. Ethan follows.

The crewmembers are all busy operating the rudder, the lines, or the sails. This gives Ethan and Megan a nice head start. However, given its valuable cargo, the ship also carries a contingent of soldiers. They take their time gathering their swords and spears, knowing that the two stow-aways have nowhere to run. Then, they fan out across the deck and begin to advance on Megan and Ethan, who are leaning against the railing at the back of the ship. Trapped with no place to go except overboard, they look down at the sea. It does not look like a pleasant option.

Their bracelets won't be fast enough to help them get away. Fighting is the third option, but against a dozen soldiers, they know they won't last more than a few seconds.

From one of the triremes trailing behind, Jared, Arjun, and Lien observe the scene on the cargo vessel. After touching their wristbands as Ethan and Megan had, they'd landed on the warship instead of on the cargo vessel. Jared, wearing his purple tunic, immediately received the respect to which any Phoenician nobleman is entitled. Arjun and Lien have also been treated well, since they are traveling with him. Now the trireme is just behind the cargo vessel, its bow in line with the stern of the other ship.

Jared easily hears the soldiers' words from across the water. He sees soldiers wielding spears and swords move toward Ethan and Megan. Then, without warning, a sailor staggers out of the cargo hold. "He opened the royal box. I saw him," the sailor cries.

"No one is allowed to open that box," yells the captain. "The penalty is death. Kill them!"

When Jared hears these words, he sprints the length of the trireme toward the bow, knocking sailors out of the way, and without stopping, launches himself off the ship and toward the stern of the cargo vessel. The ships are nearly twenty-five feet apart. He flies across the water and lands, almost standing up, on the rudder of the cargo ship. He scrambles aboard, his purple tunic barely wet.

"Did you see what I just saw?" Arjun asks in astonishment.

Lien only nods. On the other ship, Jared makes his way toward Ethan and Megan. The soldiers bow their heads and shrink away. They have never seen anything like this before. Who is this person? The rowers cower in their seats, thinking about the Phoenician gods, wondering if this is Yam, the god of the sea, or maybe even Baal, ruler of the universe, lord of the earth. The captain cowers off to the side.

"How the heck did you do that?" asks Megan in total awe. She's never seen Jared do anything even remotely close to that before.

"I don't know what came over me," replies Jared. "I thought I could do it and went for it."

Ethan looks at him jealously. He hates it when Jared impresses Megan. Then he asks skeptically, "You found an enchantment or hidden power, didn't you? I didn't know the game even had them."

Jared looks at him for a moment and thinks back to the walk through Tyre. Then he remembers: the purple dye. Since he put on the colored tunic, he's felt different, stronger, and more confident. "I guess I did."

As he turns around to look at the soldiers, a deep horn sounds across the water. The captains of the triremes order all oars in the water and tell the soldiers to get ready for battle.

Heeding the military orders, the cargo captain yells, "Forget the stowaways! We'll deal with them later!"

Megan, Ethan, and Jared look off toward the shore and see two other large triremes turning out of a hidden harbor. They are coming straight for the cargo ship, aiming to ram it. "Pirates," says Megan.

The cargo crew tightens the mainsail and speeds ahead. Unfortunately, the sun is now low on the horizon, and the wind is only moderately strong. The sail will be no match for the three tiers of rowers on the pirate vessel.

One Phoenician navy vessel stays hidden alongside the cargo ship and out of sight of the pirates. Then, on one command, it lurches forward and sprints ahead. It cuts straight across the bow of the cargo vessel, heading directly toward the pirates. The navy captain miscalculates the speed of the cargo vessel, and as he cuts in front of it, the two ships scrape each other. The navy ship's stern clips the cargo vessel's bow with such force that the cargo ship rolls sideways, almost swamping the deck. Several Lebanese cedar logs, a very valuable cargo, break free and crash through the side rail. Megan and Ethan lose their balance and fall overboard. Jared grabs a rope made of tar-covered-papyrus and dangles along the side of the ship. He sees how the ship is slowly moving away from Ethan and Megan. He's tempted to touch his wristband, but he can't leave them alone in the middle of the Mediterranean. He lets go of the rope and falls into the water.

A few of the sailors get ready to throw down ropes when the captain yells, "Leave them! We cannot slow down!"

Megan and Ethan grab onto a cedar log to use as a flotation device and watch as the cargo vessel sails past. The navy triremes take off in pursuit of the pirates, who now realize they have no chance of capturing the cargo vessel. They turn and flee. A few minutes later, Jared swims up to Megan and Ethan, having removed the purple tunic. They are all alone in the eastern Mediterranean Sea, floating many miles off the coast of present-day Lebanon and Israel. Twilight is slowly turning into dusk.

"Did you find anything?" asks Megan, as she drapes both of her arms over the log.

"Maybe. I'm not sure. I looked through the entire cargo hold."

"What do you mean you're not sure?" asks Megan. "Either you did or you didn't. The sailor said you opened a royal trunk."

"It might be another riddle," Ethan reluctantly replies. Then, not too far in the distance, he sees the dark outlines of fins sticking out of the water, and they are getting closer. With just a hint of panic in his voice, he says, "It can wait. We should get out of here now."

"Oh c'mon, don't be so evasive," replies Megan. "Just tell us already."

"Later," he says, pointing to the fins. "I'll tell you later."

Megan looks in the direction he's pointing. "Yeah. Good idea. Let's go back to the Afroeurasia Complex," she says, trying to mask the fear that has crept into her voice. She doesn't particularly like sharks.

"Let's go!" says Jared.

They each touch the thunderbolt icon on their bracelets and say, "The Afroeurasia portal." They wait and nothing happens.

"This time delay really stinks," Megan says. She kicks her feet, and her right foot hits something alive as it swims past, nudging her leg.

"Did you feel that?" she shrieks. "Something just swam under me!"

Before Ethan can answer, they all disappear, and the pod of dolphins swims on.

CHAPTER 22

IN A THIRD-STORY OFFICE, SEVERAL EXECUTIVES SIT around a conference table and wait patiently until Victor, the president of one of the cartel's businesses, finishes his phone conversation. "I don't care if the technical guys say it can't be done!" he yells into the video phone on his desk. The veins in his forehead pulsate as he runs a hand through his disheveled gray hair. "How can someone else be messing with the game? If our engineers don't fix those security problems now, tell them they'll all be fired! Guaranteed!"

The other executives and the few engineers in Victor's office have all seen his wrath before. They know it is usually best to ride it out without saying a word. Outside of the office, they call him "Victor Volcano." Best thing is to let him explode, and then eventually he'll calm down again. No one anticipated that the security of *The Ancients* game would be compromised so quickly.

"We can't have others adding code or characters, or whatever the heck they're doing, while students search for clues," he says. He takes a sip of water to calm himself down. "I want a daily status update." He jabs the disconnect button and turns to stare out his large office window at the rolling hills beyond the trees. Today, the peaceful view only makes him angrier.

One of the executives sitting at the conference table clears his throat, and Victor turns back to the group. "Any other good news?" he asks sarcastically.

"There is more news," the executive replies, "but it's not good."

"Well, what is it?" asks Victor, getting up from behind his desk to join the group. "This week started to go downhill with the failure of our drones. How could they have missed such a large target? We have to eliminate all potential risks. We have to make sure we get the artifact."

"They were jamming the drones," replies the program director responsible for the assault. "Got them to go off target."

Victor does not say a word; he only glares at the man. He hates excuses.

The head of competitive intelligence looks confused. He doesn't know anything about the drone attack. Pulling out a sheet of paper, he begins his report. "We learned that two of our biggest competitors are secretly talking about sponsoring some of the student teams and providing them with additional support."

"Do they know anything about the artifact? Or that the game is only a disguise for our search?"

"We have no idea…yet," replies the head of internal security. "We are investigating."

"Could the hacking of the game be related to this?" asks Victor.

"We don't think so," replies the head of engineering. "This looks to be some anonymous group."

"Do we know what they've done so far or how they've influenced the game?" Victor wonders aloud.

"No," says the head of game development. "We need to find the code first and then analyze what it's doing to the game. They're covering their tracks well."

"All these technical details are beyond me," says one of the other executives. "Have we decided if we're going to send our own players into the game?"

"We haven't made a final decision yet," replies the head of human resources. "We can't send teenagers, so we'll probably send adults. There are a lot guys out there with combat experience who are avid gamers. We're working on recruiting a few right now."

Impatiently, Victor asks, "Anything else?"

"We do know that a group from Globus Academy seems to be making the most progress. They're moving through the sites pretty systematically. I suspect they've found some clues," replies the head of game tracking. "The only problem is that we don't know what the clues are."

While the executive team talks, the director of game development silently debates whether he should say anything. While doing routine maintenance, his developers found an "enchantment" or power. This was not part of the original design. Somehow, as soon as they placed the game on the Internet, it started evolving. Someone or some group is adding code, changing the game as the students play it. He decides to wait and not say anything at this point. There is no need to upset the boss further.

"What do you think about leaking their position, or the progress they've made, to some of the other teams?" asks Victor. "Create some more intensity and competition."

The others are discussing the idea when they hear a knock on the conference room door.

"Enter. This better be good," Victor says loudly.

His assistant opens the door, pokes her head in, and nods. Victor knows that she would never disturb him without a good reason. He nods back. She sends in a young analyst who nervously walks toward the front of the room where Victor is seated.

"Well, what is it?" asks Victor.

"Sir, um…, anyway, our computers, the ones that scan billions of text messages, flagged a message a little while back. It looks like someone by the name of Jared Reyes, playing *The Ancients* game, sent a message to his friends."

"First piece of good news I've heard all week," replies Victor with just the hint of a smile. He turns to the young man. "What does it say?"

The young man takes his tablet computer and beams the message to the monitor in the front of the room. It says, "Besides the clue '*Seek a vanished civilization at Empire Plaza*,' there was something else. I'll tell you later."

"That's it?" says Victor with frustration. "What does that mean?"

"I don't know," stammers the young man as he shrinks back against the wall. He swallows hard. "The computer flagged it as a priority one message. You gave the order that you wanted to see all high-priority messages related to *The Ancients* game. Jared Reyes is one of the players."

Victor knows exactly who Jared is, but to the group, he says, "Let me think. Yes. I think I remember Jared Reyes. You're right. Thank you. You can go."

As the young man quickly exits, the head of engineering quietly whispers to another executive. They turn to Victor. "We can work with this," says the second executive, whose job focuses on developing innovative search technologies. "Give us a few hours."

"Good," replies Victor. He turns to look at the executives. "I want someone on the inside of that team. They always seem to be ahead of the others. Figure out how we can get one of those students to work for us. There must be something. If our competitors are sponsoring players, then we should be doing the same, secretly."

The head of engineering looks directly at Victor with a small smile. "Actually, we started to implement that strategy a few days ago." He loves being one step ahead of the boss. "I think we may have found a way to convince one of the players. He's also a programmer and avid gamer, and he doesn't get a lot of respect from his peers. We can use that. We can show him that he really belongs to an elite class. A class of individuals who will shape the future. Build up his confidence. Show him he is different than the others. Make him think he's special."

"Excellent!" replies Victor. "I don't need all the details. Do whatever it takes—and give me an update on progress at the end of every day." He turns to the others. "An update from each of you, every day! Meeting adjourned."

CHAPTER 23

MEGAN AND ETHAN STAND IN THE GLASS CUBE—THE lobby of the Afroeurasia Complex and Towers, their clothes bearing no trace of their swim in the Mediterranean. Outside, they see groups of students still trying to get in.

Ethan rubs a palm across his short hair and pulls his T-shirt over his belt. "That was a bit close for my taste. Were those sharks?"

"I didn't want to find out," replies Megan, fastening her dreadlocks with a clip. "Do you remember the riddle?"

"Do you think I have a photographic memory?" jokes Ethan. "Actually, I do." He then repeats what he read under the lid of the royal chest.

"I am the largest empire in the world. Nearly half the world lives within my borders. Once great, four events helped predict my collapse. Incubating a new power and way of thinking. Go to two of the four. At one you'll learn what you need."

"I'm impressed," Megan says. "That sounded verbatim."

Ethan grins. Finally, a compliment from Megan. With new enthusiasm, he touches the question mark button on his bracelet. "Let me see what I can find."

"Maybe we should wait for the others," suggests Megan.

"You mean Jared," Ethan says jealously.

"Not only."

They walk over to the pool at the base of the interior waterfall that cascades down many stories, and admire the two-foot-long koi.

Megan dips her hand into the water. "I don't remember these being here before," she says as the fish come up to nuzzle her fingers.

"I don't remember them either," replies Ethan.

"Hey, guys!" says Jared, coming around the corner with Lien and Arjun. His voice startles Ethan to the point that he almost falls into the fountain.

"Where did you come from?" asks Megan.

"Back there," replies Lien. "We returned here after we saw Jared's acrobatics on the trireme. Wow. Impressive!"

"Enchantments," says Ethan. "With that kind of power, anyone could have done it."

"I hope all that effort resulted in something," comments Arjun.

"It did. I found the next clue," Ethan says with pride. He then repeats verbatim what he saw under the lid of the royal box.

"That sounds interesting; let me look something up real quick," says Jared, backing away from the group. He takes less than two minutes to scan several library and education Web sites. He turns back to the group and sends them a link. "Here's something," he says, reading from the Web site in his contact lenses. "Empires are unique in that they create another level of government. There's the family, the village and elders, and the city-states. Empires are usually made up of people with different languages, laws, and religions. An empire is a state where one ethnic group or culture has dominion over populations that are ethnically or culturally diverse. They must create a sense of loyalty to a central government."

"Yeah, we've covered that before. Why don't you just search for 'largest empire' and be done with it?" says Megan. She is still sitting on the side of the fountain, dangling her hand in the water and admiring the waterfall.

Lien, seeing exactly where Jared is headed, searches as well. "There are several different views on what the largest empire is," she says. "Some say it was the British Empire; others say it was the Mongol Empire or the empires of the Romans, the Mauryans, or Alexander the Great—or even the Qing Empire in China."

"The clue said that close to half the world lived there; that suggests largest by population," Jared points out. "Isn't that right, Ethan?"

Ethan's attention is on Megan, who is still playing with the fish. "I think that's what it said," he replies, without looking up.

Talking and searching at the same time, Jared says, "Here, I found something." He shares the link with Lien. "I found a list of empires that I can sort by different criteria. If I sort by percent of world population, it looks like it's either the Mauryan Empire or the Persian, also known as the Achaemenid Empire. About 43 percent of the world's population lived in the Mauryan Empire around 250 BCE and about 44 percent in the Achaemenid Empire around 500 BCE. If I had to guess, I would say the clue refers to the Persian Empire."

"Why?" asks Arjun.

"I don't know," replies Jared, "just a feeling."

He and Lien continue to scan the site. The Persian Empire spanned three continents—Asia, Africa, and Europe—reaching from the Mediterranean Sea to the borders of modern-day India. It was the first to unite three sites of early urban civilization (the Nile Valley, Mesopotamia, and the Indus Valley) under a single government. In the process, it opened up regular communication between the three continents of Africa, Asia, and Europe.

"Interesting. Modern-day Iran, huh?" adds Lien. "It says that spanning three continents must have led to a lot of diffusion of ideas and cultural practices."

Jared does not react; he just keeps reading. "Their greatest achievement, according to this source, was the creation of the empire itself. They developed many techniques of governing that were also used by later empires."

Jared and Lien continue to scan the site. They learn that the Persian Empire was built on tolerance, often accepting subjects' varied customs and religions.

"Look at this," Lien says. "If you scroll down, you'll see some bullet points."

Achaemenid/Persian Empire History
- Persian power was based not just on brute force, although they had the army to maintain order and loyalty, but also on an advanced network of roads and professional bureaucracy.
- The empire created provinces or states headed by governors, or *satraps,* chosen from the local population. Unique for the times. Some ruled as tyrants.
- They built roads and had a highway system that communicated commands outward and brought taxes and tribute into the central government.
- They introduced standardized coins and laws, had banks and investment companies, and had a postal service.
- The Persians built underground aqueducts often several kilometers long.
- Educated bureaucrats and tax collectors existed.

- Social classes included imperial bureaucrats and free classes, and the bulk of society consisted of merchants, artists, craftsmen, farmers, and peasants.
- Society also included large class of slaves comprised of prisoners of war and debtors.
- A popular and influential religion called Zoroastrianism, based on high moral and ethical standards existed during that time.

Megan listens a little while longer, and then gets up and walks toward the elevators. "Looks like you found the next part of the clue, their greatness. Now we need to learn about the four events that started their collapse. Let's see what floor they are on. We can figure out the rest as we go. C'mon. Let's take the elevator up to the Persian Empire and get going."

They step into an ultramodern, all-glass elevator. The doors slide shut, and as the elevator car begins to ascend, Megan looks past the flowing water of the waterfall into the large atrium in the lobby. It must be close to twelve stories high—quite tall for an indoor waterfall, she thinks, when out of the corner of her eye, she notices a movement behind one of the white marble columns. She turns to the others. "Did you see that?"

They all look down at the column. Nothing.

"I think somebody might be following us," Megan says.

"How's that possible?" asks Ethan. "Those doors have been locked since we got here, and I haven't seen anyone come or go."

"We're in a simulation. Anything is possible. Don't you think it's strange that no one else has figured out how to get into this building?" asks Megan.

She continues to scan the lobby. "There! Look!" She pokes Jared with her elbow. "I'm sure that was a person; possibly more than one."

They all look down as they continue to ride up the painfully slow elevator, but do not see anything. Jared turns back toward Megan with a questioning look. She shrugs.

Lien decides to take the time to review a summary of ancient Greece from around 500 BCE. She knows that the Persians and Greeks fought quite a few battles back then. There might be a connection. She scans several sites.

Greek History: Ancient Greece

- Greece is located in a limited and mountainous geographical area between the Mediterranean and the Aegean Seas.
- It grew through commercial activity and established colonies abroad.
- It was a series of city-states that all shared a common culture and identity.
- The two major city-states were Athens and Sparta.
- Sparta was agricultural and militaristic. It was an oligarchy, where decisions were made by the ruling few.
- Athens was the political, cultural, and commercial center. A democracy, its civic decisions were made by open debate among citizens.

"Hey, listen to this," says Lien. "Even though Athens is considered to have been the first democracy, women couldn't participate. Slavery helped the Greeks develop this democracy because it allowed Greek citizens to have more time to meet, debate, create works of art, philosophize, and worship their many gods."

"Typical," replies Megan. "Women's rights went downhill after the Paleolithic Era. Why are you reading about Greece, anyway? We're headed to the Persians."

"I'm following a hunch," replies Lien. "It says here that social and economic inequalities among individuals and groups have been part of humans' daily experience since early times. A key theme throughout world history is the differences in wealth, power, or social status—the division between the haves and the have-nots."

"We know who had the power in ancient Greece, don't we?" replies Megan sarcastically.

"Just like in almost any other ancient society, except a few," interjects Jared, who joins Megan in scanning the area outside of the glass elevator while Lien keeps reading.

As the elevator car ascends, the lobby shrinks before his eyes, as does the waterfall cascading down into the gleaming, white-marble basin. Jared scans the other high-rises. Each building is unique but still similar in style. He wonders if the others are as modern and sleek on the inside as the lobby. He looks back down through the roof of the glass cube. As he is about to turn away, the elevator in the second glass tube begins to ascend. Strange, he thinks, why would a second elevator be moving? He doesn't notice that both elevators have slowed; they are now ascending at an even slower pace. He turns to Lien and notices her eyes focus on something on her contact lenses. "I see you searching. Did you find anything?"

"I might have. What drama!" says Lien, reading the text in her lenses.

"My dad used to say that real history can have more drama than a fictional story," replies Jared. "What is it?"

"Yeah. No kidding. Listen to this. From 500 BCE to about 338 BCE, a little over 150 years, Greek history was a roller coaster. First, around 499 BCE, the Ionians and people from other regions rebelled because they hated the tyrants that the Persians had put in place to rule them. Athenians and others supported the revolt, and the Persians invaded for the first time around 492 BCE. There were several battles, including the famous battle at Marathon in 490 BCE. The first invasion failed, but while Darius the Great was preparing for a second invasion, his Egyptian territories revolted, and he left Greece alone. After his death, his son, Xerxes, led a second invasion of Greece in 480 BCE. With the Greeks winning at several key battles like Salamis and Plataea, the Persian invasion was repelled. During these wars, Sparta and Athens worked together to fight off the Persians."

"Those two cities were very different. One was a totalitarian military state and the other, more of a democracy. I'm surprised they worked together," Arjun comments.

"Having a common enemy helped. They each had other reasons, too," replies Lien. "Like one city-state not wanting the other to gain too much power. The Greeks defeated the Persians around 480 to 479 BCE, ending the invasion of Greece. Athens then created the Delian League, an alliance of city-states, to fight aggression from the Persian Empire and other common enemies. From around 480 to 404 BCE, in what was called the 'Golden Age' or the 'Age of Pericles,' Athens became an economic, cultural, and military powerhouse."

"I remember this. This was the time of Socrates, Plato, and Aristotle, right?" asks Arjun.

"Yup," replies Jared. "Socrates was the teacher of Plato, who was the teacher of Aristotle, who was the teacher of Alexander the Great."

Lien continues to summarize. "As Athens increased its influence and power, the relationship between Athens and Sparta deteriorated, since Athens and Sparta had always vied against each other for power. This led to the Peloponnesian War between Athens, which was in the Delian League, and Sparta, which was in the Peloponnesian League. This war lasted for close to twenty-seven years and didn't end until around 404

BCE. Sparta won, and Athens was devastated. The 'Golden Age' ended, and the war caused huge damage across Greece. The city-states became weaker and weaker."

"The end of ancient Greece. The constant wars left the door wide open for the Macedonians," interrupts Jared.

"How do you know that?" asks Lien.

Jared chuckles. "I'm reading the same thing you are. The Macedonians under Phillip II, Alexander the Great's father, defeated the Greeks at Chaeronea, ending Greek freedom. Luckily, Phillip didn't destroy Greece but rather encouraged Greek culture and ideals to flourish. Then, Alexander the Great finally conquered the great Persian Empire and expanded the Macedonian Empire all the way to the Indus River. Alexander died in 323 BCE at age thirty-two."

"My head is spinning. Stop already," interrupts Megan. "Too much info. Just say that the Greeks had a profound impact on human history. In a little over 150 years, the Greeks, a bunch of city-states, fought the Persians several times to keep their freedom. Had a 'Golden Age' that influenced all of Western civilization. Fought among themselves numerous times, then finally destroyed their own land and weakened themselves to the point where they were taken over."

"That's essentially it," replies Jared. "There is more detail, of course."

"Of course," replies Megan. "Like Lien said, quite dramatic. But how does that relate to the clue, *once great, four events helped predict my collapse,*' and the Persians?"

"I think it has something to do with the Persian Wars leading to the end. The Greeks repelling the Persians eventually led to the collapse of the empire," Lien says.

The elevator is now rising vertically on the outside of the Middle East Tower. Jared glances at the floor numbers as they pass the fiftieth floor.

Then, without warning, their slow-moving elevator unexpectedly speeds up like a rocket leaving earth's orbit. Megan and Jared grab onto the glass railing along the side as their stomachs drop into their shoes. Ethan is slammed to the floor and grabs onto Arjun's legs, causing Arjun to topple over on top of him. Lien grabs Jared around the waist. They shoot up past the seventieth floor. Then, just as fast, the elevator begins to plummet back down toward the lobby. Within seconds, they are free-falling past the fortieth floor and heading for a spectacular crash. They speed past the twentieth, the fifteenth—back into the glass cube—and then they slowly decelerate. Just as they reach the bottom, the elevator reverses again and shoots toward the top, first vertically, then at forty-five degrees inside the glass tube back toward the Middle East Tower, and then vertically up the outside. The second elevator maintains its slow climb toward the sixtieth floor.

"I feel like I'm on an out-of-control yo-yo," cries Ethan.

The rapid changes in air pressure from zooming up and down are playing havoc with their ears. Jared is ready to throw up. He ignores his ears and steadies himself by focusing on a distant object, a technique similar to focusing on the horizon in a rocking boat at sea. "OK. When we shoot past the sixtieth floor, I'm going to flip the emergency stop button and hope we can get as close as possible." Before the words leave his mouth, they zoom past the fifty-ninth floor and Jared flips the switch. The elevator comes to a screeching halt. All five, not anticipating the instant stop, are slammed into the ceiling and then drop to the tiled elevator floor. It stops so abruptly that the elevator's glass walls and railings crack and shatter into a million little pieces, which then rain to the ground. They are no longer in an elevator, but rather sixty stories up, on the outside of a high rise. They stand on a small, wall-less platform that can accelerate or decelerate at any moment.

"We've got to get off of this thing, fast." Megan rises to her feet and pats Jared on the back. "Nice job."

The elevator floor is four feet foot below the opening. Just close enough to the sensor, the doors open automatically.

Jared boosts Megan up through the door, then Lien, who helps Ethan and Arjun. Jared is still standing on the platform when a bell chimes, signaling the closing of the doors and the elevator's departure. Jared jumps up quickly, landing on his stomach on the sixtieth floor. The doors remain open. His legs dangle down toward the plaza as the elevator, or what remains of it, plunges downward. Somewhere around the fortieth floor, it disappears into thin air. Megan and Lien look into empty space. They quickly grab Jared's arms and drag him up onto the floor, stepping back from the edge into a sparsely furnished lobby. The elevator doors slowly close.

"Someone is manipulating these sites," says Ethan.

"I think someone has been tracking us. They reprogrammed the site once we got here," adds Arjun.

"You think someone is messing with us?" asks Lien.

"What would you do in a normal video game?" asks Arjun.

"If I couldn't eliminate my competition, I'd try to slow them down," says Ethan.

"Exactly."

Jared walks down the only hallway leading away from the lobby. He scans his contact lenses as he walks. "Darius I used both the Ionian revolts, where some people rebelled against tyrant satraps, and his anger at Athens for having supported the revolts as an excuse to expand his empire into Europe. He sent his army against Greece, and given what you said, I'd guess it was the Greeks' success in the Persian Wars that was the beginning of the end of the Persian Empire. But there's a problem."

Megan wants to move on. "What?"

Jared stops walking. "The history of Persia, like that of Babylonia, is usually written by its enemies or its subjects. But all the primary sources for this information are Greek. Mainly, they're written by Herodotus, an ethnographer and some say the world's first historian. Others call him the 'father of lies.' There seem to be no surviving Persian historical accounts. Tough to get a Persian perspective on all of this, or to know where to go. Thucydides was another Greek historian. He wrote only about events that occurred during his lifetime that he could verify through examination of written records and eyewitness accounts. Some say he was the first scientific historian, because he strove for objectivity. And some say he pioneered the historical method used by historians today. But that doesn't tell us much, either. I have no idea where we need to go."

Megan frowned. "Let's just go down this hallway and maybe we'll see something."

They hear the muted chime of a bell signaling the arrival of a second elevator.

"I told you I saw something," says Megan. "Why do you think that elevator came up here? We better go." She begins to jog more quickly down the hallway. They run past the first door, labeled "Women's Rights in Persia," a second door labeled "Zoroastrianism," and then doors labeled "Art and Architecture" and "Science and Math." They keep running.

"All these doors," comments Arjun. "This was a huge empire."

As they run along the marble floor, they hear the footsteps behind them getting closer. They are sprinting, barely glancing at the doors, when they almost pass one labeled "Greco-Persian Wars."

Jared skids to a stop. "This must be it. Best we've seen."

"Yup," agrees Megan.

They grab the door handle just as the door begins to disappear from top to bottom. They quickly fling it open. Megan and Jared jump through the opening, ducking their heads. Lien and Ethan make it through on their hands and knees. Arjun, the last to go, has to do an army crawl through the last two feet of the doorway. Lien grabs his arms and pulls him through as the doorsill slowly disintegrates. They all sit on the other side, breathing hard.

Arjun is the first one to speak. "Whew! That was close. Thanks, Lien."

"No problem."

As the last inch of the door slowly disappears, they can hear muted cursing from the hallway. They all look at each other. The voices sound familiar.

CHAPTER 24

"WHAT HAPPENED TO THAT DOOR?" ASKS JARED AS HE helps Arjun up.

"It was probably a link that was being taken down," answers Arjun.

Megan raises her head above the reeds and immediately sinks back down. "I think we're actually in the middle of a battle. I see Greek soldiers on our left and a massive Persian army with the ships on the beach to our right. We better retreat back into the marsh before someone sees us."

The five teenagers are now in a boggy marshland in the Valley of Vrana outside of Marathon, twenty-four miles from Athens, in the year 490 BCE. They can hear the waves in the Bay of Marathon to their right. The plains are eight to ten miles long and maybe two to three miles wide. The great Persian army of Darius I, with its cavalry, light-armored infantrymen, and archers, is camped along the coast. The Persian force greatly outnumbers the ten thousand Greek citizen-soldiers—the hoplites.

For a brief second, Jared wonders if they are still in the Middle East Tower or if the link transported them to the Europe Tower.

For nine days, each army has waited for the other to make the first move. The Athenians have stalled for days, hoping for reinforcements from Sparta. However, the Spartans are in the middle of a religious festival and won't arrive until the end of the battle. The Persians, given their overwhelming numbers, are hoping that the Athenians will be overcome by fear and surrender.

"We can't just hide here; we need to go search for the next clue," Jared says.

They retreat to a hill in the middle of the marsh, which gives them a full view of the beach and the plain. It is before dawn, and the ten thousand Greek hoplites begin to assemble in a phalanx formation, four men deep in the middle and eight men deep on the flanks. Trumpets blare, and a tight column of Greek hoplites in full armor and carrying seven- to nine-foot spears, swords, and shining shields begins to march down the plain toward the Persians. The battle seems so unbalanced. The Persians calmly send soldiers carrying wicker shields to the front, since their cavalry is nowhere to be seen. The hoplites march, and then jog, and for the last few hundred meters, sprint at the enemy. The archers let thousands of arrows fly. They go everywhere, but mostly over the heads of the sprinting Greeks.

Jared tackles Megan as a misguided arrow sails overhead. A soldier probably fired it just as he was hit. They tumble down into the wet marsh and stay hidden for several minutes.

Megan looks into Jared's eyes, smiles, and murmurs, "Thanks."

He smiles back at her. They watch as wave after wave of arrows, thousands of them, sail over the heads of the Greek soldiers. They crawl back to the top of the mound in time to see the hoplites with their wooden shields crash into the Persian ranks, their iron-tipped spears severing flesh and bones, ripping apart the Persian army. The battlefield is a horrific, screaming, pushing, close-quarter fight between heavily armed men and light infantry.

"Ha. I know how this is going to end," chuckles Ethan. "I commanded the Greek army in this exact battle against the Persian tyrant in my war video game a few years ago. Freedom wins against tyranny."

They all watch the battle from the marsh when Lien asks, "What's happening? Do you see that? Something is off."

"Yeah, I see it, too," adds Arjun. "Everything seems to be speeding up."

"Oh, this is so cool!" yells Ethan excitedly. "The game is accelerating time. We'll be able to see the whole battle in just a few minutes. I wonder if there's a way we can control how fast time goes?"

They watch as the Greeks make forward progress when Megan points to the center of the formation, where the Athenians are starting to retreat in a disciplined and orderly fashion. Jared wonders if the Persians are overpowering the hoplites or if this retreat is a tactic. Soon, they see that it is by design. The Greek general, Miltiades, knowing about Persian battle strategy, has weakened his center and strengthened his flanks. As the Persians pursue the retreating Greeks, they find themselves surrounded on three sides. The slaughter continues. There is no exit, and the Persians panic, break ranks, and flee back to their ships.

In less than thirty minutes it is afternoon. And that is all the time the battle took—one day. By early evening, the battle is over. The rest of the Persians head back out to sea and sail toward Athens. The Athenians and their Plataean allies quickly head overland to defend Athens.

Jared, Megan, Ethan, Arjun, and Lien cannot believe what they witnessed. They get up, make their way out of the marsh, and wander among thousands of dead soldiers, staring at the brutality of the battle. Megan almost trips over a dismembered body. Although this is a simulation, she can smell and feel the horror of death. Blood is everywhere. Limbs and dead soldiers lie everywhere. Ethan, no longer chuckling, almost throws up as he maneuvers around puddles of blood that drench the ground.

Megan quietly says, "These ancient battles were brutal. Over six thousand dead Persians and fewer than two hundred dead hoplites. This was a rout."

"True," replies Jared. "Looks like General Miltiades's battlefield tactics worked."

"Too bad he ended up dying in an Athenian prison," adds Lien, scanning her contact lenses.

Jared, not allowing himself to be sidetracked, continues, "From what I remember, there is a debate about the importance of this battle. Some say that stopping the Persians here at Marathon gave birth to the Classical Age in Greece, which was the foundation of Western civilization, with ideas about philosophy, culture, science, and democracy. The achievements during this time led to the European Renaissance and Enlightenment hundreds of years later. Other historians don't necessarily agree."

They continue to walk toward the edge of the plain. Jared looks thoughtfully toward the sea and the setting sun. "It is so quiet now. You know, the more I think about the clue, the more I think it does refer to the four big battles of the Greek and Persian wars." He quickly searches on his lenses. "The first was Marathon in 490 BCE, the second and third were Thermopylae and Salamis in 480, and the fourth and final one was in Plataea in 479."

"Why do you think that?" asks Lien.

Jared begins to scan more data on his contact lenses. "Some say the wars started when the Persian Empire tried to rein in rebellion on its frontier—the Ionian Revolt."

Like many other empires, he reads to himself, the Persians always faced issues on their frontiers. According to history, Marathon was important during the first invasion of the Persians, and the battles at Thermopylae and Salamis were key in the second invasion. At Thermopylae, King Leonidas of Sparta and his army of seven thousand men held off the ten-to-forty-times-larger Persian army of Xerxes I, Darius's son, for seven days at the pass. They might have succeeded had it not been for a traitor, who showed the Persians a path behind the Greek lines. This battle was significant because although the Greeks lost, it provided a motivational example. Soldiers in the rear guard faced certain death, yet they stayed and defended the pass. After Thermopylae, the Persians went on to capture Athens. There was no real battle, since the Athenians had evacuated the city. The next big battle was at Salamis. Some historians believe that was a turning point in the Greco-Persian wars, since after losing, Xerxes retreated to Persia, leaving only a small force in Greece. Some argue that given the significance of ancient Greece in the development of Western civilization, had the Persians dominated Greece, it might have altered a major trajectory of human history.

"Let's go back to the riddle," says Lien, who is walking next to Jared. "The phrases '*I am the largest empire in the world*' and '*half the world lives within my borders*,' refer to the Persian Empire at the time. I can see how the phrase, '*four events helped predict my collapse*' might refer to these four battles with Greece?"

"Yeah," replies Jared. "And I think that '*incubating a new power and way of thinking*' refers to the rise of democracy and Western thinking."

They continue to walk along the side of the battlefield. Anyone who sees them would think that they are five young Greek villagers looking for dead relatives.

After scanning more information, Jared says, "I don't think we'll find the next clue here. As far as I can tell, most of the information comes from a few primary sources. At various points in history, the Greeks were subjects, enemies, or conquerors of the Persians, so they might not have had the most impartial view. Herodotus wrote *Histories*, and Aeschylus, an Athenian playwright, wrote *The Persians* and something known as the *Decree of Themistocles*. Other than that, there isn't much physical evidence left."

"Maybe we should look for what the Persians wrote about the wars," suggests Arjun, who is thinking that an empire as large and powerful as the Achaemenid Persian Empire must have left significant records.

"There's not much," replies Lien. "The Achaemenid rulers left very few records since most of the information was communicated orally."

"You guys can be so academic," says Megan. "The riddle said to go to 'two of the four.' We've only been to one, Marathon, so we have to go to another battle. Thermopylae, Salamis, or Plataea?"

"Thermopylae," says Ethan.

"Plataea," says Lien.

"Why those?" asks Jared.

"I don't know," replies Ethan. "From what I can remember, Thermopylae was a pretty big battle."

"But Plataea," says Lien, "was the last battle of the Greek and Persian wars to take place on Greek soil."

"I agree with Lien," adds Arjun.

"I don't know," Jared interjects. "I'm leaning toward Salamis, since it was a turning point in the wars."

The four of them debate the various options. Jared finally puts up his hand, signaling that they should all stop. "I think we need a tiebreaker. Megan, what do you think?" he asks, looking around.

But Megan is nowhere to be seen.

They call out somewhat softly, "Megan." They look in the underbrush and scan the battlefield. Finally, Ethan points and says, "There. Look up there."

One hundred yards past the marshes, they spot Megan climbing up a moderately steep, rocky hillside, heading for the entrance to a cave.

Much louder this time, Jared yells, "Megan!" He turns to the others. "She always does that."

She turns her head and signals them to join her.

"Does what?" asks Lien.

"She heads off by herself. She'll see something and go after it."

"Whoa, did you see that?" asks Ethan. "There was a strange light. For a minute, the cave entrance looked like it was shimmering."

"Shimmering?" wonders Lien.

"Yeah. The entrance glowed a faint blue."

"I think the sun is getting to you," Arjun jokes.

"Maybe that's what Megan saw," replies Ethan.

Arjun and Lien fight their way through the marsh along a narrow path that rises a few feet above the boggy soil. Jared and Ethan are several yards behind, when Jared hears a moaning sound off in the high grass. He picks his way through the mud, and as he emerges into an opening, a wounded Persian soldier smashes a Greek shield into the back of his head. Jared topples forward, unconscious. Ethan, following a few steps behind Jared, grabs an abandoned sword and stabs the soldier, quickly ending his life.

Ethan rolls Jared onto his back and slaps his face. There's no reaction. Jared is out cold. He's about to splash some water on Jared when he is interrupted by a text message on his contact lenses. He wonders who it could be and quickly scans the text. He looks up and sees that Arjun and Lien have almost reached Megan and are out of shouting range. Good. As he looks down at Jared, he's torn. He's been given a request. He sighs deeply. This could also be the perfect opportunity for him to get closer to Megan. He doesn't want to hurt Jared, just get him out of the picture for a little while. Maybe slow him down. He bends down, slips the wristband off of Jared's arm, and throws it several feet into the grass. It should take Jared some time to find it. He then rises and quickly hurries to catch up with the others.

Megan, meanwhile, reaches the entrance of the cave and looks down toward the others. She doesn't wait but rather enters through the opening. A deep, dark-blue light illuminates the interior. She saw the blue light as they were walking on the edge of the battlefield, and knew that she would have to investigate. The cave, perfectly round and a little over six feet in diameter, turns out to consists of a stone floor and rock walls. The blue light illuminates a low tunnel that extends back into the mountain and then disappears. Megan wanders in, and after fifteen feet, she realizes that the tunnel makes a sharp turn to the left. She continues to walk, staring at the walls and ceiling around her. After the turn, she spots a series of short phrases carved into the stone in a large font. They are glowing with the same blue light. On the ceiling, she sees "Battle of Thermopylae," "Battle of Salamis," and "Battle of Plataea." On the right-hand wall she sees "Persian Empire," "Darius," and "Xerxes I." The left-hand wall is labeled with "Herodotus," "Plutarch," "Thucydides," "Sparta," and "Athens." The walls are covered with many other phrases in smaller type. Megan glances at as many as she can, thinking that they remind her of neon lights.

She notices that there are two copies of each of the battles names written on the ceiling. One is written closer to the right side of the wall and the Persians. The other is closer to the left side of the wall and the Greeks. She sees two versions of the Battle of Salamis overhead. She reaches up, touches the phrase closer to the right wall, and disappears.

Lien and Arjun reach the entrance of the cave and turn around to look back down at the plain of Marathon. They see Ethan lumbering up the slope. He finally reaches them, panting and out of breath.

"Where's a glass of water when you need it?" croaks Ethan.

"Where's Jared?" asks Lien, scanning the slope.

"He said he needed to take care of some business. He'll be along," replies Ethan. He avoids eye contact and walks into the cave, breathing in the cool air—a welcome change from the hot sun outside.

"And you left him alone in the middle of a battlefield?" Lien asks with scorn in her voice.

"The battle's over; there's nothing to worry about. He said he'd be right here. Let's go figure out where Megan went," answers Ethan. He walks farther into the tunnel and looks around. "This is wild, a cave illuminated in blue," he says. He then begins to yell, "Megan! Megan! Where are you?" There is no answer. Ethan, followed closely by Arjun, turns the corner and is momentarily stunned by all the neon writing. Lien lingers at the entrance.

The boys keep walking several more feet, round one more corner, and walk another thirty feet. The cave ends abruptly. Ethan walks up to the rock wall and starts to look for a doorway or any kind of opening. Megan must have gone somewhere. A few minutes pass as he searches the ceiling, the walls, and the floor. Nothing. He begins to walk back toward the entrance. He calls out, "Megan. C'mon, Megan. Stop joking around."

Ethan and Arjun return to the front of the tunnel where Lien is waiting. "We didn't see her anywhere," Ethan says with a trace of concern. "The tunnel ends after two more turns. I don't know where she went. She's got to be here somewhere."

"What are you guys talking about?" asks Megan, coming around the corner from the back of the cave with a big smile on her face. "I'm right here."

Ethan walks up to her and gives her a big hug. "I'm glad you're safe," he says. Megan doesn't reciprocate. She stands stiffly and pats his back with one arm.

"Where were you?" asks Arjun. "We walked back there and didn't see you."

Megan tilts her head toward the side and says, "You're not going to believe this! I found something really cool." She starts to move toward one of the walls, but then suddenly turns back around. "Where's Jared?"

"He had to take care of some business. He'll be right here," Ethan answers quickly, before anyone else can say anything.

"Maybe we should wait," suggests Megan.

Ethan exhales slowly. This is not how he wanted it to go. He needs to think of something quickly. He turns to Megan. "Remember when we were in the elevator, and you thought you saw someone? Maybe it's another team. We can't slow down now. Why don't we split up? You and I can go on ahead, and Arjun and Lien can wait here for Jared."

Lien, beginning to see what Ethan is trying to do, replies, "Arjun can go with you guys. I'll wait here for Jared."

"But you shouldn't wait alone. It could be dangerous," replies Ethan, trying to sound concerned about Lien's safety. "This way, it will be two and two."

"I can wait with Lien," suggests Arjun. "As soon as Jared gets here, we'll catch up with you."

"Sounds good. Let's go," Megan states impatiently. She takes Ethan's hand and walks toward the wall. Together they touch "Battle of Salamis" on the right-hand side of the ceiling, near the word "Persia."

Seconds later, they stand on the slopes of Mount Egaleo as the sun rises.

"Wow," says Ethan. "Those blue phrases were Web links. Cool." He is overjoyed that his strategy has worked. Now he finally has some time alone with Megan.

"Pretty neat, huh?" replies Megan.

"But why two identical phrases?" asks Ethan.

"Simple," answers Megan. "One link takes you to the Persian side of the battle, and the other link takes you to the Greek side of the battle."

"Very clever," Ethan says.

"History is full of different perspectives, and in a battle, it is clear that there are at least two different views," Megan says.

"So this is the Battle of Salamis, but which side are we on?"

"It's 480 BCE. And we have the best seats in the house," replies Megan. "Look around; you're not dressed as a Greek."

Ethan uses his contact lenses to do a quick search for Salamina, Greece, on his earth-mapping program. He sends the link to Megan. "Here. Look at this."

Megan opens the link and looks at the satellite image. "That's a pretty narrow strait."

Below, in the Straits of Salamis, about three hundred Greek trireme warships wait. The much larger fleet of six to eight hundred Persian ships, consisting of Phoenicians, Ionian Greeks, and others, moves into the straits. Themistocles, an influential Greek general, knew he could take away the Persian fleet's advantage if they fought in the narrow strait, where the smaller, faster Greek ships could outmaneuver Xerxes's navy. Most of Greece was already under Xerxes's control, but Xerxes hoped that by destroying the Greek navy he could force a surrender. He wanted to finish the war as quickly as possible.

While Ethan looks down at the fleet, Megan looks up the hill. Farther up the rocky slope, on a large stone outcropping, sits Xerxes on his throne. Guards and attendants surround him, and he has a full view of the straits. She quickly scans some information from Herodotus: Xerxes witnessed the battle in order to reward those commanders who showed bravery. Those who lost their ships but made it to shore were brought to his throne to explain themselves; many were beheaded on the spot.

Megan touches Ethan gently on the shoulder, and then points toward the royal contingent. "We need to get up there."

"Now?" asks Ethan.

"With a full view of the battle, we might get a better idea of what to look for."

"I don't know," replies Ethan. "I think we should wait until evening. The whole mountain is swarming with Persians. Look—soldiers, advisers, even scribes."

"C'mon. You're already dressed like a Persian. Just put a cap on your head and pretend we belong. In this crowd, nobody should notice. We don't have a lot of time."

"The two of us walking up there is going to seem odd," replies Ethan.

"You can wait here if you want," snaps Megan. "I'm going to go look for a clue near the throne."

Down below, the battle starts. The smaller, more nimble fleet of Greek ships rams the larger Persian vessels, breaking oars, rendering them useless, or punching holes in their sides. In some cases, the ramming is not successful. and something similar to a land battle takes place with heavily armed hoplites fighting lighter-armed Persians.

Megan and Ethan casually wander toward the throne, careful not to raise the suspicions of the guards. Once there, they mill about among the many attendants.

At the beginning of the battle, King Xerxes is happy and engaged, since it seems to be going well. But over the course of the day, the Persians become entangled and disorganized in the cramped waterway. Megan overhears a conversation between Xerxes and his officers about the courage of one of the Persian commanders, Artemisia, the queen of Halicarnassus. She is one of the first woman admirals. When he sees the result of her battle, he praises her by saying that his fleet behaved like women, while the only woman in it behaved like a man. Megan smiles to herself.

Megan whispers, "I guess that was a compliment. See? Never mess with a woman."

"I won't." Ethan pauses and looks something up. "Hmm! Here in *Histories*, by the Greek historian Herodotus, it's clear there's more to the story. Xerxes didn't see how she rammed an ally to escape from a pursuing Greek ship. You want to hear it?"

Knowing full well that she won't look it up later, Megan replies, "Not now. I can read it some other time."

As the Greeks begin to prevail and Xerxes witnesses the carnage, his mood becomes worse and worse. By the end of the day, the battle is over. The ocean is covered with wrecks as far as the eye can see—sinking ships, tangled rigging, broken oars, and weapons of all kinds. The bloated, ghastly bodies of the dead float on the currents and bob in the waves. Many of the Persians conscripted into the navy couldn't swim. The Greeks lost forty ships, yet succeeded in capturing or sinking nearly two hundred Persian ships.

Xerxes leaves his throne and heads down Mount Egaleo with his contingent, passing Megan and Ethan as they make their way up the slope to try to get a better look at the throne. As they get close, Megan looks up. To her astonishment, Damian and Ivy stare back. They are standing a few feet behind the throne. The rest of their team is spread out farther up the hill. One of the royal scribes, writing down the names of brave or cowardly Persian captains, hands Damian a scroll and then disappears into the crowd of royal handlers making their way down the slope.

Megan sees Damian touch his bracelet, and she sprints uphill toward him. Damian quickly turns and runs away from the royal court down a less crowded path. One of the guards starts yelling and pointing at Damian. "Thief! Traitor! He's taken a royal scroll!"

Damian and Ivy half run, half slide down the hill with Megan and Ethan right behind them. The guard who accused Damian drops his shield and sword and chases after them. He is fast and the gap is closing. Soon, more Persians join him.

"You go after Damian and Ivy!" Megan yells to Ethan. "I'll see if I can slow down the guards." She stops and grabs a handful of tennis-ball-sized rocks and begins to throw them at the Persian pursuers. Megan's aim is terribly accurate, and she lands several rocks on the torsos and legs of the guards. She can't stop them all, however, and several guards start to get close. Megan turns and barrels down the hill past Ethan, who is struggling to keep his footing on the loose rocks. Megan is only a few feet from Ivy when she jumps feet-first like a long jumper and slams into Ivy's legs. They both go tumbling down the rocky slope for several yards until they finally stop.

Meanwhile, Lien and Arjun have helped Jared locate his wristband. The trio arrive on the site just in time to witness the Persians' pursuit of the twins. Jared looks uphill and recognizes Damian and Ivy immediately, but has no time to wonder how they've gotten here. He looks around. Farther uphill he sees the rest of their team. Down the hill he sees a rock outcropping and quickly formulates a plan. Without saying a word to Lien or Arjun, he starts to barrel down the hill, sword in hand, on an intercept course with Damian and the pursuing Persians. He runs as if he were in a cross-country race in school, jumping over rocks, avoiding bushes, and trying to maintain his balance on the steep slope. As he gets closer to the outcropping, he feels his strategy might work. It is just tall enough to shield his body, and he accelerates to get behind it.

When Damian looks back to see what has happened to his sister, Jared, dressed as a Persian soldier, steps out from behind the outcropping and slams the broad side of his sword into his stomach. Damian doubles over, gasping for air, and then falls onto his back. Jared gently takes the scroll from his hand.

As Lien and Arjun throw rocks, spears, and anything else they can find at the pursuing Persians, Jared flattens his back against the stone, trying to make himself indistinguishable from the rock. While catching his breath, he unfurls the scroll and begins to read. As he finishes, Megan passes him on the right, running and jumping over the smaller rocks. Ivy is nowhere to be seen. On Megan's heels, Arjun and Lien try to keep up. Ethan hides among a group of boulders. Not far behind, several sword-wielding royal guards, furious that an imperial scroll was stolen, close in on them.

Jared puts the scroll in his belt and starts to take off after Megan. As soon as he leaves the cover of the rock, he senses the shadow of something above him. He steps aside as a Persian, dressed in a conical hat, a shirt, and tight-fitting trousers, lands next to him. At first, he thinks it might be Ivy. The jump dislodges the conical hat, revealing a female face—but it's not Ivy. The soldier jumps to her feet and attacks Jared with a ferocious punch aimed at his face. Jared, surprised to see her wearing a wristband, moves aside just in time. The soldier kicks and then throws a barrage of punches. Jared sees the action in slow motion, and it allows him to move out of the way. His martial arts teacher in PE would be proud: for years, he has tried to teach the students how to stay calm and focused during a fight.

"Give me that scroll," the woman soldier says, throwing another barrage of punches.

Jared blocks each one and realizes that he could defeat this soldier, but it would take too much time. He lands one punch on the soldier's shoulder, propelling her backwards, then turns and follows Megan, Lien, and Arjun down the hill as fast as he can. Megan takes a route precipitously close to the edge of a cliff. One of the guards, close on her heels, has almost caught up to her. Near one of the steepest drops, she unexpectedly turns and lashes out at her pursuer with a series of kicks. He manages to block all of them, and then he punches back. With a lucky kick, Megan hits him in the chest, and he tumbles backward off the cliff, screaming all the way to the bottom.

Jared, almost upon them, wonders about the other student soldier when Ivy grabs him from behind. "Give me that clue!" she yells. Seconds later, the young woman Jared was fighting slams into both of them. Megan looks on as Jared and the two Persian soldiers roll on the ground. When they finally stop, Megan realizes it's Ivy and another player.

Jared struggles to his knees and raises his upper body. Ivy has her hands wrapped around his ankle. Farther up, he can see Damian shake off the effects of the sword strike and begin to jog down the hill.

"You want this?" yells Jared as he grabs the scroll from his belt. "Go find it!" With all his strength, he throws the scroll. It makes a large, graceful arc off the steepest side of the mountain.

"No!" screams Ivy, letting go of Jared's leg. The Globus Academy students and several students from other schools, all dressed as Persians, watch the scroll disappear over the edge.

Jared, Megan, Lien, and Arjun quickly leave the others and continue to make their way down the slope. Ethan eventually catches up. As soon as they are out of view, they each touch the thunderbolt on their bracelets and, one after the other, say, "Empire Plaza, Middle East Tower, sixtieth floor."

CHAPTER 25

THEY TURN AROUND AS SOON AS THEIR FEET TOUCH THE marble of the sixtieth-floor lobby. Jared wipes a trickle of blood from his forehead. He leans his head back and runs his hands through his hair. "Whew. Did anyone follow us?"

"I don't think so," replies Megan. "I can't believe Damian, Ivy, and the others were there. How did they get ahead of us?"

Jared shrugs. "I have no idea."

"And the way that female soldier fought," says Arjun.

"You mean the martial arts?" asks Ethan. "Did the Persians learn that from the Chinese?"

"There was trade along the Silk Road, and they must have learned some things from each other, but I don't think martial arts were one of them," Lien says.

"She wasn't a game character," interjects Jared. "She was a student from another team."

Megan shakes her hair loose and stretches her muscles. "We better get moving. By the way, why did you throw the scroll off the cliff?"

"It had the next clue, and I figured it would buy us some time," replies Jared.

"I wonder if there are different ways to get to these Web sites. Maybe they didn't come through Empire Plaza," says Arjun.

"Just like the real Web," adds Ethan.

"So what did the scroll say?" asks Megan.

Jared leans up against the inner wall of the hallway and closes his eyes to visualize the text. Before he can answer, he disappears.

"What the heck just happened?" asks Megan.

"One moment he's here, the next he's gone," replies Lien.

Several minutes pass. Lien, Ethan, Arjun, and Megan are killing time by looking out over Empire Plaza when they spot a huge airship off in the distance. They follow it for a while, when out of nowhere, Jared pops back up.

"Sorry, guys. A friend of my uncle's pulled me out of the game."

"I didn't think that was possible," says Ethan.

"I guess it is. Before I could answer your question, I was standing on the home page. I figured something was up, so I deactivated."

"Heck of a surprise, huh?" says Ethan.

"Yeah, but not compared to what you're about to hear," replies Jared. "Supposedly, a student from one of the other schools died in the game."

Megan looks at Jared with concern. "It wasn't the guard I kicked off Mt. Egaleo, was it?" asks Megan. "He wasn't a student, and he wasn't wearing a wristband. I checked."

"No," replies Jared.

"I can't believe it," says Lien. "There are supposed to be safeguards."

Arjun sits down and holds his head with both hands, "Does anyone know what happened?"

"Not really," replies Jared. "Supposedly, the guy was fighting against the Persians in Thermopylae as a Spartan. We all know what happened to the Spartans, Thespians, and Thebans at Thermopylae."

Megan, her confidence in the game now shaken, tries to keep her emotions under wraps. "Still, real-life players aren't supposed to die. This sucks."

"The game developers must be going crazy," says Ethan. "Although they did have everyone sign releases."

"Still, Ethan!" says Lien, horrified. "This is not how it's supposed to go!"

"From what I understand, almost nobody knows about this incident yet. It's not public information, and I'd be surprised if we hear about it when we deactivate," Jared says, repeating what Gia told him to say.

"And we should keep it that way," replies Ethan. "No one needs to know about this. We need to get back to the game. Other teams might be getting ahead."

Jared looks at the stunned faces of Lien, Arjun, and Megan. Their trust in the game seems to be shattered. He cannot tell them that Gia figures that if the story does break, it will be covered up. With a little disinformation here, a little rumor there, and several seeds planted on social networking sites, the story will morph into something else. Maybe the player had a pre-existing condition that was exacerbated by the battle, or maybe he decided to play the game from a chair next to a pool and accidentally fell in and drowned.

Megan is the first to speak. "This is a big setback. Do we want to continue?"

Given the gravity of the situation, Jared doesn't want to influence his teammates one way or the other. Gia did say that they should keep playing, since so much is at stake. But Jared figures that each person must come to that conclusion individually.

"If my parents knew, they'd never let me continue," says Arjun.

"Who says they have to know?" replies Ethan.

The group debates the pros and cons of letting anyone know about what happened and whether they should continue with the game. In the end, all five decide to continue. They have come too far, and there is too much at stake to quit now. They pledge to look out for each other, and to make sure this glitch or bug in the software does not affect one of them.

"By the way, if no one knows about this, how did you find out?" asks Ethan, looking at Jared with skepticism.

Jared pretends not to hear the question. "OK, if we're all agreed to continue, here is what I can remember from the clue. It said, '*I am a great emperor around the third century BCE. Find what I have left behind, my legacy, and understand my story. Only then will you know where you must go.*'"

"Can't these clues ever be easy and just say, 'Go here'?" says Ethan, still wondering how Jared found out about the player's death. He decides not to push it; he will find out soon enough.

"Simple clues would be nice," replies Jared, leaning against the wall.

Megan walks along the hallway. She looks outside through the floor-to-ceiling windows. There are dozens of walkways and water-filled canals connecting the towers of the Afroeurasia Complex above and below the sixtieth floor. Megan stops abruptly. "Ha! I got it! This is the Silk Road!" she exclaims, pointing to the walkways.

"What are you talking about? The Silk Road wasn't one road," interjects Lien. "It was a network of overland and maritime trade routes that connected most of Afroeurasia, based on the lucrative Chinese silk trade. Many of those routes are still used today."

"Exactly! That's why there are so many walkways. The canals probably represent the maritime routes."

"That's a pretty good guess," Jared says, looking down ten stories to a canal that consists of half a pipe, roughly five feet wide, suspended fifty stories in the air. "But it still doesn't tell us where to go."

"I've solved the riddle," Lien says matter-of-factly, as she shifts the focus from her lenses to the group. "We need to go to China during the rule of Emperor Qin Shi Huang. He was China's first emperor. He united

China in 221 BCE after the Warring States Period and had a profound influence on Chinese history and culture."

"Sounds good to me," says Megan. "I saw a door down this hallway that leads to one of those walkways."

"Not so fast. Hold on a second," warns Arjun. "I think we need to go to India instead. Ashoka the Great, one of India's greatest emperors also ruled in the third century BCE. He had an epiphany that changed his life and he also left a major legacy. He converted to Buddhism and that religion became a major force throughout his empire."

"Looks like we need to split up again," suggests Jared. "I'll go with Lien."

"Good. I'll go with Arjun," Megan says impatiently. She wants to get going.

"I'll go with Megan and Arjun," adds Ethan.

Jared and Lien walk toward the door that Megan had pointed out earlier, while Arjun, Megan, and Ethan head a few floors down, where a canal seems to lead to the Indus Tower.

Jared walks toward a door in the outside wall of the Middle East Tower and pulls it open. The walkway is an all-glass rectangle. Four gray steel beams, one in each corner, span the space between the two towers, six hundred feet above the plaza. The floor, ceiling, and walls between the four beams consist entirely of a crystal-clear, glass-like material.

"I hope you're not afraid of heights," says Jared as he steps through the doorway onto the walkway. Through the glass floor, he can see all the way down to the plaza below, and his stomach contracts. It looks like he's stepping into thin air. "Just don't look down," he calls over his shoulder to Lien. He continues forward at a slight upward incline as the walkway between the towers gently swings back and forth. It reminds him of one of those old suspension bridges. Halfway across, he looks back and notices that Lien, after walking out a few feet, has stopped. She is frozen in place, staring down at the plaza below.

"Lien!" he calls.

She does not respond. She doesn't move forward or backward. She doesn't even lift her head. Jared turns around and quickly heads back. His speed makes the walkway swing even more, and she begins to shiver. When he reaches Lien, he puts his arm around her shoulder and tells her to look at him. After a little bit of coaxing, she does as he says. He then gently walks her back to the entry.

"OK, you're back at the beginning. Are you OK?"

"Whew!" Lien exhales deeply. "I didn't think I was afraid of heights, but this is high."

Jared notices that she seems to have held her breath for the entire time she was on the glass. "We can get you across this," he says. "I want you to do a few things. One, keep breathing, deep inhales and exhales." He points at his eyes with his two fingers. "Two, I want you to focus your eyes on mine. Don't look anywhere else—not down, not up, not sideways. OK?"

Lien nods.

"Put both of your arms on my shoulders for stability," says Jared, taking a step out onto the glass. "I will walk backward, and you will keep looking at me, OK?"

Lien nods again.

"If the bridge begins to swing, just keep walking; don't look anywhere. I'm going to hold you tightly, right on your shoulders, and remind you to breathe," continues Jared.

She nods again, not saying a word.

They slowly step out onto the glass and begin to walk across. The entire way, Jared quietly and softly encourages Lien. He can feel her nervousness. By speaking to her in a soothing voice and gently massaging her shoulders, he lets her know that she is safe. It takes them some time to get across the long walkway to the platform on the other side. When they reach the platform, Lien breathes a big sigh of relief and drops into his arms. "No one has ever been that gentle and encouraging. Thanks, Jared." She straightens up and gives him a big hug.

"You're welcome." He gives her arm a gentle squeeze, and they step through the doors into the China Tower. They are in a different part of the world now. The dark wooden floor creaks as Jared and Lien walk across the lobby. They are a few floors higher than they were before. The walls are covered with deep-green wallpaper. Red and black lacquered beams support the ceiling. Between the beams, golden dragons watch their every move. Nine beautifully covered silk chairs in bright blue, yellow, and green are scattered around the room. Seven hallways lead away from the lobby. Above each hallway is an empty name plaque.

Jared sits down in one of the chairs and quickly looks at the seven plaques. "One chance in seven to pick the right hall."

Lien sits next to him, leans back, and closes her eyes. "I think this was around the time of the Warring States Period, from 475 BCE to 221 BCE," she says. "The Zhou Dynasty ruled for close to nine hundred years, starting around 1100 BCE. They believed in a Mandate of Heaven that meant heaven would grant the ruler power as long as he governed justly and wisely. This mandate gave the rulers a great deal of authority, and they were able to centralize power and implement a feudal system, just like the one in Europe during the Middle Ages."

Jared looks at Lien, her long, black hair cascading around her neck and across her chest. Her brown eyes sparkle as she speaks. He thinks that although he's never viewed Lien as anything more than a smart classmate, she is actually quite attractive.

She continues, "Let me give you a summary of the Zhou Dynasty. I've got it right here on my lenses." She reads:

- "The Zhou Dynasty is divided into two periods, the Western Zhou and the Eastern Zhou. In total, it ruled from around 1100–221 BCE.
- "The dynasty became huge, and rulers were appointed, by inheritance, to oversee each territory.
- "They made progress in economics, science, culture, and politics.
- "Eventually, they began to lose control over their territories, and the states became more independent.
- "The Spring and Autumn Period overlapped with the Eastern Zhou. It was a time when seven powerful states appeared, and China's feudal system became more and more irrelevant.
- "The states expanded into other territories, assimilating other cultures and technologies such as fighting on horseback.
- "Finally, the dynasty fell and gave way to the Warring States Period. This instability led to an intellectual movement in which three major philosophies emerged: Confucianism, Taoism, and Legalism."

As he listens, Jared realizes that these philosophies still affect China's role in the world today.

Lien concludes, "Out of the Warring States Period, one of the former territories emerged as a dominant power: the state of Qin." As she says the name, the letters Q-I-N emerge on the plaque over the hallway on the far left. One after another, the names of the other six Warring States, emerge over the other hallways: Chu, Qi, Yan, Han, Wei, and Zhao. Lien gets up and looks at the door signs. "We need to head this way." She walks down the hall labeled "Qin." Jared, convinced that she's right, follows along without saying a word.

As she walks, she continues to talk about the Qin Dynasty of ancient China. "Qin Shi Huang became the leader of the state of Qin at age thirteen, and was emperor of all of China by his late thirties. For over five centuries the states had competed for power, but he unified them for the first time laying the foundation for present-day China. He was brutal in his conquests, incorporating the newest arts of war. He also made shrewd political moves. He made several major contributions to the unification of China: a standardized script, uniform systems of measurement and currency, and a tax system. He codified a legal system, got rid of hereditary rulers, and used a centrally appointed administrative system. He encouraged cultural reforms, expanded the network of roads and canals, and ordered that the walls, built earlier by the other states, to be connected into one wall in the northern frontier—the Great Wall. He unified the geography and philosophical tradition. He even built a capital at what is now the city of Xi'an."

"Busy guy," Jared comments.

"That was the positive," replies Lien. "Then there's the negative. There's lots of controversy about his legacy."

"Sounds like most emperors. You get the good and the bad," Jared says. "Most emperors left a series of moral questions. They were great leaders because they achieved many amazing things, but they often sacrificed thousands of lives and trampled on people's freedom to get it done."

"During his reign," continues Lien, "he didn't allow any scholarly discussions of the past. Books that disagreed with his thinking were burned, and scholars were killed—some even buried alive. Thousands died as he connected sections of the Great Wall. About three quarters of a million forced laborers worked for close to thirty-seven years to build his tomb. It was a replica of his kingdom. It wasn't discovered until the 1970's, becoming one of the greatest archaeological discoveries of the twentieth century. Archaeologists estimate that there are seven thousand soldiers, chariots, and horses built of clay to defend him in the afterlife."

Jared, with a thoughtful look, says, "My dad used to say that a lot of stories about history have to be checked out to ensure they are accurate, especially as new evidence is discovered."

"I agree," replies Lien, "but we know quite a bit about the army that was supposed to protect him in the afterlife."

"You mean The Terracotta Army."

"Yes," replies Lien. "And that's where I think we need to go. The Qin Shi Huang Necropolis."

"I think you're right," adds Jared slowly as he thinks about the clue, "but we have to go to a site that takes us to the Necropolis today, not during the third century BCE. The clue said, '*Find the legacy.*' What better place to learn about someone's legacy than a burial ground that is also a museum and archaeological site."

After a second, Lien replies, "That's brilliant. I wouldn't have caught that." They walk a little farther down the hallway to a door on the left labeled "Excavation: Qin Shi Huang Necropolis." She opens the door and steps through.

Meanwhile, Megan, Arjun, and Ethan decide to take the stairs down to the fiftieth floor instead of using the elevator, especially after their last ride. They emerge from the stairwell directly across from the door leading to a canal. As he opens the door, Ethan calls out, "Shoot! Why now? Sorry, guys, my mom just pinged me. I've got to stop the game. Something urgent came up. Text me your next location and I'll catch up."

Odd, thinks Megan. Something about how Ethan just told them he had to leave doesn't sound genuine. She looks at him with a quizzical expression, then quickly says, "Sure. We'll let you know." Turning around, she looks out over the pipe full of water and the small two-person kayak moored to the Middle East Tower. Megan rarely feels nervous, but now, when she looks over the edge, a cold shiver runs down her spine. Paddling five hundred feet in the air in an open canal only five feet wide, with no net or side rails, sounds a bit crazy. Some of these Web sites are truly nuts.

Arjun hops into the front of the kayak, and Megan takes the seat behind him. They start to paddle on the calm water and make good progress. Then, as they pass the halfway mark, waves begin to arise—ripples at first, but then they get larger and larger.

"We've got to paddle faster!" yells Megan, as the water becomes more and more violent and waves spill over the sides of the canal. "These waves can pitch us over the side if we don't hurry." Soon, it feels as if they are riding Class IV river rapids. Megan is doing everything she can to keep the kayak centered in the canal as they race toward the Indus Tower. A wave submerges them, and they come up seconds later, soaking wet.

"This canal seems a lot longer than the walkway above," yells Arjun, trying to be heard over the roar of the water.

"Yeah. It feels like a water ride gone out of control," Megan shouts back.

Several feet from the Indus Tower, the waves abruptly stop, and the water becomes calm and clear again. Megan and Arjun paddle to a landing and drag the kayak out of the water. As they enter the tower, Arjun catches a glimpse of the sign on the door.

"Did you see that?" he asks Megan. "It said 'Himalayan River System. Beware: Possible Rapids.' No wonder it was a wild ride."

"I still think it was an out-of-control water ride," she replies. "I saw this canal from the sixtieth floor, and it was calm until we started to cross it."

Arjun walks toward the fiftieth-floor lobby. "Let's sit down for a second and figure out where we need to go." They each sit on an ornately carved Indian chair and search their contact lenses.

"Hey, listen to this." Arjun begins to read.

Mauryan Empire
- "Chandragupta Maurya, in 321 BCE, built one of the largest empires in India to date by unifying smaller Aryan kingdoms.
- "He increased the centralized government's control over regional kingdoms, and divided India into provinces.
- "They developed a single currency, assessed taxes, and enforced laws.
- "The empire had a large army of close to seven hundred thousand soldiers, and a secret police force to watch for treason and protect the government.
- "Chandragupta Maurya ruled for twenty-three years, then gave the throne to his son, Bindurasa, and became a Jain ascetic.
- "Driven by agriculture, the empire became powerful and wealthy because it was at the crossroads of a commercial network linking the Pacific Rim, Southwest Asia, and the Mediterranean."

Arjun continues, "There's a map here that shows it stretched from present-day Pakistan and Afghanistan through the Indus River Valley, eastward through the Ganges River Valley, to present-day Bangladesh and down the Indian subcontinent. That's big."

Megan, meanwhile, reads an excerpt about how some archaeologists and historians argue that the theory of an Aryan invasion in India is an invention of nineteenth- and twentieth-century British and Germans, that it is incorrect, and that it leads to distorted opinions about India. Others have different views. Where there is agreement is that the Aryan culture and beliefs did spread throughout India.

Megan is only half listening to what Arjun is reading. As he finishes, she adds, "It seems like the same patterns come up over and over again. Emperors centralize the government, divide an empire into provinces to manage the complexity, create a single currency, collect taxes, and so on. Many empires began at a crossroads of trade or as part of expanding commercial networks. But we need to find something about Ashoka. Isn't that where we need to go?"

"You're right. There's a link here to Ashoka. I'll send it to you."

Megan receives the link and opens the page in her contact lenses. It is a short summary.

Ashoka's Life

- Son of Bindurasa, Ashoka spent his early years in the Mauryan armies and was twice exiled by his father.
- After Bindurasa's death, a war of succession began. Some references suggest Ashoka killed ninety-nine of his one-hundred half brothers to ascend the throne around 269 BCE.
- After the bloody battle of Kalinga, he underwent a major transformation, converted to Buddhism, and become a just and merciful king. He made Buddhism the state religion and fostered an era of religious tolerance.
- He had thirty-three edicts and inscriptions carved into pillars of stone forty to fifty feet high, boulders, or cave walls. Built thousands of stupas (monuments) and viharas (monasteries), sent missionaries to ancient Rome and the Egyptian city of Alexandria, and pursued an official policy of nonviolence.

- He built roads, hospitals, wells, and shelters. Spent money on public works. Free medical care for people and animals.
- Ashoka left behind the first ancient language in India since the time of Harappa.
- He ruled for forty years and took the empire to its greatest level.

"Whew!" says Megan, turning off the search. "A whole life in less than a page. That was exhausting. It says that most of what we know about his life came from stone edicts and oral legends."

"Yes," replies Arjun. "In India, it is sometimes difficult to separate history from mythology. Stories often included real events, so it is hard to know where the story ends and where the myth begins."

"Not only in India," replies Megan. "Myths and stories are interpretations and don't necessarily contain facts or evidence, but they often are based on some truth. They can still be a powerful tool to help us interpret the past."

"How do you know that?" asks Arjun in surprise. Although Megan is bright, he never thought she was very interested in history.

"I enjoy the stories and myths of woman warriors and warrior goddesses. I've done a lot of reading about powerful women in all cultures. But I've done the most research on Celtic women."

"Interesting," says Arjun. "I never would have guessed," he adds facetiously, then smiles.

"I don't talk about it much," says Megan, getting up from the chair. "The riddle said, 'Understand my story.' I wonder about the stories surrounding Ashoka's conversion. That battle of Kalinga sounds horrific. Some say that more than one hundred thousand were killed on each side, and thousands were deported. I think we should go to a site that describes the story of Kalinga and the conversion."

"Yeah, I agree," replies Arjun.

CHAPTER 26

JARED AND LIEN STEP THROUGH THE DOOR AND STAND inside the rammed-earth walls of the necropolis complex that Emperor Qin Shi Huang had constructed as a microcosm of the palace, empire, and entire world.

Jared looks around. "This place is huge."

"Yeah. But for a major tourist attraction, it is strangely empty," adds Lien.

Jared pulls up a Chinese map with an English translation on his lenses. The tomb city contains administrative buildings, stables, cemeteries, and the 550-yard-by-500-yard tomb of the emperor. The entire city has an area of almost one and a quarter square miles. Historians believe that the tomb consists of seven and a half miles of city walls including thirty-foot-high outer and inner city walls. He quickly scans a description of the necropolis. Six hundred and fifty yards east of Qin Shi Huang's Mausoleum, which is larger than the Great Pyramid in Egypt, are the pits containing the Terracotta Army.

"Where do we start?" Jared wonders aloud.

"Most of the mausoleum is still unexcavated, including the tomb," replies Lien. "The interior is supposedly as big as a football field, and they used quicksilver to recreate a hundred rivers from ancient China, which were kept in motion by machines."

"Machines more than 2,200 years ago? That sounds more like a myth."

"Modern scientific analysis using earth-core samples has confirmed that there were rivers of mercury inside," says Lien, "and that they were laid out like a map of China."

"Don't want to go in there, even if we could. Why don't we head over to the Terracotta Army?" suggests Jared as he continues to scan his lenses. "I just don't know which pit. It looks like there are four main pits—and they're huge." Jared reads that the first pit is longer than two soccer fields, three times as wide, and sixteen feet deep, with sloping entrances on each side. It contains eleven corridors with an estimated six thousand buried soldiers wielding spears, halberds, bronze daggers, axes, bronze swords, crossbows, and machetes. Clusters of cavalrymen holding bronze swords, which look as sharp and smooth as the day they were created more than two thousand years ago, stand at the ready. A coating of chromium oxide helped resist corrosion and tarnish. The Qin Dynasty saw extensive developments in science and in the use of metals such as chrome, iron, and mercury. War chariots wait closely behind the infantry and cavalry. The life-size statues stand on mats. The tunnels were originally covered with logs and then buried. The second pit houses mixed military forces, cavalry and infantry units, crossbowmen—sixty standing and more than 150 squatting. More than sixty war chariots await orders. The third pit is the command center for the other two pits, but the commander-in-chief is missing. Pit Four is empty.

"Let's head to Pit One," says Lien. "It is the largest, and it was the first to be discovered."

Lien and Jared walk across a plaza and enter a massive, sixteen-thousand-square-meter building with a twenty-two-meter-high ceiling. They are the only two people inside. In front of them stand two thousand unearthed soldiers with solid, kiln-fired legs and hollow upper bodies, accompanied by twenty wooden chariots.

As the two teenagers step out of the shadows along the wall, the soldiers—no two alike—see the intruders and begin to clang their bronze weapons against each other. Jared grabs Lien and quickly jumps back against the wall, making sure not to turn his back to the soldiers. "What the heck is going on?" asks Jared as he looks at Lien with concern. "I thought they were made out of clay."

"This is not good," whispers Lien.

The noise of the clanging swords and shields is deafening. Soldiers, some with paint still on their faces, adjust their weapons, ready to march. Charioteers and cavalrymen quiet their horses as they tighten the reins. Others slowly head toward an open crossbow container. Several commanders climb out of the pit.

"Maybe it's part of the exhibit. A new, interactive way to entertain tourists," offers Lien, trying to sound positive, just as a lone spear grazes her shoulder, drawing blood. "Then again, maybe not."

"That spear was meant to kill. Let's get outta here," yells Jared as he searches along the back wall for another exit. He pounds his fist against the wall. "Not again! These disappearing doors are driving me nuts!"

The order to attack is given. The soldiers slowly and methodically march out of the pits and head straight for Jared and Lien. Luckily, the soldiers who headed to the crossbow container have to wait until the infantrymen move out so they have a clear shot at the intruders.

"We need to get out in the open and out of this enclosed area. This is a death trap!" yells Lien.

They crouch down and sprint for an exit that finally emerges at the other end of the enormous hall. They run as fast as they can. Arrows and spears begin to fly.

Jared leaps over one of the corridors just as he sees the outline of a warrior emerge. As Lien jumps, the soldier extends to his full height of six feet, two inches and grabs her leg in midair. He pulls her down into the corridor and is about to use his short sword when she kicks him in the chest with all her might. The solder crumbles like ancient pottery. Thank goodness, their torsos are hollow, Lien thinks.

Jared extends his hand to help her up. "Great, now you've destroyed a priceless artifact. The curator is going to love you," he says, trying to lighten the mood.

Lien, taking him seriously, replies, "If an ancient artifact attacks me, I don't care if it's priceless or one of a kind, I'm fighting back."

Jared looks at Lien for a moment. He's never seen this side of her. They run along an earth-rammed partition wall between two corridors, jumping over spear and sword thrusts from the soldiers below. They quickly exit the building before the next wave of arrows launches. All they hear are the marching soldiers and charioteers preparing to continue the attack.

"Let's see if we can catch that bus," yells Jared. They sprint across the open space in front of the building to a departing bus whose doors have not yet closed. As they jump aboard through the rear door, they notice that there are no passengers and no driver.

"I'm not sure this was such a good idea," replies Lien between breaths.

"At least it will get us away from those soldiers," replies Jared. "We can jump off again. Maybe over there." He points toward a clump of undergrowth and trees at the base of the mound containing the mausoleum.

"I hope no one saw us," says Lien a few minutes later, as they hide among the trees. She hopes they'll be safe for a few minutes.

Jared sinks down and leans against a tree. "What the heck is going on with these Web sites? Who reprogrammed those soldiers to attack so quickly? They noticed us as soon as we arrived."

"It's a game," replies Lien. "But it does seem odd."

Jared wonders if someone is continuing to manipulate the information or to change the game, and if so, why? Could the prophecy be coming true? Are the soldiers doing this to anyone who enters or just to him? His questions just keep piling up.

Lien sits down across from him. "You seem lost in thought. What's on your mind?"

"It's just odd that terracotta soldiers would attack us," he replies.

"Like I said, it's probably all part of the game," says Lien. "Imagine how boring it would be if all we did was come here and look for clues."

"I guess you're right," answers Jared, although he is not fully convinced.

Lien continues to describe ancient China under Qin Shi Huang. She explains how there is a lack of written historical records and how many contemporary Chinese scholars disagree with the historian Sima Qian's assessment. However, Jared isn't listening. Something behind one of the trees has gotten his attention. Holding himself very still, he keeps his head low and cautiously peers straight ahead.

"Jared, were you listening?" asks Lien.

"Shh! Keep your head down. I think someone is watching us," he whispers.

Lien scoots to his side and looks into the clump of trees, following Jared's gaze. "Where?"

Jared indicates with his chin. "There, to the left of that big tree, in the green thicket. He's hard to see, but it looks like a camouflaged terracotta soldier. He's wearing body armor and his hair is braided in a topknot. The figure's neck, face, and ears are green."

"Out of the Terracotta Warriors who still retain some of their original paint, most have pink faces. Only one is green. The initial discovery of this warrior led to a big debate in archaeology. Some thought the green was a mistake; some thought he was a spiritual leader in the military; others thought it signified youthfulness and bravery," Lien whispers behind her hand as she remembers the article in which she read the story. "One theory came from a student who suggested that this might be a sniper in camouflage."

"An assassin!" says Jared, trying to keep his voice low.

"We'd better get out of here," replies Lien, anxiously. "These assassins were deadly accurate."

Jared takes one more look at the soldier, who remains kneeling, controlling his bow. He makes eye contact with Jared, and then carefully wraps a piece of paper around the arrow, pulls the bowstring, and with one fluid motion, releases it, firing the arrow straight at Jared.

Jared sees the arrow leave the bowstring in slow motion. He looks into the warrior's eyes and senses that the arrow will miss him and embed itself in a nearby tree. The warrior is not a killer. He is trying to send a message.

A flash of light catches his eye and he looks up past the Terracotta Warrior. Several feet behind him, another warrior, dressed in a camouflaged suit, and definitely not made of terracotta, aims his repeating crossbow at Lien and fires several bronze bolts in rapid succession. Instantly, Jared yells, "Watch out!" and throws himself in front of Lien, directly into the path of the bolts.

The first two bolts go high, but the second two slam into his shoulder. One goes into the soft tissue and the other hits his clavicle. Jared grabs his shoulder and screams as he falls backward into Lien. They both tumble to the ground. A searing pain shoots down his arm and across his chest, up to his neck. He's never felt pain like this. Lien looks up and catches a glimpse of both warriors as they disappear into the thicket. She looks down at Jared, who is turning pale. She cradles him in her arms.

She hopes the bolts weren't dipped in poison, a favorite strategy of the ancient Chinese.

"Jared! Jared! Stay with me!" Tears begin to roll down her cheeks, but she pushes them back. She gently places him on the ground, gathers her strength, and pulls the bolts out of his shoulder. Jared only moans.

"Listen, Jared. I need you to do exactly as I say," Lien continues forcefully. "I'm going to put your finger next to the home button. I need you to press it and say 'home.' As soon as you get there, say 'disengage.' Can you do that?"

Jared drifts in and out of consciousness and can barely understand her. He wills his eyes open. "Yeah. I think so."

"OK, here we go. I'm going with you, but I don't know if we'll arrive at the same time."

Jared looks up at Lien, grits his teeth and with a low voice says, "Wait. The arrow. Look at the note." He breathes deeply and then continues, "Keep playing. We must win!"

Lien wants to ask him why winning is so important when suddenly he disappears.

CHAPTER 27

ARJUN AND MEGAN ARRIVE ON THE SECOND STORY OF AN almost destroyed villa. In the hallway, a sign reads "Legends and Myths of Ashoka the Terrible/Ashoka the Great." Arjun remembers that the Indian Emperor Ashoka lived from around 300 to 230 BCE. Megan strolls past the sign, out onto the second-story balcony, and looks down at a lone man walking through the city, which is filled with destroyed houses and scattered corpses. The war with Kalinga is over, and it is the next day. The man looks remarkably similar to a drawing of Ashoka that she saw on the Web. As the man walks, he becomes sick with grief and then cries out, "What have I done? If this is a victory, what's a defeat? Is this a victory or a defeat? Is this justice or injustice? Is it gallantry or a rout? Is it valor to kill innocent children and women? Do I do it to widen the empire and for prosperity or to destroy the other's kingdom and splendor? One has lost her husband; someone else, a father; someone, a child; someone, an unborn infant. What is this debris of the corpses? Are these marks of victory or defeat? Are these vultures, crows, and eagles the messengers of death or evil?"

Arjun follows Megan onto the balcony and quietly says, "That's one example of a legend about Ashoka. There are many stories about how Ashoka's epiphany occurred."

Megan waits, but nothing else happens. They both walk back into the building and out of the room. Then Megan spots a first-floor terrace on the opposite side of the building. She walks down the crumbling stairs and out through the doors onto the dirt terrace, and stares out toward a river. Arjun follows her to the terrace.

She looks out over a vast battleground and a wide river. She can see thousands of dead warriors and slaughtered horses and elephants. The river is red with blood. It is deathly silent. Ashoka walks by. He seems to be basking in his glorious victory. Suddenly, a beggar steps out of the red water of the river, carrying a dripping bundle in his arms. "Mighty King," the beggar says, approaching Ashoka and holding up his bundle. "You are able to take so many thousands of lives. Surely you can give back one life…to this dead child?"

"This is another example of the legend about the emperor," says Arjun.

Megan reflects on how difficult it is for a person to change, yet one key event can transform a human being. Arjun continues, "Some say the beggar was a Buddhist monk. Others say the beggar was the Buddha himself. All that is certain is that Ashoka never raised his sword again. To this day, this river is called Daya—compassion."

Megan says nothing. She leans against a short rock wall and reflects on the epiphany that Ashoka experienced. Oral histories are definitely another way to learn about the past, she thinks.

She is still gazing across the blood-drenched banks of the river when they hear more footsteps coming from the second-story balcony. Arjun and Megan quickly jump across the low wall separating the terrace from the riverbank and hide behind the building. Megan peeks around the corner and sees an athletic young woman with harsh features giving orders to several young people, all wearing wristbands. They are about to climb over the wall themselves, when, as if in a replay, Ashoka begins to walk by again, and they stop. Staying against the wall, Arjun and Megan quietly make their way farther around the side of the building. Although

Megan can no longer see what is happening in front of the terrace, she can hear the beggar say, "Mighty King."

She is thinking of running around toward the front of the building, when she takes one last look across the battlefield. Everything is red, drenched in blood, except for one slender rectangle. In the middle of the field lies a shimmering blue silk scarf. The shimmering blue reminds her of the blue cave in Marathon. This could be an important link. The scarf is fluttering in the warm, humid breeze, as if drawing her in. She feels she must investigate.

"Arjun, wait here, I'll be right back."

"Where are you going?"

She points to the scarf.

"It could be a trap," says Arjun. But he's a second too late.

Megan sprints out into the open, wondering how such a beautiful piece of silk got into such an ugly place. She kneels and carefully picks up the fabric, letting it slide through her fingers. It is so soft, and yet it seems to have an energy all its own. The scarf slowly and gently wraps itself around her wrists and hands. Then, in an instant, the silk draws tight— it *is* a trap after all, thinks Megan. She tries to free her hands, but with little success. The silk begins to rise. Her hands and arms rise with it. She struggles to free herself, but the silk pulls her hands above her head. As she looks down, she realizes that her feet have left the ground. The scarf is pulling her into the sky. Arjun runs across the battlefield and jumps up, trying to reach her feet, but she is a few inches too high. The scarf continues to pull her skyward. Arjun looks up after her.

"Go! I'll text you where I end up," Megan yells down. She can see several other students staring at her from the villa. Arjun nods and touches his wristband.

The initial pain she felt as her arms were pulled skyward is gone. She floats along behind the scarf as if sitting on a magic carpet, flying high above the vast lands along the Silk Road. At first, she thinks she is truly flying over Central Asia. However, as the scarf flies beneath the cloud cover, just above the ground, Megan can see information and artifacts below. They show an intermingling of cultures—Central Asian, Indian, Persian, and Greek. As she takes a closer look, she realizes that she is not flying across a physical landscape but rather across hundreds of Web sites, all linked, describing the cultural history of Central Asia. As she flies, she thinks about the pastoral nomads from the semi-arid steppes and deserts of Africa and Eurasia, and how their influence and migrations became a major force of change across the entire region. She thinks about the Mongols and the Turks, as she realizes that the scarf is taking her east, to the Far East.

CHAPTER 28

SLOWLY, MEGAN STARTS TO RECOGNIZE HER DESTINA-TION. HER GUESS is reinforced as she flies over several Web sites depicting images of the Himalayas. Then the scarf takes her above the vast, arid landscape of the Taklamakan Desert. Sand dunes rise over six hundred feet above the plains. The air is dry and sandy; it looks like one of the most hostile environments Megan has ever seen. She detects a few oasis towns with large camel caravans stopping for supplies, water, and food. This must be part of the Silk Road, trade routes along which goods are carried from the East to the West.

She then flies above the barren landscape of the Gobi Desert. She realizes that the scarf must be some kind of link, and it probably is taking her to ancient China. She remembers the short-lived Qin Dynasty around 220 BCE but cannot recall what came after it. She vaguely remembers from class that after Emperor Qin Shi Huang's death, there was significant unrest, and a subsequent emperor raised taxes and enlarged the army. Peasants were bitter over the high taxes, harsh punishments, and labor quotas. There were executions, rebellions, murders, suicides, and power struggles. The state was in turmoil. However, beyond that, she's not sure. She activates her contact lenses and searches.

At first, she finds a reference to a primary source, the *Records of the Grand Historian* by Sima Qian, the prefect of the Grand Scribes. Considered to be the father of Chinese history, he lived from 145–90 BCE during the Han Dynasty and chronicled over two thousand years of

Chinese history. It must be the Han, she thinks. Sima Qian seems similar to Herodotus, the father of Greek history. She scans further and finds that the first three chapters were first translated into English in 1894, some say with the sole purpose of discrediting Sima Qian and all of ancient history as recorded by the Chinese. As she flies over the desert, she wonders how much of history has been reinterpreted by later generations, with each interpretation colored by the era in which the historian lived.

The original text is too hard to understand, and Megan keeps scanning. She finds a nice summary of the Han Dynasty and begins to read, barely noticing that the scarf has taken her above a major dust storm engulfing the desert below.

She reads about Liu Bang, who emerged from the peasant class and founded the Han Dynasty in 202 BCE. It was the second imperial dynasty in China, and it lasted almost four hundred years. Liu Bang destroyed rival kings and centralized the government. China under the Han Dynasty was a highly structured, agricultural-based society, with the emperor at the top of the social order. Kings and governors were on the second tier; officials, nobles, and scholars were on the third, followed by peasants, then artisans, merchants, soldiers, and finally, slaves. Megan sees how a strong central government and the teachings of Confucius became key parts of Chinese life, as they remain today.

When Liu Bang's great-grandson, Wudi, took the throne, he expanded the government by increasing the civil service. Government jobs were highly desired. Whereas before they were awarded to family members, under Wudi a set of formal examinations were implemented. The Han emperors built roads and canals, expanded the army, and extended the Great Wall. For greater unification, the Han encouraged conquered peoples to become part of the empire. People intermarried, schools were established to teach Confucian principles, and several writers wrote about China and Chinese history.

As Megan continues to fly, she looks around at the brilliant blue sky and thinks about the significant role that strong central governments have played in Chinese history. She returns to scanning her lenses and learns that paper was invented in 105 BCE, leading to the spread of books and education. The Chinese collar harness for horses allowed them to pull heavier loads than horses anywhere else. A two-bladed plow, the wheelbarrow, and water mills all improved the efficiency of agriculture. Farming was considered the most important occupation since there were close to sixty million people to feed. Although commerce and merchants were considered less important, manufacturing was critical, with the government establishing monopolies in several areas such as salt, iron, and silk. China officially became a Confucian state, and it prospered.

As she browses one of the sites on her lenses, she sees a comparison of the various geographies. In 100 BCE, Rome was a republic, Celtic and Germanic tribes roamed Northern Europe, Polynesians had colonized the Pacific islands, and Indian tribes lived throughout the Americas.

She scans several more pages about how, aside from trade, there was little contact between China and other advanced civilizations, such as the Greeks, the Romans, and the Mauryans. Several articles about the Chinese Imperial Court catch her eye. It was a very dangerous place full of palace intrigues, politics, evil plots, and shifting alliances. Royal advisors and eunuchs vied for power and influence. Emperors often had several wives and concubines. This created an environment in which wives and concubines would compete with each other for power. Succession often became a major issue.

Megan is so engrossed in reading about imperial Chinese politics that she does not notice that she is no longer flying but rather hovering above the ground. Without warning, the scarf unwinds itself from her wrists, and Megan drops a few feet into the middle of a large library behind an elaborately carved, red-lacquered screen. It takes her a moment to get her bearings. She has no idea where she has landed. The sign above reads "Dongguan Imperial Library." Two young women who look to be royalty are huddled together at a nearby table, whispering. Megan can barely hear what they are saying. She sneaks closer. As she gets into hearing range, she is grabbed from behind, and a powerful hand is clamped across her mouth.

"Shh! They cannot know you are here," says a high-pitched female voice. "Empress Deng is in a foul mood today, and no one is allowed to disturb her when she speaks with Ban Zhao."

Megan thinks, Empress Deng? She's read about her.

"Will you be quiet?" asks the voice.

Megan nods. The hands release her slowly. She spins around, ready to attack, and then stops in surprise. The voice belongs to a middle-aged man with gray hair. He's about her height, and he is wearing the imperial clothes of the palace.

"Who are you?" asks Megan.

"I would rather not say," replies the man. "Only that I serve the royal court."

Megan remembers reading about eunuchs. They were employed to protect the chastity of the thousands of imperial concubines, ensuring that only the Chinese emperor had access, and to maintain an aura of sacredness and secrecy. Since eunuchs are incapable of having children, they could not start a dynasty and seize power. Scholar-officials, on the other hand, could. Tensions and rivalries between eunuchs and Confucian officials, as well as between wives and concubines, were strong. Everyone had to watch his or her back constantly. Life-threatening court intrigue and power struggles took the lives of many. These were a key theme in the ancient Chinese imperial court. Succession was always a big issue because of the high infant mortality rates. For eunuchs in imperial China, it was a great honor to serve in the palace, protecting the emperor's harem, acting as spies, and often becoming advisers. Since the emperor was the recipient of the Mandate of Heaven, which justified his rule, there was no challenge to his authority. Eunuchs were restrained enough and were allowed to see the emperor's private life, thereby gaining access and influence. They often became wealthy and powerful, mostly orchestrating things from behind the scenes.

Just then, Empress Deng and Ban Zhao end their discussion and walk toward the exit.

Megan quickly brings up the link that she had been looking at earlier on her lenses, and scans the tumultuous history of Empress Dowager Deng and Ban Zhao, poet, writer, and China's earliest known female historian. Ban Zhao, born into a family of imperial scholars, tutored the leading women of the court and taught the empress classical writing, mathematics, astronomy, history, and the classics. She completed the *Hanshu*, a history of the first two hundred years of the Han Dynasty. This work had been started by her father, Ban Bia, and continued by her brother, Ban Gu. She finished it after her brother was killed. Megan figures that the time must be around 110 CE.

As soon as the two women exit the library, Megan heads toward the table to look at what they were discussing. Maybe there will be a clue.

"Wait," orders the eunuch in a commanding tone. There is a faint trace of worry in his voice. For a minute, he wonders if Megan is a spy sent by the Empress Dowager to test his loyalty, or maybe by Emperor An. Maybe they are testing him to see how he deals with other women of the court. He dismisses his worry. This woman is too different.

As Megan begins to read the text on the table, her face becomes flushed with disbelief. She lightly pounds the table with her fist, and then turns. "What's this?"

The court servant looks around to see if anyone is watching. "This is the set of rules for young women written by Madame Zhao, *Lessons for a Woman.*"

Megan can barely contain herself. She reads some of the phrases— "implicit obedience," "womanly qualifications," "husbands controlling wives," "women serving husbands," "let her modestly yield to others, respect others, and put others first, herself last."

"Yes," replies the servant. "Confucius did not say much about women, so Madame Zhao wrote an instruction manual for her daughters on how to live a Confucian life. It is natural and proper that women are subservient to men. Come, we must go."

Megan, tense and disagreeing with what is written, wants to argue with the eunuch. A voice inside her tells her that it will be of no use. These are different views, cultural norms, and practices, and this is a different time. She has to try to understand, even if she disagrees. She remembers the discussions with her diplomat father about cultural and historical empathy. She also remembers reading that Chinese society and Confucian doctrine did accord mothers and mothers-in-law quite a bit of honor and power within the family. In addition, even though less than 10 percent of Chinese society was literate at the time, some upper-class women pursued education and even became scholars.

She takes a deep breath and slowly backs away from the table with her head bowed. Some of the ideas aren't so bad, such as respecting the elders and acting with humility. Ancient Chinese society wasn't alone in putting women in an inferior role. She remembers that even in Athens, the heart of democracy, women had fewer rights than men did. They could not vote or own property, they were not citizens, and they were controlled first by their fathers and then by their husbands.

As Megan regains her composure, she tells herself that she will not be subservient to anyone. She sees the servant's eyes following her every move. He seems quite displeased with her outburst and acts like he is not sure what to do. She must calm his concern or he might raise the alarm. She swallows her pride and apologizes, lowers her head, and bows. This seems to calm him for the moment.

"We must be careful. There are eyes everywhere, even in the women's quarters. Come, come." He quietly scampers through various hallways and rooms. Megan follows close on his heels, admiring intricate carvings and royal splendor.

As they move down a richly adorned hallway, he grabs her arm and in one swoop pulls her around himself and pushes her toward a beautifully carved wooden door. "Exit through here. Look for the exit. You will then know what to do. Let no one see you enter or leave." The eunuch opens the door and pushes her through. Only then does she see that the door is painted in a glowing, deep-blue lacquer. The door shuts behind her and disappears.

Emerging in a dimly lit room, she tries to adjust her eyes. She's in a theater with twelve silk-covered recliners in three rows of four, all facing a large digital screen. She looks around the room and notices that there are no doors or windows. She feels trapped. She explores the walls, moving curtains aside and searching with her fingers for a crack or something that would indicate a hidden door or window. After searching for several minutes, she gives up and plops herself down into one of the chairs. As her weight hits the chair, the room goes dark, and the deep voice of a commentator engulfs her.

"Welcome to the story of the Han Dynasty, 200 BCE to 220 CE." A video starts to play on the screen, and Megan watches as the Han Empire comes alive. She's already read much of the information on her lenses. But she hadn't known that the Han Dynasty fell and then returned. In the process, the rich became richer and the poor became poorer, due to the way land was divided and taxes were assessed. The first period was known as the Western Han, then it was interrupted by Wang Mang and the Xin Dynasty, and then there was the Eastern Han. The East/West nomenclature comes from the relative position of the capital.

At the palace, advisers, servants, and rival families competed for succession—chaos reigned in the palace while peasants revolted in the countryside. Wang Mang overthrew the Han rulers and tried to restore order, but with no success. After a great flood, the peasant revolts continued, and the wealthy who opposed Wang Mang's policies rebelled, eventually assassinating him. Soon thereafter, a member of the former imperial family took control of the throne. For several decades, the second Han Dynasty, the Eastern Han, was quite prosperous. The government sent soldiers and merchants westward to control the Silk Road. Besides the overland route, a maritime Silk Road started. However, the same patterns of economic imbalance, political intrigue, and social unrest also toppled that second Han Dynasty in 220 CE.

The video ends. As the credits go by on the screen, the lights come up to a dim glow. Megan gets up when she senses something behind her. A silk scarf slips around her neck. At first, she thinks it is the blue scarf that led her here, and she does not react. But then she asks herself why a link would wrap itself around her neck. She quickly jams her palm between her neck and the scarf as it draws tight, too tight. She kicks with her legs, knocking over the recliners in front of her. Slowly, she is dragged backwards across the recliner. She finds herself on her back looking up into a girl's face. It is the young woman from the terrace in Kalinga. She recognizes her hair, intense eyes, and harsh features. For the first time, Megan has a chance to study the young woman's eyes, which are cold, calculating, and full of an arrogance that assumes Megan has already lost.

The assailant pulls the scarf even tighter. "Your end has come. We will win this quest. The artifact is ours."

"Who are you?" whispers Megan, barely able to say the words.

"I am the last person you will see for now."

For a second, Megan thinks that some people take this game way too seriously. But then she remembers the prophecy. She fights for air and tries to refocus on the moment. Her hand is keeping the scarf from strangling her, but she can't match her attacker's strength. Megan knows that she only has a few seconds of consciousness left. She can't do anything with her free hand. The attacker stands just out of reach. Staring at the ceiling, Megan notices a trapdoor. That must be the exit the eunuch meant! Her mind races through options on how to fight her attacker. Finally, she decides to close her eyes and let her body go limp. Her adversary, overconfident, will believe she has won and release the tension in the scarf.

Megan senses the change when it comes. Summoning her remaining energy, she kicks her legs up toward her head, rolls back onto her shoulders, and grabs the young woman in a headlock between her legs. The attacker realizes she's just made a dreadful mistake. Megan flings her into the chairs in front. Having miscalculated, the attacker lets go of the scarf in order to protect herself, but it's too late. She hits her head against the steel frame of an overturned recliner and goes limp.

Megan notices the wristband on the young woman and thinks that although the woman looks young, her eyes are not those of a student—more like those of a seasoned warrior. Megan then stacks several recliners on top of one another and scrambles up through the trap door in the ceiling, kicking down the recliners afterwards to hide her escape route. Once through, she enters a palace room decorated with gold-and-red wallpaper. On a couch just a foot off the ground, surrounded by ivory, rhinoceros horns, tortoiseshell, and silk, sits a man who looks like a Roman emissary, reading.

Megan notices a couple stacks of books on his desk. One stack is titled *Naturalis Historia,* by Pliny the Elder, a Roman author. The second, shorter stack is titled *Geographica,* by a Greek named Strabo. The trapdoor must have been another link. She wonders if she is in Rome, even though the room looks Chinese.

Not looking up from the ancient text, the emissary says in a deep voice, "A most fascinating encyclopedia of ancient knowledge. Did you know that Pliny writes that the large trade with India, Seres—the ancient Greek and Roman term for inhabitants of eastern Central Asia, meaning silk—and the Arabian Peninsula takes close to one hundred million sesterces from the Roman Empire every year?"

Megan does not answer. She can't quite believe that there were already trade imbalances in the ancient world. Who would have thought?

The emissary lays down what he is reading and looks up. "Ah! There you are! I've been waiting." He looks at Megan carefully. "You look to have Celtic blood in you. Are you a Celt?" The emissary does not let her answer. "I was told that you would be different. Strabo, the Greek, wrote so eloquently, 'The whole race is fanatically fond of warfare. They are vociferous and act on impulse. When they are upset, they immediately gather together in groups in the open, to urge each other on to warfare, without the slightest preparation or reflection.'" He waits to see Megan's reaction.

She says nothing, holding back as best she can. She hates these stereotypes and assumptions. She recognizes that the emissary is quoting from a Greek historian who might have been a little biased. A lot of what was written at that time was sketchy and possibly biased—authors often had their own agenda. Although the Greeks and Romans did initially have peaceful trading encounters with the Celts, they also learned about the Celts' skills in battle.

The emissary is a bit surprised to find someone with Megan's heritage in ancient China, but dismisses the thought. After all, he is only following orders. "No matter," he continues. "You will be perfect. We shall leave immediately. Imperator Caesar Marcus Aurelius Antoninus Augustus awaits our return." The emissary looks at two guards who have come through a door behind Megan, and then points to her and orders, "Seize her." Before Megan can move, the guards tie her arms and hands behind her back. "We shall leave immediately," says the emissary.

Megan does a quick search for Marcus Aurelius. In less than a tenth of a second, several search results are displayed on her lenses. She learns that she must be moving forward in time. She is no longer in 110 CE, but rather somewhere around 170 CE.

CHAPTER 29

MEGAN WAKES UP AS THE MASSEUR SLATHERS HER WITH olive oil and continues with a deep-tissue sports massage. She sits up on the table and realizes that she is only wearing a linen loincloth and band top. She quickly grabs the linen sheet off the table and wraps it around herself. The masseur chuckles to himself, thinking some of these foreign slaves are so bashful.

"Where am I?" asks Megan. All she remembers is the emissary saying that she will enjoy her new school right next to the Roman Colosseum. After that, everything went black.

"You're at Ludus Magnus, the greatest gladiator school in the entire empire."

Megan groans and wonders what she is doing in a gladiator school.

"The emperor is looking forward to seeing you fight this afternoon. New sponsors from one of the far-off territories are hosting the games today. It should be spectacular. We rarely get to see a woman from Britannia." The masseur pushes her back on the table and continues working her muscles. Megan, staring at the floor through her contact lenses, texts her location to Arjun and the rest of the team. She then searches online for any information about the gladiatorial games.

She learns that the Roman Colosseum played a significant role in Roman public life. It was built over a ten-year period and was one of the first structures in which concrete was used. The games were meant to display the power and prestige of Rome. The Colosseum and the circus represented the epitome of Roman culture. The Colosseum featured eighty entrances, water, toilets, and canvas sun shelters. The gladiatorial games were used to entertain the masses and satisfy their passion for blood sports and violence. But the entertainment wasn't just gladiator games. The Romans also held public executions, killed Christians, and slaughtered exotic wild animals, all in the name of entertainment. They had festivals that could last one hundred days. Entry was free, and people would come in the morning and stay until sunset to revel in the power of Rome. They wanted to be entertained and to see fabulous spectacles. The emperor or wealthy aristocrats often financed the games. These sponsors would choose the way to end a fight among gladiators. The more popular the games, the more the sponsors' political power would rise.

As she scans the information, Megan realizes that there is a lot more to the story of gladiators than is often portrayed in the modern-day popular media. Some gladiators got rich and famous, like modern-day celebrities. Most only had to fight three to five times a year for about fifteen minutes, and if they won, they might be paid for one fight what a soldier would earn in an entire year. And not all fights were to the death. Many slaves, prisoners of war, and criminals were conscripted to gladiator schools. However, many also volunteered. For new recruits, it was strict and harsh, but if a gladiator won, his life would be a lot better than working in the quarries or fields.

In several sources, Megan reads that even emperors, senators, and women fought in the arena. Most interesting is that there is some evidence that even wealthy, aristocratic women fought at times. Unfortunately, there is little proof. Although women fought rarely, enough of them were involved that Emperor Severus banned female gladiators in the early third century BCE. Megan wonders who will watch her fight.

Arjun, who exited the game while Megan was headed to the Han Empire, receives her text message. He is surprised that a player can now send text messages from within the game to a player outside of the game. He figures that another new feature must have been released, and does not give it much more thought. He quickly forwards Megan's text to Jared, Lien, and Ethan.

After several minutes, Ethan responds that he is in the middle of debugging some computer code, but that he will be right there. Arjun is surprised; he knows that Ethan is the ultimate gamer and likes to program, but why is he debugging code while in the middle of the game? Arjun makes a mental note that they will have to talk about that sometime outside of the game, since he likes to work with computers, too.

Lien and Jared do not respond at all. Arjun wonders if they are back from the Qin Empire yet. Ethan and Arjun agree to join Megan in about an hour. After seeing the replies, Arjun turns his attention back to Rome.

At first, he wonders about the Roman emissary in China, when he remembers that ancient Chinese historians did record that Rome sent several envoys to China during the Han Dynasty. There was only indirect contact between the two empires through trade. They did not really know much about each other.

Arjun never likes to enter any situation unprepared, so he decides to take the next hour and refresh his memory about ancient Rome. He brings up several Web sites, pulls out a few books from his dad's library, and begins to take notes.

Roman History
Etruscans: ~800 BCE

- Pre-Roman civilization.

Founding Myth: ~753 BCE
- Romulus and Remus founded Rome on the Tiber River.
- Greece was in decline.

Kingdom: 753~509 BCE
- A crossroads for culture and trade. Good land and weather for crops.
- Values included loyalty to the many gods and goddesses, loyalty to family, and obedience to authority.

Republic: 509~27 BCE
- Representative government (similar to US) and complex constitution. Not direct democracy like Greece.
- Grew and expanded. Fought the Macedonians, the Gauls, the Spanish, and the Carthaginians in the Punic Wars.
- Dominated the Mediterranean, spreading its culture and influence.
- Later, social inequities and unrest, faltering economy, and political infighting between the two major political parties, the Optimates and Populares.
- Civil wars, plays for power, private armies.
- The rise of the first triumvirate, the rise of dictatorship, and assassinations.
- Assassination of Julius Caesar by senators.
- Republic collapsed around 27 BCE.

Empire: 27 BCE~476 CE (Western Empire) and 345 BCE~1453 CE (Eastern Empire)
- Era of Imperial Rome began with Octavius (Augustus Caesar), Julius Caesar's heir, and the first emperor.

- For two hundred years, the Pax Romana (peace and prosperity) reigned.
- Rome expanded to its largest geographical size, and arts, sciences, and literature flourished.
- Engineers built roads, aqueducts, and buildings.
- Persecution of Christians.

Then...

- Peace and prosperity ended and the empire declined due to many social, political, economic, and military causes.

  » Reached a limit in terms of expansion, so there was little gold or silver coming in. The economy fell apart.

  » Agrarian economy depended on slaves, led to stagnation of technological change and growth. A lack of circulating currency and trade deficits.

  » The soil, overworked, was no longer fertile.

  » Smaller amounts of valuable metal were extracted, so they put less silver in coins, hoping to create more money. Value of money dropped, and prices went up (inflation).

  » Managing the huge Roman bureaucracy became expensive so the government raised taxes.

  » Weather patterns changed, and people from the east and north migrated south to Italy in search of better land and harvests.

  » The frontiers were attacked by hostile tribes. People started to lose faith and loyalty.

- By 250 CE, Rome had 150 holidays a year. To distract and control the unemployed masses, the government provided free games, races, and gladiator contests, even building a fifty-thousand-person colosseum. Some estimate the games cost up to one-third of the Empire's total income.

Arjun is pinged by a text message from Ethan. He realizes that he has lost track of time. He quickly finishes reading that around 290 CE, Emperor Diocletian divided the empire into east and west. He tried to revive the worship of Roman gods by destroying churches and ordering Christians to change back to the old religion. Whoever refused was executed. The empire's problems were still there: huge costs for the army, taxes, and bureaucracy. When Diocletion died, succession was messy. One of the commanders, Constantine, who had converted to Christianity, secured control of the west and east.

In 330 CE, Emperor Constantine founded Constantinople at the location of the ancient Greek city of Byzantium. Constantinople, named after the Emperor, became the capital of the Eastern Roman Empire and later one of the wealthiest European cities in the Middle Ages.

Meanwhile, the west fell apart over several years as Germanic people, fleeing from the Huns, moved into the Roman provinces. Rome no longer had an army to protect itself, and so, in 410 CE, the Visigoth king, Alaric, sacked Rome. The Huns, united by a warrior chieftain named Attila, advanced against Rome as well, but disease and famine stopped that army. The Germanic tribes, however, kept coming. Around 476 BCE, the Western Roman Empire collapsed, and Western Europe disintegrated into a series of Germanic kingdoms.

Even though Attila also attacked the Eastern Roman Empire, he never succeeded in capturing Constantinople; it preserved the Greek and Roman culture for another thousand years until the Ottoman Turks conquered the city in 1453. The Turkish sultan then made it the capital of the Ottoman Empire and changed the city's name to Istanbul.

What a long history, with so many ups and downs, thinks Arjun. He looks back at his notes and realizes that he has covered over two thousand years of Roman history. He logs off his computer as his smartphone begins to ring in the kitchen. It will have to wait. He touches the wristband and activates the nanobots.

CHAPTER 30

"THIS IS JUST GREAT!" YELLS ETHAN. "WE BARELY GET here, and before we can do anything, we're taken prisoner."

Megan looks at Ethan. He does not sound convincing; what he says sounds almost rehearsed, as if he were trying to be overly dramatic.

Several Roman soldiers lead Megan, Arjun, and Ethan through the Colosseum's subterranean maze of tunnels, cells, animal pens, and vertical shafts. The heat from the day and from the burning lamps is oppressive, and the stench of animals, excrement, blood, and death is nearly unbearable. At the lowest level is the water and sewage system. They enter a long tunnel. Megan recognizes it as the one connecting the Colosseum with the Ludus Magnus gladiator school. Along the way, they pass a series of rooms where gladiators are preparing for their matches.

"Where are Jared and Lien?" asks Megan quietly.

"Don't know. They didn't respond to the message," replies Arjun.

Above their heads, the ceiling begins to open revealing the arena. Arjun and Megan quickly scramble out of the way. Large stage props are raised; some are lowered. They can see the sun setting in the sky and thousands of people cheering in the stands. They see the royal box in which the emperor is standing and looking down at the fight in the arena. He extends his right arm and puts his thumb out to the side; the crowd roars. The losing gladiator is put to death.

"I thought thumbs down meant death," whispers Ethan.

"Sometimes history gets distorted. Hollywood films and writers often misinterpret history, and then it gets into the mainstream. Everybody believes it," replies Arjun, "And yet it's not true." Arjun stares out into the arena, sees how the dead gladiator is taken from the field: dragged through the gate of death by a hook in his heel and taken to the Spoliarium. This basement room is where the dead gladiator is stripped of his armor before the body is disposed of.

The winning gladiator walks through the gate of life, down the main tunnel, directly toward them. He wields a sword that glistens red with blood and a body shield dented from battle. As the gladiator approaches, Megan notices a white band on the skin around his wrist where the game bracelet would normally be located. She thinks he's probably a player, but why isn't he wearing a wristband? He walks close to Megan and then whispers, "Beware today's two sponsors, for they have become drunk with power. Do not let them seize your wristband." Megan looks after him, wondering what he meant. She looks up at the imperial box but can only see the emperor.

As they near the gate of life, two soldiers grab Ethan by the arms and pull him to the side. "You will come with us. There are different plans for you." Ethan shrugs and goes with the soldiers—a little too easily, in Megan's view. She tries to break free from the soldiers holding her, to help Ethan, but they jab her with their spears, and she resumes walking down the tunnel. "We'll figure something out, Ethan!" she yells. A soldier punishes her with a punch to the stomach.

Ethan glances back toward his teammates but avoids making eye contact, and then calmly walks along with the soldiers, not saying a word.

As they walk, Arjun whispers to Megan, "Once we get out there, we should get ready to touch the home button, just in case."

Megan nods in agreement.

"No talking!" yells a soldier as he and his comrades prod the teenagers with spears to keep them quiet. First Megan and then Arjun enter the arena through the gate of life to the cheering applause of the audience, the "Roman mob." As they enter, each is given weapons. Megan receives two swords and a shield. Arjun receives a six-foot spear and a gladius, the primary sword of the ancient Roman foot soldier. The arena is filled with amazing props that seem to have appeared out of nowhere. In the middle of the field stands a twenty-foot-tall pyramid, modeled after the Pyramid of Djoser in ancient Egypt. It is surrounded by jungle plants, trees, and a river. At the opposite side of the arena are cages filled with wild animals and guarded by Roman centurions. To the left is another group of students, and to the right is what looks to be a group of trained gladiators. Megan looks at each student and each gladiator, assessing their possible strengths and weaknesses. As she scans the men, her jaw drops. Standing second from the end is Sizwe. He is holding a weighted net, a trident, and a dagger. Megan nudges Arjun, who catches her eye and then sees where she is looking.

"What's he doing here?" whispers Arjun in surprise.

"I have no idea. He doesn't look happy, though," replies Megan. She continues walking out into the arena toward the imperial box when she realizes what the gladiator was trying to tell her. Sizwe is not wearing his wristband. As they pass a large palm tree prop, she quickly slips off her wristband and hides it in the planter containing the tree. Several steps behind her, Arjun sees what she is doing and decides to do the same thing. He also drops his bracelet into the planter. He has noticed that although Megan is often impetuous and doesn't give things a lot of thought, she is very perceptive, has strong intuition, and is often a few steps ahead of her enemy.

As they arrive in front of the imperial box, they hear the gladiators say, "*Ave, Imperator, morituri te salutant*—Hail, Emperor, those who are about to die salute you." After the gladiators, the teenagers are told to move closer toward the box. Megan has no intention of dying, so as the others chant the phrase, all she says is "*Ave, Imperator,*" and mouths the rest. The emperor doesn't catch on. He nods and leans toward one of the senators. Megan can barely hear him as he says, "This audience is my power. I give them a spectacle, and they are enthralled. I give them what they want. While their attention is diverted, while they are entertained, I remain popular. They don't question what I do, and thus I can control them." The emperor chuckles. "They don't even notice how I take away their freedom." Arjun looks at Megan, ready to mention that this sounds more like a movie line than real history, when the emperor raises his arms and quiets the crowd. He turns and then introduces the two sponsors for today's games.

The crowd erupts in a wild cheer. Megan and Arjun stare into the imperial box, dumbfounded. How could this possibly be? Gazing down at them with smug looks are Damian and Ivy, dressed in the clothes of Roman nobility. Behind them stand Alexa, Fabio, and a few other students from their world history class. Ivy whispers to the emperor, "Well done, Caesar, finding that woman in ancient China." Caesar nods.

Meanwhile, Megan continues to scan the box, and for an instant, she thinks she sees Ethan. She quickly focuses back on the twins.

"Welcome to our games," Ivy calls out to the crowd. "This will be a spectacular event!"

Arjun tilts his toward Megan and whispers, "I can't believe Damian and Ivy! Don't they understand that what they do here in the game— sending others into the arena—also has real-world implications? If any of those players ever meet them outside of the game, they're going to be in such trouble."

"Yeah! No kidding," replies Megan. "Some just don't see that online behavior can have offline consequences. When I get out of here, they're not going like what I have to say."

Damian leans over the edge of the box and calls to four soldiers, "They should only have the weapons they were given. Make sure they are not wearing wristbands. Bring those to me." He winks at Megan. The soldiers gather the wristbands from the other students and hand them to Damian, who puts them in a bowl, which he places on the wide railing of the imperial box. He then signals to the trumpeters to open the games. The teenagers see the cages opening, and the half-starved animals that know the taste of human blood slowly come out. The students scatter for cover. The professional gladiators stand their ground and wait.

The spectators begin to boo and hiss. They are impatient and want to see a fight. Reacting to the crowd, one of the gladiators unexpectedly launches himself at one of his comrades and, with a few perfectly-targeted slashes with his curved swords, cuts across the other's chest and arms. The injured gladiator falls to the ground incapacitated, unable to move his arms. The crowd cheers wildly. At the end of the arena, a gigantic scoreboard shows 33,250 Likes, 15,024 Dislikes. Some liked the bravery and initiative shown by the one gladiator; others disliked the cowardice he displayed with the surprise attack on a comrade. The board then displays the number 41,280 and a white handkerchief. The emperor signals that the injured gladiator's life will be spared and that he should be removed from the arena. Since he is not a slave, he is carried out on a stretcher. The trumpets sound and the battle resumes.

Megan and Arjun stick together as students and gladiators attack. "We could really use the others right now," says Arjun. He watches as

Sizwe throws his net, catching another player by the feet and pulling him to the ground. Sizwe shows an amazing aptitude for the trident and the net. He easily wards off the other students, inflicting only minor wounds. With the gladiators, it is a different story. Sizwe goes all out to inflict as much pain as possible, as quickly as possible. After all, these are most likely computer-generated warriors. As the fight continues, Megan and Arjun decide to make their way to the pyramid, figuring that it will be easier to protect themselves from higher ground. However, this does take them farther from the planter where they hid their wristbands.

Every time a gladiator or a student is wounded, the scoreboard flashes the number of "likes" and "dislikes" for all to see. In one case, the number of "dislikes" is so high that the emperor has no choice but to immediately sentence the gladiator to death. He does not want to lose any popularity. This is quickly taken care of, and the dead gladiator, a slave, is dragged out of the arena by his heels.

As they continue to work their way toward the pyramid, the last rays of the sun hit the arena. Megan looks to the top of the pyramid and catches a hint of blue. Could this be, she wonders, a link like the one in the cave at Marathon? Now she has to figure out how to retrieve the wristbands and make it back. She looks around the arena for anything she can use. Then she sees it. At the edge of the arena stands a horse with a bow and arrow strapped to its side. She figures it must belong to a Sagittarius, a gladiator who fought on horseback. They were often seen as great animal hunters. This horse is probably going to be part of a specialty act, if any animals survive. Megan quickly outlines her plan and shares it with Arjun.

Before he can protest, she launches herself off the lower step of the pyramid and sprints across the arena. After thirty minutes of combat, the crowd is slowly getting bored. When they see Megan run toward the edge of the arena, many jump out of their seats and cheer wildly. She is three-quarters of the way to the horse before any of the other combatants even notice. A few feet from the animal, she jumps into the air and, with a straight-leg kick, makes short business of the centurion holding the horse. He crumples to the ground, dropping the reins just in time for Megan to grab them. She mounts the horse, grabs the bow and arrow, and gallops back toward the palm tree. The crowd goes wild, cheering louder and louder at her bravery. She slows at the planter, leans down from the horse, and grabs the two bracelets without stopping. Damian and Ivy are gesturing and screaming wildly at the gladiators in the arena to take her down. Then, instead of heading straight for the pyramid, she gallops toward the imperial box, takes aim, and fires two arrows in rapid succession into the box. Everyone, including Damian, Ivy, and the emperor, drops to the floor to take cover. The mob cheers less wildly. For good measure, she then takes two more arrows and fires them into the crowd. The cheering turns into panic as the crowd realizes that this is not a trusted Sagittarius but rather a young woman fighting for her life. Arjun throws his spear as hard as he can toward the imperial box. It flies across the arena and sticks into the emperor's wooden chair.

At the base of the pyramid, Megan jumps off the horse as the gladiators move in. She quickly ascends a few steps toward Arjun. Sizwe has also made it to the base of the pyramid, and he continues to fend off attackers. Megan hands a wristband to Arjun, and looks down toward Sizwe. Her eyes meet his. She realizes that he is trying to help them escape.

"I understand!" he yells. "I'll fight them off for as long as I can. Just make sure you come back for me."

"I can't leave you here alone," replies Megan, climbing back down and standing next to Sizwe. "Arjun, you go!"

Across the arena, Damian and Ivy, sensing that no more arrows or spears are coming, raise their heads above the concrete railing of the imperial box and see Megan, Arjun, and Sizwe at the pyramid.

"Look!" yells Ivy. "There's a faint blue light coming from the top." They watch as Arjun hesitates, and then begins to climb to the top of the pyramid. "Let's go!" yells Damian. He climbs over the railing into the arena, accidentally knocking the bowl with the bracelets to the arena floor. He runs toward the pyramid as fast as he can. Ivy follows closely behind, completely forgetting her other teammates and the spilled wristbands.

"He dropped the bowl with the bracelets," says Sizwe. "This is my chance. I'll be OK. You better follow this link. Who knows how long it will be active. Damian and Ivy are coming." Not waiting for Megan's reply, he leaves the pyramid and sprints toward the imperial box. As he meets Damian in the middle of the arena, he puts out his arm, striking Damian in the chest and knocking him to the ground, giving Arjun and Megan a little extra time. Sizwe looks back and sees Megan looking back toward him one more time, and then she begins to climb. Within seconds, she and Arjun reach the top of the pyramid and disappear. Sizwe heads to the bowl on the floor that held the wristbands. There is only one left; it must be his.

Ivy helps Damian to his feet and they run toward the pyramid. Most of the animals are focused on the gladiators and do not give chase. They reach the top of the pyramid and see that the link is still active. Without a second thought, they both jump through the opening. Seconds later, the blue light goes out.

CHAPTER 31

ARJUN STANDS IN ANOTHER ARENA. THIS TIME, INSTEAD
of the Colosseum, he is in the middle of a large masonry ball court about
330 feet long and one hundred feet wide. Two large stone rings sit six
meters off the ground on a vertical stone wall. He is dressed in a loincloth,
leather hip guards, a head covering, knee and elbow guards, and a belt.
The four other players look gaunt, undernourished, and weak, as if they'd
been locked up for months. He recognizes the ancient Mesoamerican
ball game from pictures. If there's one thing he hates, it's being dropped
into some unknown situation without any time to prepare. On top of
that, he looks around and cannot see Megan anywhere. He shakes his
head in disbelief. Great, he thinks, I go from one arena to another—I
must have terrible karma.

Crowds of noblemen, noblewomen, and children are sitting on the
tops of the walls, waiting. Arjun uses the lull to quickly look up the game
on his contact lenses and watch two short videos. He learns that the
Olmecs probably invented the game over three thousand years ago. He
has no clue as to how this game is played, except for what was described
in his textbook. He hopes that either his martial arts or surfing skills
will help, but he's not counting on it. So, he keeps scanning and learns
that Mesoamericans played the game casually for recreation, but that it
also had a significant religious and ritual purpose. The ball represented
the sun. The game signified the battle between life and death and was a
crucial part of the culture. Thousands of courts have been found around

Mesoamerica—over six thousand in Mexico alone. The layout of the courts is connected to different astronomical orientations.

He looks everywhere for information on how the game is played but can't find any rules, only theories. A few sites suggest that the game is a combination of soccer, volleyball, and basketball, but the ball can't touch the ground. You score points by hitting certain markers and getting the ball through the stone hoops. He figures that he is an average athlete in all three sports, so it should not be too difficult to learn by doing.

Finally, a procession of religious leaders, priests, and chieftains begins to take their seats. The priests lead the crowd in several sacred songs and rituals, creating an electrifying atmosphere. Arjun thinks back to the arena in Rome. He was just there. Then the singing stops, and there is deathly silence.

He's amazed at the acoustics. He can hear the other players whisper from the far side of the court. Then, as they move into the center, the crowd erupts in a cheer. The ball is in play.

He is scanning the crowd, looking for Megan, wondering where she can be, when the ball hits him in the shoulder. He winces in pain. This ball isn't anything like a soccer ball, or even a basketball. He estimates that it is eight or ten inches in diameter and close to six pounds of solid rubber. It hurts. He's going to be bruised and battered no matter how well he tries to protect himself. Plus, he has to play twice as hard. His team looks like a bunch of emaciated prisoners of war, completely outmatched by the more practiced home team. He notices that the spectators are all gambling and placing bets against his team. If they lose, they become the religious sacrifice at the post-game ritual.

After just a few minutes, his team is several points behind. The crowd is cheering every time a member of the home team touches the ball, no matter what he does. Arjun notices that two of the opposing players are built as if they belong on a football field. He looks more closely and notices that they are each wearing a bracelet similar to his own. Another school? He was sure that Ivy's team was the closest competitor, but maybe not.

He can't worry about that now though. The other team easily hits the stone markers, gathering more and more points. Seeing that they have a huge advantage, the home team begins to play even more aggressively, trying their best to get the ball through the ring to end the competition early. The heavy ball bounces off the hip of an opposing player and like a missile flies toward one of the players on Arjun's team. Arjun sees that the player isn't paying attention. He is looking into the crowd. Arjun yells. When the man looks back toward the game, it is too late. He doesn't see the ball coming, and it strikes him directly in the face, shattering every bone. He keels over dead. Arjun looks at the player's wrist. Luckily, there is no bracelet.

Arjun watches his other team members lose faith and begin to give up. They move more slowly and only go through the motions of playing. Arjun gets angry. He is a bit surprised at himself, because he rarely lets his emotions get out of hand. Then, one of his teammates fumbles the ball and passes it into an empty space. Arjun dives to the ground and keeps the ball in play with his elbow, then jumps up and fires it back toward the other side. The crowd roars its approval, and Arjun draws on their energy. He's a good athlete, but with his team of prisoners, the odds are stacked against him. He tries to fire the ball at one of the targets, but as soon as he moves his hip, he winces in pain. There is a sharp, stinging sensation all over his body as he passes the ball. He does his best to keep his team motivated and in the game. Eventually, his team scores a few points. Unfortunately, they are still several points behind, and time is running out.

And then it happens. One of the opposing players miscalculates and softly shoots the ball back into Arjun's side of the court, near the ring. Arjun aims carefully, sets up the shot, grits his teeth, and using a slight twitch of his hip, gently arcs the ball upwards. The crowd rises to its feet as the ball flies toward the ring on a perfect trajectory for the hole.

It is almost there; it is losing speed and height, but it is still heading for the hole. The ball catches the lower stone rim, spinning forward, *wanting* to get through the hole—just like a basketball spinning and wanting to go through the hoop. The arena falls silent. All eyes are fixed on the rubber ball. If it goes through, the game is over and Arjun's team wins. The ball struggles forward and then loses momentum. It stops spinning and falls back down, hitting the ground with a thump.

The crowd lets out a collective groan. So close. They all feel the fine line between life and death. Everyone stares, mesmerized. The gods have spoken. Arjun's team was not fated to win, and its players will be sacrificed to appease the gods. The crowd celebrates with the victors as Arjun and his teammates are led from the Great Ball Court at Chichen Itza. He can hear the priests saying that because of his valiant effort, he will not be sacrificed with the others at the Temple of the Jaguars and the Tzompantli or wall of skulls, but rather later that evening at the Great Pyramid of Kukulkan. Several guards, while escorting Arjun, suggest that he does not deserve the honor of a sacrifice on the Great Pyramid. Instead they should throw him into the Sacred Cenote, or Well of Sacrifice, and be done with it. Arjun remembers that the Yucatán is a porous limestone shelf with only a few inches of topsoil. Since no rivers can form, water filters through the topsoil, creating a vast network of freshwater pools. He is tempted to try to run down the trail and jump into the Sacred Cenote to escape, but it's too risky. It's like cave diving; you can get completely lost and drown. His escape will have to wait.

Coming down from his adrenaline high, for the first time since he arrived he feels the oppressive heat and humidity of the jungle. He thinks about Megan. He could use her help. What happened to her? After a few minutes of walking, the guards lock him into a tight, dimly lit, stone prison cell. He appreciates the coolness of the cell and the little bit of water in the corner. He removes his protective gear, admires the many bruises that are beginning to emerge, and stretches out on a pile of dried grass. Exhaustion sets in, and he falls asleep quickly. Thirty minutes later, he wakes up and leans against the stone. He needs to better understand Mayan history, and quickly. He begins to search, ignoring the message icon in the corner of his lenses.

The Maya

- The Mayan civilization flourished from around 250 CE to 900 CE in southern Mexico and Central America, although the Maya established settlements and cities much earlier.
- The Maya were around at the same time as the Romans, the Han Dynasty, and the Gupta Empire.
- Similar to earlier civilizations in Afroeurasia, the Mayans were a complex civilization based on a collection of city-states.
- Mayan kings were considered to be living embodiment of gods.
- They built pyramids similar to the Egyptian pyramids or Mesopotamian ziggurats, to help rulers legitimize their authority through a connection to the gods.
- They established tremendous cities, such as Tikal, with an estimated population of sixty thousand to one hundred thousand people. Many of the ancient city names have been forgotten, and later explorers sometimes invented new names.

- They built an extensive network of roads to sustain communication and commerce to various Mayan cities.
- They developed the most advanced writing system in the Americas using hieroglyphic symbols.
- As in most agricultural societies, social classes developed. The majority of people were peasants or slaves, ruled by a small elite group of kings, priests, and hereditary nobility.
- Without any large domesticated animals, the primary source for labor was humans and so there was always a demand for more slaves. Mayan wars were fought more to acquire slaves than to acquire territory.

Arjun continues to scan the text to get a sense of the Mayan culture. He looks for anything that might help him locate the next clue. Because of his interest in math, Arjun reads about the accuracy of one of the Mayan calendars. Mayan astronomers and mathematicians carefully observed the planets, the sun, and the moon, calculating the precise orbit of Venus around the sun. They calculated the solar year at 365.2420 days—only .0002 of a day short of what is accepted today. Calendars were used to determine when to plant crops. The Maya had a sophisticated mathematical system based on groups of twenty—counting fingers and toes—so it was one, twenty, four hundred, eight thousand, etc. They also had a concept of zero, represented by an oval shell.

As he reads more about how the Maya used their concept of zero, guards summon him from his cell. He is cleaned and dressed in a new loincloth, and a feather-and-shell headdress is placed on his head. If only his classmates at Globus Academy could see him now, he thinks. If he dressed like this back at school, which he wouldn't, someone would probably snap a picture and post it online. Thank goodness the players can't take any physical items like cameras across sites.

A wide cloth band is tied around his waist to hide the deep purple bruises that have started blossoming everywhere. The guards bind his arms behind his back, and then, with a guard on each side, he is escorted across the grounds, through the large crowd, toward the Great Pyramid. He looks at one of the four stone staircases, each angled at forty-five-degrees, leading to the top. The steps are steep and shallow. Arjun tries to win some time by pretending he is too sore to ascend. He acts as if he can barely move his leg muscles, given the ferocity of the game. The guards do not care. They lift him under his biceps and carry him up the stairs. He counts ninety-one steps. Four staircases mean 364 steps, and the platform equals 365 days for the year, another reference to the calendar and the cosmos. At the top, they enter the temple's north entrance, which is flanked by two carved serpents. Arjun squints as his eyes adjust to the dim light. He tries to focus, but his eyes are a bit blurry.

He remembers scanning an article that described how religion influenced almost every aspect of Mayan life. Their many gods could be good, evil, or both. They divided their cosmos into the heavens above, the human world in the middle, and the underworld below. The gods maintained the agricultural cycles in return for offerings and sacrifices. By receiving sacrifices, they kept the world in balance. Before a battle, there would be days of religious rituals. Even the leaders would participate in the battles. Some scholars suggested that the winners would have made a better sacrifice. Too bad he landed on a site where the losers are sacrificed instead. Arjun begins to wonder if the Maya even made human sacrifices at the Pyramid of Kukulkan or if this is misinformation on this Web site. Anyway, it is too late now.

The afternoon sun slowly slides down the western horizon, and Arjun still has no idea where to look next for a clue. He can hear the preparations for the evening ritual. It does not look good. He hopes something will turn up soon. He thinks about hitting the home button and getting out of here, but then he won't have the next clue. He must continue, at least for a little while.

Inside the dimly lit structure, he can barely see three priests dressed in rich, highly decorated clothing and wearing sacred masks. The head priest holds a black obsidian knife at his side. Arjun's hands are unbound, and he is laid on a large, square, stone slab. He tenses as his bare back touches the cold stone. After binding his arms tightly to the sides of the slab, the priests ask the guards to exit the temple and wait outside. Arjun quietly berates himself for being such an idiot. By allowing his arms to be tied, he's missed any opportunity for escape. This is not good. From what he remembers, the priests often cut out still-beating hearts. Sweat begins to build on his brow, and his breathing gets faster. This is no longer a game; he's truly scared. Then he sees the old message icon in the corner of his lenses and criticizes himself for not noticing it earlier. Seeing that it is urgent and from Lien, he opens it, and his heart almost stops. He scans the text and learns that Jared was shot and badly wounded in Qin China and will need to recuperate. She is staying with him to make sure he's OK, and they will join the game again later. He stares up at the ceiling, thinking that this game is definitely more than a lesson in ancient history. As he looks at the pattern overhead, he recognizes a series of dots that look like stars. He remembers that this stepped pyramid was built for astronomical purposes. He also sees that one of the dots looks more like a circle—a zero, a little blue zero. He needs to get up there somehow.

The head priest is chanting and moving closer and closer with the obsidian knife. Arjun can smell something on the priest's breadth. It smells like chocolate. Arjun reprimands himself for not getting out sooner. He struggles against the ropes, but now they are too tight. He cannot believe he is going to be sacrificed while smelling chocolate.

The chanting gets louder, and the priest lifts the knife above his head and brings it down toward Arjun's chest. Arjun sees the action in slow motion. Trembling, he closes his eyes.

When the knife is halfway to Arjun's chest, a hand reaches around from the back of the priest, grabs the priest's wrist, uses the downward energy to change the trajectory, and plunges the knife into the priest's stomach.

Arjun, anticipating excruciating pain from the knife thrust but not feeling anything, opens his eyes. He sees the priest fall toward him. An instant later, he feels that his arms are cut free. He pushes the priest's body off his chest. It falls to the ground with a thump. Arjun elbows the second priest, shattering the sacred mask and rendering him unconscious, and rolls off the stone slab. The guards rush into the temple to investigate the commotion. He is about to attack the third priest when he sees the priest strike the first guard with a karate palm punch to the forehead, propelling him backwards into the other guards.

Together with the third priest, Arjun fights his way out of the temple. The crowd below senses that something has gone wrong, and several more guards come running up the steps. Arjun looks at the priest, who is still hidden under a ceremonial mask. They have no time to talk. As two guards reach the top step, Arjun and the priest run toward them and using flying sidekicks to send them tumbling backwards, head over heels down the steep stone steps, causing several other guards to jump out of the way.

The priest removes his ceremonial mask. It's not a he, but a she. Megan gives Arjun a big smile.

Arjun is so happy to see her, he gives her a big hug. He can't believe it. "That was so close! Thanks!"

"No problem."

"What took you so long?"

"I got the message from Lien just as I arrived in Chichen Itza and immediately went to see Jared. Then, instead of sending me back to the same spot, the link sent me to El Caracol, the observatory," replies Megan. "It's almost half a mile away from here. A huge crowd was beginning to walk toward the Great Pyramid, and several people asked me if I was going to come watch the sacrifice of the man who almost won the ball game—only to be denied by the gods in the last second. I wasn't sure how to get here, but something told me this was the place to be."

"I'm glad you decided that," says Arjun. "By the way, is Jared OK?"

"Yeah. Recuperating remarkably fast, but I'll tell you more later."

"Anything happen at El Caracol?"

"Not really. Several priests were following the motions of Venus. I pretended to be a priestess for a bit, and then quickly left to come here."

"So there were female priests among the Maya?" asks Arjun.

"Yup," replies Megan.

Just then, a priest, having regained consciousness, comes running out of the temple. He grabs Megan around the waist, propelling them both over the edge of the platform at the top of the pyramid. In mid-air, Megan twists her body so that the priest is beneath her. They hit the uppermost stone terrace more than eight feet below the platform. The priest lets out a deep cry as Megan lands on top of him, slamming his head into the stone. Their momentum carries them to the edge of the terrace; they barely keep from falling down to the next terrace. The priest is still breathing, but shallowly. Megan yanks his mask off.

Arjun, looking down, recognizes him as one of the players from the ball game. "Pull up his sleeve," he yells to Megan.

She does so, revealing a wristband similar to her own.

"There's probably more of them somewhere," replies Arjun. "We'd better get going."

Arjun moves down the steps next to the terrace toward Megan. "C'mon, let me help you up." He looks down into the crowd below and recognizes Damian and Ivy trying to make their way to the pyramid. "Shoot. They're here."

"Who?" asks Megan.

"Damian and Ivy." Arjun reaches for Megan's hand and helps her onto the steep steps. "Come with me quickly. I need to show you something." Together they head back up to the temple as more guards now climb up all four sides and Damian and Ivy push their way through the crowd.

"Here, lie down on this stone slab," says Arjun.

"Arjun! We don't have time!" shouts Megan.

"Humor me. Look up."

Megan looks at the ceiling, sees the zero, and immediately recognizes it as a link. She stands up on the slab. "Get up here. Quick, give me your hand."

Arjun climbs up onto the slab, and together they touch the small, light-blue zero. Instantly, they disappear from the temple at the top of the Kukulkan-Quetzalcoatl stepped pyramid in Mexico and appear in an ancient study. They look around and suddenly hear a voice from behind.

"Hey, guys. I didn't expect you to show up here."

CHAPTER 32

IN FRONT OF A SERIES OF SHELVES, HOLDING A book titled *Āryabhatīya, a Sanskrit Astronomical Treatise,* stands Ethan with an astonished look on his face. He wasn't expecting his teammates to catch up so quickly.

"Ethan!" yells Megan as she launches herself across the desk, grabs him by the lapels of his coat, and pushes him up against the bookshelf. "What the hell are you doing? What's your game?"

Although he understands Megan's anger, he still feigns surprise. He lifts his arms in surrender. "What are you talking about?"

"You know exactly what I'm talking about! You've been acting strange lately. You tell us Sizwe is working with Damian and Ivy, which I don't think is true, and now all of sudden you're here, ahead of everyone. Something doesn't add up!"

Ethan backs away from the shelf. "Hey, I'm sorry. A lot's been happening at home, and I just told you what I saw. Sizwe was talking to Damian." He hesitates for a moment and then quickly says, "Plus, didn't you get Lien's text?"

"No!" replies Megan. "I was too busy fighting for my life."

"Well, Lien figured out the clue from the Terracotta Warrior. It said to find the blank space represented by the letter 'N' that rhymed with Nero. She didn't understand until she realized the 'N' was actually on its side. It wasn't an 'N,' but rather a 'Z.' After some work, she realized that the clue meant 'find the zero.' Two ancient societies came to the forefront—the Mayans and Āryabhata from the Gupta era, or classical age of Indian mathematics and astronomy."

Megan's anger slowly wanes. Maybe there is some truth to what Ethan is saying. Maybe she's being too hard on him. She looks out one of the windows. She's not sure anymore.

Ethan looks at Megan, and his stomach ties itself in knots. Who am I kidding? he thinks. His new friends were right. He never had a chance with Megan.

Arjun breaks the awkward silence. "So since the two ancient societies that worked with the concept of 'zero' were the Mayans and the Gupta, all you did was follow the zero."

"Exactly." Ethan chuckles, remembering that the Gupta developed the zero as an actual number, along with the number system we use today, a decimal system based on numerals one through nine, known as Hindu-Arabic numerals. He swings his arms. "Welcome to the private study of Āryabhata, one of the world's greatest mathematicians and astronomers."

"So we're at Nālandā University?" asks Arjun.

"Yes. One of the world's oldest," replies Ethan.

Megan is not convinced that it was that easy. Why would Ethan come to India and not go to the Americas? Why would he come alone and not let any of the other team members know? More inconsistencies.

"The Gupta Empire in the Golden Age of ancient India was a great time for India," Arjun says as he leans against the desk. He is proud of his rich Indian heritage. "Do you know much about the Guptas?"

"Only what I read since I got here," replies Ethan casually leaning against a desk.

A few seconds of silence pass. Sensing a bit of arrogance in Ethan's voice, Megan asks, "Are you going to share?"

"Oh…yeah, here, let me send you what I got." He focuses on his contact lenses and sends the link to Arjun and Megan.

Megan skims the information.

Gupta Empire: 320~600 CE

- After the Mauryan Empire declined because of economic woes and pressure from external attacks, India suffered political disintegration—a form of dark ages.
- The Guptas brought unity. It was a smaller and decentralized empire.
- Most people were farmers, living in patriarchal families in small villages. Craftspeople and merchants lived in specific areas within town.
- The first Gupta emperor came to power through marriage, not through battle.
- Under the Mauryans, Buddhism had partially replaced the old Vedic religion. The Guptas brought a revival of the traditional religions, Sanskrit literature, and Hindu culture. Hindu culture spread widely.
- There were extensive inventions in mathematics, science, arts, engineering, technology, religions, and philosophy.
- Indian scientists figured out the solar year at 365 days per year, similar to the Maya.
- They calculated the positions of the planets, studied solar and lunar eclipses, and more.
- The most famous scientist of the Gupta era was Āryabhata, a mathematician and astronomer. His major work covers arithmetic, algebra, plane and spherical trigonometry, continued fractions,

quadratic equations, and more. He had a theory that the Earth moved around the sun, and he studied solar and lunar eclipses.

- His most famous work was the *Āryabhatīya*, which he wrote in Kusumpura, one of two mathematical centers in India.
- The other center was the capital of the Gupta Empire, the heart of the communications network of the time, allowing information to flow in and out of India.

Ethan also includes two links to primary sources, one to the journal of Fa-hsien, or Faxian, a Chinese Buddhist monk who traveled through India around 400 CE and recorded his observations, and a second to another Chinese traveler named Yijing, who provided additional details.

"How long have you been here?" asks Megan, testing Ethan.

"I don't know. I lost track of time," replies Ethan. "I've been through almost everything in this study, but I haven't found any clues." He places several books on the desk. "Darn! I'm being pinged again. My mom. I'm sorry, but I have to go. I'll catch up with you guys later."

"You sure get pinged at the oddest times," says Megan.

Ethan shrugs. "Like I said, lots happening at home." He walks to the end of the study and exits through one of the doors.

"That was strange. He sure disappeared fast," says Arjun.

Megan walks over to the bookshelf. "Yeah, no kidding."

"So how's Jared, really?"

"He's actually doing really well," replies Megan, continuing to search the books. "He was shot in the shoulder by two crossbow bolts, but is already moving his arm."

"Wow, he's recuperating fast."

"Yes." Megan pretends to look at the titles as she debates how much to tell Arjun about the game. When she first got back home, Megan was furious at Lien for allowing this to happen until she saw how bad Lien felt and how she blamed herself for Jared's injury. Jared said that he was not taken to a regular hospital because of all the nanobots in his system. Gia and Uncle Alberto took care of him on the boat. Supposedly, the bolts were dipped in a substance that affected the nanobots. Luckily, Alberto was able to counteract it before it had any effect. Gia then glued the hole shut with a new type of medicinal adhesive and rubbed a special ointment onto the wound. Jared bounced back quickly and was able to go home in less than two days. At one point, Megan exited the game to see how he was doing, and that was when she and Jared agreed to tell Lien about the prophecy.

Arjun is a good person. She thinks that he should probably know the seriousness of the situation. She stops looking at the books and turns. "Arjun, you may want to sit down. I need to tell you something."

He puts down the book he has been scanning and gives Megan a questioning look. "This sounds serious."

"It is." Megan gives Arjun an overview of Gia, Alberto, and what happened to her and Jared on Gia's houseboat, omitting some of the more secretive details; and then she repeats the prophecy:

New Lords of the Clouds seek to dominate our world.
Choice disappears; freedom and independence are at risk.
Have the courage to use your own mind—sapere aude.
Follow clues hidden in the web of humanity's history.
Find this powerful artifact before it falls into the wrong hands.

Arjun's eyes grow wide. After spending a few minutes in stunned silence, he gets up and begins to pace the room, "I knew it!" He pounds a fist into his palm. "I knew there was more to this game. Do we have any idea what this artifact does?"

"No. All we know is that it is very powerful and that several organizations are looking for it."

"And we're right in the middle of everything."

"Looks that way," replies Megan. "I think we should search this room one more time."

"I agree." Arjun walks over to one of the bookshelves and begins to scan the titles.

Megan, meanwhile, sits at Āryabhata's table and searches through various papers with little success. She then pulls on the top drawer, only to find it locked. She pulls harder, but the drawer doesn't budge. "Hey, Arjun, any idea of how we might get into this?"

Arjun joins her at the table, and together they pull, to no avail. "Looks like it's locked," he says. "We need to find the key."

"Sure. It could be anywhere," Megan replies with disappointment. "It might even be around Āryabhata's neck on a necklace."

"Yes, that could be," Arjun says. Then he spies a statue, no more than two inches high, on the corner of the table. "Wait a minute, Āryabhata was Hindu. Why would he have a statue of Buddha on his desk?" He grabs the statue and hears the rattle of something inside. Turning it upside down, he sees a wax seal covering an opening. He peels the wax off with his fingernails, and out falls a key. "Let's try this," he says with a victorious look on his face.

They open the desk drawer. Inside is a large, leather-bound book. No title, no author. Megan pulls it out and opens it to the first page.

"Look at this!" she exclaims. A detailed picture covers both pages. It depicts a red-carpeted waiting lounge with one wall covered by a forty-foot curtain. The lounge appears to be half the size of a soccer field and has a relatively low roof. Its other three walls are dotted with large niches, each filled with a statue. Gods and goddesses from every part of the world look out from their niches. For a moment, Arjun thinks about how spiritual life and moral codes have affected history and human life—even his own life. He turns his attention back to Megan, and they examine the picture. They recognize the benevolent and kind gods of the ancient Egyptians, and the ancient Sumerian gods who were feared and obeyed no matter what. They see Minoan goddesses, who vastly outnumbered male gods, and African gods and goddesses. They spot the Olympian gods of the Greeks and the Roman gods of the Republic, Empire, and conquered lands. They pick out the Assyrian and Babylonian gods and goddesses of Mesopotamia. The Celtic Pantheon. The Germanic gods. The Hindu gods and goddesses. The gods and goddesses of Chinese folk religions. The Mayan gods.

"I can't believe there were so many ancient gods and goddesses," says Megan.

"They're not all gods and goddesses," replies Arjun, pointing to the drawings of Li Si and Shang Yang. "These were the thinkers behind Chinese Legalism. They thought of people as evil, and so everything was in terms of strict laws and harsh punishments." He then points to Confucius. "He wasn't a god, either. Confucianism was a political and social philosophy, a social belief system relying on the fundamental goodness of people. Confucius thought of everything in terms of responsibilities. These statues and pictures all depict belief systems."

"How do you know all this?" ask Megan.

"We covered this in the first half of the school year. Don't you remember?"

Megan shakes her head and shrugs.

Arjun turns the page to more pictures. "This looks to be about polytheism, the major belief systems before 600 CE, when many ancient civilizations believed in multiple gods. Hindus, for example, still believe in multiple gods."

He keeps turning the pages and then stops as he reaches another double-page picture. This time, the curtain is drawn back to reveal an enormous hangar beyond the waiting lounge. Moored inside are a dozen strange-looking airships of all different shapes, sizes, and styles. Some look like ancient ships dangling from huge balloons; others look like simple rectangular platforms attached to a series of balloons. Each is tightly moored to the ground, but they float at different heights. Several airships are moored together, and others are moored by themselves. The ceiling is so high up that it looks like it is part of the sky.

As they turn the page, they see a picture of an enormous glass globe contained within a larger glass sphere that looks as though it would be at least thirty feet in diameter. This double globe is suspended from the ceiling. The outer glass is engraved with religious symbols. Arjun recognizes the Christian cross, the Jewish Star of David, the Buddhist Wheel of Dharma, the Hindu Pranava, the Taoist yin and yang, the Baha'i nine-pointed star, and the Shinto torii, among at least thirty others.

They continue to turn the pages. "Look at these names," says Megan, looking at a picture of the airships.

Pointing, Arjun says with surprise, "It says Trimurti. I wonder if this airship is named for the three great Hindu gods: Brahma, the creator; Vishnu, the preserver; and Shiva, the destroyer."

Megan points to another part of the picture. "This one says 'Abraham,' probably referring to Judaism." She points to the airship. "And this one is called 'Emanuel.' I don't get it."

"Emanuel is another name for Jesus. That airship is probably Christian," replies Arjun.

The last of the three airships in this part of the picture is called "Qur'an." Arjun knows it must be named in honor of Islam. "Interesting that these three ships are all right next to each other."

"Maybe it's because Judaism was the first monotheistic faith, and out of it grew Christianity and Islam," replies Megan. "They are known as the Abrahamic religions. They have some similarities and many differences."

"So you *didn't* sleep through the entire first semester," jokes Arjun.

"Very funny." Megan turns to the next page. "Look, there's Lao Tzu and Taoism, Confucius and Confucianism. This is an amazing book. These ships are all named after major belief systems before 600 CE, plus Islam, which came after 600 CE." She flips to the next page and without looking, accidentally touches the picture. Instantly, Megan disappears.

To her surprise, she is suddenly standing on an enormous Chinese junk that is floating close to the ceiling. "Siddhārtha" is stenciled in red letters on its side. A rope ladder extends one hundred feet to the ground. The ship is at least four hundred feet long and has impressively many decks. She begins to climb down and learns from information displayed on the ship that Buddhism was founded by a young Hindu prince named Siddhārtha Gautama, who rejected his wealth. He went searching for a way to escape the endless cycle of suffering and rebirth described in Hinduism. She explores the storage room and finds several Syrian artifacts. Strange, she thinks. What would Syrian artifacts be doing on a Chinese junk unless the Chinese sailed to Syria in the second century BCE? She remembers from class that the ancient Chinese did really build these enormous ships. After quickly going through the ship, Megan decides to head back to the study. She touches her wristband and returns to Arjun.

"I think I accidentally hit a link," she says as she pops up behind him. Arjun almost falls out of the chair. "Don't scare me like that! I figured that; the picture had a light-blue frame around it."

Megan leans against the chair. "This book is definitely out of place. Way ahead of its time. I don't think it's a clue; it doesn't really tell us anything about where to go."

"Actually, in temple carvings and ancient Sanskrit literature, there are references to flying machines called *vimanas*," replies Arjun. "But this book of airships is more about belief systems. I think it's just part of the game. It doesn't tie to the ancient Sanskrit epics."

"Do you think it could be a game enchantment or power?" asks Megan, wondering why the book would be in an ancient Hindu scholar's study.

"I think it's possibly a false clue to lure the player away from the real clue, which is probably still in this room," answers Arjun. "Imagine how much time it would take for us to explore each of those airships. We'd be here for who knows how long."

"Agreed. We better keep looking in here."

After searching the study carefully for thirty minutes with little success, Megan decides to take a more systematic approach. She remembers seeing movies in which the characters "toss" a room when they are looking for something. She begins to pull books from the shelves, overturn furniture, lift carpets, and generally ransack the study.

"Stop! What are you doing?" cries Arjun. "This is the study of one of the greatest mathematician-astronomers of all time. We should show some respect."

"Arjun, remember, this is a game. Whenever people look for something in films, they usually ransack the place to look behind and under things." She continues to walk along the shelves, pulling books down as she goes. Halfway around the room, she suddenly stops and looks up at a shelf. It's about shoulder-height, and she can see to the back. There, tucked in the back corner, is a small book. "See! Here's something." Megan reaches for the book and returns to the table. "Great! It's in Arabic," she says in frustration.

"Wait," replies Arjun. "This is the *Arya-Siddhānta*. This is one of Āryabhata's lost works. He describes ways of measuring time with sundials and water clocks. Only an Arabic translation exists. This might be it."

"So, that still doesn't help us," replies Megan, moving back to the shelves to clear more manuscripts and books.

Arjun opens the book. "I can't read Arabic, but wait. Check this out." Megan walks back and looks at the book. Between two pages showing drawings of two types of water clocks is a bookmark. Written on the bookmark is a short phrase.

Seek the multistory water clock calibrated to the sundial—the circle of time. Change the scales of space and time, and have faith.

She turns to Arjun with a look of victory. "I think this is definitely the next clue!"

"Hmm." Arjun leans against the table. "Sundials and water clocks were used in many societies throughout the ancient world. Most were used for astrology. I've never heard of one that big, though."

"Me neither," Megan says. "What does the phrase '*change the scales of space and time*' mean?"

"No idea," replies Arjun. "But I think I know what the circle of time means. It's about the perception of time. The Western mind says that time is linear, with a beginning and an end. But other cultures, such as the ancient Hindus, some Native Americans societies, the Hebrews, and the Buddhists, see time as a circle. Like a clock, it continues without a beginning or an end. I read a novel over the holidays in which the author referred to Einstein and wrote about time as a circle bending back on itself and repeating."

"Is Einstein what you normally read during vacation?" asks Megan. "Never mind, we'd better head back, gather the team, and look for the big water clock. Nice job."

"You, too," replies Arjun with a big smile. He high-fives her. She's quite likable under that tough exterior, he thinks. Still, he does not like leaving the study of such a famous mathematician in such a mess, but as Megan said, it is just a game.

CHAPTER 33

MEANWHILE, ON THE EIGHTIETH FLOOR OF AN ULTRA-modern skyscraper somewhere in Asia, executives file into Victor's conference room and take seats at the table. They are waiting for their boss.

Victor storms into the room and plops himself at the head of the table. Without any greeting, he immediately launches into the meeting. "I heard that our security problems still exist and that someone from the outside is still manipulating the game. Is this true?"

The director of engineering speaks up. "We've brought in several security firms to help us plug the holes, but they keep moving. We're not sure if it's the work of our competition or some other group. One thing we do know is that they seem to be one step ahead of us all the time."

Victor stares at the executive. "How will we ever be able to control the Internet if we can't even get a simple game to be secure?"

"It's actually not such a simple game," replies the engineer. Then he quickly backs down under Victor's angry glare.

"Our competitors all have different strategies on how to gain power and control," Victor says. "Some want to do it with advertising, influencing people on what to buy and where to go on the Web—and they are doing it very subtly; people don't even know they are being influenced or directed to certain places. Some are building ecosystems where people can only use compatible devices from within the ecosystem, and thus they control the hardware, the software, and the information that gets presented. Others are trying to control the pipes that deliver the information. And then there are some who say that all they are doing is giving people what they want. However, in the face of overwhelming amounts of information, they provide summaries and answers to make it easier for people to make decisions—the decisions they want people to make. We need to make sure that we find this artifact if we want to stay competitive.

"In ancient times, those who controlled the media had power. In Mesopotamia, it was the clay tablets; in Egypt, Greece, and Rome, the papyrus scroll. Whoever could read, write, and control this medium had power. The priests and, in some cases, the emperors controlled the communication with the gods. This allowed the priests and temples to accumulate wealth and power. Today, the medium of choice is the Internet, and from what we've learned, this artifact will let us control it. Imagine the wealth and power we could amass. We must not fail! Too much is riding on this."

The executives have all heard this speech before. Many of the senior members know that Victor has been trying to amass this power for many years. Ever since he learned that an artifact exists that might help him reach this goal, he has been ruthless and single-minded in his pursuit.

"Give me an update on the game," he commands.

The director of human resources gives a quick update: they are still hiring former soldiers and mercenaries who are avid gamers. They have already deployed several in the game.

The head of public relations gives a summary of what happened after one of the players died. "We were able to keep the story under wraps. We negotiated with the parents and then flooded the media both online and offline with disinformation, and the story went away pretty quickly. It's lucky that people today have such short attention spans. They were onto the next thing within a few days, some even within a few hours."

"Good," replies Victor, dispensing a rare compliment. "What about in the game itself? Are teams making progress?"

The head of game tracking clears his throat. "One team from Globus Academy continues to make the most progress. They tend to pull ahead of the others quite regularly. But we also learned that they may have an idea about the importance of the artifact."

"How can that possibly be?" asks Victor, raising his voice.

The security chief speaks up. "We suspect that when the two key players on the team, Jared Reyes and Megan Kelly, went to the houseboat that our drones tried to destroy, they learned about the artifact from Jared's uncle, Alberto, and his assistant, Gia."

Victor smiles to himself. He remembers Gia from many years ago. She is a formidable adversary. "What were they doing there? I thought that Alberto's lab was shut down by the federal government and that he was captured."

The security chief shrugs. "The lab was shut down, but Alberto seems to have escaped. He was probably on the houseboat with Gia and the two students. A bad coincidence."

The veins on Victor's forehead begin to pulse. "No! I don't believe in coincidences. It's another mess-up. We penetrated the government's digital system and provided them with enough false information to lock him up for years," Victor says. "It will take them forever to fact-check everything, and only then will they learn that it was all fabricated. We need to make sure that Alberto is out of the picture for a while. Leak some more information."

"Will do," says the security chief. "Some more false information should slow him down."

"I hope you're right," replies Victor, not totally convinced. He knows Alberto. "In the end, it doesn't matter what team wins. We just need to make sure we get our hands on the artifact—no matter what it takes."

After listening to the discussion, the head of game development finally speaks up. "Given how well the team from Globus Academy is playing, I think we should let them continue. Let's see if they can find the artifact. If and when they do, we'll step in and take it. Simple as that."

As the others finish, the director of engineering clears his throat. "Yes. I agree. That sounds like a good strategy, especially now."

The others all look at the engineer.

"We were able to recruit one of the Globus Academy players. He now sees that playing for us means playing for the winning team. He can become so much more with us than he could ever become anywhere else. Plus, to seal the deal, we gave him an extra incentive."

The others all smile and look at Victor.

"Excellent! That works for me," Victor says, looking around the table. The others nod in agreement. He then looks at the security chief. "The only item I would add is that we need some insurance, a backup plan, to ensure that the artifact, once found, will be turned over to us. I'll let you figure out how to do that. Meeting adjourned."

CHAPTER 34

JARED WAKES UP IN HIS BED AS GIA CLEANS OUT HIS wound. He looks at her. "It feels like there are a million ants crawling on my arm."

Gia only smiles and places a bandage around his shoulder. "It's the special ointment. It accelerates the healing process."

"I don't understand how an arrow doesn't come back out of the game but a wound does."

"Physical items don't travel through the Web," replies Gia. "When you got shot, the nanobots essentially created the wound. A bit more ointment and you'll be fine in no time." Gia tapes the bandage tightly. Jared's shoulder twitches as he feels the coldness of the ointment penetrate the wound, and then a hot, burning sensation engulfs his entire right side. The heat slowly gives way to a constant tingling up and down his arm, shoulder, and back. Gia leaves the room and quietly closes the bedroom door.

He lays his head on the pillow, closes his eyes, and tries to remember what happened. He remembers seeing the mercenary soldier behind the Terracotta Warrior. He looked like a player, but an adult player. After Jared was shot, Lien cradled him in her lap, and then helped him returned to the home page. There, several other players stared at him in bewilderment, and then he deactivated the nanobots and was back in his bedroom. His mom called Gia.

Lien showed up at his house, and then Gia came to pick him up and bring him to the houseboat. At Gia's request, Lien went home. Jared does not remember much of what happened on the boat, but two days later, Gia drove him home to recuperate. Lien stopped by to make sure he was OK. She felt bad about what happened. Then, to his surprise, Megan came by and sat with him. He recalls how she made sure he was comfortable, making jokes and stroking his hair. She even planted a kiss on his forehead before she left. Jared smiles to himself, thinking of Megan.

Suddenly, his eyes snap open. That was at least two days ago. It must be the middle of spring break. He hasn't seen his mom since he got home. He sits up in bed. He hopes that the others have continued to play.

"Gia!" he calls, "Where's Mom? Where's Uncle Alberto?"

Gia reenters the bedroom. "Uncle Alberto had to go out of town. But as for your mom, I don't know. She wasn't here when we brought you back home. Alberto said she often has urgent out-of-town business meetings."

"She does," replies Jared. "But she never leaves without telling me, or in this case, she would have told you. Something's not right." Jared climbs out of bed and heads to the bathroom. "I'm going to wash up." He removes his shirt and leans over the washbasin, making sure he does not get the bandage wet. As he splashes his face, he notices that he has regained full range of motion in his shoulder. There is still some tingling, but he can move his arm almost like normal. He wonders how that can be. He's never healed this fast before. Maybe Gia knows.

Jared is toweling off when the secure satellite phone Gia gave to him begins to chirp. He cautiously picks it up. "Hello?"

"¡Hola!"

"Uncle Alberto, is that you?"

"Yes, I only have a little time. Things have gotten much worse—they've started a new disinformation campaign about me. I think they're getting desperate."

"Where are you?" asks Jared. "Actually, hold on, Gia's here. Should I have her listen to this?"

"Yes."

Jared calls for Gia and puts the phone on speaker. "OK, she's here. Go ahead."

Alberto continues, "I can't tell you where I am; the call is probably being traced. We only have a minute or two. A few hours ago, I learned that the FBI is renewing its focus on your dad's case."

"That's awesome," replies Jared excitedly. "I've got to go tell Mom."

"I wouldn't just yet. The FBI and the NSA think he may be working for the cartel or one of the other corporations looking for the artifact."

"You've got to be kidding! Why would they say anything like that?"

Alberto clears his throat. "Well, you know that they have high-powered computers that can stitch together video images. I guess the kidnapping was filmed by someone and posted online. No one took it seriously, because there are so many staged films on the Web today. No one knows what's real and what's not. It took the FBI, with the help of the NSA, several days to connect the dots—to link this specific event with the specific person they've been looking for. I never saw the images, but supposedly they've been searching the globe for the guy who kidnapped your father. He had been wanted for questioning in regard to several global incidents. Then he happened to turn up in your neighborhood."

"Yeah, OK. But why do they think the kidnapping was staged? It didn't feel staged to me."

Alberto sighs deeply, and then after a few seconds says, "I don't know. All we know is that the authorities think something was off."

"My God," replies Jared, too stunned to reply. "Staged? Do they think Dad was in league with the kidnappers? I don't believe it. Who is this guy?"

"We couldn't get that information, but we'll keep trying. This battle just keeps escalating," replies Alberto.

"Do you think the government is interested in this artifact, too?" asks Jared.

"Governments, plural," Gia says.

"Gia's right. There are probably several groups that are interested. Rumors are starting to spread like crazy about what this thing can do. Make sure your mother is safe, and check on Megan. I don't trust anything anymore."

Jared takes several breaths, still shocked by the news. He looks at Gia and then says, "Mom's not here. Gia thinks she might have gone on a business trip, but she didn't leave any word, so I'm not sure."

"Damn!" replies Alberto. "We'll check it out. That sounds suspicious. She always lets someone know."

Jared looks at the phone. This is the first time he has ever heard his uncle swear.

"Jared, I've got to hang up. Time is almost up. Gia, find out what's going on with his mom. Jared, you go check on Megan. I'll be in touch. Oh…and, Jared?"

"Yes."

"Make sure you find that artifact."

Jared hears a click and then only static. He turns off the phone, takes the battery out of it, and hides the phone in his desk drawer.

"I'll check on Megan," he says as he heads out of the bedroom, completely forgetting about his wound.

"You can reach me on the satellite phone if you need me," replies Gia.

In the garage, Jared sees both cars, his mom's and his dad's. He hasn't driven his dad's car in a while, and this is as good a time as any. He jumps in and pushes the ignition button.

"Good afternoon, Master Jared. It's been a while," says Jeeves, the onboard computer, in a British accent. "Where would you like to go?"

"Megan's house, and quickly."

The car automatically adjusts the seat, mirrors, and radio to Jared's preferences. It's ready to back out of the garage when Jared interrupts. "Jeeves, on second thought, let me drive." He pulls out of the garage, and as soon as the car is out in the open, it locks onto several wireless towers and a satellite. The car is now connected to the network. Jared flies down the street, doing more than fifty in a twenty-five mile-per-hour zone. Jeeves continually sounds the alarm that Jared is going too fast. As he swerves around cars, collision sensors and proximity alarms go off constantly. Jared can't find the disable button, so he just lets them blare. He has a dreadful feeling. His uncle would never risk calling if he didn't think something serious was happening.

Several miles away in a nondescript four-story building, software sends an automatic alarm message to a technologist. Many months earlier, software engineers had hacked into the car manufacturer's system and located the information on Jared's dad's car—not only vehicle-health information, but also contact information synched to the cell phone. The "drive automatically" function allows the driver to mention a name, and the car will locate that person. The driver can then instruct the car to drive to a specific address or hook up with the friend wherever he or she happens to be. The network knows where everyone is at any given point in time. After a person leaves his or her car, the network traces that person wirelessly through all of his or her other devices. Now that implanted devices, such as medical record chips, are getting more common, tracking is becoming even easier.

The computer recognizes that Jared's dad's car has stayed in one GPS location for months—the garage—but today it is moving, and moving fast. Someone is driving erratically and surpassing the posted speed limit on every street. The technologist speaks a few commands, and an algorithm starts to calculate probable destination based on who could be driving, the locations of the driver's friends, and the car's driving patterns, current speed, and direction. As the technologist looks at the information flowing in, he taps into the traffic infrastructure, which is also networked. He hopes that when the driver crosses a major intersection, the surveillance cameras will capture an image of the driver. He decides that there is no need to engage satellite surveillance yet.

Jared races to Megan's house and skids to a stop in the driveway while Jeeves protests and lectures him on how to slow down and park a car correctly. He suggests that maybe Jared needs to go back to driving school. Jared jumps out without turning off the engine, bounds up the steps to the front door, and bangs on it with both fists. Nothing. He jumps the side fence and heads to Megan's bedroom window. The glass is gone, and the sharp edges have been removed. He gets on his toes and peers inside. The room is trashed. Megan is not there, and neither is her mattress.

He thinks about calling her parents, but they are on a diplomatic mission somewhere in Africa. He looks back at the large window. Someone must have carried her out on the mattress so as not to disturb her while she was in the Web. She must have never known what was happening. For a second, he wonders how doing something to someone's body in the offline world affects that person in the online world. He then sprints back to the car and tries to call Gia on the secure satellite phone. Luckily for him there is no answer, since the car is listening to all conversations and routing the information to the remote monitoring station. Had he used his normal phone, which is wirelessly hooked up to the car, the monitoring station would have also known the number he dialed, in addition to what he said.

Jared needs to get back into the game, now. He speeds home, parks the car in the garage, and heads to his room. He texts his team and touches the wristband.

CHAPTER 35

JARED ARRIVES IN THE AFROEURASIA COMPLEX AND TOWERS JUST as a massive tremor lasting a few seconds shakes the glass cube lobby, knocking him off his feet. What is going on? he wonders. The lobby is swarming with students and sinister-looking men. He ducks his head and scans the lobby for his teammates. Finally, he sees them huddled together, trying not to stand out, near the large indoor waterfall. He slowly makes his way over to them. "Hey, guys."

"Jared!" Lien's face lights up, and she gives him a big hug, careful not to squeeze his shoulder too hard.

Arjun comes over and shakes his hand gently. "Good to have you back."

Ethan only nods, thinking it was so nice *not* having him around.

Megan waits until last and then embraces him gently. "I'm so glad you're OK," she whispers in his ear. She then plants a quick kiss on his cheek. Ethan turns his head and walks away.

"Me, too," whispers Jared, holding her tightly. "We need to talk." He needs to tell her what happened to her offline.

"OK, but not now. Something strange is happening." As Megan finishes her sentence, they hear a slight rumbling, similar to a thunderstorm, and the ground shakes again. Megan, Jared, Lien, and Arjun try to maintain their balance on the rolling marble. Ethan steps behind a column a few feet away and fiddles with a mini-tablet-like device. A few seconds later, the rumbling and the shaking stop.

"What's going on?" asks Jared, frustrated. He needs some private time to talk to Megan.

"I don't know," replies Arjun. "It's been happening every few minutes since we got here."

"Earthquake?" asks Jared.

"I'm not so sure," replies Lien.

"We'd better hurry and figure out where to find this water clock," Arjun says, explaining the details of the clue he and Megan found in Āryabhata's study. "I'm going to check out the directory."

Arjun mingles with the crowd and makes his way to the entrance of the lobby. Megan follows a few steps behind. As the others begin to trail after them, she turns. "Maybe some of you should stay here so it doesn't look too obvious."

"I'll wait here," Lien says. She makes herself comfortable on the concrete edge of the fountain pool and sticks her hand into the water to play with the koi. Jared sits down next to her. Ethan quickly catches up to Megan, and they push through the throng of students. Ahead, they see Arjun looking intently at the names on the directory.

"What's up?" asks Ethan.

"I don't know. These names aren't the same as before," says Arjun, pointing to the bronze directory mounted on a large stone pedestal. They hear the loud rumbling again, and this time they grab onto the sides of the stone to balance themselves. As a tremor, larger than before, rolls through, several entries on the directory begin to evaporate. Megan, Arjun, and Ethan watch in surprise as "Egyptians" disappears from the directory, followed by "Kush," "Minoans," "Phoenicians," "Persian Empire," "Greek City-States," "Alexander the Great," "Roman Empire," "Mauryan Empire," "Gupta Dynasty," "Qin Dynasty," and "Han Dynasty."

"What's happening?" asks Megan.

"If I had to guess, I'd say all these great civilizations came and then went. They are now going, that's why the names are disappearing," answers Ethan.

"That theory makes no sense," says Megan. "These civilizations didn't disappear completely; they were absorbed, they changed, they evolved. They became something different or part of something else. I mean, the Persian Empire no longer exists, but their values, practices, technologies, and other aspects of their culture might continue on in other ways."

"Since these are Web-based reconstructions, I would think they should stay up as long as their pages stay up," says Arjun. "Plus, these civilizations all rose and fell at different times."

"OK, OK, it was just an idea," replies Ethan.

Megan looks at the names and wonders aloud, "But why do great empires or civilizations fall apart?"

Ethan jumps in. "That's simple." Thinking that Megan wants an answer, he continues. "There's not just one reason; there are many. There are internal reasons—like territorial overextension, corruption, angry peasants, too many or too few taxes, social unrest between the classes, lack of trade, economic issues, infighting, greed, bad leaders, succession issues, overpopulation, drought, natural catastrophes, and rebellions from conquered provinces." Ethan does not stop, but keeps reciting reasons, in some way still trying to impress Megan. "Then there are the external reasons, like invading armies. Nomads challenging empires. Think about the Huns, the Arabs, and the Uyghurs."

"How do you know all this?" asks Arjun.

"Before playing *The Ancients* game, I was playing an empire game, and I totally messed up. My empire fell apart after only a few days," Ethan says with a laugh. "Lesson learned."

Back at the waterfall, Lien continues to dangle her hand in the water, absentmindedly trying to attract the koi, when she yells out in pain, "Ouch!" Jared looks into the pool, immediately grabs her arm, and pulls it out of the water. A section of the tip of her small finger is missing. "What the heck!" Lien yelps. "These aren't koi! They look more like piranhas."

Jared tears off part of his shirt and ties it around Lien's finger. "Are you sure they were koi?"

"Yes, I'm sure! One minute they're koi, then all of a sudden they're piranhas."

"Maybe someone is rewriting the game code," replies Jared, making sure that the bleeding stops.

"You mean while we're sitting here?"

"Yes." Jared looks around, wondering where Ethan went. He was here just a minute ago. He spots him over with Megan and Arjun.

Across the lobby, Arjun turns away from the directory. "Well, this isn't going to help us much," he says. "I have no idea how we're going to find a water clock. I assume a lot of old civilizations used them." As the three walk back toward Lien and Jared, they fail to notice that new names have appeared on the Afroeurasia Tower and Complex directory: "Byzantine Empire," "Holy Roman Empire," "Tang Dynasty," "Song Dynasty," "Yuan Dynasty," "Ming Dynasty," "Delhi Sultanate," "Mongol Empire," "Ghana," and "Mali Kingdoms," among others. As a matter of fact, in all of the towers the directories are changing—new names are being added. In the Americas Tower lobby, besides the Mayan name, the directory now includes the "Aztecs" and "Incas." Even the large numbers engraved into the stone at the front of Empire Plaza change from 2000 BCE to 1500 CE. Empire Plaza is entering another phase of construction.

As they push their way through the mingling students, Arjun looks up at the glass elevators filled with people going up or coming back down. Suddenly, his mouth falls open and he can barely speak. "Oh my God!" He grabs Megan's arm and points to the elevator over on the outside of the Middle East Tower. Ethan stops as well and tilts his head back to see what they are looking at. One of the elevators, filled with people, is slowly disintegrating from the top down. The elevator is literally dissolving into thin air.

"What is happening with this game?" cries Megan.

Arjun thinks that someone is probably cleaning up loose ends. "I don't think there were any students or players in the elevator," he says, hoping that's true. They return to Lien and Jared.

"Anything?" asks Jared.

"Nope," says Arjun, as he sits on the concrete edge of the pool next to Jared. Lien gently massages her finger, staring absentmindedly out the fifteen-story windows. She watches the clouds and looks across the water at the large glass blocks. The sun casts a long shadow. "What time is it?" she asks, all of a sudden.

"I have no idea," replies Megan. "I haven't thought about time since I started playing this game." She then looks around the lobby and sees a wall clock. "It looks like it's a few minutes before noon."

Lien keeps her eyes focused on a shadow out in the plaza as it moves toward one of the glass blocks. As the glass block is engulfed by the shadow, the enormous waterfall behind her roars even louder as more water cascades over the edge. The volume of water splashing down into the pool is now so great that she can feel a fine mist on her head and hair. She jumps up. "I've got it! It's been right here in front of us, or behind us, the whole time!"

"Got what?" asks Jared.

"The clue! What Arjun described. It's been here all along!" says Lien.

"OK, what is it?" asks Megan.

"The multistory water clock synchronized with the sundial is right here. Those big glass blocks out in the plaza belong to an enormous sundial, and this waterfall is the water clock. It's twelve, and the amount of water coming over the edge just increased. The two are calibrated relative to each other."

"Hmm," says Arjun. "That's strange. The idea with a water clock is to make the flow of water as constant as possible. Not vary it."

"Yeah. I agree," adds Ethan.

Lien, upset at how quickly her idea has been shot down, replies with a trace of irritation in her voice, "Well, do you have a better idea?"

"It's the best idea we've had so far. I think we should check it out," replies Megan. "What floor is that waterfall coming from?"

"I agree with Megan and Lien," Jared says. "I think it's probably on the twelfth."

"Stairs or elevator?" asks Megan jokingly.

"Real funny," replies Jared.

"What? You didn't like our earlier yo-yo ride?" Megan says, moving toward the door leading to the stairwell.

"Or the disintegrating elevator from a few minutes ago?" adds Arjun. "I don't think we have a choice."

As they all leave the lobby, Jared sees Megan stumble on the smooth floor. She recovers, and then an instant later she stumbles again. That's strange. There's nothing here that should cause her to trip. He wonders if they are moving her body in the offline world. He needs to talk to her as soon as he can. Jared thinks about telling Arjun and Lien, but with Ethan around, he's not sure now is the right time.

The five teenagers, with Megan in front and Jared bringing up the rear, enter the stairwell, making sure that no one else sees them. They begin the long climb to the twelfth floor.

CHAPTER 36

THE STAIRWELL DOOR OPENS AUTOMATICALLY, BUT instead of a lobby, the teenagers exit onto a dock that extends over a canal. Where the other floors had hallways, this floor has a twenty-foot-wide, six-foot-deep canal filled with water. The exterior walls are glass, just like on the other floors. The inner wall consists entirely of a seamless, ten-foot-tall, high-resolution monitor that curves around the inner core of the building. It also extends from the water line of the canal, up the curved inner wall, and across the ceiling. They notice several industrial-size green inner tubes piled up on the dock, as well as a control console.

"Welcome to Level Three. Congratulations. You are the first team to arrive," booms a voice that seems to emanate from everywhere all at once.

"I guess this is the place," Megan says nonchalantly.

"It looks like one of those amusement-park water rides," adds Arjun. The others look around. To their left, the canal disappears as it curves around the inner wall, and then it reappears again to their right.

"Not like any ride that I've ever seen," Ethan says. "Especially with that screen."

"Probably a big circle with the screen in the middle. I wonder if the screen goes all the way around. I say we try it out," suggests Megan. She grabs one of the inner tubes, and before anyone can stop her, she jumps into the canal. She floats on the water, looking up at the others. "Water's warm. There's got to be a way to turn this thing on."

"Maybe it's one of those lazy river rides," jokes Jared as he walks over to the control panel, which is covered with semitransparent black glass. Arjun and Ethan join him. Embedded in the glass is a dimly lit, slowly-spinning 3D globe depicting the Earth. "Wow! Look at this," says Jared.

"It's really dim. How do we turn it on?" asks Ethan, looking everywhere for a switch.

"I've read about this technology before," Arjun says. He reaches between Jared and Ethan and places his palm on the glass over the globe.

Seconds later, the globe lights up and the booming voice returns. "I'm sorry; you don't have enough experience points to access this feature. Only those who understand will be granted access."

"Understand what?" yells Megan, still floating on the inner tube.

The voice returns. "You must rise above the details, understand the rich tapestry that is human life on Earth. Only when you understand the threads that wove this tapestry will your eyes be opened to how patterns repeat. Although there are answers, there are many more questions. Your eyes do not yet see; therefore you lack the experience points to continue on this level."

"I think you're wrong!" Jared says with a confidence that surprises even Megan. "We have traveled to sites showing how humans populated the entire globe, and how a great revolution ushered in the era of farming and the emergence of complex societies, and how networks of trade, exchange, and encounter began to emerge in a time when great empires covered the earth. So don't tell us we don't have the experience points to continue."

Silence engulfs the room. Arjun nudges Jared and prompts him to take a closer look at the dark glass. Barely visible under the surface, three drawings emerge that look as though they've been copied from a prehistoric cave painting. One consists of stick figures and trees, the second consists of two groups of stick figures, and the third consists of two groups of stick figures with circles merging above their heads. Jared quietly calls Lien over to take a look.

"Confident aren't we, young man?" says the voice. "Well, if you and your team can answer a few questions, maybe I will give you the experience points necessary to continue."

"Agreed," replies Jared. He and his father often discussed the major patterns that shaped the world. He and his team should be able to figure this out.

"You have traveled to many time periods and places during this quest, experienced different cultures, learned a great many details. If you had to pull all this together in three essential questions that any student of history should ask, what would they be?"

Arjun points to the three drawings. Looking at the first one, he whispers, "The first one looks like people and trees. Trees usually mean the environment."

Jared nods and then says, "The first question is, How has the relationship between humans and the natural and physical environment changed over time, and how will this pattern continue in the future? During the Paleolithic Age, the relationship was very different, but as humans evolved, they extracted more and more resources and energy from the natural environment." He pauses.

Once again, the room is silent. "Yes," the voice says, and then it goes silent again. Meanwhile, Megan clambers out of the canal. Soaking wet, she stands behind Lien.

Lien looks more closely at the second drawing. "This one looks like two groups of people. It probably means how we interact."

"That's as good an answer as any," says Arjun. Jared nods. Megan agrees. Ethan hangs back.

Lien leans toward the console. "The second question is, How has the relationship between groups of humans changed over time?" She then steps back.

Jared quickly adds, "It used to be bands of hunters in scattered communities. Now there are billions of people, with more showing up all the time, interacting online—instantly connected. Relationships seem to have gotten so much more complex."

"Yes. Very good," replies the voice. Silence again engulfs the space.

The team looks at the last image, which shows people and little round circles coming from their heads. "I have no idea on this one," says Lien.

"That one's simple," says Megan. "Break it down. Usually, something coming out of someone's head indicates speech, or it shows a thought or ideas."

"That's it!" says Lien. "It's about sharing ideas."

"Are you sure?" asks Arjun. "That sounds a bit lame."

"I think so," replies Lien. "Ideas drive everything—science, technology, everything."

"Sounds good," says Jared. "Give it a shot."

Lien steps to the front and leans toward the console as if she's speaking into a microphone on a podium. "The third question is, how have the relationships between different views of the world, nature, and the cosmos changed? Humans think and share ideas with language. We share ideas about living, like new technologies, science, organization, morality, and spirituality."

"Yes again," replies the voice. "It looks like you have done well. All of history can be summarized by these three questions. Correct?"

Ethan is about to blurt out, "Correct," when Jared clamps a hand over his mouth. "Wrong!" he says thoughtfully. "These are only one set of lenses through which to look at history. Truly understanding requires one to look at history from multiple perspectives. For example, there are major themes such as population patterns, economic networks and exchange, the uses and abuses of power, and the haves and have-nots. These themes transcend time. Understanding them and looking at information from multiple perspectives is critical. We need to ask the tough questions, analyze the information and the evidence, and substantiate conclusions."

Ethan wrestles himself free, steps back, and glares at Jared. How dare he try to shut him up?

"Yes. I have underestimated you. You have spoken beyond your years," replies the voice. "Maybe you are worthy to continue the quest. Experience points granted." With that, the entire console lights up, and a portion of the glass slides to the side, revealing a digital keypad and a digital dial with an arrow, narrow on one end and thicker on the other. While his teammates' attention is focused on the console, Ethan exits through the stairwell door. He's had enough. He'll track them remotely.

Arjun gently touches the globe with his fingers and steps back as the globe emerges and floats above the console. The circular screen across the canal powers on. Arjun is about to touch the globe again when Jared steps in. "Here, let me try. Now I recognize this technology, too." He gently nudges the globe; then he pulls his hands apart and the globe expands. He pushes his hands together, and the globe shrinks.

Remembering the projections in Gia's houseboat, he says, "This is so cool. Watch."

He expands the globe to three feet in diameter. As he expands it, more and more details emerge. Instead of landmasses and continents, he can now see individual villages. The globe continues to float above the control panel.

"This is like one of those earth software programs, only it's in 3D form," Arjun says.

"Yes," replies Jared. "Except this globe is fully interactive. It allows you to see different scales of geographical space at different times. You can see a community or an entire civilization based on how you size the globe." Jared uses the keypad to enter a date. The globe becomes blurry for just a few seconds, and then refocuses itself with the way the world looked on that date. Jared types in several other dates, and the globe keeps changing.

"Watch this." Jared types "~" for "approximate" and then "2000 BCE." He expands the globe so he can see the island of Crete and the detail around the ancient city of Heraklion on its northern coast. He points. "There, can you see it? Just south of the city is the Palace of Knossos." He touches the globe, and the screen displays the story of the Palace of Knossos.

"Wow. How do you know so much about this technology?" asks Lien.

Jared hesitates. "I, umm, I read about it in a magazine."

"This is cool," Arjun says. "Ethan, you should see this. You were at the Palace of Knossos earlier, right?" There is no reply. Arjun and the others look around the dock. Ethan is gone.

"Maybe his mom pinged him again," says Megan as she grabs a tube and climbs back into the canal. "It seems to be happening a lot lately."

"What do you think this dial does?" Arjun asks, turning it from the off position. As he turns the dial, the water in the canal begins to move very slowly, and the screen begins to project images of Knossos that become more and more recent. After a few minutes, they see images and hear the story of how the Palace of Knossos was excavated by Sir Arthur Evans in the early twentieth century.

"This dial seems to control scales of time," Jared says. "If you keep it turned down, the water will move very slowly, and you can examine something in great detail, like the events during one year or one day. Watch what happens if you turn it up. I suspect the water will move faster and you can blast through hundreds of years." He turns the dial up. "Yup. The images tell a much bigger story."

"Careful!" Lien calls out. "Stop this thing! Where's Megan?"

Jared quickly turns the dial to the off position, and the water stops flowing. "Megan!" he yells down the canal.

"Are you all right?" Arjun calls.

"There's no reverse on this thing!" Jared yells. "You're going to have to paddle back!"

From around the corner they can barely hear Megan's voice. "Just like I thought. This goes in a circle," she yells. "Turn it on and let me go around."

Jared does as she says but keeps the dial turned down low. As they wait, Arjun can't resist touching the first set of stick figures. The screen changes color again and projects another series of images. He waits for a minute or so and then touches the next set of figures. The same thing happens again. He does it one more time with the third engraving, and then touches it again to turn it off.

"This is absolutely amazing," Lien says, moving toward the control panel. "These are the lenses you were talking about, Jared. When Arjun touched the first one, all of the images were of humans and the environment throughout time. Above the pictures were key themes. I didn't see them all, but one of the first themes was about patterns of population and how that changed over time."

Jared nods and contemplates the power of such a device in helping people to understand history. It would give people the ability to recognize details, relationships, and patterns. He sees what his dad meant when he said that it's important to understand how the past can inform the present. With this device, someone could trace past events to the present and use knowledge about the past to ask critical questions, in order to make better decisions. Like how the Greeks' fight for freedom affected all of Western thinking. Could this be the artifact that everyone is seeking? It is a powerful device. His thoughts are interrupted as Megan comes floating around the corner on her inner tube.

"That was awesome, but I'd like to go faster," she says as she scrambles out of the tube and back onto the dock. "Who's next?"

The others take turns exploring different parts of the globe at different speeds (time scales). Jared is the last to go. He takes the inner tube and jumps into the water. "I wonder if this is the artifact," he calls out. "But we haven't figured out how to change the scales of space and time. Plus, I'm still not sure what 'have faith' means."

Megan smiles. "What are you talking about? We know how to change the scales of space and time." She turns the dial almost to full. The water in the canal erupts into a raging flood, and Jared shoots along the rapids. The images on the screen cover large swaths of time. Megan lets him go around several times before she sees him signaling for her to stop. She turns the dial, but by the time Jared slows, he has floated far beyond the dock. He has to go around one more time. Three minutes later, he emerges.

"This is some awesome technology," he says, climbing out of the canal soaking wet. "Even though I was going fast, the images stayed in synch with my eyes, and I could understand the information. But even better, I may have figured out the 'have faith' part."

"Really?" asks Megan.

Jared explains, "When you're traveling at a high speed on the other side of the building, a big silver push button appears on the outer wall. It's similar to those old-fashioned automatic-door buttons that haven't been used since sensors were integrated into all entry doors, years ago.

"Written above an arrow that points to the button, it says, 'Falls of Faith,'" continues Jared. "This larger channel has a narrow, five-foot tunnel off to the side. A steel gate blocks it. I suspect it leads to these falls."

"Why didn't we see that?" asks Lien.

"I think it only shows up when you're going really fast, looking at lots of history or big patterns of time," replies Jared.

"You can't be serious," Arjun says. "You can't expect us to take an inner tube over a twelve-story waterfall into the lobby. That's nuts. It's suicidal. It's like fifty feet higher than the highest wave ever surfed. It will crush you."

"No kidding," adds Lien.

"I don't know if that's where the tunnel goes," Jared replies defensively. "It just says Falls of Faith."

"Where else could it go?" asks Arjun. "I haven't seen any other big waterfalls."

Megan calculates that twelve stories would be over one hundred feet high. High divers often jump from greater heights, but they are trained professionals and they do not have an inner tube along. Something else must be going on. Because of the inner tubes, she cannot get the notion of a water-park ride out of her head. "I'll try it," she says finally. She takes one of the inner tubes and jumps into the water. "Who's going to turn this thing on?"

"I'm not sending her over a twelve-story waterfall," Arjun says as Megan slowly floats away.

Lien wonders for a split second what it would mean for her and Jared if Megan were out of the picture. Then she immediately berates herself for even thinking that way and dismisses the thought. "Me neither," she says.

Megan looks into Jared's eyes, and as if communicating telepathically, Jared instinctively knows that she'll be fine. Megan is a risk taker, but she does not take careless risks. She takes calculated risks and usually thinks through the consequences ahead of time.

Megan yells something, but no one can hear it over the roar of the water as Jared turns the dial. Thirty seconds later, she races around the corner again. From several feet away, she yells, "Missed the button." She then passes the dock and yells something over her shoulder as she disappears around the corner again.

"What did she say?" asks Lien.

"Have faith!" answers Jared.

"What's that supposed to mean?" asks Arjun.

"One always has to have faith," answers Jared.

"This is nuts! I don't think it's faith; it's suicide," Arjun says, worried about his friend.

Thirty seconds pass, then sixty, then ninety. Soon, five minutes have gone by without them seeing Megan.

"Who's next?" asks Jared.

No one says anything.

"OK. I'll go," says Jared as he jumps into the canal with his inner tube. "Will you turn it on, Lien?"

Lien hesitates. "I still don't think this is such a good idea."

"Someone has to go see what happened to Megan," yells Jared.

Lien takes a deep breath and turns the dial. The water in the canal erupts. Arjun and Lien watch as Jared is grabbed by the strong current and propelled around the building. Jared sees the button for the gate coming up quickly. He's torn. On the one hand, he thinks he should go for it. On the other hand, it is a big risk. Megan could be lying in the pool at the bottom of the falls, dead. He realizes that it's a simulation, but death is real, and Gia can't fix a broken body.

He hears a voice from deep down saying, "Have faith, faith in yourself, faith in the divine." He floats closer to the button, debating with himself. He's almost past it when, at the last second, he reaches back and punches it with his fist. The outlet opens, and his inner tube races into a narrow tunnel about five feet wide and four feet high. In the distance, he can hear the roar of the falls. The current in the side channel is extremely slow, which gives him more time to think about his decision. Finally, when he has resigned himself to his choice, he notices a blinking dot on his contact lenses.

It is a message from Megan. "Stop! Don't go! Worked for me, but now a trap. Someone is rewriting the code on the Web site as we speak!"

Great, thinks Jared. Now what? He tries to slow himself down by paddling against the current. He rolls off the inner tube and begins to swim, and then he realizes that his feet will touch the bottom. The canal is only four feet deep, but the volume of water is slowly pushing him closer and closer to the falls. He tries to grab the walls, but they are smooth, just like in the canal at Chavín de Huántar. As he tries for another handhold, he sees his wrist and realizes how stupid he has been. With all the action of the last few hours, he completely forgot about his bracelet. He touches the home button, figuring that he can always come back later—if those nanobots do not take forever to activate.

He paddles harder, but the current takes him around a corner, and he sees the edge of the falls ten yards away. The roar becomes louder and louder. A few feet from the edge, he sees two other canals merge into his, bringing much more water and increasing the current. He now understands how the waterfall can have so much more water cascading over its edge. Three canals merge into one. The canal in which he is paddling flows slowly—but he can't make any headway against the current. It is too strong.

He watches his inner tube float toward the edge, expecting it to drop over. But suddenly, it drops out of sight before reaching the edge of the falls. Now he's even more worried. Those nanobots had better get him out of here soon! As he continues to fight the current, a rope made of shirts, pants, deflated inner tubes, and jackets all knotted together comes floating toward him. He grabs it and slowly pulls himself hand over hand against the current. As he gets close to the larger canal, he sees Lien and Arjun hanging onto the gate. They are holding onto their improvised rope with all their strength as the current of the main canal behind them races by.

"I hate these canals," says Jared as he grabs onto the gate.

After a few minutes of letting their muscles rest, they close the gate and float back toward the dock. They climb out and flop onto their backs, exhausted.

Jared cancels the home command and turns toward Lien and Arjun. "I don't know what to say. You guys saved my life."

"You did it for me in Qin China," replies Lien, breaking out into a tired smile. "Now we're even," she adds jokingly.

"How did you know I was in trouble?" asks Jared.

"Didn't you see? Megan sent the message to all of us," replies Arjun.

"No. I didn't look at it that carefully—hey, wait a minute," says Jared, looking at them both. "I didn't know you guys wore bathing suits under your clothes."

"Very funny," replies Lien. "This is not my bathing suit."

"Oh, I'm sorry," replies Jared, a bit embarrassed.

"Just remember what we had to sacrifice to save your life," Lien says as she unknots her wet clothes and puts them back on. "And don't you dare tell anyone."

"Oh, I wouldn't dare," Jared replies with a grin.

They take the stairs down to the lobby, and Megan meets them at the base of the waterfall. "This is a gigantic water slide," Megan says. "As I was circling in the big canal, I did a quick online search and learned that Empire Plaza had recently installed one of these slides to attract more visitors. After learning that, I figured it must be safe. You actually don't go over the falls. Right before the edge, the inner tube drops onto a steep water slide and you fly down a near-vertical drop right behind the water-fall. The slide continues in a translucent tube that goes under the lagoon and toward the island. It dumps you into a turtle-shaped pool under the plaza sundial."

"That's why I saw the inner tube drop away," Jared says.

"Exactly. I wouldn't want to go over a twelve-story waterfall in an inner tube, either," replies Megan.

"A turtle-shaped pool, though?" asks Lien.

"It's a big circular stone room under the island with light cascading in through the glass blocks on the island above. As the sun shone through the blue blocks of glass, it created a blue, rectangular space in the center of the pool. I guessed that it might be another link and waded over to it. As I stepped into the center, a message emerged on the ceiling. It wasn't a direct link this time."

"What did it say?" asks Arjun.

"*Offline, find the Indian legend of the great turtle. Enter its throat and you'll see the net, where it all began, and there you will find what you seek,*'" says Megan repeating the phrase.

"That sounds strange, but it's consistent with the other clues," says Lien. "They always tell us to seek something."

"It looks like the quest continues in the real world," adds Jared.

"What happened next?" asks Arjun.

"It took me a bit of time to get back. Luckily, I found a maintenance corridor next to the water slide that led back here to the lobby. As I got here, I realized that I had not closed the search screen on my lenses. I had only minimized it. I was about to close it when I noticed that the page for the water slide was now listed as 'under construction.' I found a way to get behind the waterfall and noticed that the top section of the slide had disappeared. Anyone going down that slide would be toast. You would have dropped twelve stories. I sent the message immediately."

"Good that you did; I was almost over the edge," Jared says. "If it hadn't been for Lien and Arjun, I would certainly have been toast."

"That sounds close," adds Megan. "Something else: as I was walking through the maintenance corridor, I saw a person in a hood and coveralls working on a palm-size device. His face was obscured by one of the columns, but I did see his hands. I was going to go investigate, but then figured that I needed to get back here."

Jared and Arjun look at each other. "Palm-size tablet?" asks Arjun. "Ethan had one in his hands went he left us."

"He was also holding a similar device earlier," Jared says. All of a sudden, he puts two and two together. "Arjun, you know computers. Could a device like that alter the code on a Web site while someone is on that site?"

"Anything is possible. If that device gave him access rights, he could change the code on any site. And he is a good programmer," replies Arjun.

Jared ponders Arjun's answer. "Yeah, but how did he get a device like that into the game? You can't bring in physical items from the outside."

Scrunching his forehead, Arjun replies, "I know. Unless someone programmed…"

"Damn!" says Megan. "I knew it. He's been acting weirder and weirder. Now, he knows our next step and is manipulating the game."

"Nothing we can do about that now. We just need to be extra vigilant," Jared says.

"I can't believe he would actually go that far," adds Lien.

"We need to get going," Megan says. "Looks like this quest continues in the offline world."

"You mean the real world," Jared says with a worried look. If they are going to search in the real world, then where is Megan? He gently pulls her away from the others. "I need to tell you something in private, right now," he says thinking he can fill in Arjun and Lien later. "And I'm not taking no for an answer." Jared then looks at the others. "We'll be right back."

Megan sees the intensity in his face and follows him.

As Jared tells Megan what has happened to her body offline, construction noise begins, and hordes of workers stream into the Empire Plaza Lobby and head toward the elevators. "We'd better get out of here," yells Jared as he and Megan return to the others.

"Yeah! I think something is happening to the game," replies Arjun.

CHAPTER 37

JARED DEACTIVATES THE NANOBOTS. LYING ON HIS BED, he reflects on what has happened. It is as if the game is reliving history. Between 200 and 500 CE, migrations and invasions brought down the classical empires of Rome, the Han, and the Gupta. The Classical Age was ending. He looks around his bedroom, and then slowly gets up. He gathers his hair in a ponytail and walks out into the kitchen, glancing at the clock. Yikes, he's been in the game for several hours. Strange, he thinks, he doesn't even know what day it is. The flat-screen monitor embedded in the refrigerator door tells him that it's Friday afternoon. Spring break is almost over. He grabs an orange juice from the refrigerator and wanders out into the living room. With his dad gone, and now also his mom, the house feels very empty. He grabs the satellite phone and dials Gia. After several rings, his call goes to voice mail, and he leaves a short message about the latest clue. He then plops himself onto the couch and stares up at the ceiling, thinking about Megan. He feels so helpless. The last time he had this feeling was when he hid behind the car the day his dad was kidnapped. Back then, he felt scared and helpless. He's not scared today, only angry.

Alberto said that the best thing to do is to find the artifact, but will that be enough? Jared punches the cushion in frustration. Then he sighs and tries to focus on the clue. He closes his eyes. He is thinking about turtles when a memory slowly emerges from the back of his mind. Didn't Gia say something about a turtle? Yes! The memory returns. It was while they were in his father's study on the houseboat. She had said that some Native Americans believed the world was created on the back of a sea turtle.

He jumps up from the couch and hurries to the computer to look up Native Americans and turtles. After close to thirty minutes of searching, he finds some general information but nothing he can use. He is wondering what he should research next when he hears his smartphone chirping in the bedroom. He races to grab it and looks at the screen. It's Lien.

"Hey, Lien. What's up?"

"You're not going to believe this, but we're exactly where we need to be," she says excitedly over the phone.

"What! How do you mean?"

"The artifact is somewhere around here, in the Bay Area."

"How can that be? We go roaming through virtual history all around the globe and end up where we started? Explain. Actually, wait. Why don't we set up a conference call with Arjun so he can hear it, too?"

"OK. But what about Megan?"

"She can't make it. I'll tell you about it later."

Lien hears the change in Jared's voice and asks, "What's going on? Anything wrong?"

"I'll tell you when we get on the call."

Several minutes later, Jared places his smartphone on the living room table, and two holograms appear. This new hologram technology allows users to choose to project their full-body image and several feet of surrounding environment. All participants in the call can see that Arjun is in his bedroom, Lien is in her kitchen, and Jared is in his living room. Ethan and Megan do not join the call.

"Isn't this a bit dangerous?" asks Arjun. "This call is probably being monitored."

"I know. But I don't think we have a choice. We need to move fast," replies Jared.

"At least let me try activating my white-noise generator," adds Arjun. "Maybe it will give us some privacy."

Jared goes on to explain that he thinks Megan was taken from her home while she was playing the game. Arjun and Lien are stunned. Jared goes on to explain that Alberto and Gia both have the same hypothesis. Someone is going to use her as a bargaining chip if Jared and the team find the artifact first. With her parents out of town, no one is going to ask any questions. Jared then switches topics. "Let's stop talking about Megan. Best thing we can do for her is find the artifact. Lien has some interesting information. She thinks the artifact is somewhere in the Bay Area. Fill us in."

"Well, after searching unsuccessfully online, I decided to call our local reference librarian."

"I didn't know libraries still had reference librarians," says Arjun.

"Of course they do. And they can be really helpful," replies Lien. "I got this really nice lady, and I was telling her about this research project I was doing about a turtle legend and Native Americans. It didn't take her more than a few minutes. She said that many tribes have legends about how we all live on the back of a great turtle."

Jared remembers what Gia told him.

"And guess where the head is?" Lien asks rhetorically.

"Let me take a wild guess," interrupts Arjun. "Here!"

"Exactly," replies Lien. "Mount Tamalpais is the holy right eye, and Mount Diablo is the left eye. The San Francisco Bay is the mouth."

"If the Bay is its mouth and we have to go down its throat, do we go north or south?" asks Arjun.

"Let me see," replies Lien. "The librarian also said that the tail was in Florida. So my guess is that its throat is south."

Arjun realizes it immediately and blurts out, "Silicon Valley."

"Yeah, but Silicon Valley is a pretty big place," Jared says. "Where do we go?"

"What did the clue say, again?" interrupts Arjun.

"Enter its throat and you'll see the net, where it all began, and there you will find what you seek," Jared recites. "Does that make any sense to you?"

Arjun rubs his lips and stares off into space. He brainstorms several words, calling them out as they pop into his mind. All of a sudden, he yells, louder than necessary, "Yes! 'Net' doesn't mean fishing. Silicon Valley, technology—'Net' means the Internet. It must have something to do with the Internet," he says more quietly. "The forerunner of the Internet was a network that connected only four computers. One of those computers was here in Silicon Valley. But they shut that network down decades ago. It became obsolete and was replaced by another."

"That makes sense," Lien says. "I was stuck thinking it was a fishing net. But I think you're right."

"I'm not so sure," says Jared hesitantly. "It might be a bit of a stretch."

"Think about it," Arjun argues. "Remember the prophecy? Lords of the Clouds. Those could be corporations that are trying to dominate the Internet. It's history repeating itself. Pharaohs dominated civilizations, the Phoenicians dominated trade networks, and emperors dominated their empires. Today it's about businesses and the Internet."

"But wait a minute," says Lien. "Couldn't it also be governments trying to control the Internet? Look how many governments censor the Internet and try to control or suppress information."

Jared reflects on the prophecy. Weird, he thinks. His dad was right. Big patterns do repeat themselves, just in different ways and with different technologies. The use or abuse of power seems to be a recurring theme. His eyes light up as an insight strikes him. "I think you're both right. The lords could be corporations or governments. It's really up to us. If we don't think critically about the information we are exposed to and what we consume, then we do lose our freedom."

"Hmm! 'Sapere aude' does mean 'dare to be wise' or 'dare to know,'" adds Lien. Jared looks at her with a hint of surprise. "What?" asks Lien. "I know a little Latin—actually I looked it up when you first told me the prophecy." She smiles.

"Yes!" says Jared. "If people don't dare to question things, if we believe everything we see or read, then we become lemmings—or worse, dependent on these lords. They'll control our lives. We maintain freedom by asking the critical questions, by challenging."

"There's a Chinese proverb my parents always told me," says Lien. "He who asks a question is a fool for five minutes; he who doesn't ask a question remains a fool forever."

"So this is about the Internet," Arjun says. "I think the clues lead us back to the beginning—to the start of the Net."

Jared thinks for a moment. "You may be right. My dad used to tell me that Aristotle supposedly said that if you want to understand anything, observe its beginning and its development."

Lien sighs and leans against her kitchen counter. "OK. So, unlike in ancient times when battles were fought over territory or slaves, today it's a battle for the Internet. But where did the Internet start?"

"I don't know, but I'm sure we can find the place," replies Arjun, pacing his room in excitement. "If the place still exists."

Before anyone says anything else, Jared notices a strange movement in the window behind Arjun. The holographic projector has captured a shiny reflection.

Jared yells, "Arjun, watch out!" just as a large insect the size of a fly on steroids comes through the bedroom window. Arjun recognizes it from his techno-science magazine as a micro-aerial vehicle. A second later, he jumps out of the way, grabs his wetsuit from a nearby chair, and smothers the insect inside the neoprene. He throws the wetsuit onto his bed, grabs a book, and bashes the intruder until he hears a crunch. Then he slowly unwraps the suit, ready to hit it again if the fake insect isn't dead. But its wings are broken and it isn't moving. Arjun examines the device. It looks just like an extra-large fly, but it is metallic, has ultralight wings, has cameras instead of eyes, and is remote-controlled. Arjun has read that most of these devices are used for reconnaissance, but this one is nasty. It has a capsule on its abdomen, along with a needle. This particular device has an altogether different purpose: carrying poison or chemicals. Arjun slumps to the floor and leans against the edge of his bed, breathing heavily. He doesn't want to think about whether this "fly" was meant to kill or just immobilize.

Suddenly, he hears a mechanical sound behind his head. He jumps up as the insect tries to crawl toward the edge of the bed, right to where he was resting his neck. No longer fully functional, it falls over the side. It hasn't given up. Arjun grabs the book from his bed, smashes it numerous times against the insect, and then grinds what's left into the floor. "Now you're dead!" he says quietly.

"Oh my God! Did you see that!" yells Lien with panic in her voice. "Someone just tried to get Arjun!"

"Yeah! I'll make sure he's OK," says Jared, pulling out his satellite phone.

"We'd better go find this artifact before our whole team disappears," Lien says. "These guys don't mess around."

CHAPTER 38

EARLY SATURDAY MORNING, JARED RECEIVES A TEXT from Arjun indicating that he thinks he's located the site. He and Lien will be by to pick Jared up within the half hour.

Jared showers and looks at himself in the mirror. The wound in his shoulder is almost completely healed. He wonders what Gia used to help him heal so quickly. One of these days, he's going to ask her. He throws the bandage in the garbage and puts on a fresh shirt. A few minutes later, he hears Arjun pull into the driveway in a four-door sedan. Jared grabs his jacket and satellite phone and heads out the front door. He looks at the car. It is not the coolest, he thinks, but at least Arjun has a car. Jared's still trying to convince his mother that if he had one, it would make her life so much easier.

"Hey, Lien," Jared says as he climbs into the backseat behind her. "Hey, Arjun. Yesterday was crazy. You OK?"

"I'm good. Couldn't sleep much last night, but I'm good. We have a bit of a drive," Arjun says. "And I'm not totally positive that this is the place, but I think so."

They drive down the highway for close to twenty minutes, commenting on how light the traffic is on the weekend. They take a west exit and drive through a residential neighborhood nestled under huge oak, sequoia, willow, and magnolia trees, and continue into the more industrial section of town. They pass many one- and two-story office buildings and warehouses. Some look deserted, some are for lease, and others house professional businesses, including law firms, accountants, architects, biotech labs, and engineering firms. It's the weekend, and the area is nearly deserted, except for the occasional car using the streets as a shortcut. They pass several abandoned office buildings, and then Arjun makes a sharp right turn into the driveway of an old, two-story building consisting of offices, warehouses, and industrial space.

"This is it," he says, pulling into the parking spot closest to the door. The place looks deserted. "They usually kept the computers in the basement." They try the door, but it is locked. They look through the first-story windows and see office furniture that dates back to the end of the last century. The place looks as though it has not been used in years. They walk around the building to one of the chain-link gates that restrict access to the industrial section. It has a thick chain wrapped around it several times, and a large lock.

"I'm sure this is the place," says Arjun. "But how are we going to get in?"

Thinking about what Megan would do, Jared jumps up and starts climbing the chain-link fence; luckily, there is no razor wire on top. "C'mon. They might have left something open in the back."

"I'm not sure this is such a good idea," Arjun says. "This used to be a restricted facility. I don't want to be arrested for trespassing."

"OK. Why don't you wait here and text us if something happens?" Jared replies, glancing at Lien as he reaches the top. He jumps down ten feet to the other side.

Lien does not think twice. She climbs the gate and is over the top and standing next to Jared in less than half the time it took him. He looks at her with surprise. He knew that Lien was athletic, but this is more than athleticism.

"Remember, text us if something comes up. Don't call," Jared says to Arjun.

"Forget it. I'm coming, too." Arjun jogs toward the fence, climbs it just as fast as Lien had, and gracefully jumps to the ground. Jared looks at both of them, wondering where they learned to move like that. It can't be an enchantment; they're not in the game anymore. Jared dismisses the thought as they move toward the building.

They try all the doors, only to find them locked. Next, they try all of the ground-floor windows. They're all locked, too—except for the last one, hidden by a big bush at a corner of the building. It looks locked, but Lien pushes on it anyway. The glass moves upward an inch. The window frame is so corroded that they can't get it to move any farther. Jared grabs a broken branch from a nearby tree and, using it as a lever, pushes the window up two feet.

"Now we're breaking and entering," says Arjun, stepping back a few feet as if he is trying to distance himself from the action.

"We haven't broken anything...yet," replies Jared. "We're just exploring."

"Now you sound like Megan," says Lien as she helps push the window. Jared stops for a moment. He realizes that he misses Megan, especially now.

The three teenagers climb through the window into a large office space. The carpet hasn't been vacuumed in decades, cables dangle from the ceiling, and old cubicle walls stand at odd angles. They walk down a wide staircase into the basement and enter another enormous room. It's the size of five or six classrooms combined. Here, the sixty-year-old linoleum floor, yellow and cracked, still looks better than the old acoustic ceiling tiles. Several bundles of cables hang from the ceiling next to dusty air vents and a series of over-sized 220-volt electrical plugs. More old office furniture is piled in the corners of the room. Otherwise, the space is empty.

Jared is the first to speak, and disappointment is clear in his voice. "Nothing here! Empty!"

"Can't be," says Arjun. "One of the four computers that was part of the first Net was here."

"Not anymore. Dead end," Lien says.

After looking around the room for several minutes, the teenagers give up. They are climbing the stairs when they hear a jingling sound.

"I think someone's coming," whispers Jared. "That sounds like a key ring."

"Quick, hide!" says Arjun. He turns and runs back down the stairs into the large room. They try to hide among the old office furniture, and hope that the guard does not come down the steps.

Minutes later, the jingling stops, and they sigh with relief. They slowly make their way back toward the stairs. They round the corner and stop in their tracks.

"And who do we have here?" asks a guard sitting casually on the steps as if he had been waiting for them. He has one hand on his gun holster. "You do realize this is private property and you're trespassing."

The guard looks more than eighty years old. He's wearing a security guard's hat over his longish white hair. Jared contemplates bolting for the exit. But the guard looks to be in decent shape and can probably reach his holster faster than they can run. The guard holds up a tablet on which Jared can see images of himself, Lien, and Arjun. Hidden security cameras. He should have known. The guard erases the image and looks at the teenagers suspiciously.

Jared thinks fast. "Umm...we're doing a school research project. We were told that an old computer is supposed to be here."

"Yes, one of the original Internet computers, from the original network," says Arjun, stepping closer to the guard.

"We wanted to see a bit of history," adds Lien.

The old guard chuckles, not sure if he should believe the teenagers, but he appreciates anyone who values events of his era. "Ah, yes. The first network," he says. "I still remember when we created the first link. That machine hasn't been here for decades. When they shut the place down, they moved all that old technology elsewhere—it was outdated." He sees the disappointment on the teenagers' faces.

"See? Dead end!" Lien whispers to Arjun. Jared slowly moves behind Arjun and Lien.

The guard relaxes a bit. "Why do you want to see that old thing anyway?"

Arjun thinks for a moment, and then says, "The Greek philosopher Aristotle once said, 'If you would understand anything, observe its beginning and its development.'"

"Someone who can still quote an ancient philosopher. I'm impressed," replies the guard. "We never imagined where it would all go. Just like it's hard to imagine where it will be tomorrow." He then remembers that they're in a locked facility. "By the way, how did you get in here?"

"Through one of the windows," replies Arjun truthfully.

"No. I mean onto the property. You know you are trespassing," he repeats.

"Yes," Lien says. "We're sorry. We couldn't resist."

"Well, all right. If you leave right away, I'll let you off with just a warning. Just don't let me catch you again."

"Thank you!" Arjun says, thinking about what his parents would do to him if they ever found out he was arrested for breaking and entering.

"Yes, thank you," says Lien, extending her hand toward the guard as she walks up the steps.

The guard takes her hand and shakes it vigorously. "Remember, no return visits."

Lien and Arjun make their way past the guard, who keeps looking down into the room. "I guess we need to keep looking and fight the battle for the Internet another day," Arjun says quietly. "Freedom will have to wait."

The guard spins around and says, "Excuse me! Young man, what did you just say?"

"Oh, nothing," Arjun replies. He keeps walking.

"I heard you say something about the Internet and freedom," says the guard, climbing the steps toward them.

Arjun hesitates for a moment, and then figures that there's nothing to lose. "I said freedom will have to wait and we'll fight—"

Jared's yell interrupts him. "Hey guys! Quick! I think I found something!" Jared is standing in the far corner of the room. As Lien and Arjun look down the staircase toward him, he slowly disappears between two desks. Lien and Arjun bolt past the guard toward Jared.

"Wait! Wait!" yells the guard in a near panic. "You can't go there! It's restricted!"

CHAPTER 39

LIEN AND ARJUN SEE THAT JARED HAS DISAPPEARED down a spiral staircase leading to another basement room.

"We've played this game way too much," says Lien, as she heads down the narrow steps. "For a minute, I thought this was another link."

"Me too," says Arjun, following closely and ducking to make sure he is out of the guard's line of fire. However, Arjun does not think the guard will shoot. There is something different about this guard.

At the bottom of the spiral staircase, there's more old furniture. A few yards away, Jared stands in front of double doors held shut by an old padlock. "Listen. I hear a soft humming coming from behind these doors. Something's in here."

Lien wonders why there's a set of double doors after such a narrow staircase. When they catch up with Jared, she and Arjun both put their ears to the door.

"You're right," Arjun says. "A slight humming."

They hear the guard at the top of the spiral staircase. "There isn't anything down there," he yells. "Just some old fluorescent lights. The ballasts in those things make a heck of a racket. Come back up."

"Sounds bigger than that," replies Arjun.

"Let's take a look," Jared says. "Look for anything we can use to pry open the padlock." Arjun and Jared search frantically, but there's only old office furniture, nothing they can use. The old guard slowly makes his way down the stairs, careful not to fall.

"Guys! Look!" Lien takes the lock and gently lifts the bar out of the locking mechanism. "It was unlocked the whole time."

As the guard enters the basement room, Lien and Jared pull on the doors. The guard stops, closes his eyes for a moment, and sighs. It is too late, he thinks. He cannot guard this place any longer. Looking for the key every time he came down to check on the machine had driven him crazy, so he had left the padlock unlocked most of the time.

Jared, Lien, and Arjun look into a pitch-black room with blinking blue lights off in the distance. As the door swings all the way open, dim ceiling lights come on.

"Wow," mumbles Arjun as he steps through the doorway. He leans against the door and stares into the room—it's a huge computer-server room. Computers six feet tall stand along concrete walls the length of the basement, at least fifty feet. Several flat-screen monitors attached to the wall indicate the status of the servers. The power is on, lights are blinking, and a faint humming sound fills their ears. The room is cool and well-ventilated. They walk along a highly polished floor, similar to the one in the Empire Plaza lobby. Reflections make the computers look even larger. At the end of the room is another door. As they walk closer, they see bundles of cables running from the last set of servers through the wall into the back room. They realize that they are only in an anteroom.

Jared hesitantly touches the doorknob. He turns it slowly and pulls. As the light spills into the next room, he can see a device lying on a rectangular pedestal twenty feet away. As the three teenagers enter the room, the pedestal turns a deep, icy blue. Jared feels along the wall next to the door and locates the light switch, bathing the room in a deep red, similar to the inside of an old photography darkroom. Behind the cube stands a cabinet with a computer, at least eighty years old, attached to another flat-screen monitor. A single cable runs from the flat screen to the device on the pedestal.

Arjun, Lien, and Jared stare at the high-tech device in amazement. It's a clear, glass sphere a little larger than a tennis ball. A green gel-like substance floats inside. On the bottom is some type of cable port. Arjun recognizes it as an old Ethernet port.

Could this be it? The artifact that everyone has been searching for? Jared walks closer. He sees computer code, ones and zeros, swirling around within the gel. "What is this?" is all he manages to say.

He's about to lift it off the pedestal when the guard calls out, "Don't! You'll set off the alarms. It's very fragile."

"What is it?" Jared repeats.

"I suppose it's over now," laments the guard, sinking into a chair near the sphere. "The time has come." He becomes thoughtful. Except for a slight humming sound, the room is quiet. Finally, the old guard says, "It all started so innocently."

"What did?" prods Jared.

"We were a bunch of young engineers—driven, idealistic. The world was entering the Internet Age, the Communication Age. Everything was going digital and online—all the information you can imagine. It was the era of big data when the amount of data about people and things was exploding and analyzing it became a basis for competition. News, articles, books, information about every aspect of life...the entire world's information was being digitized. Health records, personal information, communication with family and friends. Anything that could be collected about a person was being collected and stored in millions of computer servers around the world. People were getting exactly what they wanted. They did not have to listen to anything they didn't want to hear or read anything they did not want to see. It was the personalization of information. People saw specific ads based on their online behavior and information based on their interests, values, and viewpoints. They loved it. It was a way to deal with the overload of information. Social pressures drove it to extremes. It seemed like the perfect world. Except there are always two sides to everything, even nirvana." The guard gets up, takes off his cap, and begins pacing the room.

"Soon, some people realized that all this personal information float-ing in cyberspace could be used against them by others. Things they'd done years earlier would come back to haunt them. For example, a stu-dent wouldn't get into law school because she'd been tagged in a few inap-propriate pictures her friends posted on the Web years earlier, back when it was just fun. Or a man would be denied services based on what an organization had learned about him online, and he'd never know why he was denied. Companies would deny insurance coverage based on what they learned about a person's genetic risk factors – stored online. People thought that information was deleted when in reality, it was still stored on some computer server, and it was being analyzed. People lost control over information forever. It would live on endlessly. The Internet never forgets." The guard closes his eyes and shakes his head as he remembers.

"Security firms tried their best to close any gaps, to stay one step ahead of hackers, corporations, and even governments that might use this data maliciously, but they couldn't keep up. Hackers, individual, orga-nizations, and even governments kept causing mischief. Corporations wanted more information so they could sell more products or reduce their risks. Governments wanted to know more about their citizens, often for security purposes. Like I said, it was the era of big data; more and more information was collected about everything and everyone. So, several people who saw how this was spinning out of control turned to us for help." The old man looks at the ceiling.

"That sounds like a major historical pattern repeating itself," says Jared. "Since ancient times, the control of information has represented power."

"Yes. And it is still that way today," says the guard.

"The uses and abuses of power. That key theme again," adds Lien.

"So who turned to you?" asks Arjun.

"Several organizations who focus on protecting people's privacy wanted a solution. Many citizens around the globe started to understand the risks. They wanted a solution, too. They wanted to be able to control what others saw about them. They wanted privacy. They wanted to delete information that they had made public on the Web but now regretted, or information that was being collected without their knowledge. We worked day and night for months and finally developed a computer application that would erase a person's history. It was beautiful. A person could use this program and erase their presence on the Net. The program would scour the Web like a spider, looking for anything about that person. It would penetrate the most sophisticated and secure databases and servers and come back with information about every place their name, picture, or identification numbers showed up. They could then decide to erase whatever they didn't want public, and the spider would go erase it. Privacy advocates would have been thrilled." The guard runs a gnarled hand through his hair.

"We called it the zero-day application, meaning you could turn the clock back to day zero, when there was no information about you on the Web. We never thought about the risks, or the other consequences." Several tears emerge as the old guard thinks about what they created.

Lien gently places her hand on the old man's shoulder. "You said 'would have been'...What happened?"

"We don't know." The guard wipes away the tears with his thumb and shakes his head. "Somehow the code mutated. It started to rewrite itself. It started to act less like computer code and more like a biological virus. Soon, it was out of control, morphing into something we had never seen before."

"What did it do?" asks Arjun.

The guard closes his eyes again and breathes deeply. "It not only allowed a person to erase personal history; it now allowed the user to erase and rewrite any aspect of *human* history."

"What?" asks Lien removing her hand. "How is that even possible?"

"Almost all of the world's information is now digital. There are very few hard copies of anything left. The virus goes out onto the Web, finds all the information about a particular subject, and lets the user erase it or change it."

"Oh my God!" Lien covers her mouth. She completely understands the power of such a device. She remembers how the first emperor of China, Qin Shi Huang, ordered all histories burned, except for those he favored. This sounds like a high-tech way of doing even more.

"No wonder everyone wants to get their hands on this thing," says Jared. "Imagine the power. You could erase the knowledge that democracy started in Athens. Change the outcomes of ancient battles. People would repeat the same mistakes over and over again. Within a few decades, you could manipulate an entire population to do what you want because they would have no idea of what happened before."

"Rulers have used symbols of power to control their people for millennia," adds Arjun. "Pharaohs and the ankh, Chinese emperors and dragons, even the arrow has been used a symbol of power throughout history."

"Yes, but this sphere is more than a *symbol* of power," replies the guard. "It *is* power. A technology, a tool of power. Whoever controls it becomes most powerful. We could never let this get out. After the mutation, we started calling it the zero-day history virus. It was so powerful that it would find a previously unknown vulnerability in a system, and it could set any part of history to zero—day zero, zero awareness of the vulnerability—and then add different information. Once we saw what we'd created, each of the original team members swore an oath to take a turn guarding the sphere and this secret virus. I am, unfortunately, the last of the original team members—the last guardian."

In the silence that follows, Jared reviews the prophecy in his head. "So, the prophecy is true. Any corporation, government, or individual— the Lords of the Clouds—could rule the world with this type of power. Freedom and independence would be at risk."

"Why didn't you just destroy it?" asks Lien, looking at the guard.

"We couldn't. It would be like destroying one's child. We hoped that someday humanity would evolve to the point where such a device could be used positively."

"Positively?" asks Jared, shaking his head. "Still idealistic, aren't you? There are key themes that have accompanied humans through all of history and they aren't likely to change anytime soon. The use and abuse of power is one of them. The world has always been filled with have and have-nots, one group controlling another. These themes haven't changed in millennia. Why should they change now?"

The guard chuckles. "Well said, young man. Perhaps you're right and we have been naïve. Maybe we haven't learned from the past, and the sphere should be destroyed." He glances over at the glass sphere.

Suddenly, they hear loud clapping from the back of the room. "Bravo! Bravo! I couldn't have said that better myself."

They all turn. The outlines of several men are visible in the light that washes in from the anteroom. Jared has heard that voice before. However, he cannot see who it is. The light in the room is too dim.

"Yes, Jared, well said, but you are also a bit naïve," the man says. "We have a much better plan for this little device. Whoever has the power will always rule. And this device will give us the power. You are right: there will always be haves and have-nots. In this case, we will have the sphere and you will not." The man laughs at his own play on words. He and the other men begin to walk toward Jared, Lien, Arjun, and the guard. "By the way, thank you for finding the artifact for us. Game well played!"

CHAPTER 48

"KEEP THAT DEVICE SAFE," JARED WHISPERS TO THE guard without taking his eyes off the oncoming men.

Unseen and unheard, a micro-aerial device, similar to the one that attacked Arjun, strikes the guard in the neck. The old man does not reply. His breathing slows; he slumps over in the chair, and then falls to the floor.

Jared, Lien, and Arjun watch as the men slowly come into focus. Jared's eyes grow wide. He will never forget the face or the name. The man standing in front of him is Victor, the one who kidnapped his father. A few feet behind Victor, with a lopsided smirk on his face, stands Ethan. Jared is too stunned to speak.

Lien shakes her head. "Ethan! What are you doing? You traitor! You're our classmate!"

"Sorry, guys, but I have my reasons," replies Ethan with a newly developed arrogance. "The Lords of the Clouds will eventually rule the Net. There is no way to stop them. I decided to join the winning team early." Ethan steps in front of Victor and turns to Arjun. "Arjun, you're bright. I knew it the first time I met you as a freshman. You like technology. Don't you see? We programmers, gamers, coders, and mathematicians are the priests of the future. In ancient times, priests were the gatekeepers of communication. Today, we are. We are the new elite, the ones who control what people see. We write the algorithms that guide searches, that can filter reviews, that determine what people see. We can make or break a Web site, a product, a service. Businesspeople have to come to us to translate the real world into the online world. We can even start and stop political movements across the globe. We design viruses and cyber weapons. Imagine the power! Join me. Join us. We are the new priests of the online world. The rewards are immeasurable: money, power, and prestige. You'll be part of creating the future!"

Arjun looks at Ethan with disgust. "Oh, I'll be part of creating the future all right," he replies with confidence. "But not the future you see. Listen to yourself, Ethan. You sound like one of those ancient tyrants who tried to control the world. Eventually, they all failed. People want freedom."

"Ha! That's where you're naïve," Ethan says. "Freedom must be fought for. Fighting on the Net means people have to work to seek the truth, to understand the sources of information, to question, to challenge. They don't want to do that. They want it easy. They want only the information they desire delivered to them. They don't want to listen to other views."

"I guess I have more faith in humanity than you do," replies Arjun. "I think your moral compass is a bit off."

"Suit yourself," Ethan says. "Maybe I misjudged you."

"You sure did!"

"Enough of this philosophical debate!" shouts Victor. "Step aside and let me have my sphere."

"I'm sorry," Jared says, stepping forward. "I let you take something I cared for last time. I don't think that's going to happen again."

"Just as stubborn as your father," replies Victor. "Soldiers! Take care of these kids, and bring me that sphere." As three mercenary soldiers move toward Jared, Lien, and Arjun, Victor adds, "Oh, by the way. If for some reason you get lucky and beat my men, remember: I always have a backup plan." He pulls a tablet computer from his jacket and touches the screen. "In this case, it's your girlfriend, Megan."

Ethan mockingly adds, "Yeah, your girlfriend," then looks at Lien with a snide grin, because he knows that she likes Jared.

Jared glares at Ethan and remains silent.

Victor brings up a video feed of Megan, hands and feet tied, mouth gagged, lying on the floor of a van. "She's right upstairs, in a van parked outside."

Jared looks at the video and sees Megan staring at the camera. Jared and Megan's eyes meet. He sees her wink and then shake her head vigorously from side to side. Then a hand belonging to an unseen person slaps her.

"See, eventually, no matter what, I will get that sphere. It's that simple," says Victor, chuckling. "Once I have the sphere, maybe I'll let her go."

"And if you don't get it?" asks Jared defiantly.

"That's not an option," replies Victor, stepping farther back.

Expecting little resistance from the teenagers, the first mercenary attacks Arjun without hesitation. Arjun deftly steps out of the way, his motions fluid and quick. He focuses his breathing and mental energy. He imagines himself as a snake and goes on the attack. His first two punches and two kicks are blocked, but the fifth strike somehow penetrates the soldier's defenses. Everyone hears the two bones of the man's forearm snap. The soldier grimaces in pain, takes a step back to catch his breath. The soldiers regroup. This might not be so easy after all.

Lien steps toward Arjun. "I didn't know you could fight like that. Where did you learn?"

"It's called *Kalaripayattu*, one of the oldest forms of Indian martial arts. My parents thought it would be good for me to learn it as part of understanding my Indian heritage. I started several years ago. They said I should never use it unless my life is threatened. This counts, right?"

She nods, keeping an eye on the other soldiers. "Funny. My parents did the same."

"You know Kalaripayattu?" Arjun asks with astonishment, briefly glancing at Lien.

"No, I meant that I started Chinese martial arts several years ago." She turns her attention to a soldier as he attacks. She can immediately tell that he also has some martial arts training. She tries to focus and put herself into the dragon mindset of Shaolin Kung Fu. She forms her hand into a claw and lands a blow to the soldier's face, using her waist to generate power. Lien's lucky strike surprises even herself. Blood begins to trickle down the soldier's cheek. He licks it and his eyes flare with rage.

The third soldier, a head shorter than his comrades, focuses on Jared, lowering himself into a crouching position. At that moment, Jared wishes he'd paid more attention in PE when they did martial arts training. The man attacks, and Jared is able to block the first kick and punch, but then he leaves his midsection exposed. The soldier throws a punch, landing it squarely, with full power, in Jared's gut. Jared feels as if he has collided head-on with a freight train. Keeling over and gasping for air, he drops to his knees. Lying next to the still-passed-out guard, he is sure every rib is broken.

Seeing that Lien and Arjun are good fighters but not yet experts in martial arts, the attackers decide to work in tandem. The third soldier, having made short work of Jared, helps where he can. The men, matched almost evenly with Arjun and Lien, know enough to block most of the attacks. After a few minutes of parrying, strikes, and counterstrikes, several blows get through Arjun and Lien's defenses. Arjun, with blood dripping from his lips and with his curly black hair matted in sweat, miscalculates a punch. The counterstrike hits him squarely on the side of the head, instantly knocking him unconscious. He crumples to the floor next to Jared, who is still struggling to breathe normally. Now it's three against one. Lien, who is now exhausted, has no chance. The men grab her and tie her legs and hands with an electric cord from an old office lamp.

Ethan steps past Victor and walks toward the sphere. "Well done, but not good enough." He steps over Arjun and gives Jared a good kick in the chest. "That's for always showing me up around Megan!" He grabs the sphere off the blue pedestal. "I think I'll take this now," he says, grinning.

"Not so fast, young man," says Victor, quickly moving forward and snatching the zero-day history virus from Ethan's hands. "I think this is mine." He looks at the teenagers sprawled on the floor. As Arjun and Jared slowly come back to their senses, he says, "Oh, and thanks again for finding the artifact for us."

Victor turns and walks out of the room, followed by Ethan and the three mercenaries. As they step through the doorway into the anteroom filled with computers, Ethan glances over his shoulder. "Have a nice life!" He turns off the red light and closes the door.

Seconds later, Jared, Arjun, and Lien hear the desperate scream of one of the mercenaries. Jared slowly gets up and fumbles for the light switch. Arjun rubs his temples, and then crawls over to Lien and unties her. The three move toward the door as fast as their injuries will allow. Arjun jerks the door open, steps over the threshold, and then almost loses his balance.

Instinctively, Jared grabs the back of Arjun's shirt collar and yanks him to safety. The room is gone. Arjun would have plunged fifty meters into a river below.

CHAPTER 41

THEY ARE NO LONGER STANDING IN A LARGE COMPUTER room. They are now on a battlement walkway in a medieval castle. The castle is under siege, with one parapet already destroyed. It is being attacked from all sides. One of the mercenaries floats facedown in the sewage-filled moat below.

"What's going on?" yells Jared, just as a catapult launches a burning ball of hay over the wall. He ducks in the nick of time, avoiding a burning ember that would have taken off his head. "Are we back in the game?"

"No idea," replies Arjun, ducking behind another parapet. "We'd better get out of here, though." Beyond the castle walls, soldiers are loading large siege engines. Knights are having their men prepare long ladders. Arjun, Lien, and Jared keep low and run along the battlement toward a set of stone stairs leading down to the inner courtyard. They see Victor, Ethan, and the two soldiers sprinting past the water well and heading toward the main building. "They still have the sphere," yells Jared.

As they descend the stairs, a knight squeezes past them, running up toward the battlements. "I am the guardian!" he yells. "The sphere must be protected! We are under attack!"

Arjun and Jared look at each other. "Did that knight look familiar?" Arjun asks.

"Yeah!" replies Jared, "A little like the guard. We have no time for him. We need that sphere!"

Arjun and Jared enter the main building a few steps behind Lien as everything begins to flicker like an old light bulb losing power. They continue to run after Ethan, but the floor is no longer stone. Instead, it is a highly polished wooden floor. Shōji screens partially block the doorways to rooms with tatami mats on the floor. Arjun glances out of an open window and notices curved rows of clay roof tiles. "I think we just entered a Japanese feudal castle."

As the words leave his lips, the castle flickers again, and the walls and floor change to adobe. Persian art and weapons are strewn about. They see Ethan up ahead, trailing the others as they leave the fortified building. Again the castle flickers, and as they emerge into daylight they can see a city four hundred feet below. The architecture has changed dramatically again. Instead of Persian artifacts, they now see Sanskrit writing on the walls and realize that they are in a Hindu fortress. Running along a stone alley, they see intricately carved facades of palace apartments on the left and the forty-foot-high outer wall on the right. Ahead, Ethan ducks into a doorway on the left.

The flicker comes again, this time lasting almost twenty seconds, and the castle morphs back into a medieval European fortress. They are back in the main building.

Jared can see Victor and his soldiers heading to the castle keep. Then, something in the chapel catches his eye. He hesitates for a moment. "Go after the sphere," he tells Arjun and Lien. "I'll catch up with you in a minute." He enters the sanctuary of the chapel. It's not much larger than a bedroom. The floor is rough wood, and the walls and ceiling are stone. The wooden pulpit is stained a dark brown and illuminated by the windows behind it. On it is a bright, shiny pendant. It has a more luxurious patina than silver, gold, or platinum—a bluish hue. This is what caught his eye. He has never seen anything like it. Around the pendant's perimeter is a circle made with one fast brushstroke. The circle has a small opening at the bottom. He recognizes it as the *ensō* circle, associated with Zen. It often means enlightenment, connection, and strength. He remembers that his father once told him that the Japanese word "Zen" is linked to the Korean, Chinese, and Sanskrit languages. In the center are the three interlocked spirals of the triskele symbol, surrounded by spheres, all connected by tiny metal rods. The spheres and rods look similar to the view from the home page of *The Ancients* game—a representation of the World Wide Web. The triskele seems to be trapped in the web. Jared lifts the pendant carefully and cannot resist putting it around his neck, if only for a minute. For an instance, he feels a strange daring.

Jared is captivated by what he finds on the pulpit, despite the need to go after Victor and the sphere. He tells himself to only linger for a few more seconds. He sees a booklet titled "Feudalism Never Existed." It looks like a newer document. Jared opens it to the first page and reads that the word "feudalism" was never used during the Middle Ages and that historians are now debating the term. Some go so far as to say that feudalism did not depict actual medieval society. As the discipline of history has grown more rigorous over the years, more critical questions are being asked. Jared wonders why such a new text would be lying on this old pulpit when he hears Arjun and Lien yelling his name.

He's about to put the booklet down when he notices an old sheet of paper. It must have been under the booklet. On it, an artist has drawn a large replica of the pendant with a few minor additions. Inside the spiral of one of the branches of the triskele is a drawing of a sphere with something inside of it. Tucked inside the second branch of the triskele is a faint drawing of an old medieval key with a spiral handle and a tiny magnifying glass on the end. It's embedded in a book, a diary maybe.

The third branch of the triskele also wraps around a drawing, but it has faded and is unrecognizable.

Next to this symbol, written in the flowing handwriting of a scribe, is a paragraph about the triskele symbol. It is often interpreted as a symbol of man's progress, or the three aspects of life: body-mind-spirit, earth-sea-sky. It is most closely associated with the Celts, who spread out over much of continental Europe, the Iberian Peninsula, Ireland, and Britain.

Seeing the triskele makes Jared think of Megan, and a smile tugs at the corner of his mouth. He hears Arjun and Lien yell as the castle flickers again, this time for close to thirty seconds, and then stabilizes. Jared takes the triskele pendant from around his neck, places it on the paper, and covers it with the booklet. He quickly leaves the chapel to catch up with Lien and Arjun.

The three teenagers enter the castle keep. Tired after running through castle after castle, Jared feels his ribs every step of the way. He pants heavily as he reaches the rooftop of the keep. He comes through the doorway and sees Victor and Ethan taking cover behind the battlement wall. Only one mercenary is still standing. The other lies dead with multiple arrows in his body.

Arjun and Lien crouch next to the doorway. A barrage of arrows coming from the curtain wall below force Ethan to stay put. The invaders have penetrated the castle, and the keep is the only safe place left. Several siege engines slowly move toward the castle walls. Ethan, not sure what to do, gets up to back away when two arrows fly across the castle grounds behind him. Men with longbows have climbed onto the roof of the tower diagonally opposite the keep. From their higher elevation, they have a clear shot at anyone on the roof. One arrow hits Ethan in the back of the thigh and the other in the back of the shoulder, propelling him forward and over the wall.

Lien watches Ethan fall. She runs, crouching, to the edge of the keep wall and pokes her head above it. "Guys! Over here! He's still alive." Ten feet below, on the tile roof of a small projection in the keep wall, Ethan is sprawled, clutching his leg and moaning. He is protected from below, but if any knights look down at him from the keep, he will be an easy target.

"We need to see how we can get him back up here," says Lien.

"He was a traitor. You said it, too. We should just leave him there," Arjun replies in anger. A few seconds later, he adds, "Maybe not."

While Lien, Arjun, and Jared look down at Ethan, Victor, clasping the sphere tightly, sprints across the roof of the keep. Suddenly, a barrage of arrows comes from the castle tower. Miraculously, they miss him by inches. He lunges toward the exit and charges directly into the chest of an enormous, hooded figure. The impact knocks the sphere from his hands, and for a moment, time appears to stand still as he and Jared watch the glass ball fall toward the stone floor.

Instead of shattering, however, the sphere bounces and rolls toward the last remaining mercenary a few feet away. The hooded man steps past Victor and shoves him down through the doorway.

Meanwhile, the remaining mercenary scoops up the sphere in his left hand and brandishes a sword in his right as three robed warrior monks step from behind the hooded man. Bows drawn, they scan Jared, Lien, and Arjun, who stand perfectly still, barely breathing. Then the monks turn toward the mercenary, who is standing against the battlement wall with a look of defiance on his face. In unison, two of the monks fire. One arrow hits the mercenary in the stomach; the other strikes his side. He staggers backwards and sits on the short stone wall, the two arrows form-ing a horizontal line across his abdomen. Still holding the sphere and the sword, he slowly tips backwards, 150 feet above the moat. Then the third monk fires. His arrow penetrates the mercenary's heart, killing him instantly. The sword drops from the mercenary's hand, the stare freezes on his face, and he topples backwards off the keep, the sphere locked tightly in his left hand.

Jared ignores his pain and dives toward the mercenary, grabbing his ankle before he disappears over the side. The man's bulk pulls Jared over the edge. He can't hold on for long. Before Lien and Arjun can reach him, he and the soldier begin to fall down the side of the castle.

The castle flickers again, this time for just a second, and then everything goes dark. Jared stops falling. A couple of seconds pass without anyone moving. They hear the low roar of a generator off in the distance, and a dim safety light comes on. Jared, holding the man's ankle, is lying on a glass-like floor. The three arrows form the shape of a triangle in the man's abdomen. Arjun and Lien, a few feet away, look at Ethan, moaning. He has several broken bones, and is covered with cuts and bruises. Scattered about the room are the three mercenaries, all dead. Victor is gone. They are in a huge, square room with grids on all the walls, floor, and ceiling. On one end is a door that looks like the one they entered when they ventured down the spiral staircase. Behind them is the second door leading to the basement's back room where the sphere was found.

Jared gets down on his hands and knees and climbs over to the dead mercenary. He pries open the soldier's hand and takes the sphere.

Lien runs her hands through her hair, straightens her clothes, and fixes her ponytail. "What just happened?" She looks at Arjun, and then at Jared.

"Beats me," replies Arjun.

Jared shrugs. The door to the back room opens, and the white-haired guard, holding his head as if he has an awful headache, stumbles through. He looks around the room and smiles weakly. "It worked. I can't believe it. The first and only time it's been used, and it worked," he says in a tired but excited voice.

"What worked?" asks Jared.

"My guardian program. This room. It's a holodeck."

"A what?" asks Arjun.

"A holographic environment simulator. It's an advanced form of a virtual-reality simulation. It was described by an author in his stories about space travel in the late 1980s. When I became the last guardian for the sphere, I had to come up with another way to protect it. I started tinkering with a holodeck-like security system, based on those fictional stories, but I only got so far. I wonder how it became so sophisticated."

"Unless…" His voice trails off as he walks toward the back room. "I didn't even notice." He peers into the back room. The old computer and the rectangular pedestal where the sphere rested are both switched on. He smiles to himself. "Never mind."

The three teenagers follow him into the room. "I have no idea what you're talking about," Jared says.

"Me neither," adds Arjun.

"Let me try to explain," says the guard, sitting back down in the chair. "This computer was part of the first-ever Internet, or the forerunner to the Internet. It was shut down in 1990. By then, it may have encountered the story and theories about holodeck technology, through one of its many network connections. I mean, initially, there were only four computers, but by the time this computer was deactivated, there were probably three hundred thousand computers on the network. Now there are millions."

"So this network that was shut down decades ago comes back to life and does all this?" Arjun asks.

"When it was shut down, many of the computers connected to it were moved to another network. The torch was passed from the old to the new," replies the guard, chuckling. "Maybe the old Net thinks that the modern Internet is under threat."

"You're not suggesting that it's a living, thinking network, are you?" asks Arjun, not sure how seriously to take the guard.

"I don't know what I'm suggesting," replies the guard. "More likely, someone or something is using this network to try to maintain a balance of power—battling to keep the Internet free and not beholden to any one group, like these Lords of the Clouds. By hiding the clues in the Web, maybe they figured that only someone who practices historical thinking and can see recurring patterns and themes has the moral strength to guard the artifact. Only such a person or persons would be worthy to handle the sphere. Maybe you are the new guardians."

The three teenagers look at each other, stunned. The new guardians? Them? "Oh...I don't think so," they say in unison.

"I'd have to agree with that!" adds Megan, standing at the door.

"Megan!" they shout, breaking into big smiles. Jared runs toward her, she moves toward him, and they embrace. He whispers in her ear, "I'm so glad you're safe," and gives her a peck on the cheek. Then he releases her and steps back. "How did you get here? How'd you escape?"

Megan smiles. "I pretended to be subdued, and they left me with only two guards. When one of the guards went outside to talk to someone, I hit the second guy with a pipe I found in the van, and ran. When we first drove here, I'd noticed a lot of power lines coming into this building and a backup generator. It looked like too much power for a building that was so old. I figured that something must be going on, and looked for a way to shut down the power and disconnect the generator. I thought that if you guys were in darkness, it might give you an advantage."

"Was that where the flickering was coming from?" asks Lien, also giving Megan a hug.

"I assume so. Why, what happened?"

"We'll tell you later," says Jared. "It's just good to see you safe."

"It did take me a while, since this place has more redundant power sources than a hospital." Turning to the guard, Megan says, "Right, Doctor?"

"Doctor?" says Arjun.

"Yes," says Megan. "As I searched for how to turn off the power, I came across this old file in one of the desks." She turns to the guard. "Great picture, by the way. It says here that you were one of the original thinkers and technologists who worked on the Net. You always liked to be in the background, so that no one even knew that you existed."

The old man sinks back in his chair. "True. That's how I wanted it. But things are moving so quickly nowadays. Like in ancient times, whenever a new technology is introduced, it changes society. Today, we debate the definition of Internet freedom. I'm getting too old for this. There are the Internet optimists and the Internet pessimists, all clamoring to present their points of view and convince the others that they are right. Our world has become so bipartisan. It's black or white, right or wrong, no shades of gray. And yet things are actually so much more complex."

Jared looks at the technologist. "When your application mutated into this day-zero history virus, you knew that you had another technology that could change the world forever, especially if the wrong person got their hands on it," says Jared. "You devoted your life to guarding it because you couldn't destroy it."

"Yes." The old guard takes out a handkerchief and blows his nose.

Jared and Megan, followed by Lien, Arjun, and the old guard, are about to leave the room when Jared's satellite phone chirps.

"I need to take this." Jared hits video and walks away. At first, he is too stunned to react. Gia is wearing the triskele pendant he saw in the chapel.

"Why don't you guys go up?" says Megan, turning to the others. "Get Ethan out of here, as well. I'll wait for Jared."

The others leave, and Megan is leaning against a desk, when one of the flat-screen monitors on the wall comes on. The image of Victor emerges. He is sitting in front of a modern desk in some kind of mobile command center. "Hello, Megan. I must commend you on your escape."

Megan is surprised. How did he get on that monitor? Finally, she pulls herself together and replies, "Thanks. It's always good to have some luck."

"Indeed. By the way, where's Jared?" asks Victor as he scans the room through the monitor. "Ah, there he is in the back."

Jared looks up at the screen. Holding his hand over the satellite phone, he moves to Megan's side. "You again!" he says angrily. "Sorry, but this time you lose. The sphere stays with me." Triumphantly, he pulls it from his pocket.

Victor begins to laugh. Jared is beginning to hate that laugh.

"Oh, Jared, we're in the real world now. It's no longer a game. You think that Megan would be my only insurance policy? Who do you think has your mom and dad?" he says condescendingly.

Jared drops the phone. "That can't be," he murmurs. Too stunned to speak, he stares blankly at the screen while Megan picks up the satellite phone.

Victor continues to chuckle, and then says in a smug tone, "I'm sure we can work out a deal—a trade maybe—a set of parents for a small sphere."

Megan brings the phone to her ear. "Yeah. Hi, Gia. It's me, Megan. I can hear you fine. Wait. Let me put you on speaker."

Gia's powerful voice emanates from the small speaker. "Jared! Are you OK? Are all of you OK?"

Jared can barely answer. "Yes," he says weakly. "We were so close, and now this. You heard, didn't you?"

"Yes, I did. Hold on. Let me patch in Alberto. He's at a different location."

A few seconds of crackling noises on the line is followed by *"¡Hola!* How's my favorite nephew?"

"Been better, Uncle," mumbles Jared. "We got the sphere, but they still have Mom and Dad."

"That's what I wanted to tell you. Your mom and dad are here with me. Safe."

Before Alberto can continue, Jared drops to his knees and buries his face in his hands. Tears stream down his face. "They're safe?" he stammers.

"Yes. My team rescued them this morning. That's why I had to leave quickly—we got a tip."

Megan joins Jared on the floor and wraps her arms around him. Tears stream down her cheeks as well. It's been an intense time.

On the screen, Victor's face contorts, and all the smugness disappears. "That can't be!" he yells. "That's impossible!"

"Hello, Victor. We meet again," says Gia toward the screen. "And yes, it is possible. I see you didn't find our trap. We figured you might go after Jared's mom, so we implanted a little device in her—the advantage of tracking technology. That, plus the tip we got, led us right to her and George. I can't believe that your team would keep husband and wife together in the same location. Tsk, tsk. Our benefit, I guess. An assault team freed both Jared's mom and dad less than an hour ago. You must not have heard yet."

As he listens, Jared thinks about how, in this case, there was a real benefit to using a tracking device. There are always two sides to the use of technology.

Victor balls his hand into a fist and punches one of his desk drawers, shattering it into splinters. He then takes his tablet computer and hurls it across the room. The screen in the basement room goes dark.

"Gia, are you still there?" asks Jared

"Yes, I'm still here."

"I think you upset him," says Jared, filled with such relief to know that his parents are safe.

"I've got to sign off," says Alberto. "We need to make sure it's safe, so we should be back in a few days." They hear a small click as Alberto disconnects his line.

"I can't believe it. We actually did it," says Megan, still holding Jared.

"Victor wanted this artifact more than anything," replies Gia. "You, Megan, and the others did a great job. We'll be right there to take the sphere off your hands and put it in a safe place."

Jared sighs, covers the mouthpiece of the phone, and stares at Megan, silently debating with himself. This virus is incredibly powerful, both in a good way and in a bad way. There should be a way for people to delete their own personal information from the Web, to erase data that maybe was put out there by mistake or in a weak moment, to give people a level of control over their information, to create a mechanism by which the Web also forgets. This program could do that. Yet if it were to fall into the wrong hands—if misused—it could be catastrophic. If a person were erased from cyberspace, it would be as if he or she did not exist. By changing history, someone could manipulate thousands of people into believing anything. If someone did not like what someone else said, the opinion could just be deleted. People could be manipulated like lemmings or even enslaved. As the prophecy said, choice, freedom, and independence could disappear.

Jared runs his fingers through his hair. Just minutes earlier, he'd thought about the pros and cons of tracking devices. Why do these technologies always have two sides? There's never a simple answer. He breathes deeply and thinks about his values, what his intuition tells him to do. Power, and technologies that provide power, are often abused. He is reminded of another quote his father would cite. This one from Lord Acton, who wrote, "Power tends to corrupt, and absolute power corrupts absolutely." This device could provide someone with absolute power. He has to be true to himself.

He then turns to Megan and whispers in her ear. Megan listens intently as Jared quickly describes the purpose of the sphere and the zero-day history virus, his dilemma, and his plan. She nods in complete agreement Then, on cue, he drops the phone and fires the sphere like a baseball pitch into the blue rectangular pedestal. Both shatter into a thousand pieces. The green Jell-O-like substance oozes to the floor.

Jared takes several breaths and then picks up the phone.

"What happened?" asks Gia.

"I destroyed the sphere."

The phone line goes quiet. Then, after almost a minute, Gia's voice returns. "I understand. Here is what you need to do. We're going to have to talk about how to communicate this to your friends, to the school, and to the public. We'll do that tomorrow. My team will be there in a few minutes to clean up the scene. Why don't you and your teammates go home now? Tell them not to say anything until we talk." She quickly explains what he and Megan need to do next and then hangs up.

Jared and Megan look at each other and embrace. He plants a big kiss on her cheek. "Thanks! I don't think humanity is ready for a device that can erase and alter human history at the touch of a button," says Jared. "At least not for a while."

"I agree—a long while," replies Megan. "The question is, will it ever be?" She takes Jared's hand, and together they head up the spiral staircase and leave the basement.

CHAPTER 42

IT'S MONDAY MORNING. SPRING BREAK IS OVER, THE blogosphere is abuzz, and social networks are filled with chatter. Text messages and tweets fly as students comment on how a team from Globus Academy finished *The Ancients* game and found the artifact. Strangely, over the weekend *The Ancients* game has captured the attention of a worldwide audience. Jared wonders how the information got around so fast, especially since only ten schools were involved initially. Maybe someone has been feeding information to the media. But why? he asks himself.

Megan and Jared drive to school in Megan's Spitfire. "By the way, did you kiss me when I was shot by those arrows?" Jared asks shyly.

Megan looks over at him, slightly embarrassed. "Maybe just a peck on the forehead." She didn't think he'd remember.

"It was nice," replies Jared, looking at the road ahead.

Megan slowly pulls into the campus drive, and students immediately mob them. They can't open the car doors, so they climb over them. Everyone at school knows that they finished *The Ancients* game and found the artifact. Students begin to chant, "Team Globus, Team Globus," as Megan and Jared make their way toward the building.

"Not a bad name, eh?" asks Jared.

"Works for me," replies Megan.

Just then, someone yells out, "There's Lien and Arjun!" and the crowd of students splits in two as some head over to welcome the other two team members.

Jared can't quite believe the reception. As he walks toward the building, he reflects that just a few weeks ago he was not considered to be in the "in" group. He never really knew where he stood with most people in his class. And now this. He's amazed at how quickly opinions can change. He realizes that this new status might only last a few days. It will die down again as the focus shifts to something else. But for now, he decides to enjoy the attention. He now understands the power of communication and information, the power that the Lords of the Clouds seek, the power of influencing the masses. There are examples in every century throughout history.

The school warning bell rings and Megan, Jared, Lien, and Arjun separate to go to their first-period classes. They'll see each other again in sixth-period world history. Jared reaches his first-period classroom and enters to a round of applause. He grins and squeezes himself into one of the desk-chairs that always seem too small. As he settles in, the principal makes a short announcement over the public-address system, congratulating the team, citing the team members by name, including Ethan, and reminding students that there are only eight weeks left until summer break.

In each class, students mob Jared and the others, congratulating them and peppering them with questions about the quest and the artifact.

At lunch, Jared, Megan, Arjun, and Lien decide to head off campus to a small deli for lunch and some peace and quiet. Being so popular can be exhausting, even if it's only been for such a short time. As they enter, Megan sees Ethan sitting by himself in a corner booth. He's nursing his leg and trying his best to go unnoticed.

Megan, with the others closely behind, storms over. "How dare you!" she yells at him and slaps him hard across the face. Ethan shrinks back as she's about to hit him again. All his bluster and arrogance are gone.

Jared grabs her arm. "Stop! That won't help."

Ethan, barely able to look up, says, "I'm sorry. I screwed up. A lot was happening, but it's still no excuse."

"Yes you certainly did screw up!" replies Megan and storms off. Jared and Lien look at Ethan with pity. What a way to turn on your friends, they think, and they turn to follow Megan out the door.

Arjun stays behind and looks at Ethan quietly, wondering why he's not angrier. He should be just as angry as Megan. When Ethan finally looks up, Arjun looks him straight in the eye. "Ethan, I'm hurt. Why? I don't get it."

Ethan looks away. "I don't know what happened. I got in way over my head. Everything they said sounded so good."

"You were naïve."

"I understand that now. Some woman, Gia, came to me yesterday, and we talked all afternoon. I was such a fool."

"Gia talked to you?" asks Arjun with surprise.

"Yeah. She explained. She said that with power comes great responsibility and—anyway, I don't want to get into it now."

"All right. I'll talk to the others, but we're *all* hurt. We thought we were a team. That we could trust each other."

Ethan stares down at his plate. He doesn't make a sound.

"It's going to take a long time to rebuild trust, Ethan, if ever." Arjun turns and walks away.

Sixth-period history rolls around, and as the students enter her classroom, Ms. Castro beams with pride. She didn't much care about the competition; she's just happy that some of her students did so well, learned something, and completed the quest so quickly. She announces that today will be a celebration of her students' effort and that in a few minutes the principal and vice principal will join them. There are paper plates and cups, finger foods from different parts of the world, and various juices.

Cool, thinks Jared. Class will be a party.

Several minutes later, Jared glances out the door and sees the principal and vice principal walking down the hallway, talking intently. Ms. Castro welcomes them into the classroom as they make their way to the front of the room. First, the principal says a few words about how proud he is of the caliber of students at Globus Academy and how truly gifted they are. He goes on to say how thankful he is that their school was chosen to be one of the first to play this new game.

Then Dr. Jones, the vice principal, steps forward and thanks the team. Because they found the artifact first and won, Globus Academy will receive a generous grant. Dr. Jones asks Megan, Jared, Lien, Arjun, and Ethan to come forward. The others exchange knowing glances as Ethan hesitates to come to the front. Finally, all stand in front, and Dr. Jones shakes hands with each, congratulates them, and then quietly lets them know that a token of appreciation has been deposited in their scholarship accounts. Few notice that Ethan doesn't seem as happy as the others. As the five return to their seats, others congratulate them on winning the reward.

Sizwe shakes Megan's hand and gives her a small hug. "Nice job! You guys make a good team."

"Thanks for your help in the Roman Colosseum. We need to talk sometime soon."

Sizwe smiles and nods.

Some, with a twinge of jealousy in their voices, offer halfhearted congratulations. Damian and Ivy say nothing.

One of the students raises his hand and asks, "Can we see the artifact? All we heard was that it was some kind of sphere." Dr. Jones reaches into his pocket and pulls out a clear-glass sphere the size of a tennis ball with a blue globe inside. When they see the artifact, Jared, Megan, Lien, and Arjun exchange looks and knowing smiles. This sphere looks familiar, but it is definitely not the sphere they found. Gia has been working hard on the public relations front—on communicating and *not* communicating the information. No one needs to know about the zero-day history virus.

"Can you believe it was hidden here locally the whole time," says another student. "Who would have thought?"

This is Silicon Valley, thinks Jared. Anything can happen.

The others all look at the artifact in admiration. But Jared has a strange feeling. He senses that the atmosphere is already changing in the classroom. He can feel students' interest beginning to wane, their focus already turning to other things now that the quest is over and a winner has been declared. He'll be surprised if students are even talking about *The Ancients* game by the end of next week.

"Thank you all for your participation," Dr. Jones continues. "We appreciate any feedback or comments you might have on how we can improve this game. I will pass them on to the developers. They can then make some major enhancements to the next game." He pauses for just a second to let the phrase sink in.

"Next game?" a few students ask.

"Yes. The developers told me that just before summer, another game will be released. It's called *Codex*. It will take place during the Middle Ages and the Renaissance. The developer will have software patches and upgrades for the nanobots, bracelets, and lenses within the next few months."

Jared now knows why the information about the first game and its victors was spread so quickly. There must be a second artifact. And the developers must be using a different game strategy. If they can generate more enthusiasm, then more teams will search, the search will go faster, and they can get their hands on the next artifact more quickly. He wonders what could be so important. Could it be even more devastating than the zero-day history virus? Is the Internet still under threat? Is the prophecy still in effect?

And sure enough, Dr. Jones's brief mention of *Codex* reignites the students' interest level. There will be a second game, a second search. Students will get another chance to win. The enthusiasm is back. Even while the vice principal is speaking, Megan, Jared, Lien, and Arjun receive text messages from other students. They want to join Team Globus in the next game.

Codex, thinks Jared. This should be interesting—especially with a larger team. He then remembers the piece of paper in the castle chapel bearing the triskele symbol with the faint drawing of a medieval key embedded in a book on its second branch. "Codex" is another word for "book," isn't it?

As soon as class is over, Jared walks toward Megan. "This game is not over. We may have won a battle, but I'm afraid the war continues."

➲ *The End* ➲

APPENDIX
CURRICULUM ENHANCER /
CONVERSATION STARTER

The following information is meant to help:

- Readers
  - » Understand the big, historical patterns that shape our world.
- Young Adults
  - » See relationships to solve problems and to build persuasive points of view in the context of an interesting story.
  - » Develop and nurture inquiry-based habits of mind and historical-thinking skills.
- Parents
  - » Start worthwhile, interesting, and relevant conversations with their sons and daughters.
- Educators
  - » Supplement the curriculum they already teach with an exciting and entertaining story that will engage students and motivate them to explore further.
  - » Facilitate students in working with big questions that will help them see the relationships and patterns in historical facts and themes, thereby better understanding the world of today.

>> >> >>

With the massive amounts of information in the twentieth-first century, we need to help people, especially students, see and understand the facts but also look beyond them to see and understand the underlying patterns that affect the world. Only in this way can they see the connections, understand the relationships between the parts, and make informed decisions.

≫ ≫ ≫

The Ancients: A Few Big Questions
Patterns that Transcend Time,
enhancing historical, critical, and creative thinking

These big questions tie story events to what occurred during ancient times (<10,000 BCE to approximately 600 CE) to questions and themes (big patterns) that shape our world. These questions are intended to help enhance readers' historical, critical, and creative thinking skills.

I am sure that after reading the story, many more questions will come to mind. The ones below are meant to help kick-start the process—to help you explore further.

World History for Us All¹ ldhistoryforusall.sdsu.edu/	The Ancients: A Game A TeamGlobus™ Adventure	Chapter
Three Essential Questions	*Sample "Big" Discussion Questions that Tie to the Book²*	
Humans and the Environment	Jared and Megan's world-history teacher said that the Neolithic/Agricultural Revolution changed nutrition, health, and social relations. Did early humans make a critical decision way back then that put us on a different trajectory? • What could that decision have been? • What is the argument on each side? How would you defend one or the other point of view?	5
	In ancient times farmers used slash and burn agriculture. Some societies still use that today. • How did humans try to dominate, harness, or control the environment in ancient times? • Are any of those techniques still used today? Describe.	6
Humans and Other Humans	During the quest, Megan, Jared, Arjun, Lien, Ethan, Sizwe, and all the other characters encountered many different societies and cultures in different times. They saw how human relations have changed over the years. • How would you characterize the change in human relations between 10,000 BCE and 600 CE? • How have human relations changed up until today? • Why have relations become so complex? • How did the role of women change from the Paleolithic Era to the Neolithic Era?	Throughout
	Throughout the quest, the characters learned that the ancient world was full of authoritarian regimes with kings, dynasties, and emperors. • How did those ancient regimes control information? • How do autocratic regimes control information today? • How can the Internet support the intentions of these regimes? • How can the Internet work against those intentions?	Throughout

Humans and Ideas	Megan had to write a paper on cultural-mindedness. • What is cultural-mindedness and why is it important?	2
	Humans share ideas because they have language. When Megan and Arjun visited the Web site about the myths and legends concerning Ashoka's transformation, she realized that myths and legends are powerful stories. • Why are myths and legends so powerful?	25, 27
	Many people think about the past; some focus on a specific detail and others on grand sweeps of time. • Why do you think humans continue to construct, reconstruct, and dispute the past?	Throughout
	Today, media is a primary vehicle for sharing ideas and information. • How was the sharing of information in ancient times similar or dissimilar to the way it works today? • What is media literacy? Did any of the ancients need to be media literate? Is it more important today? Why?	Throughout
	Jared read the statement "Technology is neither good nor bad, nor is it neutral." • What do you think that statement means? Can you give an example?	19
	The old guard said, "Just like in ancient times, anytime a new technology is introduced we debate its effects on society. Today we debate the definition of Internet freedom." • Pick a technology and describe how it has affected human society positively and negatively. • What do you think he means by Internet freedom?	41

Seven Key Themes	*In World History for Us All, a theme is defined as a topic that addresses a particular sphere of human activity over time. The major themes presented here concern broad aspects of change that have been enduringly important in the human experience.*	
Patterns of Population	Throughout the book, Jared and Megan noticed how much population has increased and changed over the millennia and how relations between people changed as they moved from small clans to complex societies to great civilizations. • How have relations between humans changed and/or stayed the same over time? • The world population in Megan and Jared's time will be over nine billion. How will this affect how the world operates? What problems will arise? What are potential solutions?	Throughout
	Jared explained that with the use of new scientific techniques there is some new evidence that links Australia with India. Human migration is a major pattern in ancient times, as well as today. • Why do humans migrate? What effect do migrations have? • How does genetics help better understand past migrations? • Do you see any other scientific techniques or evidence that might help explain global migrations?	19

Economic Networks and Exchange	In the story, Jared, Megan, Arjun, Ethan, and Lien learned about the Phoenicians and their trading network, and they learned about the monopoly that the Chinese had on silk. • What types of economic networks and monopolies does the world have today? How do they affect the global economy?	20
	Megan learned that even in ancient times there was a trade deficit between the Roman Empire, India, China, and Arabia. • How do trade deficits arise? Why do we still have them today?	28
	Economic networks and exchange have driven the world economy since ancient times. • What are the similarities and/or differences between trade in ancient times and today?	Throughout
	During the Han Empire, legend says Emperor Han Wudi looked toward the lands of the West and said they placed great value on the rich produce of China. One of the first steps in opening the Silk Road(s) came with Alexander the Great's expansion into Central Asia. • How was the relationship with China during ancient times similar or dissimilar to today? • How are trade and the old Silk Road being renewed today?	28

Uses and Abuses of Power	Changing power relations and the desire to have more power are central themes that started in the earliest times and continue today. • In the book, how is the cartel trying to gain power? • How did the role or power of women change throughout ancient times?	Throughout
	In the ancient world, much of the power was concentrated in the state, dynasty, or empire, often personified by an emperor. Today non-state, often private, power is of great significance. • How has this notion of power changed? • What other entities have power across the world today? • How do these other entities influence the world around us?	Throughout
	Computer viruses have become more and more prevalent today. • How are viruses used to assert power today? • Look up "zero-day virus" and "flame virus" (not referenced in the story). How were they used?	39
	Megan got frustrated because in most ancient societies, women had less power than men did. Jared replied that there were a few exceptions. • Can you name the ancient societies where women had less power and those few societies where they had more? Explain. • Why do you think that was the case?	23
	• In the Roman Colosseum, Megan and Arjun overheard the emperor speak to a senator about power, popularity, entertainment, and controlling the mob. Arjun commented that it doesn't sound too far off from modern politics. • What do you think he meant by that statement? • How is modern politics similar to or dissimilar to the politics of ancient Rome	30

Haves and Have-Nots	The characters noticed the number of slaves used in the ancient world to do much of the work. • Is slavery still part of our society in the twenty-first century? How so?	Throughout
	The social pyramid is a concept that emerged as soon as humans moved out of the Paleolithic Era and has been part of human society ever since. • How did the social pyramid manifest itself during the time of the ancients? • How does the social pyramid manifest itself today? What affect does it have on how people live and work together?	Throughout
	A key theme that emerged in ancient times was the notion of inequality. Recently, Nobel Prize-winning economist Joseph Stiglitz wrote a book titled *The Price of Inequality* (not referenced in the story). • Look up his work. What is Stiglitz's argument about inequality, and how does it compare to inequality in ancient times? • What's changed? What has stayed the same?	Throughout
Expressing Identity	Societies, groups, and individuals all express their identity in some way. • How did societies, peoples, or individuals in ancient times express their own unique identity? Give examples.	Throughout
	Expressing who we are, what group we belong to, and a sense of individuality is core to humans. • How would Megan, Jared, Ivy, or some of the other characters answer the question "Who am I?" • How does the modern trend toward social networking help us express our unique identity? How does it hinder us from expressing our unique identity?	Throughout

Science Technology, and the Environment	Throughout the book, the characters encountered ways humans used science and technology to exploit their physical and natural surroundings. In fact, the entire game is based on some sophisticated technology. • Although the concept of nanobots sitting at synapses is fictional, more and more technology is being integrated with the human body. What are some of these devices today, and what do you see coming in ten, twenty, or fifty years? • What dilemmas or ethical questions arise from the use of some of these advanced technologies (e.g., devices in the body, tracking devices, etc.)?	Throughout
	In the book, Jared learned that the government has declared the Internet "an operational domain of war." • Throughout history, nation-states have engaged in war. Why? • How do you think war will be fought in cyberspace? • How do you think nation-states will try to control the Internet? Why?	Throughout
	The old guard said, "There are the Internet optimists and the Internet pessimists, all clamoring to present their points of view and convince the others that they are right." • What are these viewpoints? What are the arguments of each group?	41
	There seem to be three main laws that govern technology today: Moore's Law, Gilder's Law, and Metcalfe's Law. • What are these laws, and how do you think they will evolve? • How will they affect society?	Prologue

Science Technology, and the Environment	In covering over ten thousand years of history, Jared and Megan encountered many different technologies (e.g., new tools, new weapons, writing, etc.). Technological change often causes problems for the old order. • Pick one or two technologies that came into existence in ancient times and describe how they helped society develop. • What types of problems might they have created for the society or the people of the time? • The Internet is a new technology in our time. How does it help society, and what problems might it create for society?	throughout

Spiritual Life and Moral Codes	Throughout the book, life, death, and the afterlife were central concerns for the ancient Egyptians, Chinese, Mayans, and others. • Why was immortality so important? What does it say about humans? • Compare and contrast our views about immortality today with those of the ancients.	Throughout
	In this chapter, Jared learned how Göbekli Tepe challenges the way archaeologists think about the rise of civilizations. • Using the Internet, what is the significance of Göbekli Tepe? Explain.	5
	In Āryabhata's study, Megan and Arjun found a book about airships in which each airship depicts one of the major belief systems that arose during 10,000 BCE and around 600 CE. • Why do you think organized religions came into being and grew? • Why do humans often seek a spiritual life?	32
	Throughout ancient times, as religions grew they also dealt with the theme of power and the theme of haves and have-nots. • What is the relationship between religions and the theme of power, and the theme of haves and have-nots? • How did this play out in ancient times? • How does this play out today? Anything in the current news?	Throughout
Historical Thinking	Jared had to write a paper on historical thinking. • What is historical thinking, and why is it important?	2

Chronological Thinking	Jared's father and uncle developed a tool that allowed them to see big swaths of time as well as drill down into a single event. • How would you create a timeline that provides a true and visual understanding of the time spans since the beginning of the universe until today?	16
	Megan explored a Web site where Paleolithic hunters were chased by dinosaurs. This is historically inaccurate. • Can you draw a timeline that shows when dinosaurs existed and when humans first appeared on Earth? How far apart where they?	4
	On the houseboat, Gia commented, "Even though it seems like a long time, all of human history is only a fraction of geologic time, and ancient history is a fraction of human history." • Can you draw an explanation of this statement with actual numbers?	16
	The ancient empires often lasted many years. Lien pulled up a comparison table on her screen. • Can you draw a timeline of six to eight major societies of the ancient world? Of the major empires until around 600 CE? • How would you compare and contrast the big empires of the ancient past? Pick any two. • How does the length of time that these ancient empires existed compare with the duration of modern-day empires? • Why do empires rise and fall?	17

Historical Comprehension	Megan, Jared, and their team constantly wrestled with the information they found on various Web sites and its credibility. • How can a reader assess the credibility of the information he or she finds on the Internet, in books or articles, and in other sources?	5
	Megan read about Tour 5: Attend a Play, *Who Wrote Africa's History?* • What impact did this have on history and the perceptions of Africa? Discuss and develop a persuasive argument.	13
	As they encountered various Web sites, the team saw some sites filled with facts and other sites filled with interpretations. • What is the difference between historical facts and historical interpretation?	Throughout
Historical Analysis and Interpretation	In the video about Göbekli Tepe, Jared saw archaeologists and historians debate the findings. • Historians routinely debate history to this day. Why do you think that happens?	5
	The characters often encountered multiple perspectives about the same event. • Why does that occur? Herodotus wrote *Histories*, and Aeschylus, an Athenian playwright, wrote *The Persians* and something known as the *Decree of Themistocles*. • What was the Greek perspective on the wars? The Persian?	23, 24
	As they journeyed through the Web, Jared and Megan realized that rarely did an event have just a single cause. • Why do you think that was? Give an example or two. • Why are there often different interpretations of the same event?	Throughout
	When Megan was in the study with Empress Deng and Madame Zhao, she remembered past discussions with her diplomat father about historical and cultural empathy. • What is historical empathy? Why is it important? • What is cultural empathy? Why is it important?	28

Historical Research Capabilities	In this chapter, Jared said, "We'll have to look at the information and the sources very carefully." Ms. Castro explained searching: "Before we begin, remember that search engines rank material based on what they think is relevant. It may not be what you want, so don't just go to the first thing you see. Second, I suggest that you always check the resources, reliability, or credibility of the site. Understand the source of the information." • Why is it important to look at information so carefully? Explain. • How can you improve the validity of the information you find?	5
	When Jared looked for information, he often brought up multiple screens and used multiple search engines or sources. He sometimes tapped directly into library databases. • Why did he do this? • What are some of the risks or issues that come up when conducting historical research?	Throughout
	The team often encountered primary sources. • What are primary and secondary sources? • What are the challenges when interpreting the data from each? Think about Sima Qian or Herodotus. • What are the advantages and disadvantages of using primary sources? • How can you increase the validity/credibility of the historical evidence you find?	Throughout

Historical Issues, Analysis, and Decision Making	The fall of the Roman Republic is one of the most famous events in European history and has been written and talked about for two thousand years. • What is your analysis of the fall of the Roman Republic? What were some of the causes? What is the evidence? • What is your analysis of the death of Tiberius Gracchus at the hands of a mob of senators in 133 BC? Or of the killing of Julius Caesar by senators in 44 BC?	29, 30
	Think about what you have just read. Pick any historical character (e.g., King Leonidas of Sparta, Xerxes, senators who killed Julius Caesar, Alexander, Emperor Qin, etc.) and a moment in that character's life where s/he faced a problem, dilemma, or decision. • Who was the character and what problem did s/he face? Then from that person's perspective, answer the following: • What decision did the character(s) make, and what were the consequences? • What alternatives were available, and what would the consequences have been?	Throughout
	The first three chapters of the *Records of the Grand Historian* by Sima Qian, the Chinese historian, were first translated into English in 1894. Some say the sole purpose was to discredit Sima Qian and all ancient history as recorded by the Chinese. • Why would this happen? What evidence is there? • What is your position on this topic? • What is bias? How can future readers of history ensure they understand potential biases? How can you reduce bias? Megan thought about how each interpretation of history is often colored by the era in which the historian lived. • Can you explain and give an example?	28

Historical Issues, Analysis, and Decision Making	Jared saw a booklet titled "Feudalism Never Existed" and read that the word "feudalism" was never used during the Middle Ages and historians are now debating the term. Some go as far as to say that feudalism did not depict actual medieval society. Jared learned that as the discipline of history grew more rigorous over the years, more critical questions were asked. • Why did this happen? • Research and analyze this issue, and provide your point of view. Make sure to support your assertion.	41
General		
Critical Thinking	Throughout the book Jared, Megan, Arjun, Lien, and Ethan worked together as a team. • How did they work as a team? • What are the characteristics of a good team? • What makes teamwork hard? • How can these lessons be applied to your work at school?	Throughout
	In his novel *1984*, George Orwell wrote, "He who controls the past, controls the future; and he controls the present, controls the past." • What do you think he meant? • How does this still apply today?	2
	More and more technology is being integrated into the human body. Jared had mixed emotions about that aspect of the game. He was excited about the potential of the game. He'd never played anything like it before, but he hated the idea of having thousands of tiny nanobots in his body. • Why do you think Jared was reluctant? Would you be? Why or why not? • What are the pros and cons of this developing trend?	3
	At the end of the chapter, Jared was reminded of a Mark Twain quote that his father would recite: "Courage is resistance to fear, mastery of fear—not absence of fear." • Can you explain what is meant by this quote in your own words and give an example?	3

Critical Thinking	Uncle Alberto said that today, people live in an always-on, always-connected society. Humanity is moving toward a world where everyone is connected to everyone and everything is connected to everything, everywhere. This new world is full of new opportunities and full of new dangers. • What do *you* see as the new opportunities? Explain. • What do you see as the new dangers? Explain.	9
Creative Thinking	• If you were Jared or Megan and had to create or develop a classroom activity or set of activities that got everyone involved and showed how the three key relationships (humans and the environment, humans and humans, and humans and ideas) affected the ancient world and affect the world today, what would you do? • Think of the world fifty years from today. Take one or more of the three essential relationships and look into the future. Develop a hypothesis or scenario of how the world might deal with that question or theme in the future. • How would you create a cool smartphone app that would teach geography in a fun way? • If you wanted to come up with a not-too-obvious way to make people forget about ancient history, what would you do? • Megan noticed a travel brochure in the seat pocket in front of her and pulled it out. The title on the cover page said "Adventures in Ancient Egypt." It described seven tours. Create something (a brochure, video, song, poem, drawing, or painting) that describes each tour in such a way that it includes the important information and is impactful.	Throughout

1 – Three essential questions and seven key themes taken with permission from "World History for Us All" at http://worldhistoryforusall. sdsu.edu/.

2. There are more specific questions related to the Three Essential Questions and the Seven Key Themes at the World History for Us All Web site, http://worldhistoryforusall.sdsu.edu/.

The Ancients: History ➲ in ➲ Reverse
Patterns That Transcend Time—
Linking Topics from Today to the Past

The Greek philosopher Aristotle once said, "If you would understand anything, observe its beginning and its development." This quote is even more important today when we think about the overload of information.

This section helps readers look at today's issues, developments, and current events and link them to concepts and developments that arose in the ancient world. It also helps readers look at these developments and link them to big patterns that transcend time. Again, these examples are meant to provoke conversation. I am sure teachers and students can come up with many more linkages.

- Take a current event, something that is happening today or an issue that is affecting human society, and try to link it back to what happened in the ancient world (<10,000 BCE–600 CE). Discuss the big pattern that might explain the linkage.
- Recognize that the patterns often link to each other and show up under other topics.

For example:

Topic Today Twenty-First Century	Linkage to the Ancient World <10,000 BCE–600 CE	Sample Patterns That Transcend Time
Population growth, number of people on the planet, overpopulation.	How human populations grew and declined during ancient times. How human migrations affected different regions.	How population growth and movement affects the world.

410

Rainforest and/ or environmental stewardship. Drilling for oil and natural gas.	Humans' desire to intervene in the environment and extract resources since the Paleolithic/Neolithic Eras and to understand, dominate, and control the environment. Domestication of plants and animals.	How humans interact with the environment. How population growth and movement affects the world.
Industrialized farming and the use of genetically modified foods.	Agricultural Revolution—the move to agrarian societies. Continuous development of tools and techniques to increase agricultural productivity (e.g., plow, hybrid food crops, etc.). Population increase and the need to feed more and more people. The use of science and technology.	How humans interact with the environment. How population growth and movement affects the world. How the Agricultural Revolution changed life.
Even on the Internet, entities still try to control the information people see and thereby influence their behavior.	Controlling information and communication meant having power over those who did not. Ancient priests and emperors controlled the communication with the gods; scribes controlled the information that was written.	How humans use and abuse power. How the differences between the haves and have-nots show themselves. How humans use information.
Military spending. Most countries in the world have a military	Battle and warfare between groups was a way of life from early tribes in the Paleolithic age to city-states of Mesopotamia and the large empires of the classical age. Military developments and history are key to understanding ancient societies and civilizations.	How humans use and abuse power. How militarization of society affects life and the world.

411

Partisanship in representative governments.	Greeks' development of direct democracy, citizens' rights, freedom of speech and religion. Rome's creation of a representative government different from the Greeks' to manage the size and complexity of the empire. Roman political leaders known as the Populares and the Optimates.	How humans interact with other humans. How humans use ideas to improve life. How humans use and abuse power. How humans express identity.
Immigration and migration.	Population increase. Rise of complex societies and the multiplying of overcrowded cities.	How population growth and movement affects the world. How civilizations emerge. How agrarian societies spread.
The dominance of science and technology in society	The Greeks' development of scientific and moral questioning known as natural philosophy. Development of science and math in societies around the world, including India, China, Americas, etc. The human desire to understand and explain the world.	How humans use ideas to improve life. How science and technology affects human lives.
The global economy, trade imbalances among different countries. The amount of national debt in various countries.	Expanding networks of exchange and encounter during 1200 BCE to 500 CE. Increased trade and desire for goods. Egyptians opening sarcophaguses to obtain treasures to fund government debt and spending. Ancient Romans having a trade deficit with Ancient China.	How humans interact with other humans. How humans use ideas to improve life. How economic networks and exchange shape the world.

The religious tensions around the world—among Jews, Christians, Muslims, Hindu, etc. Within Islam—Sunni and Shia differences.	The rise of big religions. The split in Islam over Mohammed's successor.	How humans interact with other humans. How humans express identity. How spirituality and moral codes shape life. How major religions grow.
Innovation and change continues to accelerate.	Innovation and change increasing in speed between 10,000 BCE and 600 CE.	How humans use ideas to improve life.

These sample patterns tie in to the three essential questions and seven key themes from "World History for Us All" at http://worldhistoryforusall.sdsu.edu/ and the World History Content Standards at the National Center for History in the Schools at UCLA at http://www.nchs.ucla.edu/Standards/world-history-standards.

REFERENCES

The historical and Internet aspects of this book draw on a variety of sources. I have separated the information into two major categories: key sources and additional sources. I would encourage readers to explore both. I also encourage readers to engage, explore, and think about the wealth of information on the Internet and the importance of thinking critically about what they find. I suggest they can take various terms found throughout the chapters, such as "biological nanoelectricalmechanical systems" or "bioNEMS," and plug them into several search engines to see what comes up. When you see the results, think about the information, the source, and its credibility.

Key Sources for the Novel:

<u>About History</u>

Armstrong, Monty, et al. *Cracking the AP World History Exam. The Princeton Review*, New York: Random House, 2009. Print.
SDSU World History for Us All: www.worldhistoryforusall.sdsu.edu.
UCLA National Center for History in the Schools: www.nchs.ucla.edu.

<u>About the Internet/Technology</u>

Arthur, Charles. *Digital Wars*. London: Kogan Page Ltd., 2012. Print.
Innis, Harold. *Empire and Communications*. New York: Roman & Littlefield, 2007. Print.

Johnson, Clay. *The Information Diet*. Cambridge: O'Reilly, 2012. Print.

Kaku, Michio. *Physics of the Future*. New York: Random House, 2011. Print.

Lanier, Jaron. *You Are Not a Gadget*. New York: Vintage Books, 2011. Print.

Steiner, Christopher. *Automate This*. New York: Penguin, 2012. Print.

Wallace, Patricia. *The Psychology of the Internet*. Cambridge: Cambridge University Press, 1999. Print.

Wu, Tim. *The Master Switch: The Rise and Fall of Information Empires*. New York: Alfred A. Knopf, 2010. Print.

Zittrain, Jonathan. *The Future of the Internet*. New Haven: Yale University Press, 2008. Print.

Other

Bellanca, J., and Ron Brand. *21st Century Skills: Rethinking How Students Learn*. Bloomington, IN: Solution Tree, 2010. Print.

Encyclopedia Britannica: www.britannica.com.

Peace Corps. *Culture Matters: The Peace Corps Cross-Cultural Workbook*. Washington, DC: US Government Printing Office, 1999. Print.

Wikipedia: www.wikipedia.com.

Additional Sources for the Novel

About History

Black, Jeremy. *The Atlas of World History*. New York: Doring Kindersley, 2005. Print.

Brown, Cynthia Stokes. *Big History*. New York: New Press, 2007. Print.

Crabtree, Charlotte, et al. *Lessons from History*. Los Angeles: National Center for the History in the Schools, 1992. Print.

Harrison, T. *Great Empires of the Ancient World*. Los Angeles: J. Paul Getty Museum, 2009. Print.

History Matters: www.historymatters.gmu.edu.

Roman Empire and Colosseum: www.roman-colosseum.info.

About the Internet/Technology

Aboujaoude, Elias. *Virtually You*. New York: W. W. Norton, 2011. Print.

Berners-Lee, Tim. *Weaving the Web*. New York: Harper Collins, 2000. Print.

Blum, Andrew. *Tubes: A Journey to the Center of the Internet*. New York: Harper Collins, 2012. Print.

Carr, Nicholas. *The Shallows: What the Internet Is Doing to Our Brains*. New York: W. W. Norton and Company, 2011. Print.

Carr, Nicholas. *The Big Switch*. New York: W. W. Norton and Company, 2008. Print.

Clark, Andy. *Natural Born Cyborgs*. Oxford: Oxford University Press, 2003. Print.

Dutton, W., et al. *Freedom of Connection—Freedom of Expression*. Oxford: Oxford Internet Institute for Unesco Publishing, 2011. PDF.

Emmons, Sally, and Jim Ford. *Fantasy Media in the Classroom*. Edited by Emily Dial-Driver. London: McFarland, 2012. Print.

International Human Rights and Conflict Resolution Clinic. *Living Under Drones*. Stanford Law School and Global Justice Clinic at NYU School of Law, 2012. PDF.

Lunenfeld, Peter. *The Digital Dialectic*. Cambridge: MIT Press, 1999. Print.

Mayer-Schönberger, Viktor. *Delete: The Virtue of Forgetting in the Digital Age*. New Jersey: Princeton University, 2009. Print.

Murray, Janet. *Hamlet on the Holodeck*. New York: The Free Press, 1997. Print.

Morozov, Evgeny. *The Net Delusion*. New York: Public Affairs, 2011. Print.

Pariser, Eli. *The Filter Bubble: What the Internet Is Hiding from You*. New York: Penguin Press, 2011. Print.

Prensky, Marc. *Brain Gain: Technology and the Quest for Digital Freedom*. New York: Palgrave MacMillan, 2012. Print.

Rheingold, Howard. *Smart Mobs*. Cambridge: Perseus Publishing, 2002. Print.

Rosen, Christine. "Virtual Friendship and the New Narcissism." *The New Atlantis* (Summer 2007): www.TheNewAtlantis.com.

Rosen, Larry. *iDisorder*. New York: Palgrave Macmillan, 2012. Print.

Shirky, Clay. *Cognitive Surplus*. New York: Penguin Group, 2010. Print.

Sieberg, Daniel. *The Digital Diet*. New York: Three Rivers Press, 2011 Print.

Szoka, B., and Adam Marcus. *The Next Digital Decade*. Washington, DC: TechFreedom, 2010. www.NextDigitalDecade.com.

Wagner, Mark. "Massively Multiplayer Online Role-Playing Games as Constructivist Learning Environments in K-12 Education: A Delphi Study." PhD diss., Walden University, May 2008.

Other

Hammond, Ray. *The World in 2030*. Zarautz, Spain: Itxaropena, 2007. PDF. www.editions-yago.com.

Huxley, Aldous. *Brave New World Revisited*. New York: Harper Perennial, 2006. Print.

Kurzweil, Ray. *The Singularity Is Near*. New York: Viking. 2005. Print.

Lightman, Alan. *Einstein's Dreams*. New York: Warner Books, 1993. Print.

Orwell, George. *1984*. New York: Harcourt Brace, 1983. Print.

Ritzer, George. *The McDonaldization of Society*. Thousand Oaks, CA: Sage Publications, 2013. Print.

INDEX

Bantu, 109
basis for the world economy, 182, 398
battle for the Internet, 351, 358
Big Bang, 147
biological nanoelectricalmechanical systems, bioNEMS, 21, 415
booby-traps, 115
British Empire, 207
Bronze Age, 64, 71
Buddhism, 241, 249, 303, 309
Byzantine Empire, 328

Caesar Marcus Aurelius Antoninus Augustus, 273
Carthage, 176, 184, 190, 192, 278
Çatalhöyük, 45, 47, 48, 49, 50, 51, 94, 97
cedars of Lebanon, 182, 196
Celts, 250, 265, 272, 273, 307, 376
censor, 165, 350
central government, 102, 107, 206, 208, 248, 264, 265
Chaeronea, 213
Chavín, 103, 105, 119, 120, 121, 122, 124, 128, 134, 135, 178
Chavín de Huántar, 120, 121, 122, 128, 134, 341
Chichen Itza, 292, 298
China, 22, 41, 55, 87, 90, 96, 103, 112, 149, 161, 175, 177, 207, 237,
    240, 241, 243, 244, 245, 251, 252, 255, 257, 263, 264, 265, 266,
    267, 268, 272, 273, 277, 284, 296, 304, 307, 309, 342, 351, 364,
    370, 375, 398, 403, 407, 412
Chinese Imperial Court, 265, 267
Chinese silk trade, 240
Christianity, 20, 109, 276, 279, 280, 308, 309, 413

Made in the USA
Charleston, SC
11 September 2013